Leon ~~wanted~~ ~~to~~
mother.

That had to mean something, didn't it?

He was the most marvelous man. To think he trusted her with his prized possession!

Even if she was a virgin who'd had no experience with men she could do the mothering part right. Maybe their marriage would help heal the wound between Leon and his family.

Marriage to Leon would ensure a close relationship with Belle's mother for the rest of their lives.

But what if Leon met another woman and fell in love?

She knew the answer to that. It would kill her. But would their marriage be so different from the many marriages where one of the partners strayed? It was a fact of life that millions of married men and women had affairs. There were no guarantees.

By the time morning came she'd gone back and forth so many times she was physically and emotionally exhausted. But one thing stood out above all else. The thou... of being back... life in New York sounde...

They had to marry someone, didn't it?

He was the most unforgiving man. To think he wished her death in cold blood...

Bianca! She was unique when it had no experience with men she stand on the moral high road right. Maybe their marriage would help heal the wound between George and his family.

Marrying Bianca would create a close relationship with Bella... it back for the rest of their lives.

But what if George once anything wrong and killed him love?

She knew the answer to that. It would kill him... but would their marriage be so different from the many marriages where one of the partners doesn't... it was a fact of life that millions of married men and women had affairs. They were no guarantees...

By the time morning came she'd gone back and forth as many times as she was physically and emotionally distraught that one thing stood out above all else. The thought of going back to her life in New York looked like living death...

A MARRIAGE
MADE IN ITALY

BY
REBECCA WINTERS

First published in Great Britain 2013
by Mills & Boon, an imprint of Harlequin (UK) Limited,
Eton House, 18-24 Paradise Road, Richmond, Surrey TW9 1SR

© Rebecca Winters 2013

ISBN: 978 0 263 90139 9
ebook ISBN: 978 1 472 00523 6

23-0913

Harlequin (UK) policy is to use papers that are natural, renewable and recyclable products and made from wood grown in sustainable forests. The logging and manufacturing processes conform to the legal environmental regulations of the country of origin.

Printed and bound in Spain
by Blackprint CPI, Barcelona

Rebecca Winters, whose family of four children has now swelled to include five beautiful grandchildren, lives in Salt Lake City, Utah, in the land of the Rocky Mountains. With canyons and high alpine meadows full of wild-flowers, she never runs out of places to explore. They, plus her favourite vacation spots in Europe, often end up as backgrounds for her romance novels, because writing is her passion, along with her family and church.

Rebecca loves to hear from readers. If you wish to e-mail her, please visit her website: www.cleanromances.com.

CHAPTER ONE

BELLE PETERSON LEFT the cell phone store she managed,
and took a bus to the law office of Mr. Earl Harmon in
downtown Newburgh, New York. The secretary showed
her into the conference room. She discovered her thirty-
year-old, divorced sibling, Cliff, had already arrived and
was sitting at the oval table with a mulish look on his
face, daring her to speak to him. She hadn't seen him
since their parents' funeral six months ago.

On the outside he was blond and quite good-looking,
but his facade hid a troubled soul. He'd been angry enough
after his wife had left him, but the deaths of their parents
in a fatal car crash meant he was now on his own. Today
Belle felt Cliff's antipathy more strongly than usual and
chose a seat around the other side of the table without
saying a word.

Now twenty-four and single, she had been adopted
fourteen years ago. The children at the Newburgh
Church Orphanage had liked her, as had the sisters.
But out in the real world, Belle felt she was unlovable,
and worked hard at her job to gain the respect of her
peers. Her greatest pain was never to know the mother
who'd given birth to her. To have no identity was an
agony she'd had to live with every day of her life.

The sisters who ran the orphanage had told Belle that Mrs. Peterson had been able to have only one child. She'd finally prevailed on her husband to adopt the brunette girl, Belle, who had no last name. This was Belle's chance to have a mother, but no bonding ever took place. From the day she'd been taken home, Cliff had been cruel to her, making her life close to unbearable at times.

"Good morning."

Belle was so deep in thought over the past, she didn't realize Mr. Harmon had come into the room. She shook his hand.

"I'm glad you two could arrange to meet here at the same time. I have some bad news and some good. Let's start with the bad first."

The familiar scowl on Cliff's face spoke volumes.

"As you know, there was no insurance, therefore the home you grew up in was sold to pay off the multitude of debts. The good news is you've each been given fifteen hundred dollars from the auction of the furnishings. I have checks for you." He passed them out.

Cliff shot to his feet. *"That's it?"* Belle heard panic beneath his anger. She knew he'd been waiting to come into some money, if only to make up delinquent alimony payments. She hadn't expected anything herself and rejoiced to receive this check, which she clutched in her hand before putting it in her purse.

"I'm sorry, Mr. Peterson, but everything went to pay off your father's debts and cover the burial costs. Please accept my sincere sympathy at the passing of your parents. I wish both of you the very best."

"Thank you, Mr. Harmon," Belle said, when Cliff continued to remain silent.

"If you ever need my help, feel free to call." The attorney smiled at her and left the room. The second he was gone, an explosion of venom escaped Cliff's lips. He shot her a furious glance.

"It's all *your* fault. If Mom hadn't nagged Dad for a daughter, there would have been more money and we wouldn't be in this mess. Why don't you go back to Italy where you belong?"

Her heart suddenly pounded with dizzying intensity. "What did you say?"

"You heard me. Dad never wanted you."

"You think I didn't know that?" She moved closer to her brother, holding her breath. "Are you saying I came from Italian parents?" All along she'd thought the sisters at the orphanage might have named her for the fairy-tale character, or else she came from French roots.

Her whole life she'd been praying to find out her true lineage, and she'd gone to the orphanage many times seeking information. But every time she did, she'd been told they couldn't help her. Nadine, her adoptive mother, had never revealed the truth to her, but Belle had heard Cliff's slip and refused to let it go.

He averted his eyes and wheeled around to leave, but she raced ahead of him and blocked the door. At twenty-four, Belle was no longer frightened of him. Before they left this office and parted ways forever, she had to ask the question that had been inscribed on her mind and heart from the time she knew she was an orphan. "What else do you know about my background?"

Cliff flashed her a mocking smile. "Now that Dad's no longer alive, how much money are you willing to pay me for the information?"

She could hardly swallow before she opened her

purse and pulled out the check. In a trembling voice she said, "I'd give you *this* to learn anything that could help me know my roots." While he watched, she drew out a pen and endorsed it over to him.

For the first time since she'd known him, his eyes held a puzzled look rather than an angry one. "You'd give up that much money just to know about someone who didn't even want you?"

"Yes," she whispered, fighting tears. "It's not important if they didn't want me. I just need to know who I am and where I came from. If you know anything, I beg you to tell me." Taking a leap of faith, she handed him the check.

He took it from her and studied it for a moment. "You always were pathetic," he muttered.

"So you don't know anything and were just teasing me with your cruelty? That doesn't really surprise me. Go on. Keep it. I never thought we'd get that much money from the auction, anyway. You're one of the lucky people who grew up knowing your parents. Too bad they're gone and you're all alone now. Knowing how it feels, I wouldn't wish that on anyone, not even you."

Belle opened the door, and had started to leave when she heard him say, "The old man said your last name was the same as the redheaded smart-mouth he hated in high school."

Her heart thundered. She spun around. "Who was that?"

"Frankie Donatello."

"Donatello?"

"Yeah. One day I heard Mom and Dad arguing about you. That's when it came out. He said he wished they'd never adopted that Italian girl's brat. After he left for work, I told Mom she ought to send you back to where you came from, because you weren't wanted. She said that would be impossible because it was someplace in Italy."

What? "Where in Italy?" Belle demanded.

"I don't know. It sounded something like Remenee."

"How did he find out? The sisters told me it was a closed adoption."

"How the hell do *I* know?"

It didn't matter, because joy lit up Belle's insides. Her leap of faith had paid off! Without conscious thought she reached out and hugged him so hard she almost knocked him over. "Thank you! I know you hate me, but I love you for this and forgive every mean thing you ever said or did to me. Goodbye, Cliff."

She rushed out of the law office to the bus stop and rode back to work. After nodding to the sales reps, she disappeared into the back room and looked for a map of Italy on the computer. She was trembling so violently she could hardly work the keyboard.

As she scrolled down the list of cities and towns that popped up, the name Rimini appeared, most closely matching "Remenee." The blood pounded in her ears when she looked it up and discovered it was a town of a hundred forty thousand along the Adriatic. It was in the province of Rimini.

Quickly, she scanned the month's schedule of vacations for the employees. They all had one week off in summer and one in winter. Belle was on summer break from college, where she went to night school. Her vacation would be coming up the third week of June, ten days away.

Without hesitation she booked a flight from New York City to Rimini, Italy, and made arrangements for a rental car. She chose the cheapest flight, with two stopovers, and made a reservation at a pension that charged only twenty-eight dollars a day. No phone, no TV. The coed bathroom was down the hall. Sounded like the orphanage. That was fine with her. A bed was all she needed.

Since she'd been saving her money, and roomed with two other girls, she'd managed to put away a modest nest egg. All these years she'd been guarding it for something important, never dreaming the money would ever help her to find her mother.

"Belle?"

She lifted her head and smiled politely at her colleague. "Yes, Mac?"

"How about going for pizza after we lock up tonight?"

"I'm sorry, but I have other plans."

"You always say that. How can someone so gorgeous turn me down? Come on. How about it?"

Her new assistant manager, transferred in from another store, was good-looking and a real barracuda in sales, but he irritated her by continually trying to get her to go out with him.

"Mac? I've told you already that I'm not interested."

"Some of the guys call you the Ice Queen." He never gave up.

"Really. Anything else you want to say to me before you finish the inventory?"

She heard a smothered imprecation before the door closed. Good. Maybe she *was* an ice queen. Fine! So far she hadn't seen examples of love in her personal life and didn't expect to.

Her birth parents had given her away. Her adoptive parents had suffered through an unhappy marriage. Her adoptive brother was already divorced, and angry. He'd used her pretty mercilessly as an emotional punching bag. Belle always felt she was on the outside looking in, but never being part of a whole.

She thought about the single girls at the store, who all struggled to find good dates and were usually miserable with the ones they landed. Two of the four guys were married. One of them was having an affair. The other was considering divorce. The other two were players. Both spent their money on clothes and cars.

Her own roommates were still single and terrified they would end up alone. It was all they talked about when the three of them went running in the mornings.

Belle didn't worry about being alone. That had been her state from the moment she was born. The few dates she'd accepted here and there outside the workplace had fizzled. It was probably her fault, because she didn't feel very lovable and wasn't as confident as she needed to be. Marriage wasn't an option for her.

She didn't trust any relationship to last, and cut it off early. Belle hadn't met a man she'd cared enough about to imagine going to bed with. No doubt her mother had experimented, and gotten caught with no resources but the church orphanage to help her. Belle refused to get into that circumstance.

What she *could* depend on was her career, which gave her the stability she craved after being dependent on the orphanage and her adoptive parents. She was a free agent now. Her store had been number one in the region for two years. Soon she hoped to be promoted to upper-level management in the company.

But first she would take her precious vacation time to try to find her mother. If Cliff had gotten it wrong or misunderstood, then maybe the trip would be for nothing, but Belle had to think positive thoughts. Romantic Italy, the world of Michelangelo, gondolas and the famous tenor Pavarotti, had always sounded as delightful and as faraway as the moon. Incredible to believe she'd actually be flying there in ten days.

Tomorrow she'd see about equipping herself with a company GSM phone and SIM card, the kind with a quad-band. Once in Rimini, she'd find a local library and work from the latest city phone directory to do her research.

She was in the midst of making a mental list of things she'd need when Rod, one of the reps, suddenly burst in on her. "Hey, boss? Can you come out in front? An angry client just threw his cell phone at Sheila and is demanding satisfaction. He said it broke after he bought it."

She smiled. "If it wasn't broken, it is now. No problem." No problem at all on the first red-letter day of her life. "I'll be right there."

It was seven in the morning when thirty-three-year-old Leonardo Rovere di Malatesta, the elder son of Count Sullisto Malatesta of Rimini, finally got his little six-month-old Concetta to sleep. The doctor said she'd caught a bug, and he'd prescribed medicine to bring down her temperature. It was now two degrees lower than it had been at midnight, and she hadn't thrown up again, *grazie a Dio!*

After he'd walked the floor with her all night in an attempt to comfort her, he was exhausted. The dog ought to be exhausted, too. Rufo was a brown roan Spinone, a wedding gift from his wife's father.

Rufo had been devoted to Benedetta and had transferred his allegiance to Concetta when Leon had returned from the hospital without his wife. Since that moment, their dog had never let the baby out of his sight. Leon was deeply moved by such a show of love, and patted the animal's head.

There was no way he'd be going in to the bank today. Talia and Rufo would watch over his daughter while he slept. The forty-year-old nanny had been with him since Benedetta had died in childbirth, and was devoted to his precious child. If the baby's fever spiked again, he could count on her to waken him immediately.

He kissed Concetta's head with its fine, dark blond hair, and laid her in the crib on her back, out of habit. She never stayed in that position for long. Her lids hid brown eyes dark as poppy throats. She had Benedetta's coloring and facial features. Leon loved this child in a way he hadn't thought possible. Her presence and demanding needs filled the aching loneliness in his heart for the wife he'd lost.

After tiptoeing out of the nursery, he told Talia he was going to bed, then went to find his housekeeper, who'd always worked for his mother's family. She and Talia were cousins, and he trusted them implicitly.

"Simona? I've turned off my cell phone. If someone needs me, knock on my door."

The older woman nodded before Leon headed for his bedroom. He was so exhausted he didn't remember his head touching the pillow. The relief of knowing the baby's fever had broken helped him to fall into a deep sleep.

When he heard a tap on his door later, he checked his watch. He'd slept seven hours and couldn't believe it was already midafternoon! He came awake immediately, fearing something was wrong.

"Simona? Is Concetta worse?" he called out.

"No, no. She has recovered. Talia is feeding her." Relief swamped him a second time. "Your assistant at the bank asked if you would phone him at your convenience."

"Grazie." Leon levered himself off the bed and headed for the shower, surprised that Berto would call the villa. Normally he would leave a message on Leon's cell. Maybe he had.

After he'd shaved and dressed, Leon reached for his phone. There was a message from his father asking him to join the family for dinner.

Not tonight.

Another message came from his friend Vito, in Rome. Leon would phone him before he went to bed.

Nothing from Berto.

Leon walked into the kitchen, where he found Talia feeding plums from a jar to his daughter, who was propped in her high chair. Rufo sat on the floor with his tail moving back and forth, watching with those humanlike eyes.

Concetta's sweet little face broke into a smile the second she saw her father, and she waved her hands. Whenever she did that, it made him thankful he was alive. He felt her forehead, pleased to note her fever was gone.

"I do believe you're much better, *il mio tesoro.* As soon as I make a few phone calls, you and I are going to go out on the patio and play." It overlooked his private stretch of beach with its fine golden sand. Concetta was strong and loved to stand in it in her bare feet if he braced her.

Yesterday he'd bought a new set of stacking buckets for her, but she hadn't felt well enough to be interested. Now that her health was improved, he couldn't wait to see what she'd do with them. First, however, he phoned his father to explain that the baby had been sick and needed to be put down early.

When Leon heard the disappointment in his voice, he made arrangements for dinner the following evening *if* she was all better. With that accomplished he called his secretary at the bank.

"Berto? I sent you a text message telling you my daughter was ill. Is there a problem that can't wait until tomorrow?"

"No, no. I'll talk to you in the morning, provided the *bambina* is better."

Leon rubbed the pad of his thumb along his lower lip. "You wouldn't have phoned if you didn't think it was important."

"At first I thought it was."

"But now you've changed your mind?" Berto was being uncharacteristically cryptic.

"*Sì.* It can wait until tomorrow. *Ciao,* Leon."

His assistant actually hung up on him! Leon clicked off and eyed the baby, who'd eaten all her plums and seemed perfectly content playing with her fingers.

"Talia, something has come up at the bank. I'll run into town and be back within the hour. Tell Simona to phone me if there's the slightest problem."

"The little one will be fine."

He kissed his daughter's cheek. "I'll see you soon."

After changing into a suit, Leon alerted his bodyguard before leaving the villa. He drove his black sports car into the most celebrated seaside resort city in Europe, curious to understand what was going on with Berto.

After pulling around to the back of the ornate, two-story Renaissance building, partially bombed during World War II and later reconstructed, he let himself in the private entrance reserved for him and his family. He took the marble staircase two steps at a time to his office on the next floor, where he served as assets manager for Malatesta Banking, one of the two top banking institutions in Italy.

Under his father's brilliant handling as wealth manager, they'd grown to twenty-five thousand employees. With his brother, Dante, overseeing the broker-dealer department, business was going well despite Italy's economic downturn. If the call from Berto meant any kind of trouble, Leon intended to get to the bottom of it pronto.

His redheaded assistant was on a call when Leon walked into his private suite of rooms. Judging from his expression, Berto was surprised to see him. He rang off quickly and got to his feet. "I didn't know you were coming."

Leon's hands went to his hips. "I didn't expect you to hang up so quickly from our earlier conversation. I want to know what's wrong. Don't tell me again it's nothing. Which of the accounts is in trouble?"

Berto looked flustered. "It has nothing to do with the accounts. A woman came to the bank earlier today after being sent from Donatello Diamonds on the Corso D'Augosto."

"And?" Leon demanded, sensing his assistant's hesitation.

"Marcello in Security called up here, asking for you to handle the inquiry, since your father wasn't available. The manager at Donatello's told her she would have to speak to someone at the bank. That's when I called you.

"But after I heard it was some American wanting information about the Donatello family, I figured it was a foreign reporter snooping around. At that point I decided not to bother you any more about it."

Leon frowned in puzzlement. Someone wanting to do legitimate business would have made an appointment with him or his father and left their full name.

Was it one of the paparazzi posing as an American tourist in order to dig up news about the family? Leon's relatives had to be on constant alert against the media wanting to rake up old scandal to sell papers.

Leon had seen it all and viewed life with a cynical eye. It was what came from being a Malatesta, hated in earlier centuries and still often an object of envy.

"When I couldn't get you or your father, I tried your brother, but he's out of town. I told Marcello this person would have to leave a name and phone number. With your daughter sick, I didn't consider this an emergency, but I still wanted you to be informed."

"I appreciate that. You handled it perfectly. Do you have the information she left?"

Berto handed the notepaper to him. "That's the phone number and address of the Pensione Rosa off the Via Vincenza Monti. The woman's name is Belle. Marcello said she's in her early twenties, and with her long dark hair and blue eyes, more than lives up to her name. When she approached him, he thought she was a film star."

Naturally. Didn't the devil usually appear in the guise of a beautiful woman? Of course she didn't leave a last name....

"Good work, Berto. Tell no one else about this. See you tomorrow."

More curious than ever, Leon left the bank. A few minutes later he discovered the small lodging down an alley, half hidden by the other buildings. He parked and entered. No one was around, so he pressed the buzzer at the front desk. In a moment a woman older than Simona came out of an alcove.

"I'm Rosa. If you need a room, we're full, *signore*."

Leon handed her the paper. "You have a woman named Belle registered here?"

"Sì." With that staccato answer he realized he wouldn't be learning her guest's last name the easy way.

"Could you ring her room, *per favore?*"

"No phone in the rooms."

He might have known, considering the low price for accommodations listed on the back wall. "Do you know if she's in?"

"She went out several hours ago and hasn't returned."

He spied a chair against the wall, next to an end table with a lamp on it. "I'll wait."

The woman scrutinized him. "Leave me your name and number and she can call you from the desk here after she returns."

"I'll take my chances and see if she comes in."

With a shrug of her ample shoulders, the woman disappeared through the alcove.

Rather than sit here for what might be hours, he phoned one of his security people to do surveillance. When Ruggio arrived, Leon gave him the American woman's description and said he wanted to be notified as soon as she showed up.

With that taken care of, he walked out to the alley and got in his car. He was halfway to the villa when his cell phone rang. It was Ruggio. Leon clicked on. "What's happening?"

"The woman fitting the description you gave me just entered. She's driving a rental car from the airport."

"Which agency?"

When Ruggio gave him the particulars, Leon told him to stay put until he got there. On the way back to the pension, he called the rental agency and asked to speak to the manager on a matter of vital importance. Once the man heard it was Signor di Malatesta investigating a possible police matter to do with the bank, he told him her last name was Peterson, and that she was from Newburgh, New York. Leon didn't often use his name to apply pressure, but this case was an exception.

He learned she'd made the reservation nearly two weeks ago and had rented the car for seven days. It seemed she'd already been in Rimini three days.

Leon thanked the manager for his cooperation. Pleased to be armed with this much information before confronting her, he made a search on his phone. Newburgh was a town sixty miles north of New York City. What it all meant he didn't know yet, but he was about to find out.

He saw the rental car when he drove down the alley and parked. Ruggio met him at the front desk of the pension, where Rosa was helping a scruffy-looking male wearing a backpack and short shorts.

"She's been in her room since she came in. She's *molta molta bellissima,*" Ruggio whispered. "I think I've seen her on television."

Marcello had said the same thing. "*Grazie.* I'll take it from here," Leon told him. If she was working alone or with another reporter, he planned to find out.

Once Ruggio left, he sat down. By now it was quarter after six. Without a TV, she'd probably leave again, if only to get a meal. If he had to wait too long, he'd insist Rosa go knock on Signorina Peterson's door. To pass the time, Leon phoned Simona, and was relieved to hear his little girl seemed to be over the worst of her bug.

As he was telling his housekeeper he wasn't sure what time he'd get home, a woman emerged from the alcove. Without warning, his adrenaline kicked in. Not just because she was beautiful—in fact, incredibly so. It was because there was something about her that reminded him of someone else.

She swept past him, so fast she was out the door before he was galvanized into action. After telling Simona he'd get back to her, he sprang from the chair and followed the shapely woman in the two-piece linen suit and leather sandals down the alley to her car.

He estimated she had to be five feet six. Even the way she carried herself, with a kind of unconscious grace, was appealing. Physically, Leon could find nothing wrong with her, and that bothered him, since he hadn't been able to look at another woman since Benedetta.

"Belle Peterson?"

She wheeled around, causing her gleaming hair, the

color of dark mink, to swish about her shoulders. Cobalt-blue eyes fringed with black lashes flew to Leon in surprise. If she already knew who he was, she was putting on a good act of pretending otherwise.

She possessed light olive skin that needed no makeup. Her wide mouth, with its soft pink lipstick, had a voluptuous flare. He found her the embodiment of feminine pulchritude, but to his surprise she stared at him without a hint of recognition or flirtatiousness. "How do you know my name? We've never met."

With that accent, she was American through and through. He found her directness as intriguing as her no-nonsense demeanor. Some men might find it intimidating. Leon's gaze dropped to her left hand, curled over her shoulder bag and resting against the lush curve of her hip. Her nails were well manicured with a neutral coating. She wore no rings.

If in disguise for a part she was playing—perhaps in the hope of infiltrating their family business in some way to unlock secrets—he would say she looked...perfect.

He pulled the note Berto had given him out of his suit jacket pocket and handed it to her.

She glanced at it before eyeing him again. "Evidently you're from the bank. How did you get my last name?"

"A simple matter of checking with the car rental agency."

Her blue eyes turned frosty. "I don't know about your country, but in mine that information can only be obtained by a judge's warrant during the investigation of a crime."

"My country has similar laws."

"Was it a crime to ask questions?"

"Of course not. But I'm afraid our doors are closed to all so-called journalists. I decided to investigate."

"I'm not a journalist or anything close," she stated promptly. Reaching in her shoulder bag, she pulled a business card out of her wallet.

He took it from her fingers and glanced at it. *Belle Peterson, Manager, Trans Continental Cell Phones Incorporated, Newburgh, New York...*

He lifted his head. "Why didn't you leave this card at the bank with the security man you talked to?"

Without hesitation, she said, "Because a call to my work verifying my employment would let everyone know where I am. Since my whereabouts are no one's business, I wish it to remain that way. The fact is, I'm on vacation and it's almost over."

He slipped the card into his pocket. "You'll be returning to Newburgh?"

"Yes. I've talked to as many people with the last name Donatello as I've been able to locate in Rimini. So far I haven't found the information I've been seeking."

"Or a missing person, maybe?" he prodded. "A man, perhaps?" The question slipped out, once again surprising him. As if he cared who she was looking for...

Her gaze never wavered. "I suppose that's a natural assumption a man might make, but the answer is no. Not every woman is looking for a man, whether it be for pleasure or for marriage...an institution that in my opinion is overvaunted."

She sounded like Leon, only in reverse, increasing his interest.

"To be specific, the manager at Donatello Diamonds directed me to the Malatesta Bank, but it seems I've come to a dead end there, too. Since you prefer not to tell me your name, at least let me thank you for the courtesy of coming to the pension to let me know you can't help me. I can cross Donatello Diamonds off my list of possibilities."

Like a man concluding a business meeting, she put out her hand for Leon to shake. His closed around hers. Unexpected warmth shot up his arm, catching him off guard before he released her. "What will you do now?"

"I'll continue to search until my time runs out in three days. Goodbye." She turned and got in her rental car without asking him for the card back. He watched until she drove to the end of the alley and turned onto the street.

Her card burned a hole in his pocket. He pulled it out. If he phoned the number on the back of it, he'd find out if she'd been telling the truth about her job. But since he was a person who always jealously guarded his own privacy, he could relate to her desire to keep her private life to herself.

No matter what, this woman meant *nothing* to him. If she'd come on a fishing expedition, he hadn't given her any information she could use to cause trouble.

By the time he'd driven back to the villa, his thoughts were on his daughter. It wasn't until later, after he'd kissed her good-night and was doing laps in the pool, that images of the American woman kept surfacing. There was something familiar about her that wouldn't leave him alone.

A nagging voice urged him to phone the head office of TCCPI, wherever it was located, to find out if she'd fabricated an elaborate lie including a business card. Leon could do that before he went to bed. If he didn't make the call, he'd never get to sleep.

CHAPTER TWO

EARLY WEDNESDAY MORNING, Belle came awake after a restless night. The tall nameless man in the light blue silk suit who'd tracked her down in the alley last evening was without question the most dangerously striking male she'd ever met in her life.

With those aquiline features, he embodied much more than the conventional traits one normally attributed to a gorgeous man, such as handsome, dashing or exciting. She couldn't believe it, but she'd been attracted to him. Strongly attracted. It had never happened to her before.

Once he'd called out to her, she'd felt his powerful presence before she'd even turned to study his rock-hard physique. His black hair and olive skin provided the perfect foil for startling gray eyes.

For him to come from the bank armed with information no one could have known meant he was someone of importance. The fact that her inquiry had brought him to the pension convinced her she'd unwittingly trespassed on ground whose secrets were so dark, they had to be well guarded.

Who better than the man who'd suddenly appeared like some mysterious prince from this Renaissance city?

Just remembering their encounter sent a shiver down the length of her body.

She was being fanciful, but couldn't help it. His deep voice with barely a trace of accent in English had agitated her nervous system. Even after twelve hours she could still feel it resonating. Though she'd never forget him, she needed to push thoughts of him to the back of her mind. Her flight home Sunday would be here before she knew it, which meant she needed to intensify her search.

Once she'd showered down the hall, and had slipped on a short-sleeved, belted white cotton dress, she left the pension armed with her detailed street map and notebook. She'd kept a log of every Donatello name so far. Her destination for the last Donatello she could find in the city of Rimini was Donatello's Garage.

After following the directions she'd been given on the phone yesterday, she talked to the manager, who spoke passable English. He told her a man by another name now owned the shop. The original owner, Mr. Donatello, and his wife had both died of old age. They'd had no children who could inherit the garage.

This was the way it had been going since last Sunday, when she'd started working through the list of Donatellos in the Rimini phone directory. In most cases the people she'd talked to were willing to help her, even going to the trouble of finding someone to help them understand her English.

They were proud of their genealogy. Many of them told her she could come by their house. The others told her their information over the phone, but so far there were no leads on a woman with the middle or last name Donatello, in her late thirties or early forties, who'd been to New York twenty-six years ago. It was like looking for a needle in the proverbial haystack.

Resolving not to be dispirited, Belle thanked him and headed for the library near her pension, to do more research on the other nineteen cities and towns within Rimini Province. They were ten to twelve miles apart and had much smaller populations, so there wouldn't be as many Donatellos to look up. That could be bad, if nothing was discovered about her birth mother.

En route to the library, Belle stopped at a trattoria for breakfast and filled up so she wouldn't have to eat until dinnertime. She would be doing a lot more driving over the next few days. Before she left Rimini, she approached the woman in the research department, who spoke excellent English and knew she was looking for Donatello names.

"I have one more question, if you don't mind. Could you tell me anything about the Malatesta Bank?" The striking Italian who'd shown up at the pension had refused to leave her mind.

"How much time do you have?"

That's what Belle had thought. "Yesterday the manager of Donatello Diamonds directed me to the bank to get information, but I learned nothing. Why would he do that? I don't understand the connection."

"The House of Malatesta was an Italian family that ruled over Rimini from 1300 to 1500. There's too much history since then to tell you in five minutes. But today a member of that old ruling family, Count Sullisto Malatesta, runs the Malatesta Bank, one of the two largest banks in Italy. They own many other businesses as well.

"Another, lesser ruling family of the past, the House of Donatello, made their fortune in diamonds, but over years of poor management it started to dwindle. Some say it would have eventually failed if Count Malatesta, then a widower, hadn't merged with the House of Donatello.

"He saved it from ruin by marrying Princess Luciana Donatello, the heiress, whose father was purported to have died of natural causes." The woman lowered her voice. "I say *purported* because some people insisted both he and his wife had been murdered, either by another faction of the Donatello family, or by the Malatesta family. Soon thereafter, the count made his power grab by marrying her, but nothing definite came of the investigation to prove or disprove the theories."

Belle shuddered. The dark stranger from the bank had looked that dangerous to her.

"The Donatello deaths left a question mark and turned everything into a scandal that rocked the region and made the wedding into a nationwide event."

"You're a fount of knowledge, and I'm indebted to you," Belle told her. "Now I'm off to the other towns in Rimini Province to look up more Donatellos. Thank you so much for your time."

The woman smiled. "Good luck to you."

Belle was glad to be leaving the city, to be leaving *him*. Before she left, she would pay her bill at the pension and turn in her rental car. In case the man from the bank made more inquiries about her, he'd be thrown off the scent. Leaving no trail, she'd take a taxi to another rental agency and procure a car for the rest of the week.

She left the library and walked out to the parking lot to get in her car. As she opened the door, she heard a deep familiar voice say, "Signorina Peterson?" Her heart jumped.

It was déjà vu as she looked around and discovered the man who'd been responsible for her restless night. This time he was dressed in a blue sport shirt that made him even more breathtaking, if that was possible. His eyes played over her with a thoroughness that was disarming.

"Why are you following me, *signore?*"

"Because I overheard your conversation with the librarian and am in a position to help you in your search if you'd allow me."

"Why would you do that, when you won't even tell me your name?"

"Because you're a foreigner who has suffered two frights. The first from me, because I put you through an inquisition yesterday. The second from the librarian, who increased your nervousness just now when she answered your question."

He'd been listening the whole time? That meant he'd followed her from the pension. Belle held on to the door handle for support. "What makes you think I'm nervous?"

"The pulse in your throat is throbbing unnaturally fast."

Those silvery eyes didn't miss a detail. "I imagine it always does that when I'm being stalked."

"With your kind of beauty, I would imagine it's an occupational hazard, especially at your workplace." While she tried to catch her breath, he said, "I had you investigated."

"I knew it," she muttered.

He cocked his dark head. "Not in a way that anyone from your store could ever find out. I called headquarters in New York and explained our bank was doing the

groundwork to sponsor an American cell phone company in Rimini, to see how it would play out."

"That was a lie!"

"Not necessarily. American cell phone companies
are one asset we've had an idea to acquire for some
time. When I asked which store manager might be equal
to the task, you were mentioned among the top five
managers for your company on the East Coast."

"What did you do? Talk to the CEO himself?" she
demanded.

"Actually, I did."

Good heavens. He was handsome as the devil and
just as cunning.

"I find it even more compelling that you started with
that company at age eighteen and six years later are still
with them. That kind of loyalty is rare. I was told you're
going to be promoted to a regional manager in the next
few months. Perhaps it might land you in Rimini."

What?

"My congratulations."

Who was this man with such powerful connections?
Belle needed to keep her wits. "Just so you know, I
have no interest in moving overseas. So now that you've
learned I'm not one of the paparazzi, I'd like your word
that you'll leave me alone, whoever you are."

"I'm Leonardo di Malatesta, the elder son of Count
Sullisto Malatesta."

Her heart thudded too fast. It all fit with her first
impression of a dark prince, and explained the signet
ring with a knight's head on his right hand. There was a
wedding ring on his left. "I understand that name con-
notes someone sinister."

His smile had a dangerous curl. "If it would make you feel more comfortable, call me Leon."

"The lion. If that's supposed to make me feel any better…"

A velvety sound close to a chuckle escaped his lips. "I want to apologize for my unorthodox method of getting to know you, and frightening you. Considering the fact that you plan to return to the States on Sunday, perhaps if you told me exactly what you're hoping to find, I could help speed up the process. I really would like to assist you."

"I doubt your wife would approve."

Those gray eyes darkened with some unnamed emotion. "I'm a widower."

"Yet you still wear your wedding ring. You must have loved her a great deal. Forgive me if I'm being suspicious. The truth is, I wouldn't dream of bothering a busy man like you, one with so many banking responsibilities. The only thing I was hoping to get from the manager at Donatello Diamonds was a little information about the female members of the Donatello family. It would take just a few minutes."

"So you're looking for a woman…"

"That's very astute of you."

A gleam entered his eyes. "Considering the very attractive female I'm talking to, surely I can be forgiven for my earlier assessment of the situation."

Don't let that fatal charm of his get to you, Belle, even if he is still in mourning.

"That depends on what you can tell me," she retorted with a wry smile back at him.

After a pause, he said, "Obviously you haven't found

her yet. Why is she so important to you that you would come thousands of miles?"

The small moment of levity fled. "Because the answer to my whole existence is tied up with her. My greatest fear is that she's no longer alive, or that I'll never find her." Sorrow weighed Belle down at the thought.

He studied her with relentless scrutiny. "Is she a relative?"

This was where things got too sensitive. "Maybe."

"How old would she be?"

"Probably in her forties." Again, maybe. According to Cliff, her adoptive father had called her mother "that Italian girl." Belle took it to mean she was young. "I learned she was from Rimini, Italy, but that could mean the city or the province."

His black eyebrows furrowed. "My stepmother, Luciana, was an only child, born to Valeria and Massimo Donatello here in Rimini. Valeria died in a hunting accident on their estate when Luciana was only eleven. As the librarian told you, some people still believe it wasn't an accident."

"What she told me sounded positively Machiavellian."

"You're right. It was only a few months ago that the police finally solved the case. The shooting was ruled as accidental."

"I see. It's still tragic when any child loses its mother."

"I couldn't agree more," he said in an almost haunted voice. Their eyes held for a moment. "My father was fifteen years older than Luciana, and he married her against my brother's and my wishes. She was only twenty at the time and could never have replaced our mother."

Four years younger than Belle's age now. "Of course not." She could only imagine this man's pain. Suddenly he'd become more human to her. He'd lost his own mother and his wife.

"She's forty-two now," Leon added. "There must be quite a few Donatello women between those ages you've met while you've been here in Rimini."

"Yes, but so far I've had no luck, because none of them ever traveled to New York in their late teens or twenties."

Leon's heart gave a thunderclap. "New York is the connecting point?" he rasped.

Belle nodded.

What had she said in answer to his earlier question about why this was important to her? *Because the answer to my whole existence is tied up with her. My greatest fear is that she's no longer alive, or that I'll never find her.*

As Leon stared at Belle, pure revelation flowed through him. He *knew* why she looked familiar to him. Had Marcello picked up on the resemblance? Or the manager at Donatello Diamonds? Probably not, or they would have said something, but he couldn't be sure. Ruggio thought he'd seen her on television.

Madonna mia!

"I told you I'd like to help you, and I will, but we can't talk here. Leave your car in the library parking lot and come with me. It will be safe."

"I don't need your help. Thanks all the same."

She opened her shoulder bag to get her keys, but

he put a hand on her arm. "If you want to meet your mother, I'm the person who can make it happen. But you're going to have to trust me."

Her gasp told him everything he wanted to know. Those fabulous blue eyes were blurry with tears as they lifted to his. "Are you saying what I think you're saying?" Her voice shook.

"Let's find out. Is there anything in your car you need?"

"No."

"Then we'll drive to my villa, where we can talk in private. I have some pictures to show you."

She moved like a person in a daze as he escorted her to his car and helped her inside. At a time like this, the shape of her long, elegant legs shouldn't have drawn his attention, but they did. Her flowery fragrance proved another assault on his senses.

"Do I look like her?"

"When I saw you come out of the alcove at the pension yesterday, you reminded me of someone, but I couldn't place you. It's bothered me ever since. Not until a few minutes ago, when you mentioned New York, did everything click into place." He started the engine. "You'll need to buckle up."

Leon wove through the streets to the villa, not really seeing anything while his mind played back through the years to the time he'd first met Luciana. He remembered his father telling him and Dante that she'd lived in New York for a year and could help them improve their English. How much had his parent known about the sober young princess he'd brought home to the palazzo, besides the fact that she had money and was beautiful?

Yet even if she'd told him nothing about having a

baby, his father would have guessed, if she'd had a
C-section or stretch marks. If not, he might still be in
the dark. Her terrible secret might explain why she'd
always seemed so remote and elusive to Leon.

Before they reached the house he phoned Simona.
After learning Concetta was back to normal and playing
with her new buckets in the kitchen, he told his housekeeper to prepare lunch for him and a guest. They'd be
arriving shortly and could eat out on the patio.

Engrossed in her own thoughts, the woman seated
next to him hadn't said a word during the drive. Once
upon a time she'd been a baby, separated at birth from
her mother by an ocean. When Leon thought about his
little daughter and how precious she was to him, he
couldn't fathom Belle's or Luciana's history. Leon had
so many questions he didn't know which one to ask
first.

When the white, two-story villa built along neoclas-
sic lines came into view, he pressed the remote to open
the gates and drove around to the back. When she saw
the flower garden there, Belle gave a gasp of admiration.

Leon helped her from the car and led her up the steps
into the rear foyer that opened into the dayroom. "At the
end of the hallway is a guest bedroom with bath, where
you can freshen up. When you're ready, come and find
me in here, and we'll eat lunch on the patio, where we
won't be disturbed."

"Thank you."

The second she disappeared, he hurried through the
main floor to the kitchen, where he found Concetta in
her playpen with some toys. She made delighted sounds
when she saw him, and lifted her arms. He gathered her

up and kissed her half a dozen times against her neck, causing her to laugh. Again he was reminded that his lunch guest had never known her mother's kiss. Obviously not her father's, either.

Talia smiled. "She's had her lunch and is ready for her nap."

"I brought company, so I can't give her all my attention, but I will when she wakes up." He kissed her once more and handed her back to Talia. His daughter didn't like being separated from him, and shed a few tears going down the hall to the staircase.

Much as he wanted to put her to bed himself, he was aware someone else was waiting for him, someone who'd been waiting years for any word about her parentage.

Simona looked over her shoulder. "Do you want lunch served now?"

"Please."

He retraced his steps to the dayroom and found Belle holding a five-by-seven framed photo she'd picked up from a grouping on one of the credenzas. Her back was turned to him, but even from this distance, he could see her shoulders shaking.

"I won't pretend to say I understand what you're feeling. I can only imagine what it must be like to see yourself in Luciana's image. Though you're not identical, anyone who knows you well would notice certain similarities."

Belle put the picture back and whirled around, her lovely face dripping with tears. She used both hands to wipe them off her chin. "My mother is a princess? *Your* stepmother? I—I can't take it in," she stammered. "In the orphanage I used to dream about what she would be like. I had to believe she gave me up because of a life-and-death reason. But my dreams never reached heights like that."

Leon put his hands on his hips. "I'm still in shock from the knowledge that she had a baby, yet there's never been a whisper of you."

He heard his guest groan. "When Cliff told me my mother was from Italy, I wanted it to be the truth. But I never thought I'd really find her. Why did you bother to come to the pension?" The throb in her voice hung in the air.

It was the question Leon had been asking himself over and over. He rubbed the back of his neck. "I can't honestly tell you the reason. It was a feeling that nagged at me to the point I had to investigate."

She clasped her hands together. "If you hadn't come, I would know *nothing,* and I would be flying back to New York without ever getting an answer. Thank heaven for you!" she cried. "I'll never be able to repay you."

A strange shiver chased through his body at the realization he might not have heeded the prompting. He'd tried to ignore it, until he'd been swimming in the pool. Then it wouldn't leave him alone.

Belle's gorgeous eyes searched his. "But now that I see her picture, I think I'm frightened. It's like that old expression about being careful what you wish for, because you might get it."

She wasn't the only one alarmed. Already she was important to him in ways he couldn't begin to explain.

"Is it because you've discovered you're the stepsister through marriage of the infamous Malatesta family?"

He'd thrown the question at her in a silky voice to

combat her pull on him. His attraction to her was sucking him in deeper and deeper. He didn't want this kind
of complication in his life, not after having lost Benedetta. Too many losses convinced him it was better
not to get involved. Leon had his daughter. She was
all he needed.

His guest stared at him through haunted eyes. "What
are you talking about? When the couple who adopted
me brought me to their house, they broke their birth
son's heart. He hated me from the first day. If anything,
I'm afraid of being the orphaned offspring of the woman
your father brought into your home, thereby breaking
your heart."

Her words touched on Leon's deep-seated guilt, and
confounded him. She really was frightened. He could
feel it. "You're pale and need to eat. Come out to the
patio with me."

Leon showed her though the tall French doors on
the far side of the dayroom. Simona had set the round,
wrought-iron table with a cloth and fresh flowers from
the garden. She'd prepared bruschetta and her *bocconcini*
salad of mozzarella balls and *cubetti di pancetta* ham he
particularly enjoyed.

He helped Belle to a seat where she could look out at
the Adriatic. With the hot, fair weather, he spotted half
a dozen sailboats and a few yachts out on the water. It
was a sight he never tired of, especially now with the
view of her alluring profile filling his vision.

Once he'd poured her some iced tea he said, "If you'd
prefer coffee or juice, I'll ask Simona to bring it."

But Belle had already taken a long swallow. "This
tastes delicious and is exactly what I needed. Thank
you."

After drinking half a glass himself, he picked up his fork and they started to eat. "I'm assuming Cliff is the son you referred to."

She nodded. "The Petersons adopted me when I was ten. Mr. Peterson never wanted me, but Nadine had always hoped for a daughter and finally prevailed on him to adopt me. They already had a sixteen-year-old son, who had no desire for a girl from an orphanage to move in on what he considered his territory."

Leon's stomach muscles clenched in reaction. He could relate to Cliff's hatred at that age. Leon had been eleven when his father had installed the twenty-year-old Luciana in the palazzo, a world that had belonged to him and his brother, Dante. *No one else.*

Now that the years had passed, and Leon had his own home and was a father, he understood better his parent's need for companionship. At eleven he'd been too selfish to see anything beyond his own wants.

From the beginning he'd rebuffed any overtures from Luciana, but he had to admit she'd never been unkind to him or Dante. Anything but. As the years went by, he'd learned to be more civil to her. Maturity helped him to see that her cool aloofness at times masked some kind of strange sadness, no doubt because she'd lost both her parents under tragic circumstances.

To think she'd had a baby she'd been forced to give up! The knowledge tore him apart inside. He could never give up Concetta for any reason.

"How did it happen that Cliff told you about your mother?"

After putting her fork down, Belle told him what had transpired at the attorney's office. Leon was astounded by what he heard. For her adoptive brother to take the money before telling her what she'd been desperate to know all her life sickened Leon. What made Cliff more despicable to him was to learn he hadn't let her keep the money that was legally hers.

"Tell me about your life with the Petersons. I'd like to hear."

She looked at him for a minute as if testing his sincerity. Then she began in a halting voice. "The day I was taken to their house, Cliff followed me into the small room that would be my bedroom. He grabbed me by the shoulders and told me his dad hadn't wanted a screaming baby around the house. That's why they'd picked me. But I'd better be good and stay out of his dad's way or I'd be sorry, Cliff said. And in fact his father was so intimidating, I tried hard to be obedient and not cause trouble."

Leon grimaced. "They should never have been allowed to adopt you."

"Laws weren't so strict then. The orphanage was overcrowded. You know how it is."

As far as Leon was concerned, it was criminal.

"Ben was a car salesman who loved old cars and had restored several, but it took all their money. He lost his job several times because of layoffs, and had to find employment at other car dealerships. The money he poured into his hobby ate up any extra funds they had. He was an angry man who never had a kind word. The more I tried to gain his favor, the more he dismissed me."

And destroyed her confidence, Leon bet.

"Nadine held a job at a dry cleaners and was a hard worker who tried to make a good home for us. She took me to church. It was one of the few places where I found comfort. But she was a quiet woman unable to show affection. It was clear she was afraid of her own son and stayed out of her husband's way as much as possible. I never bonded with any of them."

"How could you have under those circumstances?" Leon was troubled by her story.

"One good thing happened to me. As soon as I was old enough, I did babysitting for people in the neighborhood to earn money. I'd helped out with the younger children in the orphanage and knew how to play with them and care for babies. I love them." Her voice trembled.

There was a sweetness in Belle that got under his skin.

"To tell you the truth, I liked going to other people's houses to get away from Cliff and his father, who were so mean-spirited. He constantly asked me for money, telling me he'd pay me back, but he never did. I didn't tell on him for fear Ben would take out his anger on me."

With each revelation Leon's hands curled into tighter fists.

"Finally Cliff got a job in a garage after school, and in time bought himself a motorcycle. That kept him away from me, but from then on it seemed he was always in trouble with traffic tickets and accidents.

"He was often at odds with both his parents because of the hours he kept with girls they didn't know. Sometimes he barged into my room, to take out his frustration on me by bullying me. He never lost an opportunity to let me know I'd ruined his life," she whispered.

"I can't begin to imagine how you made it through those hellish years, Belle."

"When I look back on it neither can I. The day I turned eighteen, I got a job in a cell phone store and moved in with three others girls, sharing an apartment. It saved my life to get away from my nightmarish situation."

"Did Cliff follow you?"

"No. I left while he was gone. He had no idea where I went, and could no longer come after me for money and badger me. The few times I went to see Nadine, I went by her work at the dry cleaners so Cliff never saw me. She knew things were out of control with him and never pushed for me to come home again, because I was over the legal age."

Certain things Belle had just said brought home to Leon how mean-spirited he'd been to Luciana when she'd first come to live at the palazzo. He'd been an adolescent and had ignored any overtures on her part. Dante had done the same thing to her, following in his big brother's footsteps.

"I only ever saw him at the church funeral and the attorney's office after that," Belle explained. "When he told me my last name, I didn't know if it was the truth. But I wanted it to be true, so badly that I flew to Rimini on a prayer, knowing I'd seen the last of him, and was thankful."

Shaken by her revelations, Leon wiped the corner of his mouth with a napkin. "You didn't learn anything about your birth father through Cliff?"

She drank the last of her tea. "No. I decided he must have disappeared before my mother took me to the orphanage. What other explanation could there be…unless something horrendous had happened and she'd been raped? I shudder to think that might have been the case, and would rather not talk about it."

"Then we won't." If Luciana had been raped, and

Leon's father knew about it, how would he feel about Belle, the innocent second victim? The more Leon thought about it, the more it was like a bomb exploding, the resulting shock waves wreaking devastation. "What's the name of the orphanage?"

"The Newburgh Church Orphanage. Why do you ask?"

He put down his fork. "Despite the public's opinion of the Malatesta family, we give to a number of charities. Your story has decided me to send an anonymous donation to the orphanage where you were raised. That's something I intend to take care of right away."

A gift no matter how large wouldn't take away his guilt over his treatment of Luciana, but he realized the only reason Belle was still alive was due to the generosity of others who gave to charity.

"If you did that, the sisters would consider it heaven sent, but you don't need to do it."

"I want to. They gave you a spiritual and physical start in life. No payment would be enough."

"You're right," she said in a quiet voice. "One of the sisters in charge reminded us that we were lucky to be there where we could get the help we needed, so we shouldn't complain. The priest at the church where Nadine took me told me I was blessed to have a birth mother who loved me enough to put me in God's keeping."

Hard words for a child to accept, but Leon could only agree. Whatever Luciana's circumstances at the time, she'd at least had the courage to make certain her baby would be looked after. His admiration for her choice when she could have done something else changed his perception of her. But why had she given up her baby?

Had Luciana loved that baby with all her heart, the way he'd loved Concetta from the moment he'd learned they were expecting? He knew enough about Luciana's strict upbringing to realize she would have been afraid of letting anyone find out about her baby, causing a scandal that would tarnish the Donatello family name.

Unbelievable that her offspring had grown up into a beautiful, intelligent woman eating lunch with *him,* no less! *You're enjoying it far too much, Malatesta.*

Luciana had lived through a nightmare, and had gone on to make a home for his father and the boys despite Leon's antipathy. An unfamiliar sense of shame for his behavior over those early years crept into his psyche. He was now paying the price.

"Their goodness to you needs to be rewarded," he murmured, still trying to digest everything.

"Sometimes I felt guilty for wanting to know about my parents when the sisters tried so hard to keep our spirits up. When Cliff asked me why I wanted to find someone who didn't want me, I told him it wasn't important if they didn't want me. I just needed to know who I am and where I came from. But I'm not your responsibility, and I've taken up too much of your time as it is."

She pushed herself away from the table and stood up. "Now that I have answers to those questions, I can go back to New York. Needless to say, I'll be indebted to you for the rest of my life. Thank you for bringing me to your villa, and please thank the cook for the wonderful food. If you'll drive me back to the library, I'd be very grateful."

Leon got to his feet. "We haven't even scratched the surface yet."

"Yes, we have. You and I both know there are reasons why she gave me up. I would never want to cause her pain by showing up uninvited and unwanted."

"You could never be unwanted!" he declared. He refused to believe it, but that was the father in him speaking, the father who idolized his little girl. Ever since Belle was born, she'd never known the love of her own parents. He couldn't fathom it.

CHAPTER THREE

"YOU SAY THAT with such fervency, Leon, but we know the facts, don't we. My mother came back to Italy and married your father. Unless you're aware of other information, I'm sure she has never tried to find me."

"I have no idea and neither do you. Nevertheless—"

"Nevertheless, she and your father have made a life for themselves," Belle interrupted. "Last year I went to the orphanage for a final time to beg them to tell me something about my roots. I had a talk with the sister in charge." The tremor in Belle's voice penetrated to Leon's insides.

"What did she say to you?"

"She told me she wasn't at liberty to tell me anything, because my adoption was a closed case. Then she handed me a pamphlet to read. It was called 'A Practical Guide for the Adopted Child.' The material was based on research gathered by the psychiatric community. She said we'd discuss it after I'd finished it."

"And did you?"

"Yes!" she cried. "The whole brochure described me so perfectly, I went into shock."

"Explain what you mean."

She moistened her lips nervously. "I've always had

issues of self-esteem. Not to know who you are because you were given up for adoption means you don't have an identity. All my life I've wanted to know if I looked like my birth parents, or acted like them.

"What if I had sisters and brothers I knew nothing about? What if I came from a large family with half siblings or extended family I would never meet or get to know? It used to drive me crazy, wondering."

"Belle…at least now you know you have a mother and a stepfamily who are very much alive."

"Yes," she whispered, staring blindly out to sea. "If I do meet her I'll be able to learn about my birth father. I longed for a father, too, and spent many hours day-dreaming about him. But I'm terrified, Leon, because I *was* abandoned. Being abandonable meant I wasn't good enough to be kept and loved. That's a very hard thing to accept."

What she was telling Leon made him sick inside. "Since you don't know the circumstances of being left at the orphanage, don't you realize your adoptive father and brother have contributed to a lot of those negative feelings?"

"Of course." She took a shaky breath. "But to meet my own birth mother after all this time and find out from her own lips I hadn't been loved or wanted would shatter me. I don't know if I could handle it. The risk is too great."

Leon shook his head. "That's not going to happen to you. If you could see the loving way Luciana treats people…" Luciana was very loving to his daughter when he took Concetta over for visits. "You would see that your mother has an innate tenderness that goes soul deep." Leon had seen and felt it, but in the beginning he hadn't wanted to acknowledge it.

"Even so, I know I'm setting myself up to learn that everything I've ever thought or dreamed of about her and my father won't be as I assumed. You've told me she hasn't had other children, but she's a princess who has lived a life completely different from mine in every way, shape and form. The chances of her even wanting to meet the daughter she gave up are astronomical."

"That's not true. You don't know her as I do."

"I know you want to believe she'll be happy to see me, but you can't know what's deep in her heart. And there's your father to consider. The more I know about her and their life, the more I fear a permanent reunion could never be realized."

"It's true I don't know her inner thoughts." Leon's mind reeled when he compared the two women's worlds. And he had no idea how his father would react upon hearing the news that Luciana's daughter was in Rimini.

"Even if she's willing to meet me, how will she handle it? She thought she gave me up and would never see me again. Even if meeting me could satisfy the question of what happened to me, it wouldn't solve the issues she had for giving me up in the first place.

"What if seeing me exacerbates problems that bring new heartache?" Belle sounded frantic. "This meeting might result in trouble between her and your father, and they'll wish this had never happened…"

She wheeled around, her face white as parchment. Tears glistened like diamonds on those pale cheeks. "What if I brought on a crisis like that?"

Tortured by the fear and pain in her voice, Leon reached for her and rocked her in his arms like he would

Concetta when she was upset and frightened. "Shhh. That's not going to happen, Belle. I swear it." He kissed her hair and forehead without thinking.

"I—I don't want it to happen, but you can't guarantee anything."

Much as Leon hated to admit it, everything she'd revealed from her heart and soul made a hell of a lot of sense. But suddenly he had other things on his mind. When he'd pulled her to him, his only thought had been to comfort her. Yet the feel of her curves against his body invaded his senses, sending a quickening through him, one so powerful he needed to put her away from him. As gently as he could, he let go of her.

Belle took a step back before looking up at him through red-rimmed eyes. "The sister warned me my time would be better served by getting on with my own life rather than wasting it trying to find my birth mother, who obviously didn't want to be found.

"I left the orphanage with the renewed resolve to get on with my career and put my dreams away. Then came the moment in the attorney's office when Cliff made that slip about my birth mother being Italian."

"A providential slip, in my opinion," Leon muttered. He was beginning to believe some unseen power had been at work on both sides of the Atlantic. Otherwise how could he account for going to her pension to talk to her, when normally he would have left it alone?

"I agree, Leon. The second it happened, I ignored the sister's warning and the words in the pamphlet. I thought I knew better, and left for Italy, determined to keep looking. Now I wish I'd listened to her."

To his consternation, Leon was thankful she hadn't obeyed the sister in charge.

Belle's pleading eyes trapped his. "My mother's secrets are safe with me, and they have to remain safe with you, Leon. They *have* to." The desperation in her voice pulled on his chaotic emotions.

"They'll be safe as long as you do something important for me."

"What?" Her breathing came in spurts.

"I insist you stay in my house as my guest until you return to the States. If you don't let me do anything else, at least accept my hospitality. Our parents are married. That one fact bonds us in a way you can't deny."

"I wasn't going to, but since I got the information I came for, I'm planning to fly back to New York either tonight or in the morning. Every second I'm here, it's worse. The possibility that she could find out I'm a guest in your villa terrifies me. Whether she wanted me or not doesn't matter. She gave me life and I'd rather die than hurt her."

Leon's admiration for Belle grew in quantum leaps. "I believe you would," he murmured, before making a quick decision. "Your mind appears made up, so I'll see you back to your rental car."

"Thank you."

"I'll meet you in the foyer after I let my housekeeper know I'm leaving."

She nodded, and he went to find Simona. On his way back through the house he stopped in the dayroom to pick up the photograph Belle had been looking at. It showed Luciana and his father on their wedding day, outside the church. At twenty she bore an even stronger resemblance to her daughter.

When he reached the foyer, he found Belle studying

a large oil painting of his family. "That's my brother leaning against my mother."

"You look about six years old there. How old was Dante?"

"Five. We're just fourteen months apart."

She turned to him. "What a handsome family. You resemble both your parents."

"Genes don't lie, do they?"

"No. Your mother has the most wonderful smile."

"She was the most wonderful everything."

Belle stared at him. "You were very lucky to have a mother like that. What was her name?"

"Regina Emilia of the House of Della Rovere in Pesaro."

"A princess?"

"Yes." He opened the door so she could walk past him. After he helped her into the car, he handed her the photograph. "I want you to have this. No one deserves it more than you do."

Tears sprang to Belle's eyes. "I couldn't take it."

"There are dozens more where this came from." He shut the door and walked around to get behind the wheel.

Belle was still incredulous over what had happened. She hugged the photograph to her chest in wonder that she'd come to the end of her search. It was all because of Leon Malatesta, who was the most remarkable man she'd ever met. But it wasn't his generosity that had caused her to tremble in his arms just now.

While he'd been holding her, kissing her like he would to comfort a child, feelings of a different kind had curled through her like flame. The need to taste his mouth and let go of her feelings had grown so intense, she knew she was in deep trouble. He was her *stepbrother!*

In the past, when her friends had talked about desire, she'd never experienced it. Until a few minutes ago she hadn't known what it felt like. Shame washed over her to think she hadn't wanted him to stop what he was doing to her. By easing away from her before she was ready, he'd sent her into another kind of shock.

"Are you all right, Belle?"

"Yes. I—I'm just feeling overwhelmed," she stammered.

"Who could blame you?"

If he knew her intimate thoughts, he'd drive her straight to the airport right now. Earlier, he'd been ready to run her out of town, when he'd thought she was some gutter reporter out to dig up something salacious about his family. Instead he'd come after her at the pension and had single-handedly led her to her dream of finding her mother.

To tell him she was indebted to him couldn't begin to convey what was in her heart. To think that after all these years of aching to know anything about her origins she had her answer...

With one glance at the amazing man behind the wheel, Belle knew she could trust him to keep his silence. It was herself she didn't trust. There was such a huge part of her that wanted to visit her mother while she was still in Rimini; it was killing her.

The sooner Belle left Italy the better. But that meant she'd never see Leon again. How would she stand it?

You have *to handle it, Belle.*

Before they reached the library, she put the picture in

her shoulder bag and pulled out her car keys. The minute he turned into the parking space next to her rental, she opened the door and got out, before he could help her. It only took a moment before she was ensconced in her own vehicle and ready to drive off.

As his tall, powerful frame approached, she opened the window. "Thank you for everything, Leon. I'll never forget your kindness or the photograph."

"I'll never forget *you*," he said in his deep voice. "Good luck in your future position at TCCPI. Have a safe trip home."

Home. The word didn't have the same meaning anymore. "Goodbye." She started the engine and drove out to the main street. As soon as she reached the pension, she would phone to change her flight plans.

Through the rearview mirror she could see Leon standing there watching her, a bold, dynamic throwback from an earlier time in Italian history.

When she turned the corner and he was no longer in sight, a troubling thought came to her. He'd given her no grief about leaving Italy immediately. Her heart jumped all over the place because he'd made their parting far too easy. In truth, she knew the dark, mysterious son of the count could move heaven and earth if he felt like it.

Once Belle's rental car had disappeared, Leon pulled out his cell phone and gave Ruggio instructions to go to the pension and keep a close eye on her. If she went anywhere, he was to follow her.

After making a call to Simona to find out how his little girl was doing, and let his housekeeper know he might not be home until late, he headed for the bank to talk to his father. Leon found him in his suite on a business call. His parent waved him inside.

While Leon waited, he poured himself a cup of coffee from the sideboard and paced the floor with it. Whether his father knew about Belle's existence or not, what Leon had to tell him was going to come as a shock.

"It's good to see you," his father exclaimed after hanging up the phone. "Have you dropped in to tell me you're willing to consider ending your mourning period and start looking at another woman I have in mind for you?"

"No, Papà."

By marrying Benedetta, Leon had foiled his father's plan for him to marry a woman of rank he'd carefully picked out for him. The hurt hadn't been intentional, but Leon had always cared for Benedetta and refused to honor his father's wishes in the matter of his marriage. No argument the count raised had made any difference to Leon.

In that regard he wasn't so different from his widowed parent, who'd married a second time while Leon and Dante had begged him not to. But their pleading fell on deaf ears, and there'd been tension with their father ever since he'd brought Luciana into their home.

"I'm here to discuss something of a very delicate nature." Leon locked the door to his suite so no one could interrupt them. "Since I know you just passed your annual medical exam without any major problems, I feel you can handle this."

The count's dark brows met in a distinct frown. "You're beginning to make me nervous, Leonardo."

"Not as nervous as I am." He stared at his father. "This has to do with Luciana."

"Do you think she's hiding something from me since her medical exam?"

Leon heard the worry in his father's voice, revealing how much he cared about her. "I thought you told me she's as fine as you are. I'm talking about a secret she might have kept from you before you married her." Leon never was one to beat about the bush.

His last comment brought his father to his feet. Their gazes clung. *"You know?"*

The coffee cup almost fell out of Leon's hand. That one question told him his father had known about Luciana's baby all these years. He put the cup back on the sideboard. "If we're talking about a child she had out of wedlock, then yes."

Sullisto's gray eyes bordered on charcoal and were dimmed by moisture. "How did you find out?" he asked in a shaken voice.

Leon took a fortifying breath. "Before I answer that question, just tell me one thing. Did she want to give it up, or did she have to? I need to know the absolute truth before I say another word."

A look of sorrow crossed over his father's face. "She *had* to."

"Was she raped?"

The question hung like a live wire between them.

The older man took a deep breath. "No."

"Do you know the name of the father?"

A nerve throbbed in his cheek. "Yes. But *I* wasn't the father, if that's what you're thinking."

"I wasn't thinking it," Leon replied with total honesty. "I know you're an honorable man."

"Thank you for that." The count cleared his throat. "To answer your first question, Luciana wanted her little girl more than life itself. A day doesn't go by that she's not missing her, wanting to be with her. She doesn't talk about it all the time, but even after all these years, I see the sadness and witness her tears when she doesn't know I'm aware."

Hearing those words brought such relief to him for Belle's sake, it broke the cords binding Leon's chest. "How could she have given her up?"

"You have to hear the whole story, *figlio mio*."

"I'm listening."

His father paced the floor. "Luciana's father had many enemies and believed his wife was murdered. Afraid his daughter was in danger, he sent Luciana to a special college in New York at eighteen, under an assumed name, while he had his wife's death investigated.

"While she was away, she met a student. They fell in love and soon she found out she was expecting. Her situation became desperate because she knew her father would never agree to a marriage between them."

"But she was pregnant! Was he that tyrannical?"

"That's a harsh word, Leonardo. Let's just say he was a rigid man. Luciana and her lover decided to be married by a justice of the peace in a town an hour away from New York City, where she was in school. But on the day before the wedding could take place, he was killed in a hit-and-run accident. The driver was never apprehended."

Leon grimaced. "Luciana must have thought she was in a nightmare."

"Exactly. Because of what had happened to her mother, she was afraid she'd been hunted down and her lover murdered."

Aghast, Leon said, "When did she tell you all this?"

"When I asked her to marry me. You see, despite all the rumors about my wanting to take over the Donatello Diamonds empire, the reason I married her was because I'd learned to care for her a great deal."

"It's all right, Papà. You can call it what it was. You loved her."

"So you've guessed it."

"Yes."

His father breathed deeply. "Her sorrow was so great, I thought that having two stepsons to help raise would ease a little of her pain. You boys were only ten and eleven, and needed a mother, especially Dante." His voice trembled. "As for me, I needed someone who could share my life. Naturally, it wasn't like the feelings I had for your mother, but then, you can't expect that."

Leon couldn't believe what he was hearing. They'd never had this conversation about his mother before. Belle was the catalyst to force a discussion that should have taken place years earlier.

"Luciana's father was overjoyed, because he knew I would take care of her. Before she gave me an answer, she said she had something to tell me that no one else knew about, not even her father. If I still wanted her, then she would accept my proposal.

"I listened while it all came pouring out. After bitter anguish and soul searching, she'd felt she had no choice but to give up the baby for adoption so nothing would happen to her precious daughter.

"When she gave her up, she had to sign a paper that meant she could never see her child again or take her back. It was a sealed document. Luciana signed it because she was positive her own days were numbered, but at that point she didn't care about herself. When she returned to Rimini, she wasn't the same vivacious girl I'd known before she left."

Again Leon stood there, dumbfounded by the revelations.

"Her honesty only deepened my respect for her."

It appeared Belle had inherited that same admirable characteristic from her mother.

"Not long after our marriage, her father died of heart failure. She needed me more than ever." Sullisto eyed his son soberly. "But you still haven't answered *my* question."

Leon shook his head. "After what you've told me, I'm not sure it would be the wise thing to do."

"You don't trust me?"

"That's not it. I'm thinking of her daughter, who came to Rimini this week looking for the mother who gave her up."

"What?"

Leon nodded. "Sit down, Papà, while I tell you a story about Belle Peterson."

A few minutes later his father was wiping his eyes. "I can't even begin to tell you what this is going to mean to Luciana when she finds out."

"Except that Belle doesn't want Luciana to know anything." For the next few minutes he told his father what had been contained in that pamphlet, and Belle's fear of hurting her mother.

"Hurt her?" Sullisto cried out. "It would have the opposite effect! I know what I'm talking about. The one thing in our marriage that has kept us from being truly happy has been Luciana's soul-deep sadness. We tried to have a baby, but weren't successful. She's always believed God was punishing her for giving up her child."

"Incredibile—"

"Not until two months ago did we learn that Valeria's death was ruled accidental. That very day I begged Luciana to call the orphanage and find out what had happened to Belle. At least inquire if she'd been adopted. But she said she didn't dare, because she was afraid her daughter would hate her. I told her I'd hire a private investigator to locate her, but Luciana was convinced Belle would refuse to talk to her, after she'd given her up."

"Belle has the exact same fear, that her mother won't like her."

His father rubbed his hands together. "To know she has come all this way looking for her mother will be like a dream Luciana never thought could come true."

"Then you don't have a problem if they're united?"

"Mind? How can you even ask me that?" he cried. "It's my dream to make Luciana happy, but it has always been out of my hands."

That was all Leon needed to know. He could only imagine Belle's joy when the two of them finally met. "I have a plan. Bring Luciana to the villa for dinner this evening. Tell her the baby is better."

His father nodded. "She's been waiting forever for an official invitation from you."

"I know. I'm sorry about that, but it's something I plan to rectify."

It was regrettable, but true, that though his father had come by the villa on occasion, Leon had never invited them over as a couple. His cool attitude toward Luciana had prevailed all these years. He wished he'd known early on that she'd given up her child. It wouldn't have changed his feelings over his father's remarriage at the time, but he might not have been so quick to judge her because of false assumptions and the many rumors that had reached his teenage ears.

"It doesn't matter, Leonardo. I know how much your mother meant to you and Dante, and I've understood. As for Luciana, we both know how much she loves your Concetta and will rejoice at the opportunity to be with her in your home."

Leon did know that. "Come at seven. By then Concetta will have been fed."

His father seemed more alive as they walked to the door. He gave Leon the kind of hug they hadn't shared in years. It wasn't just the fact that Leon had broken down and invited them both over for dinner. Only now was he beginning to understand how much his father had suffered in his second marriage because of Luciana's pain.

Once Leon left the bank, he alerted Simona about the plans for the evening, then drove to the pension. Ruggio was parked two cars behind Belle's rental near the entrance. Leon walked over to thank his security man, and told him he wouldn't need him any longer for surveillance.

A feeling of excitement he hadn't known in over a year passed through him as he went inside the pension and pressed the buzzer to announce his arrival. Before long Rosa appeared. *"Signore?"*

"Forgive me for not introducing myself before. My name is Leonardo di Malatesta, *signora.*" The older woman's eyes widened in recognition of his name. "I need to see Signorina Peterson on a matter of life and death." He'd spoken the truth and felt no guilt about it. "I know she's here. Ask her to come out to the foyer, *per favore.*" He put several bills on the counter for the woman's trouble.

After a slight hesitation she nodded and hurried through the alcove. Leon didn't have to wait long before Belle appeared, with a tear-ravaged face and puffy eyes. He wasn't surprised to see her in this kind of pain.

"Leon?" Her breathing sounded ragged. "What are you doing here? We've already said goodbye." Maybe he was crazy, but he had the gut feeling she was glad to see him.

"Yes, we did, but something's come up. Let's go to your room and I'll tell you what's happened."

She nodded. "All right." Any fight she might have put up seemed to have gone out of her for the moment.

Leon thanked Rosa before trailing Luciana's daughter into the alcove and down the hall to her small room. She was still dressed in the white dress she'd been wearing, but it looked wrinkled.

When they went inside and he'd shut the door, he saw the indention on the single bed, where she'd been sobbing. Leon knew she couldn't bear the thought of having to leave Italy without meeting her mother.

He came straight to the point. "I went to see my father after I left you."

"Oh no—"

"Before you get upset, hear me out. I learned that he knew all about you before he married your mother." Belle's eyes widened as if in disbelief. "I asked him if Luciana had wanted to give up her baby, or if she'd *had* to."

Belle's fear was palpable. "W-what did he say?"

"I'll quote you his answer. He said, 'She had to, but she wanted her little girl more than life itself. A day doesn't go by that she's not missing her, wanting to be with her.'"

Belle turned away from him to hide her emotions. Without considering the ramifications, he grasped her shoulders and turned her around to face him. Her body trembled like a leaf in the wind. Earlier when he'd held her, it hadn't been long enough. This time he drew her against him and wrapped his arms around her.

Her gleaming dark hair tickled his jaw as he murmured, "Whatever plans you've already made to fly back to New York will have to be put on hold, because he's bringing her to my villa tonight for dinner so you two can meet."

An unmistakable cry escaped Belle's lips. She tried to get away, but he wouldn't allow it, and crushed her to him. "She won't have any idea you're going to be there. My father believes this is the best way to handle it, and I do, too. He wouldn't want this if he didn't believe she'll be overjoyed. If you need more convincing, I'll phone and tell him to come over here."

Belle's head was burrowed against Leon's chest, reminding him of the way Concetta sought comfort when she was upset. He rubbed his hands over her back.

"How can you possibly leave and not see her?" he argued. "This is the opportunity you've been waiting for all your life. You've been so strong. You've survived an existence that would have defeated anyone else. Don't you realize how proud your mother's going to be of you and what you've accomplished?"

"I want to believe it."

"Would it help if I told you *I'm* proud of you? When the head of your company sang your praises, I could have told him what a remarkable woman you really are.

How you survived in that household is beyond me. The methodical way you've gone about trying to find your mother in a foreign country, with no help from anyone but yourself, defies description."

He heard sniffing. "Thank you for those kind words." *Belle*...

"I'll wait while you gather all your belongings. For the rest of the time you're in Italy, you're going to be my guest. Don't worry about your rental car. If you'll leave the key at the desk, one of my staff will return it to the agency. When we arrive at the house, you'll have the rest of the day to get ready for this evening."

"You're far too good to me."

He pressed his lips against her temple. "Why wouldn't I be? For you to find your mother with my help after all these years brings me great happiness." *It's a gift I couldn't give my daughter, but I can give it to you.* "You wouldn't deprive me of it, would you?"

Slowly she lifted her head. One corner of her lovely mouth lifted. "No. Of course not, but I'm so nervous. What if—"

"Don't go there," he interrupted in a quiet voice, kneading her upper arms. "I can promise you that if she knew what was ahead for tonight, her fear would be much greater than yours.

"Papà told me that for years she has grieved because your case was sealed when she gave you up. Even if she could get a court order for information, she's been afraid you would find it unforgivable, what she did, and would reject her out of hand."

"Is this the truth?" Fear mixed with hope in Belle's voice.

"Ask my father. He wouldn't lie to me and is excited

for the two of you to meet. It can't happen soon enough for either of us."

"Then he's truly not upset?"

"Anything but. He believes this reunion will help solve certain problems in his marriage."

"What do you mean?"

"Her sadness for having to give you up, and his inability to take it away."

"Oh, Leon…" Belle's heart was in her eyes.

Unable to deny the attraction, he cupped her face in his hands, but it wasn't enough. He needed to taste her, and lowered his head, kissing her fully on the mouth. Right or wrong, she'd been a temptation from the outset.

As he coaxed her lips apart, wanting more, he drew a response from her that shot fire through him. What should have been one kiss deepened into another, then another. He should have been able to stop what was happening, but she'd aroused too much excitement in him.

"Belle…" He moaned her name, hungry for her. But in the next instant she tore her mouth from his and backed up against the door. He felt totally bereft. "Why did you pull away from me?"

"Someone has to stop this insanity!" she gasped, obviously trying to catch her breath. "I'm not blaming you. I could have resisted you, but I didn't because… I enjoyed it."

An honest woman.

"I could say I didn't know what got into me, but that would be a lie," she added. "The fact is I've never been this intimate with a man and I forgot myself."

"You're saying…"

"Shocking, isn't it? At twenty-four?" she blurted. "When I didn't try to stop you, I—I can understand why you kept kissing me. You enjoyed a happy marriage and miss your wife. As for me, I have no excuse, so let's just agree that this was a physical aberration that shouldn't have happened, and promise we'll never find ourselves in this situation again. Promise me, Leon. Otherwise I can't go through with anything, even if it means never meeting my mother." She had fire in her eyes.

"I swear I'll never do anything you don't want me to do. Does that make you feel any better?"

"No."

More astounding honesty. "While you pack, I'll go out to the lobby and take care of the bill."

She moved away from the door. "I don't expect you to pay for me."

"I know. That's why I want to," he murmured. She didn't have a mercenary bone in her beautiful body. Just now her mouth had almost given him a heart attack. Belle Peterson had many parts to her, all of them unexpected and thrilling. After Benedetta died, he thought he'd never desire another woman.

He left the room and paid her account through Sunday, adding a healthy bonus that brought a faint smile to Rosa's dark eyes.

Belle appeared sooner than he would have thought, carrying her shoulder bag and suitcase. Evidently her nervous anticipation over seeing her mother had made her hurry, but he had a hunch she'd always been a punctual person. Another trait he couldn't help but applaud.

He took the luggage from her and ushered her out to his car. For the second time in two days he was taking her home. A great deal had changed since yesterday morning, when he'd gone to bed after being up all night with Concetta.

Leon no longer questioned why his assistant's phone call to the villa had prompted him to get dressed and go down to the bank for an explanation. It appeared there'd been a grand design at work in more ways than one. Even so, the thought raised the hairs on the back of his neck.

CHAPTER FOUR

AN HOUR AFTER getting settled in the fabulous guest bedroom she'd only glimpsed yesterday, Belle heard a tap on the door. She'd been drying her freshly washed hair with her blow-dryer, and turned it off to go answer. Dinner wouldn't be for another hour.

"The *signore* sent me to find out if you need laundry service or would like something ironed for tonight," said the maid standing there.

Belle had never had service like this in her life. Since she wanted to look perfect for her mother, she decided to take advantage of Leon's incredible hospitality. But she couldn't forget for a second that his life and the lives of their parents were unique in the annals of Italian history.

"Just a moment, please."

She hurried over to her suitcase, which he'd placed on a chest at the end of the king-size bed. After opening it, she pulled out the short-sleeved, lime-colored suit with white lapels and white trim.

"This needs a little touching up to get out the wrinkles," she explained as she handed it to the maid.

"I'll be right back."

"Thank you very much."

While Belle waited, she finished brushing her naturally curly hair and put on her pearl earrings. Fastening the matching pearl necklace presented problems because she was all thumbs. Tonight would be the culmination of her dreams. Despite Leon's compliments, the fear that she'd be a disappointment to her mother wouldn't leave her alone.

She was glad she'd brought her low-slung white heels. When she'd packed for her trip, she hadn't really imagined having an opportunity to wear them.

Before long, the maid brought Belle's suit to the bedroom. "The *signore* said you should join him on the patio whenever you're ready," she announced.

Just the thought of him sent Belle's heart crashing to her feet. She could still feel his mouth on hers, filling her with an ecstasy she didn't know was possible.

Trying to pull herself together, she thanked the maid again. One more glance in the ornate, floor-length mirror after fastening the buttons, and she felt ready to join her host. Would he approve?

What if he didn't? Did it matter to her personally?

Yes, it mattered. Horribly. Those moments of intimacy at the pension had been a revelation to her. The way he'd kissed her had brought every nerve ending to life. The fact that he was her stepbrother didn't matter once they'd crossed the line. What happened between them had shaken her so badly she could hardly function right now, but she had to!

Not wanting to keep Leon waiting, she gave one more glance to the photo she'd placed on the dresser, then left the room and started down the hall. She knew her way out to the patio, but before she reached the open French doors, a darling brown dog rushed over to greet her. As she paused to rub his head, she saw that Leon wasn't alone.

Her eyes traveled to the dainty, dark blonde baby he held in his arms. She was wearing a pink pinafore and tiny pink sandals, the colors of which stood out against the black silk shirt he was wearing. The child cuddled to his chest couldn't be more than six or seven months old and possessed features finer than bone china.

He was walking her around the patio. As he talked to her, he kissed her cheek and neck over and over again. The scene with the baby was so sweet it brought hot tears to Belle's eyes. To be loved like that...

She shivered. She knew what those lips felt like on her mouth. To her shame, she hadn't wanted him to stop. Right now she longed to feel them against her own neck.

Was the baby *his* child? Or could she be Dante's? Belle didn't know much about his family. Their coloring was so different, given Leon's vibrant black hair, but his affection for the little girl touched Belle to the core.

He must have sensed Belle's arrival. When he turned, their gazes fused. She felt him taking in her appearance. In that moment his eyes glowed a crystalline gray that made her legs go weak in response. It was that same smoldering look she'd glimpsed back at the pension after she'd pulled away from him.

"I can see you've already met Rufo. Now come and meet my daughter, Concetta."

"*Your* baby?" Belle cried in wonder. That explained the love he showered on her. "Oh," she crooned softly, "you sweet little thing." She touched the hand clutching her daddy's shirt.

"I've seen a lot of babies in my life at the orphanage, but I never saw one who had your exquisite features and skin. You're like a porcelain doll." She looked up at Leon. "She must have gotten those dark brown eyes from her mother."

"Concetta inherited my wife's looks."

"Obviously she was a beauty."

He pressed a kiss to his daughter's forehead. "Before you judge me too harshly, I didn't mention my daughter to you before now because we had a greater issue on our minds. I planned to introduce you after you agreed to follow through and meet Luciana."

"You don't have to explain. I understand. Would you think me too presumptuous to ask how your wife died?"

"No. She passed away giving birth."

"Oh no! How awful for her—for you…" Belle's gaze traveled back to the baby. "You lost your mommy? No little girl as sweet as you should grow up without your mother. I—I'm so sorry, darling." Her voice broke. "At least you'll always know who she was, because you have your daddy, who loved her so much. And you have pictures."

Without conscious thought Belle kissed that little hand before she looked up at Leon. "What went wrong during the delivery?"

He cuddled his daughter closer. "Soon after our marriage Benedetta was diagnosed with systemic lupus."

A moan escaped Belle's lips before she could prevent it. "One of the sisters at the orphanage had that disease."

He kissed the baby's head. "My wife was the daughter of the now deceased head of the kennel on my father's estate. She and I had been friends throughout childhood. Later on, after I came home from college and had been working at the bank for several years, we fell in love, and got married in a small, quiet ceremony, out of the public eye.

"Before long her illness became more aggressive. She developed a deep vein thrombosis in the leg, which was hidden at the time. A piece of blood clot broke off and ended up in her lung. It caused it to collapse, and heart failure followed."

"Oh, Leon…"

"Concetta came premature. My great sadness was that Benedetta's life had been snuffed out before she'd been able to hold our baby."

Belle's heart ached for them. "Will Concetta get lupus?"

"No. Thankfully, the pediatrician says my daughter is free of the disease. It doesn't necessarily follow that the child inherits it."

"Thank heaven!" Belle exclaimed. "How lucky she is to have her daddy! Every girl needs her father."

Leon's glance penetrated to the core of her being. "You think it's possible to do double duty?" he rasped.

In that question, she heard a vulnerability she would never have expected to come from him. The dark prince who'd kissed her hungrily had a weakness, after all. A precious cherub, the reminder of the woman he'd loved and lost. "With her father loving her more than anyone else in the world, she won't know anything else, and will have all the love she needs, to last her a lifetime and beyond."

He hugged his daughter tighter. "I hope you're right."

"I *know* I am. Do you think she'd get upset if I tried to hold her?"

"She isn't used to people except my staff and family. If you try, you'll be taking your life in your hands, but if you want to risk it…" He didn't sound unwilling, just skeptical.

"I do." The operation at the orphanage was such that the older children always helped with the infants and toddlers. Belle had no hesitation as she plucked the baby from his powerful arms.

By now Concetta had started to cry, but Belle whirled around with her and sang a song that so surprised the baby, she stopped crying and looked up at her. The dog followed them. It was then Leon's little girl discovered the pearls, and grabbed them. Belle laughed gently. "You like those, don't you."

At this point Leon attempted to intervene. She felt his fingers against her skin while he tried to remove his daughter's hands, but she held on tighter. After a slight tug-of-war, the necklace broke and the pearls rolled all over the patio tiles. The sound sent Rufo chasing after them.

"Uh-oh." Belle chuckled again, because the surprise on the baby's dear face was priceless. "Where did they go?" Concetta turned her head one way, then another, trying to find them.

"I'm sorry about your necklace, Belle," Leon murmured, while his gaze narrowed on her mouth. Heat radiated through her body to her face.

"It's nothing," she said in a ragged voice.

"Once the pearls are gathered, I'll have them restrung for you."

"Don't you dare," she said, to fight her physical attraction to Concetta's father, who suddenly looked frustrated. His baby made him so human, her heart warmed to him. "This is costume jewelry I bought for twenty dollars on sale. We don't care, do we, Concetta." She kissed her head and kept walking with her, to put Leon out of her mind. Of course, it didn't work.

"Let's watch that boat with the red-and-white sail." She pointed to it, but by now the baby was staring at her. There were no more tears. "I bet you're wondering who I am. My name is Belle Donatello. I can't believe I know my last name. Your generous daddy is letting me stay here for a few days."

I'm staying at my peril.

She lifted her head to find Leon standing a few feet away. "How do you say *daddy* in Italian?"

"Papà," he answered in a husky tone.

Belle turned so Concetta could see him. "There's your *papà*."

All of a sudden his daughter started to whimper, and reached for him. Belle closed the distance and gave her back to him. But the baby quickly looked around and kept staring at Belle in fascination.

Leon's sharp intake of breath reached her ears. "If I hadn't witnessed it with my own eyes, I wouldn't have believed what just happened."

"What do you mean?"

"She didn't break into hysterics with you. Anything but."

Belle's mouth curved upward. "I learned in the orphanage that all babies have hysterics. It's normal. The trick is to get their attention before they become uncontrollable. The sisters were lucky, since between their habits and crucifixes, they were able to quiet the babies down fast. My pearls did rather nicely, don't you think?"

Leon had a very deep, attractive chuckle. "I think the next time you hold her, you'd better keep her hands away from the pearls in your earlobes. Inexpensive as they might be, the rest of you is…irreplaceable."

A certain nuance in his voice made her realize he'd been remembering what had gone on earlier. It wasn't something you could forget.

"Did you hear that, Concetta?" She poked the child's tummy and got a smile out of her. Lifting the hem of the pinafore, she said, "Pink is my favorite color, too. I bet your *papà* bought this for you because he couldn't resist seeing you in it." The gleam in his eyes verified her statement. "Even if you weren't a real princess, you look like one."

For the first time since she'd joined him, his features hardened. "There are no titles under this roof and never will be."

Meaning even after his father died? It followed that, being the elder brother, he *would* be Count Malatesta one day, but he'd just made it clear he wanted no part of it.

"After what I've learned of my mother's tragic history, I think that's the wisest decision you could make as her father."

He switched Concetta to his other compact shoulder. "Before she and my father arrive, this little one needs her dinner. I'll take her to the kitchen."

"Can I come, too, and help feed her?"

A quick, white smile transformed him into the kind of man her roommates would say was jaw-dropping gorgeous. He *was* that, and so much more Belle couldn't find words. "If you do, you may have to change your outfit."

She sent him a reciprocal smile, attempting like mad

to pretend she hadn't experienced rapture. "That'll be no problem."

Together with the dog, they walked through the day-room and down another hall. Belle glimpsed a library and an elegant dining room on their way to the kitchen. From one of the windows she could see a swimming pool surrounded by ornamental flowering trees. A vision of the two of them in the water after dark wouldn't leave her alone.

In the kitchen three women were busily working. Leon introduced her to his housekeeper, Simona, the maid, Carla, and the nanny, Talia, who reached for the baby. If they knew who Belle really was, rather than simply being a guest, they showed no evidence.

After tying a bib around Concetta's neck, Talia placed her in the high chair next to the table and drew a chair over to feed her.

Belle shot Leon an imploring glance. "Could I give her her dinner?"

He looked surprised. "You really want to? Sometimes she doesn't cooperate."

"That's all right. I'd love it! I moved out of my adoptive parents' house at eighteen and haven't tended a baby since."

To her joy, he said something to Talia in Italian. She smiled at Belle, then brought the baby food jars to the table. Belle opened the lid on the meat.

"Hmm…smells like lamb." She glanced down at the dog, who sat there begging her with his eyes. "Sorry, this food isn't for you, Rufo." The other jar contained squash. "Oh boy, Concetta. This all looks nummy." Belle took the spoon and dipped it in the vegetable. "Here it comes."

Slowly, she lifted it in the air and did a few maneuvers. Those black-brown eyes followed the action faithfully. Belle brought the spoon closer to the baby, who'd already opened her mouth, waiting for her food. Belle saw Leon in the shape of his daughter's mouth and felt an adrenaline rush that almost caused her to drop the utensil.

He burst into laughter. "You're a natural mother."

"Not really." She began feeding Concetta her meat while the women watched. "I fed the babies at the orphanage. This is the only thing I have a natural aptitude for."

"The CEO at TCCPI has told me otherwise," he stated.

If she wasn't careful, she might start wanting to hear more of his compliments. *And believing them, Belle?*

"When you're on your own and forced to earn a living, you learn a trade fast."

A troubled expression entered his eyes. "Your adoptive father never helped you after you left home?"

She shook her head, with its dark, shiny mass of flowing hair, and continued to feed the baby. "But I'd be ungrateful if I didn't acknowledge that he and Nadine fed and clothed me for eight years while I lived under their roof. Some of my friends in the orphanage never got adopted, and lived their whole lives there until they were old enough to leave. I was one of the luckier ones."

Concetta hadn't quite finished her food when she put her hands out as if to say she was full. She was so adorable, Belle could hardly stand it. "I think you've had enough." Without thinking about it, she untied the bib. After wiping Concetta's mouth with it, she put it on the table and lifted the baby out of the high chair.

"Uh-oh. I can tell you need to be changed. Where's your bedroom?"

Leon had been lounging against the wall, watching them. "Upstairs."

Belle darted him a glance. "If you'll show me, I'll change her, but only if it's all right with you."

One black brow lifted. "Since you've got her literally eating out of the palm of your hand, I have a feeling she'd have a meltdown if anyone else dared to interfere at this point."

"Leon…" The man had lethal charm. It had been getting to her from the first day and had worked its way beneath her skin.

"Follow me."

The only thing to do was concentrate on the baby. "You have the most beautiful home, Concetta. I always wanted to live in a house with a staircase like this. I wonder how long it will be before you slide down the banister when your *papà* isn't looking."

She heard the low chuckles trailing after him, and it was impossible to keep her eyes off his hard-muscled frame. She knew what it was like to be crushed against him, and came close to losing her breath, remembering. In father mode, Leon was completely different from the forbidding male she'd first met. Like this he was irresistible.

Rufo darted ahead of them. They entered the first room at the top of the stairs. "I might have known you'd live in a nursery like this. Your father has spoiled you silly, you lucky little girl." Belle felt as if she'd entered fairyland. He'd supplied everything a child could ever want.

There was a photograph on the dresser of a lovely,

dark blonde woman who had to be Leon's deceased wife. Concetta would always ache for the mother who hadn't lived through childbirth. The thought made Belle's heart constrict. She knew what it felt like to want your mother and never know her.

She carried the baby over to the changing table against the wall and got busy. After powdering, she put a clean diaper on her. Concetta's cooperation made it an easy operation.

Leon stood next to Belle. The scent of the soap he used in the shower lingered to torment her.

"You've mesmerized my daughter."

"It's the lime suit." She picked up the baby. After giving her a kiss on her neck, she placed Concetta in her father's arms. "I'm wearing a different color than she's used to seeing."

"So that's your secret weapon?"

When Belle raised her head in query, the crystal gray eyes she remembered had morphed to a slate color. Just now she'd detected an edge in his tone, and didn't understand it. If he hadn't wanted her to feed or change the baby, he should have told her.

As her spirits plummeted, she heard a male voice, and spun around to discover Leon's father in the nursery doorway. Rufo had already hurried over to him. She recognized him from the photographs, but since the time those pictures were taken, his dark hair had become streaked with silver.

His presence meant Belle's mother was here! Her mouth went dry.

Leon saw the shock on his father's face. Normally, he headed straight for Concetta, but not this time. The count was staring at Belle. Her beauty stopped men in their tracks, but he'd also seen the resemblance to Luciana and was obviously speechless for a moment.

His father wasn't the only one. Leon had felt out of control since their first meeting. Just now her easy interaction with Concetta, and his daughter's acceptance of Belle, had caught him unaware. It had to be because Belle reminded her of Luciana. To his chagrin he'd experienced a ridiculous moment of jealousy.

"Papà? May I introduce Belle Peterson. Belle? Meet my father, Sullisto."

The older man walked over to Belle with suspiciously bright eyes. "It's like seeing your beautiful mother when she was in her twenties." He kissed her on both cheeks and grasped her hands. "My wife's not going to believe it. I'm not sure I do."

"I don't believe it, either," Belle answered in an unsteady voice. "It's like a dream. I'm so happy to meet you."

He studied her features for a long moment. "How do you want to do this, my dear?"

Leon appreciated his father's sensitivity and stepped in. "Where's Luciana?"

"I left her in the living room, playing the piano."

"Why don't you entertain Concetta up here while I take Belle downstairs to meet her?" He kissed the baby and handed her over. "I'll come back for the two of you in a few minutes and we'll go down together."

His father hugged the baby to him before looking at Belle. "Take all the time you need."

"Are you sure this is the right thing to do, *signore?*" Her question went straight to Leon's gut.

"Call me Sullisto. You're going to make a new person of my wife," his father reassured her.

A hand went to her throat. "Thank you for being so kind and accepting."

Leon could only wonder at the emotions gripping her. "Let's go."

She followed him out of the room and down the stairs. The sound of the piano grew louder. When they reached the front foyer, he turned to her. "Ready?"

Belle nodded. "I've been waiting for this all my life, but I'd like you to go first."

Taking a deep breath, he opened the French doors. "Good evening, Luciana."

The playing stopped and she got up from the baby grand piano looking lovely as usual in a draped midriff jersey dress in a blue print. Though her daughter wasn't wearing Versace, Belle had the same sense of style and good taste as her mother.

She hurried across the Oriental rug toward him. "Thank you for inviting us, Leon. Where's your precious baby?"

He noticed the two women had the same little tremor in their voices when they were nervous. They were both the same height, but Luciana wore her hair short these days in a stylish cut. After giving her a kiss on both cheeks, he said, "Upstairs with Papà. But before he brings her down, there's someone I want you to meet."

"A special woman?"

He knew what she was thinking. His father had Leon's love life on his mind and no doubt had been discussing the list of eligible titled women with Luciana. "This one is very special. You'll have to speak English. Come in," he called over his shoulder.

After Belle stepped into the living room, he watched Luciana's expression turn to incredulity, then shock. She went so pale he put an arm around her shoulders and helped her to the nearest love seat. "Your daughter has come all the way from New York looking for you."

A stillness enveloped both women before Luciana cried, *"Arabella?"*

Tears splashed down Belle's cheeks. She, too, had lost color. Fear that she might faint prompted Leon to help her sit next to her mother.

"That's my real name?" she asked in wonder. "Arabella?"

"Yes. Arabella Donatello Sloan. Your father was English. Arabella was his grandmother's name. She told him it meant beautiful lion. You *are* so beautiful. I don't know how you ever found me, but oh, my darling baby girl, I've missed and ached for you every moment since I gave you up. You've been in my every prayer. Let me hold you."

It was like a light had gone on inside, bringing Luciana to life, illuminating her countenance. Like her mother, Belle glowed with a new radiance. They weren't aware of anyone else.

The sight of the two women clinging desperately while they communicated and wept and made dozens of comparisons brought a giant-size boulder to Leon's throat.

The explanation of Belle's name reminded Leon of his conversation with her the day before, about his own name meaning lion. Belle remembered, too, because she darted him a quick glance. It was an odd coincidence.

"I want you to know about your father. I have pictures of him back at the palazzo."

Belle flashed Leon a smile. He knew what seeing a picture of him would do for her.

"Arabella was the grandmother who raised him before she died. We talked about names before you were born. That's the one we liked the best. You would have loved him, but he was killed before we could be married. I was so terrified he'd been murdered that, when I had you, I made the decision to give you up because the danger you might be killed, too, was too great."

Leon moved closer to them. "We now know that no one was murdered, and Robert's death had to have been an accident."

"Yes, but I didn't know it until a few months ago. When I think about the years we've lost…" Her mother broke down sobbing.

Belle held her for a long time. "What happened to my father?"

"Robert and I had been in downtown Newburgh and we'd just left each other. He'd started across the intersection when this car crossed over the lines and came at him at full speed. The driver just kept going, leaving Robert lying there lifeless."

Belle's groan filled the room.

"It was so horrifying I went into labor and was taken to the hospital. You came a month early, Arabella. You were still in the intensive care unit when I had a graveside service for Robert. The police never found the man who killed him."

"How terrible for you." Belle reached out to hug her harder.

"It *was* terrible, since I couldn't tell my father. He didn't know about Robert. I knew if I took you back to

Italy, he wouldn't let me keep you at the palazzo. Worse, I was afraid you wouldn't be safe with me anywhere.

"When I made arrangements for you at the orphanage, you still needed a lot of care. But my father sent for me to come home. He wasn't feeling well, because of his heart, and hinted that he wanted me to meet Count Malatesta, who'd recently lost his wife to cancer. My father wanted him for a son-in-law.

"We married on my twentieth birthday. The fact that he still wanted me after I confessed everything to him in private proved to me he was a good man. But while I was still in New York, I couldn't imagine ever marrying again. It was agony, because I had to rely on the sisters to watch over you. I told them I'd named you Belle. That way no one could ever trace you to Robert or me. I also told them they had to promise that whoever adopted you would take you to church."

"Nadine always took me."

"Thank heaven for that."

In all the years Leon had known Luciana, she'd never made such long speeches. In one breath he'd already learned enough about her past to erase the lies he'd heard whispered by the staff and others who lived on gossip. Those lies about her being shallow and of little substance had colored his thinking for years.

He left the living room and remained outside the doors for several minutes to get a grip on his emotions, before taking the stairs two at a time. When he entered the nursery, he found his father helping Concetta stack some blocks. Sullisto saw him in the doorway. "Well…I guess I don't have to ask how it went. Your eyes say it all."

Leon nodded. "You were right. This was one reunion that was meant to be. Come downstairs and see for yourself."

He plucked his daughter from the floor, still clutching one of her blocks, and they headed out the door with Rufo. When they'd descended the staircase and entered the living room, he discovered the two women still seated on the love seat, deep in conversation punctuated with laughter and tears.

"Forgive us for barging in on you, but my daughter wants to join in."

"Concetta…" Luciana rushed over to take her from Leon's arms. Belle was right there with her. Both women fussed over his daughter, laughing, and his little girl broke out in smile after smile. She'd never had so much loving attention in her life.

Leon glanced at his father. They shared a silent message that left no doubt this watershed moment had changed the fabric of life in both Malatesta households.

"Dinner's ready. Let's go in the dining room. Tonight we'll all eat together." Leon's words delighted the women.

After he brought the high chair in, they both begged him to put Concetta between them at the candlelit table. Happiness reigned for the next hour, with most of the attention focused on the baby.

Leon looked around, realizing he hadn't felt this sense of family since before his own mother had died. His father hadn't seemed this relaxed and happy in years, either. As for Luciana, being united with her daughter had transformed her to the point Leon hardly recognized her. Gone were the shadows and that underlying look of depression.

But it was the new addition to his table that filled

him with emotions foreign to him. Since Benedetta's death, Concetta had been the only joy in his life. Having lost his wife, he hadn't been able to think about another woman. As for marriage, he had no plan to marry again. His daughter was all he could handle, all he *wanted* to handle.

Before Benedetta had died, she'd been Leon's comfort. With two losses in his life, plus Dante's aloofness, it was Concetta who was the beat of his heart now. Though she was loved by his staff, he guarded her possessively, afraid for anything to happen to her.

He'd been functioning on automatic pilot at work, unenthusiastic about the pleasures he'd once enjoyed. His good friend Vito had phoned, no doubt to make some vacation plans, but Leon hadn't even called him back yet.

While he'd been going along in this whitewashed state, Belle Peterson had exploded onto the scene. Her presence reminded him of someone who'd come along his private stretch of beach and purposely destroyed the sand castle he'd made for his daughter with painstaking care.

In Belle's case it wasn't intentional. Far from it. But the damage was just as bad, because nothing could be put back the way it was before. Leon didn't like having his world turned upside down, leaving him with inexplicable feelings percolating to life inside.

He should never have kissed her. Obviously, he needed to start dating other women. There were many he could choose from if he wanted to. But it was disconcerting to realize that none of them measured up in any way to Belle.

When Carla came into the dining room to pour more

coffee, he asked her to tell Talia to come and put the baby to bed. Concetta was too loud and squirmy, a telltale sign she was tired. But after the nanny arrived and pulled her out of her high chair, his daughter cried and fought not to be taken away. To his astonishment, she reached for Belle and quieted down the second his houseguest grasped the baby to her.

Diavolo! He couldn't blame it on the green suit *or* the shape in it. Belle herself, with her creative ways of doing things, had captured his daughter's interest.

Those dark blue eyes sought his with a trace of concern. "If it's all right with you, I'd love to get her ready for bed."

This wasn't supposed to happen, but what could Leon say? "I'm sure that will make Concetta very happy." When he saw the way she interacted with Belle, it came to him that his daughter needed a mother. Until now he'd been thinking only of his own needs. It had taken Belle's advent in their lives for him to realize a father wasn't enough for Concetta, who deserved two parents to make her life complete.

"Oh good! Come with me," she said to Luciana. "We'll do it together."

"You'll find a stretchy suit in the top drawer of the dresser," Leon suggested.

"A stretchy suit?" Belle said to the baby. "I wonder how many pink ones you have."

"It's a beautiful color on her, but then she's lovely in every color," Luciana said as they left the dining room, chatting together like a mother and daughter who'd never been apart. "She's already a great beauty."

Once they were alone, Sullisto eyed Leon. "I can see that Luciana won't want to be separated from Belle now that they've found each other. You say she's flying back to New York on Sunday?"

"That was the plan," Leon muttered, not able to think that far ahead.

"Well, as long as she's in Rimini, she'll stay with us at the palazzo. I'm anxious to get them both home." After a slight hesitation, he said, "I haven't told Luciana this yet, but I'm planning to adopt Belle so she'll be an integral part of the family."

After learning how much Luciana had suffered since giving up her daughter, Leon wasn't surprised by the announcement. What it did do was convince him how deeply his father had learned to love Belle's mother.

Feeling restless with troubling thoughts he hadn't sorted out yet, Leon got to his feet. "I'll go up and make sure Concetta is settling down without problem. Have you told Dante about Belle?"

"No. Pia has been so upset because she hasn't conceived yet, he took her to Florence for a little break. They won't be back until sometime tomorrow afternoon. It's probably a good thing. I want to give Luciana and Belle the next twelve hours or so together before we break the news to them.

"They don't have your advantage of getting to know Belle first, and her reasons for coming to Rimini. It will take time for him and Pia to absorb everything that's happened while they've been gone."

Dante wouldn't be the only one. Leon was still attempting to deal with the reality of Luciana's daughter, whose response had almost sent him into cardiac arrest earlier. Sullisto had been brilliant at keeping his wife's secret from their family. But for some reason his plan to adopt Belle didn't sit well with Leon.

He left his father at the table and went to the kitchen to find Talia, asking her to get Concetta's bottle ready and take it upstairs. "You outdid yourself on the dinner," he said to Simona, before bounding up the staircase.

He found a beaming Luciana holding his daughter, who'd been changed into a white stretchy suit with feet. Belle stood next to them, playing with his daughter's toes. The baby was laughing out loud.

Luciana saw him first. "Oh, Leon, she's the dearest child in the whole world." There was a new light in her eyes.

Belle's expression reflected the same sentiment. "We wish she didn't have to go to bed."

"I'm sure she doesn't want to be put down, either, but it's time." He walked over and reached for his daughter, who clung to him with satisfying eagerness. Talia wasn't far behind with the bottle.

She sat down in the rocker, so he could hand her the baby, who'd started to fuss the second he let go of her. "*Buonanotte,* Concetta. Be a good girl for Talia." He kissed her cheeks before following the two women out of the nursery.

Sullisto met them at the bottom of the stairs. He reached for Belle's hand. "Your mother and I would like you to stay at the palazzo with us while you're in Rimini. Would you like to come with us now?"

Leon sensed her slight hesitation. He was pleased by it when he shouldn't have been. Though he didn't know what was going on in her mind, he made the instant decision to intervene.

"Belle has already settled in as my houseguest for tonight, Papà. As it's late and I know she's exhausted, why don't I bring her to the palazzo in the morning for breakfast, and we'll discuss future plans?"

Luciana hugged her daughter. "Of course you're tired. After the shock of coming face-to-face with my beautiful daughter, whom I thought would always be lost to me, I confess I am, too. Tomorrow we'll spend the whole day together. I can't wait."

"Neither can I."

"I love you, Arabella."

"I love you, too." Belle's words came out in a whisper.

They hugged for a long time before letting each other go. Together everyone moved to the front foyer. Luciana's gaze moved to Leon. "Please bring Concetta when you come. We can't get enough of her."

Leon nodded to his stepmother and father before the two of them disappeared out the door. When it closed he turned to Belle.

"Did I speak too soon for you? It's not too late to go with them."

She shook her head. "Actually, I'm very grateful you said what you did. No matter what you say, this meeting put my mother and your father in a difficult position. By my staying here in your home, they'll have time to talk alone tonight. She put on a wonderful front, but—"

"It was no front," Leon contradicted. "I've known her close to fourteen years. The joy on her face when she saw you changed her to the point that I hardly recognized her."

Belle bit her lip. "But that doesn't alter the fact that she gave me up and no one knew about it. Now that I'm here, she has to worry about people finding out she had a child before she married your father."

"Do you honestly believe that matters to either of them now?"

"I don't know. She said she gave me up to keep me safe. But since that's no longer a concern and I've shown up, she'll have to deal with gossip. I'm not worried for myself, but the last thing I want is to bring more unhappiness to your family."

"That's very noble of you, Belle, but she's already let you know you're welcome with open arms."

Her chin lifted. "Maybe. I think it would be better if she comes over here in the morning, where we can talk in private before I go back to New York. Her presence in your home won't draw attention. If I thought my coming to Italy could upset her life in any way…"

He raked a hand through his hair. "Come out on the patio with me and we'll talk."

Without saying anything, she followed him down the hall to the other part of the house. When he opened the doors to the patio, they were greeted by a sea breeze scented with the fragrance of the garden flowers. Belle walked over to the railing. "How absolutely heavenly it is out here."

"It's my favorite place."

"I can see why."

Leon stood next to her, studying her stunning profile, which was half hidden by her dark hair. "Forget everything else for a minute and answer me one question."

She turned her head in his direction. "You want to know how I feel."

Belle had the disarming habit of being able to read his mind. "Can you put it into words yet?"

"No," she answered promptly. "Luciana is wonderful. More wonderful than I could have ever hoped. So's your father. But over these years, this need to find her has been all about me and what I want. Sitting with her on the love seat while she explained her life to me, I realized what a terrible thing I've done to her."

Leon looked into those blue eyes glittering with tears. "I don't understand."

"She didn't deserve to have me sweep into her world, bringing up all the pain and unhappiness she's put behind her. No—" Belle put up her hands when he would have argued with her.

"The sister in charge warned me I could be taking a great risk in trying to find my birth mother. I thought I knew better when you told me I could meet her at dinner tonight. When I met your father, I still felt good about it. But I don't anymore."

Leon had to think fast. "I'm guessing the part of you that feels unlovable has taken over for the moment. You're terrified that any more time spent with her and she'll see all your flaws."

Belle gripped the railing tighter. "I'm nothing like her. She's lovely and refined. I never met anyone so gracious. She's not the kind of person to tell you what she's really thinking inside. She and your father have made a life together. There's no place in it for me and there shouldn't have to be."

"You're wrong about that, Belle." If his father had his way, it wouldn't be long before she found herself being adopted for the second time in her life.

"It's hard to explain, but I feel like I've trespassed on their lives."

"Trespassed... If you feel like that, then blame me for facilitating the meeting."

Tears again sparkled in her eyes. "I could have decided not to go through with the plans for this evening. Of course I don't blame you. You've been wonderful. You *all* have. I'm the one who doesn't belong in Rimini."

"That's another part of you talking, the part that feels you don't deserve this outpouring of kindness and acceptance. You're going to have to give this time, Belle. In the past you've been too used to rejection from your adoptive father and brother. If you turn away now, after one meeting, you'll be giving in to old habits. Consider your mother's feelings."

"She's all I'm thinking about right now."

"How do you imagine she'll feel if you let your fear of rejection prevent her from really getting to know you? It works both ways."

Belle shook her head. "I don't know what to do."

"Do you think *she* does?"

A troubled sigh escaped her lips. "I'm not sure. If she'd begged me to come with her tonight…"

Ah. "What if she was afraid to pressure you, in case you had reservations? I'm the one who mentioned your fatigue, and she grabbed on to it for an excuse, in case you didn't feel comfortable going with them. Don't you see?"

"I—I don't know what I see," Belle stammered. "I love her so much already, Leon, but I'm more anxious than ever." Her eyes met his, full of despair and confusion.

He wasn't immune to her pain, but he couldn't take her in his arms again, not after he'd sworn to keep his distance.

Yesterday, when he'd drawn her against him, he'd become instantly aware of her as an alluring woman, but he'd fought those feelings. He couldn't handle the complication of a woman in his life. Yet when they'd been at the pension, he'd reached for her again, because he couldn't help himself. Much more of this and he would lose every bit of objectivity.

Already her presence was making chaos of the well-ordered existence he'd been putting back together since Benedetta's death. Otherwise why would he have stepped in to suggest Belle remain under his roof tonight?

CHAPTER FIVE

BELLE LOOKED AWAY from Leon's dark gaze, trying desperately to pull herself together. After priding herself on being able to handle her life on her own, why did she keep falling apart like this?

She should have jumped at the opportunity to go home with her mother earlier, but Leon had read her hesitation with uncanny accuracy and had offered another solution. When she'd confided her reason to him for holding back, she'd told the truth. She'd wanted to give her mother space.

But she feared there'd been another reason to stay with Leon, not so readily discernible until this moment, now that she was alone with him again. Reflecting back to that interlude in her bedroom at the pension, she was angered by her need for comfort from the last person she should have turned to.

For her to have lost control and kissed a man who still had to be grieving the loss of his wife was humiliating. It was madness.

Feigning a calm she didn't feel, she managed to dredge up a smile. "Thank you for helping me work through my angst. Concetta is the luckiest little girl in the world to have you for her father. And like *your* father, you're a virtual bulwark of strength and reason, Leon Malatesta. I've gotten over my jitters and can go to bed now with the hope of getting some sleep. Good night."

Without looking at him, she left the patio and went straight to the guest bedroom, shutting the door.

A good sleep? That was hilarious.

"Signorina?"

Belle came out of the bathroom the next morning, where she'd been putting on her makeup. Earlier, Carla had brought her coffee. "Yes, Simona?"

"Signor Malatesta says to come to the rear foyer. He's ready to drive you to the palazzo whenever you're ready."

"I'll be right there. Thank you."

She'd been up for an hour, unable to stay in bed following a restless night's sleep. After some experimenting, she drew her hair back at the nape. In her ears she'd put on her favorite pink topaz earrings. Luciana was so elegant, Belle wanted to look her best for her mother.

This morning she'd dressed in a short-sleeved, three-piece suit of dusky pink, with a paler pink shell. Whenever she wore it to the regional meetings for her work, it garnered compliments.

When she stepped outside the door, she saw Leon in a light tan suit, fastening his daughter in the back car seat of a dark blue luxury sedan. Concetta was dressed in a blue-and-yellow sunsuit. With those dark brown eyes that saw Belle coming, she was a picture.

"Good morning, you adorable thing!"

He stood up, transferring his gaze to Belle. *"Buon giorno,* Arabella," he murmured, while his eyes traveled over every inch of her. When he did that, she melted on the spot.

"Buon giorno," she responded, sounding too American for words. "Do you mind if I sit in back with her?" During the night Belle had decided that the only safe way to be around Leon was to stay close to his daughter. It was no penance. Belle was already crazy about her.

Without waiting for an answer, she walked around to the other side and climbed in back. Rufo had already made his place on the floor at the baby's feet. Belle rubbed his head behind his ears. He licked her hand before she turned to Concetta and fastened her own seat belt.

"How's my little sweetie? I love those cute seashells on your top." As she touched them, the baby smiled and reached out to pull her hair.

Leon was still looking in from the other side. Could there be such a striking man anywhere else in existence? "Like I said last night, you keep that up at your own risk."

"After the pearls, what's a little hair?" she teased.

He chuckled. "She's already got her sights set on your earrings. They're stunning on you, by the way."

"Thank you." *Please don't keep saying personal things like that to me.*

In seconds he got behind the wheel and drove them away from the estate toward the city. This was the first time since coming to Rimini that Belle was actually able to see it through a tourist's eyes. Until now her thoughts had been so focused on finding her mother, she'd been pretty much unobservant.

He drove her along the autostrada and played tour guide. On one side were hundreds of fabulous-looking hotels. On the other were hundreds and hundreds of colorful umbrellas set up three rows deep on the famous twelve-mile-long stretch of beach.

"It's a sun lover's paradise, Leon!"

"If you don't mind the invasion of masses of humanity," he drawled over his shoulder.

But he didn't have to worry about that. His private portion of beach was off-limits, and no doubt strictly watched by his security men.

After a few minutes they climbed a slight elevation where an incredible period residence in an orangey-pink color came into view. "Oh, Leon…"

"This is the Malatesta palazzo. Our family purchased it in the nineteenth century. It's of moderate size, but over the years has been restored and transformed. Like many of the elegant patrician villas along this section of the Adriatic, it combines modern technology with old-world charm." He drove through the gates, past cypress trees and a fantastic maze.

"It's breathtaking. When you were little, your friends must have thought they'd died and gone to heaven when you invited them over to play."

His eyes gleamed with amusement as he looked at her through the rearview mirror. "I don't know about that, but Dante and I enjoyed hiding out from the staff. Guests have been known to get lost in there."

"I don't doubt it."

They continued on and wound around the fountain to the front entrance. Thrilled to see her mother come out the door and rush over to her side of the car, Belle hurriedly got out to meet her. They hugged for a long time.

"Now I know last night wasn't a dream." Luciana cupped her face. "My dearest girl, do you think you could ever bring yourself to call me Mom? You don't have to, but—"

"I wanted to call you Mom last night," Belle confessed.

"Then it's settled. Come on. Let's get Concetta and go inside." Belle looked around, to discover Leon had his daughter in his arms. "We're eating on the terrace," her mother announced. "I've got Concetta's high chair set up."

Rufo ran ahead to where Sullisto stood in the elegant foyer. He sought out Belle with such a warm smile that she had to believe it was a sincere reflection of how he felt about her. It went a long way to dispel some of her fears for her intrusion in their lives.

She felt Leon's gaze. When she looked up, his gray eyes seemed to encourage her to embrace what was happening.

Once she was inside, the palazzo's sumptuous tapestries and marble floors left her speechless. Belle particularly loved the colonnade with its stained-glass windows. Leon explained that before the destruction in the war, they'd formed part of the chapel.

After following the passageway, they came out to the terrace, where a veritable feast awaited them. But Belle couldn't hold back her cry of wonder at the sunken garden below. Grass surrounded a giant black-and-white chessboard. Statues of Roman gods were placed in the odd squares, each depicting one of the twelve months of the year.

"I've never seen anything like it! The whole estate is unreal." Her gaze unconsciously flew to Leon's. "To think this was your playground, growing up."

His eyes smiled back at her.

"Come and sit by me, darling. Here are some pictures of your father."

Belle did her mother's bidding. Her hands shook as she studied the half-dozen snapshots. "He looks so young and handsome!" She couldn't believe she was gazing at her own father.

"He was both. Keep those photos. I have more."

After studying them, Belle put them carefully in her purse. Over the delicious meal, she lost track of time, answering her mother's questions about life at the orphanage. Then the subject turned to the Petersons.

Sullisto shook his head. "I can't understand why you weren't adopted right off as a baby."

"I used to ask the sisters the same thing. They told me that because I was premature, I was very sickly. It seems I took a long time to get well, and was underdeveloped. My speech didn't come until I was about four. By then, I was too old."

"Darling…" Luciana hugged her for a long time before she let Belle go.

"It's all right. I finally did get adopted, but I didn't see love between Nadine and Ben. I guess somewhere deep down he cared for her, enough to go along with my adoption. But I wished I'd been placed in a foster home, so I could have left when things got difficult."

"You had no advocate?" her mom asked, sounding horrified.

"Not after being adopted. But at one point I gathered enough courage to talk to her about it. She said she'd wanted me to feel like I belonged. Nadine had the right instincts, but there was too much wrong in their marriage, and I know for a fact they didn't consult Cliff. He was so angry, I got out of the house the second I turned eighteen. As you know, they were killed in a car crash later on."

Her mother's eyes had filled with sadness. "Where did you go, darling?"

"I'd been scanning the classifieds and found a want ad for a roommate. I went to meet three single girls who'd rented part of an old house and could fit one more person. I told them that if they'd give me a month, I'd get a job and move in. Since I needed a cell phone, I applied for work at TCCPI and they hired me. That was my lucky day."

"Now she's a manager," Leon interjected. He'd just gotten up from the table to walk Concetta around. "In fact, the corporation is taking her in to the head office in New York City in two months."

Belle's head flew back. "You didn't tell me that earlier. You only said I was going to be promoted."

His features sobered. "I overstepped my boundaries when I contacted them, and didn't want to give away all the surprises in store for you."

He'd surprised her again.

"That's wonderful!" Luciana exclaimed, but a look of pain had crossed over her face, belying her words. "Do you love your work?"

Bemused by the question, Belle turned to her mother. She knew what she was really asking. They'd met only last evening. After finding her parent, the idea of separation was unthinkable to her right now, too. "I like it well enough. It's been a way to earn a living, and they've been paying for me to go to college at night. Another semester and I'll get my business degree."

"I'm so proud of you! Are you still living with roommates?"

"Yes. It's cheaper and I've been able to save some money." Belle pulled the wallet out of her handbag and passed around some pictures of her friends. She had one photo of the Peterson family to show them.

After studying the photos, Sullisto leaned forward. "I must admit I'm surprised you didn't show us the picture of your latest love interest. Why aren't you married? Are the men in America blind? Who's the miserable man you're driving crazy at the moment?"

Belle laughed quietly. "I've been too busy with studies, along with trying to put my store on top, to get into a relationship."

"You sound like Leonardo," he grumbled.

"Concetta keeps me so occupied, there's no room for anyone else."

She sensed a certain friction between him and his father. Belle happened to know how deeply enamored Leon was of his little girl. It surprised her Sullisto would touch on that subject, when he had to know his son was still grieving over his wife's death. No wonder she'd detected an underlying trace of impatience in Leon's response.

Belle could only envy the woman who would one day come into his life and steal his heart. As she struggled with the possibility that he might always love Benedetta too much to move on, she heard footsteps in the background, and turned her head to see an attractive man and woman dressed in expensive-looking sport clothes walk out on the terrace.

"Ah, Dante!" Sullisto got to his feet to embrace his son, who bore a superficial likeness to him and Leon. "We didn't expect you until this afternoon," he said in English. "You've arrived back from Florence just in time to meet our home's most honored guest. Belle Peterson from New York? This is my son Dante, and his lovely wife, Pia."

Belle agreed Pia was charming, with amber eyes and strawberry-blond hair she wore in a stylish bob. They walked around and shook her hand before taking their places at the table. But already Belle felt uncomfortable, because Leon's brother had seen her sitting next to Luciana, and had to have noticed the resemblance. He kept staring at them. So did his wife, who whispered something to him.

Sullisto turned to his wife. "*Cara?* Why don't you carry on from here?"

Luciana cleared her throat and got to her feet. Belle's gaze collided with Leon's oddly speculative glance. She had the impression he didn't know how this was going to play out, and she felt an odd chill go through her.

"After all these years, my greatest dream has come true." She reached for Belle's hand and clung to it. "Years ago my father sent me to New York, because he thought I was in danger here.

"You know the family history, but there are some things no one ever knew except your father, who loved me enough to marry me anyway. You'll never know what that love did for me and how much I've grown to love him since then."

Her mother's revelations brought moisture to Sullisto's eyes and touched Belle to the depths of her soul. But as she saw a bewildered look creep over Dante's face, the blood started to throb at her temples.

"While I was there, I met a man from England named Robert Sloan, and we fell in love. When we found out we were expecting a baby, we planned to be married with or without my father's permission. But Robert was killed in a hit-and-run accident. At the time I was convinced he'd been murdered, and it brought on early labor for me."

Dante looked like a victim of shell shock. As Luciana continued talking, he transferred his cold gaze to Belle. It reminded her of Cliff's menacing eyes when his mother had first introduced them. That memory made her shrink inside as Luciana came to the end of the story.

"Her real name is Arabella Donatello Sloan. She flew to Rimini this week to try and find me. If it weren't for Leon, we would never have been reunited."

Dante turned to his brother. A stream of unintelligible Italian poured from his mouth.

"Our guest doesn't speak Italian," Leon reminded him. For an instant his gray eyes trapped Belle's as reams of unspoken thoughts passed between them. This was the crisis Belle had prayed wouldn't happen.

Sullisto intervened and in English told Dante how she'd researched the Donatello name until it came to Leon's attention at the bank.

"It's an absolute miracle," Luciana interjected. "It's one that has brought me the greatest happiness you can imagine. Sullisto and I talked it over last night. We're hoping she'll decide to make her home here at the palazzo with all of us, permanently."

"Mom..."

While Belle was still trying to absorb the wonder of it, Sullisto tapped his crystal goblet with a fork. After clearing his throat, he said, "We want to take care of you from here on out. Now that you're united with your mother, we don't want anything to keep you two apart."

He reached for Luciana's hand. "I'm planning to adopt you, Arabella."

"Adopt?" Belle gasped. "I—I hardly know what to say—" Her voice caught.

A smile broke out on his lips. "You don't have to say anything."

Belle was so overcome with emotions sweeping through her, she hardly noticed that Dante had gotten to his feet. With one glance, she saw that he'd lost color. He stared around the table at all of them. The dangerous glint coming from those dark depths frightened her.

"That's quite a story. The resemblance between mother and daughter is extraordinary, thus dispensing with a DNA test," he rapped out. His gaze finally fastened on Belle. "Welcome to the Malatesta family, Arabella. We truly do live up to our name, don't we?"

"Basta!" his father exclaimed. Belle knew what it meant.

"Mi dispiace, Papà," he answered with sarcasm. "Now if you'll excuse us, Pia and I have other things to do." He strode off the patio with an unhappy wife in pursuit.

"Don't look alarmed," Sullisto advised Belle the minute they were gone. "Your mother and I discussed it last night. There's no right way to handle a situation like this. We didn't expect them home until later, but since he walked in on us, we felt it was better to let Dante know up front. When he and Pia have talked about it, he'll apologize for his bad behavior."

Belle got up from the table. "For you to welcome me into your home leaves me thrilled and speechless, but I'm afraid the shock of hearing your plan to adopt me was too great for Dante. I'm not so much alarmed as sad, Sullisto. It's because my adoptive brother, Cliff, had the exact same reaction when Nadine brought me to their house from the orphanage. He was unprepared for it."

"But it's not quite the same thing," Sullisto impressed upon her. "You're flesh of Luciana's flesh. Dante is flesh of mine. Both of you are beloved to me and your mother." His words touched her to the core. "The difference lies in the fact that Dante's not a teenage boy. He's a grown man who's married, with expectations of raising a family of his own. Your being brought into the family has no bearing on his life except to enrich it."

"E-even so—" her voice faltered "—he has lived under your roof all his life and has sustained a huge shock that will impact your family and create gossip. If it's all right with you, I would feel much better if the two of you had the rest of the day to be alone with him and his wife. They're going to need to talk about this."

With an anxious glance at Leon, Belle implored him with her eyes to help her out of this, and prayed he got the message. "Since Concetta is ready for a nap, I'll go back to the villa with Leon." She leaned over to kiss her mother, then Sullisto. "Thank you for this wonderful morning. I don't deserve the gift of love you've showered on me. You have no idea how much I love both of you. Call me later."

Leon had already lifted the baby from the high chair and was ready to go. They left the palazzo and she climbed in the back of the sedan to help him fasten Concetta in the car seat. Rufo hopped in and lay down.

Belle kissed the baby's nose. "You were such a good girl this morning, you deserve a treat." She reached in her bag and pulled out her lipstick. The baby grabbed the tube and immediately put it in her mouth. It kept her occupied during the drive.

If Belle hadn't made the suggestion to escape, Leon would have insisted they leave the palazzo immediately. The shattered look on Dante's face had revealed what Leon had always suspected.

Like a volcano slowly building magma, his quiet, subdued brother had hidden his feelings beneath a facade. But today they had erupted into the stratosphere, exposing remembered pain and fresh new hurt.

"When we get back to the villa, I'll ask Talia to put the baby to bed so you and I can talk about what's happened."

"I can't bear that I've brought all this on. It's disrupting your life and everyone else's. I didn't want to hurt Mother's feelings by leaving so fast, but when I saw poor Dante's eyes..." Belle buried her face in her hands.

"You can be sure she and Papà understood. Dante finally reacted to years of suppressed pain. His behavior wasn't directed at you. It's been coming on since the day our father told us he was getting married again."

"I feel so sorry for him."

So did Leon. He eyed her through the rearview mirror. "Do you have a swimming costume?"

She blinked. "Yes."

"Good. When you've changed back at the house, meet me on the patio and we'll go down to the beach. We both need to channel our negative energy into something physical."

Belle nodded. "You're reading my mind again. A swim is exactly what I crave."

"In that case, you'll want a beach towel. There are half a dozen on the closet shelf in the guest bathroom."

"Thank you."

The drive didn't take long. When they entered the villa he showered his loving daughter with kisses before turning her over to Talia. Once upstairs in his room he changed into his black swimming trunks.

His last task was to phone Berto and tell him he wouldn't be coming in to work. Unless there was an emergency, Leon was taking time off until tomorrow. On his way out the door he grabbed a towel.

It didn't surprise him to find Belle in bare feet, waiting for him on the patio. The woman needed to talk. He could sense her urgency when their eyes met.

She'd swept her hair on top of her head, revealing the lovely stem of her neck. As he was coming to learn, every style suited her. The pink earrings still winked at him. His gaze fell lower. He knew there was a bathing suit underneath the short, wispy beach jacket covering her shapely body. It was hard not to stare at her elegant legs, half covered by the towel she was holding.

"I'm glad you suggested this, Leon. Like you, I'm anxious for some exercise before I lose it. Let's go."

Lose it was right. Dante's behavior at the table had cut like a knife.

Together they descended the steps to the sand. She removed her jacket and threw it on top of her towel before running into the water. He caught only a glimpse of the mini print blue-and-white bikini, but with her in it he felt a rise in his own body temperature despite the sorrow weighing him down.

"The sea feels like a bathtub," she cried in delight while treading water. He decided it had been a good idea to come out here. They both needed the distraction. Her dark sapphire eyes dazzled him with light.

He swam closer. "You've come to Rimini when the temperature is in the eighties."

"No wonder the city is a magnet for beach lovers. This is heaven!" For the next hour she kept her pain hidden. While she bobbed and dived, he swam lazy circles around her.

Leon held back bringing up the obvious until they'd left the water and stretched out on their towels. He lay on his stomach so he could look at her. She'd done the same. Belle had no idea how much her innate modesty appealed to him. It didn't matter how ruthlessly he tried to find things about her he didn't like in order to fight his attraction. He couldn't come up with one.

"What's going on in that intelligent mind of yours?"

"Flattery will get you nowhere," she said in a dampening voice, "especially when we both know you've been able to read me like a book so far."

He turned on his side. "Not this time."

She let out a troubled sigh. "I learned a lot after living with Cliff for those eight years. Whether justified or not, he felt betrayed by his parents. The family should have gotten professional counseling to help him. When I saw Dante's expression, he reminded me so much of Cliff, I got a pain in my stomach."

"The news definitely shook him."

"It was more than that, Leon." Slowly she sat up and looped her arms around her raised knees. "All I saw was the little boy who a long time ago fell apart at the loss of his mother. Your father said he's a grown man now, with a wife, and can handle it, but I'm afraid Dante's world has come crashing down on him again."

Leon nodded slowly. "If I don't miss my guess, his turmoil came from the fact that Papà wants to adopt you. Call it jealousy if you like. He and I suffered a great deal in our youth over his remarriage."

"Now he's reliving it. He sees how devoted your father is to my mother. When he said he planned to adopt me, maybe you couldn't see Dante clearly from where you were sitting, but his face went white."

"I noticed," Leon muttered. "There's no question her sin of omission has caught up with my brother."

In that moment he'd realized Dante had disliked Luciana perhaps even more strongly than Leon himself had years ago. But Dante had held back his feelings until this morning, when she'd revealed news about her secret baby. To make it even more painful, Belle had been sitting next to her mother at the table, bigger than life and more beautiful.

"I can see only one way to stop the bleeding."

Her thoughts were no longer a mystery. He rolled next to her and grasped her upper arms. "You can't go home yet—"

That nerve in her throat was throbbing again. "I have to. Don't you see? As long as I'm in Rimini, I'm a horrible reminder of his past. Mom and I have the rest of our lives to work things out. I have a career, Leon. In a few days I'll be back at my job. She can fly to New York and visit me. If I leave, then there'll be no gossip, and Mom's secret will remain safe."

His jaw hardened. "There are two flaws in your argument. In the first place the damage has already been done to Dante. Secondly, now that you've been united with her, she won't be able to handle a long-distance relationship. I've already learned enough to know a visit once every six weeks will never be enough for you, either. You can forget going anywhere," he declared.

Her chin trembled. He had the intense desire to kiss her mouth and body, but sensing danger, she eased away from him and got to her feet. "To remain in Italy for any length of time is out of the question. Don't you see it will tear Dante apart? It's not fair to him! He didn't ask for this. None of you did, but he's the one at risk of being unable to recover."

Leon stood in turn. "He'll recover, Belle, but it's going to take time."

"I don't know. I keep seeing his face and it wounds me. I have to leave. As for the rest of this week, I couldn't possibly stay at the palazzo while I'm here. That's always been Dante's home. My only option is to fly back to New York ASAP."

"No. For the time being you're going to stay with me, where you'll be away from Dante and yet still remain close to Luciana."

A small cry escaped Belle's throat. She shook her head. "I…couldn't possibly remain with you, and you know why. If I stay anywhere, it will be at a hotel."

Before he could think, she backed away farther. In a flash she'd gathered up her jacket and towel and darted across the sand to the steps leading to the villa.

Long after she'd disappeared inside, Leon was still standing there trying to deal with a tumult of emotions regarding his brother. But he also had been gripped by unassuaged longings, and realized he had a serious problem on his hands.

Just now he'd wanted to kiss Belle into oblivion. The chemistry had been potent from the first moment they'd met. Though Benedetta hadn't been gone that long, Leon found an insidious attraction for Luciana's daughter heating up within him.

Like father, like son?

Something warned him it could be fatal. How was that possible? If she'd sensed it, too, that could be the reason she'd run like hell.

CHAPTER SIX

In a panic over feelings completely new to her, Belle raced to her room and jumped in the shower to wash her hair. In getting what she'd wished for by finding her mother, her world and everyone else's had been turned upside down. Nothing would ever be the same again and it was *her* fault!

Since she turned eighteen she'd been leading her own life as a liberated adult, in charge of herself and her decisions. No matter the situation now, she refused to be a weight around Leon's neck.

Her roommates would tell her she was stark staring crazy to run from the situation. They'd kill for the chance to stay with a gorgeous widower in his fabulous Italian villa. What was her problem?

Belle could only shake her head. What *wasn't* her problem? When Leon had driven her away from the palazzo earlier, she'd left it in an emotional shambles. After trying so hard not to hurt anyone, she found out that every life inside those walls standing for hundreds of years had been changed because of her driving need to know who she was.

Are you happy now, Belle?

In a matter of minutes Dante's life had been turned

into a nightmare. She couldn't live with herself if something drastic wasn't done to staunch the flow of pain for him.

But she couldn't stay with Leon any longer, either. Through an accident of marriage, he was her *stepbrother,* for heaven's sake! Yet she had to face the awful truth that her feelings for him were anything but sisterly. She could be arrested for some of the thoughts she'd been having about him.

Just now on the beach, the ache for him had grown so acute she'd literally melted when he'd grasped her arms. It wouldn't be possible to stay with him any longer and not act on her feelings for him.

She finished blow-drying her hair and slipped on the only pair of jeans she'd brought, along with a khaki blouse. It was time to play tourist while she decided what she was going to do.

Before leaving the room in her sneakers and shoulder bag, Belle dashed off a note, which she propped on the dresser. In it she explained she'd gone for a walk and would be back later.

No one was about as she retraced her steps to the beach. It was the only way to leave his gated property. She hurried past a lifeguard tower. For all she knew, the guy on watch was one of Leon's security people. But she wouldn't worry about that now, because she'd reached the crowded public part of the beach. From there she entered one of the hotels.

After taking a couple of free pamphlets printed in English from the lobby, she walked out in front to get a taxi. She told the driver where she wanted to go. In a few minutes he dropped her off at the ancient Tiberius Bridge.

The leaflet said it was begun by the Emperor Augustus in AD 14, and completed under Tiberius in AD 21. It was a magnificent structure of five arches resting on massive pillars. Incredible to think that she was here in such a historic place, but she couldn't appreciate it.

Tormented because she didn't know what she should do, Belle crossed the river to the city center to window-shop and eat a late lunch. The brochure indicated the Piazza Cavour was once the area of the fish and vegetable markets during the Middle Ages.

It was fascinating information, but partway through her meal she lost interest in her food. Sightseeing hadn't been a good idea and there were too many tourists. She decided to find a taxi and return to the villa. As she got up from the table, she almost bumped into Leon, who was pushing Concetta in her baby stroller.

"Leon!" Belle cried in utter surprise. The sight of his tall, powerful body clothed in jeans and a white polo shirt took her breath. "Where did you come from?"

A seductive smile broke out on his firm lips. Her gaze traveled to the cleft in his chin. The enticing combination was too much for her. "We've been following you."

Belle might have known Leon's security people would keep him informed of her every step. In spite of knowing she'd been watched and followed, a rush of warmth invaded her. To offset it, she knelt down to give the baby kisses. "So *that's* what you've been doing. Are you having a wonderful time?"

Concetta kept smiling at her as if she really recognized her and was happy to see her. That sweet little face had a lock on Belle's emotions.

"When we found your note, we thought we'd join you."

No... To spend more time with him and the baby wasn't a good idea. "I was just going to find a taxi and go back."

"Fine. My car is parked right over there on the side street."

Caving to the inevitable, Belle said, "May I push her?"

"Go ahead, but you'll have to dodge the heavy foot traffic."

She rubbed her hand over Concetta's fine hair. "We don't mind, do we, sweetheart."

As they navigated through the crowds toward his car, every woman in sight feasted her eyes on Leon. His black hair and striking looks compelled them to stare. Belle felt their envy when they glanced at her. She had to admit that if she'd been a tourist and had seen him with his little girl, she would have found him irresistible. There was nothing that captured a female's attention faster than an attractive man out with his baby and enjoying it, especially this one.

"On the way home we'll stop by the Delfinario."

"That's an intriguing word."

With half-veiled eyes, he helped her and Concetta into the backseat of the sedan. "I think you'll be entertained."

"Is it animal, vegetable or mineral?"

Leon burst into rich laughter. "You'll get your answer before long."

Her heart went into flutter mode, something that had started happening only since she'd been in Leon's company.

He drove along the beach until they came to what appeared to be a theme park. After they got out he said, "I'll carry Concetta. Come with me."

Belle followed him to a large, open-air pool. She spotted some mammals leaping out of the water. "Dolphins?"

"Sì, signorina. Delfino." Leon paid the admission and found them two seats in the packed arena where they were performing. Belle could pick out a few familiar words spoken by the man narrating the show in Italian. She loved the sound of the language. The children in the audience were enraptured by the sight.

"Look, Concetta!" Belle pointed to them. "Can you see the *delfino?*"

The baby got caught up in the excitement and clapped her hands like the kids surrounding them. More enchanted by her reaction than by the remarkable tricks happening in the water with the trainers, both Leon and Belle laughed with abandon.

After one spectacular feat, their eyes met and she flashed him a full, unguarded smile. Belle found it impossible to hold back her enjoyment in being here like this with the two of them, as if they were a family. It wasn't until later, on their drive home, that she was brought back to reality, knowing she had a huge decision to make.

"I think my little *tesoro* needs her dinner."

"Would you let me feed her and put her to bed?" Being with the baby brought Belle comfort, the kind she needed right now.

"Of course. It will give Talia a break."

"Oh goody. Did you hear that, Concetta?" Belle was

sitting next to her in the back of the sedan and kissed her half a dozen times.

Once they arrived at the villa, Leon carried her in the kitchen to her high chair and got out the baby food for Belle. Another fun-filled half hour passed while the child ate and played with her food, smearing some of it on the traytop as well as herself.

Laughter rumbled out of Leon. "I had no idea she could be this messy an eater."

"Most babies make a huge mess when you make a game out of eating. She's so happy. Look at the way she beams at you, Leon. It's the cutest thing I ever saw. But let's be honest. She's in need of a bath big-time."

"You took the words out of my mouth. Her little plastic tub is under the sink in the bathroom."

"I'll get everything set up." As Belle turned to leave the room, Concetta started to cry, causing Belle to turn around. "Oh, sweetie, I'm just going upstairs."

Leon darted her a piercing glance while he cleaned the baby off. "My daughter is already so crazy about you, she's not going to want Talia's attention."

Belle's heart thudded. "I hope that's not true," she whispered. "See you in a minute, Concetta." She hurried through the house and up the stairs to the nursery. Once she'd started filling the tub, she found the baby shampoo and a towel.

"Leon?" she called out. "Everything's ready!"

"Here we come!" He breezed into the bathroom, carrying his daughter in the altogether and lowering her into the water. Concetta talked her head off and splashed water everywhere.

"Already you're a water baby, aren't you, sweetheart? That's a good thing, because you've got a swimming pool and the Adriatic right in your own backyard." Leon grinned as he poured a little shampoo on her head.

Belle massaged it in. "Are you having fun, my little brown-eyed Susan?"

"What's that?" Leon asked. His command of English was remarkable, but once in a while he could be surprised.

"A yellow flower like a daisy with a center just like her incredible eyes."

He nodded. "The first time I looked into them, they reminded me of poppy throats."

Spoken like a father in love with his little offshoot. "They're both apt descriptions. One day she's going to grow up and drive all the Rimini *ragazzi* wild."

A burst of laughter broke from his throat. "Your knowledge of Italian is impressive. But let's hope that eventuality is years away yet."

"I don't know. They grow up fast." Belle kissed the baby's neck. "Are you having fun, sweetheart? I know *I* am." Truly, she'd never had so much fun in her life.

"That makes two of us," Leon said in his deep voice.

He made a wonderful father. If every child could be so lucky...

Once the bath was over, she slipped a diaper on Concetta and Leon found a light green sleeper. "Here's the bottle." He handed it to her. "Would you like to give it to her?"

"You know I would."

Belle sat down in the rocker with the baby and sang to her. So much playtime had made Concetta sleepy. Her eyelids drooped almost at once while she drank her formula. The long lashes reminded Belle of Leon's. Before long the child stopped sucking and fell sound asleep.

Leon watched as Belle put the baby down in the crib on her back. After they'd left the nursery he turned to her.

"Now that we've got the evening to ourselves, I'm taking you out on the cabin cruiser so you can get a view of the coast from the water. It's a sight you shouldn't miss. The pier is a few steps down the beach, in the opposite direction from where you went earlier today."

"I figured the lifeguard was one of your security people, but he didn't try to stop me."

Leon's lips twitched. "While we're out, I'd like to discuss something of vital importance with you. I've worked out a solution to our problem."

"So have I." She was going home on Sunday as planned, with no interference from him.

His black brows lifted in challenge, as if he could read her thoughts. "Then we'll compare notes," he said in an authoritative tone. His hauteur came naturally to him, because it was evident few people had ever dared thwart him. "Meet me on the back patio in twenty minutes. Bring a wrap. It will get cool later."

She nodded before hurrying downstairs to her room. She couldn't imagine what kind of solution he'd worked out, and didn't want to listen to him, not when Dante's happiness was at stake. But she was a guest in Leon's home and couldn't forget her debt to him. It was one she could never repay.

Without him acting on his uncanny instinct to follow through on her inquiry at the bank, she would have gone on searching for her mother in vain. The situation was untenable any way she looked at it.

A tap on the door a few minutes later brought her head around. *"Signorina?"* Belle rushed over to open it and discovered Carla. "The Countess Malatesta phoned while you were bathing the baby. She would like you to call her." The maid handed Belle a note with the phone number written on it.

"Thank you, Carla."

After she left, Belle pulled the cell phone out of her purse and called her mother. Two rings and she answered. "Arabella?"

It was still unbelievable to Belle that she was talking to the mother she'd ached for all her life. "Mom— I'm so glad you called. To hear your voice…it's like a miracle to me."

"I was just going to tell you the same thing, darling. What have you done with your day?"

Belle bit her lip. "I went sightseeing and Leon took me and the baby to see the dolphins. Then we fed her and bathed her. Now she's just gone to sleep." But Belle didn't want to talk about Leon and the way he made her feel. Her mouth had gone so dry thinking about him, she could hardly swallow. "How's Dante? I've been worried sick about him."

"To be truthful, we've been worried, too. They've stayed in their wing of the palazzo all day. Since they have their own entrance, they could have gone out without our knowing it. Sullisto and I thought we'd done the right thing to tell him the truth this morning…" Her voice trailed off. "I know my husband's hurt by this."

Belle gripped the phone tighter. "If it's any consolation, I don't think it would have mattered when you told Dante. The outcome would be the same. Maybe tonight he'll decide to talk to you, so I'm not planning to come over. Can we see each other tomorrow?"

"That's why I phoned you. I'll pick you up in the

morning and we'll take a drive. I want to show you my world. We'll talk and eat our heads off. How does that sound?"

She smiled. "Like heaven."

"Let's say eight-thirty."

"Perfect. I'll be ready. I love you, Mom."

"I love *you*. Isn't it wonderful to be able to say it to each other?"

"Yes." *Oh yes.*

After they hung up, Belle threw herself across the bed and thought about the day Cliff had let her know she wasn't wanted or loved.

She'd been a child then, with a child's reaction. But she was a woman now, and understood Cliff's behavior, just as she understood Dante's. In both cases Belle had been the one to bring on more suffering. This time she had the power to end it.

When it was time to meet Leon, she grabbed her sweater and hurried down to the patio. She would listen to what he had to say, but it wouldn't change her mind about leaving on Sunday.

Leon knew something was up the minute he saw her. "What's happened since you went downstairs?" he asked as they headed for the dock.

"I just got off the phone with Mom. They haven't seen Dante all day."

"My father told me the same thing a few minutes ago, but it isn't surprising. His way is to hide out."

"What do you mean, *his* way?"

Leon sobered. "There are things you don't know."

She took a shuddering breath. "Well, I know one thing. My arrival in Rimini has hurt him."

"It's not personal, Belle. *I'm* the one who has hurt him."

Her brows met in a frown as she looked at him. "How can you say that?"

"Because it's true. You saw and heard what happened at the table when Father said I was the one who made the reunion possible. Dante couldn't handle it and blew up at me in Italian."

She shook her head. "The whole thing is tragic. Mom's going to take me for a drive tomorrow. Maybe if Dante knows she's out of the palazzo, he and your father will be able to talk."

"I don't think so."

"Why do you sound so sure about that?"

"Once we're on board, I'll explain." Leon couldn't let Belle go on thinking she was the cause of everything.

He helped her climb over the side of the cruiser. After giving her a life jacket to put on, he undid the ropes and started the engine. They moved at a wake-less speed until they were past the drop-off before he opened it up.

She knelt on the bench across from the captain's seat, looking out to sea. "Is it always this placid?"

"It is this time of evening. Much later a breeze will spring up."

"You weren't exaggerating about the view. With the blue changing into darkness, all the lights twinkling along the shoreline make everything magical."

"Your eyes are the same color right now. Twilight eyes."

His words seemed to disturb her, because she turned around to face him. "You said you would tell me about Dante. Let's talk about him." She was a businesswoman who'd been fending off men's advances for years and knew how to probe through to the marrow.

He shut off the engine and lowered the anchor. After turning to her, he extended his legs. "When Dante and I lost our mother to cancer, he was ten and I eleven. For several years we were pretty inconsolable. Father had always been so preoccupied with business, she was the one who played with us and made life exciting. No one could be more fun. We could go to her with any problem and she'd fix it."

"You were blessed to have her that long."

"We were, but at the time all we could realize was that her death left a great void. Sometimes Benedetta saw me walking on the grounds and she'd join me with her dog. She wouldn't say anything, but she was a comfort, and I found myself unburdening to her the way kids do. Unfortunately, Dante didn't have that kind of a confidante. All he had was me, and I was a poor substitute."

"Don't say that, Leon. Just having a sibling, knowing you're there, makes such a difference. There were several siblings at the orphanage. They had a special bond without even talking. If you could discuss this with Dante, I'm sure he would tell you how much it meant to have a brother who understood what he was going through."

Leon studied her for a moment. "You have so much insight, Belle, there are times when I'm a little in awe of you. But you haven't heard everything yet."

She smiled sadly. "I was the great observer of life, don't forget. You've seen people like me before. We hover at the top of the staircase, watching everyone below, never being a part of things. But I eventually grew out of my self-pity. I had to!"

"Look at you now, a successful businesswoman."

Belle leaned forward. "What happened to your relationship with Dante? I want to know. Was it terrible when your father told you boys he was getting married again?" The compassion in her eyes was tangible.

"The truth?" She nodded. "We both felt betrayed."

"You poor things."

"To be honest, I couldn't fathom him marrying anyone else. Our mom was a motherly sort, the perfect mother, if you know what I mean. She made everything fun, always laughing and lively, always there for us.

"Her death brought a pall over our household. Dante came to my room every night and cried his heart out. I had to hold back my tears to try and help him."

"That's so sad, Leon. I believe the heartache you two endured had to be worse than anything I ever experienced at the orphanage. To be so happy with your mother, and then have her gone…"

He sucked in his breath. "Things got worse when Papà brought Luciana to the palazzo to meet us. The diamond heiress looked young enough to be his daughter. In fact, she didn't look old enough to be anyone's mother. I found her cool and remote."

Belle's heart twisted. "I can't picture her that way."

"That's because meeting you has changed her into a different person. At the time I hated her for being so beautiful. Anyone could see why she'd attracted our father. As you heard through the librarian, there'd been rumors that both Luciana's mother and her widowed father might have been murdered."

Belle nodded.

"Some of those rumors linked my father to the latter

possible crime. I knew in my heart Papà couldn't have done such a thing, but I was filled with anger."

"Why exactly?"

"Because I was old enough to understand that love had nothing to do with his marriage to her. He'd done what all Malatestas had done before him, and reached out to bring the Donatello diamond fortune under the far-reaching umbrella of our family's assets.

"Gossip was rife at the time. People were waiting to see if he produced another heir. It felt like he'd betrayed our mother, and I couldn't forgive him. Dante felt the same way and threatened to run away."

"How terrible," Belle whispered sadly.

"I told him we couldn't do that. But when we turned eighteen, we would leave. Until then we had to go along with things and deal with the ugly rumors surrounding the Donatello family. But I let him down when I made the decision to go away to college."

"You had to live your own life."

He raked his hair back absently. "This morning's explosion lets me know I made a big mistake in leaving." Pain stabbed his insides, forcing him to his feet.

"What do you mean?"

"I left Dante on his own to deal with his pain. I should have stayed and helped him, but I didn't. Papà's marriage to a princess shrouded in gossip and mystery was so distasteful to me, I couldn't get out of the palazzo fast enough. I could have gone to college in Rimini, but instead I went to Rome in order to get away.

"During the years I was gone, Dante's pain turned to anger. When I returned, he was involved with his own friends. I moved to the villa, one of the properties I inherited from our mother's estate, and dug into business at the bank. Later on I began to spend more time with Benedetta. My brother and I had grown apart, but that was my fault."

Belle put a hand on his arm. At the first contact, tiny sensations of delight he couldn't ward off spread through his body. "You couldn't help what happened then," she murmured.

Leon looked down at her hand. "Oh yes, I could have, but I was too caught up in my own pain to reach out. Dante didn't display any outward signs of rebellion, but obviously, he was riddled with turmoil once our father's marriage was a fait accompli. I didn't see it manifested until I came home from college."

"Didn't your father try to prepare you for his marriage to my mother?"

"No, but to be honest, if he *had* tried, it wouldn't have done any good. Be assured I'll always love my father, but there was a gulf between us. While I was gone I stayed in touch with him and Dante, even made a few short visits on holidays. But it was four years later before I returned to Rimini to live.

"By that time Dante no longer shared his innermost thoughts with me. The closeness we once enjoyed seemed to have vanished for good. I'm afraid that for him, it was a hurt that never went away.

"He married Pia Rovere, a distant relative from our mother's side of the family. They chose to live in another wing of the Malatesta palazzo. That arrangement pleased my father and suited me, since I preferred living on my own at the villa."

"She's lovely."

"And very good for Dante, I think. Since then the three of us work in the family banking business. Unfortunately, the relations between my father and me continue to be frayed because of my marriage to Benedetta."

Belle's delicately arched brows met. "I don't understand."

"When I married her, I did something no other Malatesta has done, and took a woman without a title for my wife. I made it clear I wanted nothing to do with such an archaic custom. My father has had no choice but to look to Dante to follow in his footsteps."

"Which he has done by marrying Pia, who's from a royal house."

Again Leon frowned. "But now that Benedetta is gone, Papà is counting on my marrying a titled woman he has in mind to be Concetta's new mother. He's made no secret about it. Every time he brings it up in front of Dante, which is often, I keep reminding him that even if I weren't in mourning, I would never do as he wants. I've told him I'm not interested in marriage and only want to be a good father to my daughter."

Belle let out a troubled sigh. "Why do you think he's so intent on it?"

"Because I'm the firstborn son and the firstborn is supposed to inherit the title."

"In other words, he would prefer you to receive it over Dante."

"Yes. It isn't that he loves Dante less, but he's a stickler for duty. Luciana's father was of that same ilk. It's the one area where Father and I don't get along."

"I'm surprised he didn't forbid you to marry Benedetta."

"He did, but we got married in a private ceremony before he knew about it, and his hands were tied."

Belle studied him for a minute. "I'm sure you must miss your wife terribly. Tell me about her."

"I knew her from childhood. She was Dante's age. Our mother was an animal lover. We spent hours at the kennel playing with the dogs. Benedetta was always there, helping her father. She'd lost her mother to pneumonia, and our mom took her under her wing. It was like having a sister."

"So your love for her was based on long-standing friendship first."

He nodded. "It wasn't until several years after I returned from Rome that my feelings for her underwent a change."

"What happened?"

"She worked for her father and had a Spinone who'd been her devoted pet for a long time. I happened to be at the palazzo one day in the fall when word came to us that her dog was missing. I knew how much she loved him, so I gathered some staff to go look for him. We found him shot dead by a hunter we presumed had trespassed on the property."

"What a dreadful thing to happen. I can't bear it."

"Neither could I. When I saw him lying there, I felt like I'd been the one who'd received the bullet. Benedetta was so heartbroken, I didn't think she'd recover. I dropped everything to be with her for the next week. We comforted each other. She'd always had a sweetness that drew me to her."

"You must have had a wonderful marriage."

"For the short time we were given, I was the happiest I'd ever been."

Leon heard Belle take a deep breath. "One day your daughter is going to love hearing about your love story."

After a slight hesitation, she added, "How hard for both of you to find out she had that disease. What was it like? I hope you don't mind my asking."

For the first time since it happened, Leon felt like talking about it. "At first she grew very tired, and then suffered some hair loss. I came home from the office early many times to be with her, console her. After a while she couldn't go out in the sun. As time passed, more symptoms occurred. She had painful swollen joints and fever, even kidney problems."

"That must have been so awful, Leon."

"I didn't want to believe it would get worse. We prayed she'd get it under control, and were both looking forward to the baby. I never dreamed I'd lose her during the delivery. I was in shock for days."

"Of course. I'm so sorry. Did she suffer a long time?"

"No, *grazie a Dio.*"

"Then you received two blessings, one of them being your adorable daughter." Belle shifted position and lowered her head. "How did you cope with a newborn?"

"You've met Simona and Talia. They worked for my mother's family and I trusted them implicitly. They fell in love with the baby and have been with me ever since. I couldn't have made it without them."

"Did your father help?"

"Yes. Everyone did what they could. Their love for Concetta brought us all a little closer together."

"Then you'd think that after a marriage like yours, and that sweet baby, your father would give up his futile desire and leave you alone to decide what you want from life."

Leon nodded. "That's what a normal parent would do. Perhaps now you're beginning to understand what

I've always been up against. The point is, I would never choose a woman of rank."

"Why do you feel so strongly about it? I'm curious."

"My parents were officially betrothed before they ever met each other. They made their arranged marriage work. From what I saw, they were kind and decent to each other, sometimes showing each other affection. But until Mother was dying, I didn't know she'd loved another man and had to give him up."

His mother had told him something else, too.

"I can't begin to imagine it," Belle was saying.

"After realizing the sacrifice she'd made to marry for duty, I made up my mind that her situation wasn't going to happen to me. When the time came, I proposed to Benedetta without hesitation."

Belle shifted restlessly in her seat. "I guess that meant your father had to sacrifice, too."

Leon nodded. "You know what's interesting? The other night Father told me that when he asked Luciana to marry him, he said, 'Naturally, it wasn't like the feelings I had for your mother, but then you can't expect that.'"

"So what do you think he was really saying?"

"That he was still trying to protect me by pretending he'd loved our mother, but I knew it wasn't true. They were never in love with each other. Do you want to know something else?"

Her eyes fastened on him, revealing her concern in the reflection of the cruiser's lights.

"I think the real truth is he fell deeply in love with Luciana, enough to overlook everything in order to make her his wife."

After a slight hesitation, Belle said, "I'm pretty sure

she has learned to love him, too. The way she talked to him at the table convinces me they are very close."

"So close, in fact, he wants to adopt you to make her completely happy."

"He mustn't do that…" Her features screwed up in pain. "Think of the damage it would do to Dante. I can't handle that. You've got to stop him, Leon!"

Her reaction was even more than he'd hoped for. "I agree, and I've thought of a foolproof plan. I failed my brother when I went away to college in Rome, but this will be a way to atone for my sins."

"What can you do?" she cried. "Tell me."

"It involves your cooperation, but it has to be so convincing to everyone, and I mean *everyone,* no one will believe it's not true."

Determination filled her gaze. "I'll do anything."

"I hope you mean that."

"I swear it. Since Dante left the table, I've been dying inside."

Leon reached out to squeeze her hand before letting it go. "First you have to phone your boss and tell him you need to take family leave. Let him know you're in Italy visiting the mother you were just reunited with. Tell him an emergency has arisen that prevents you from returning to work Monday. They have to give you the time off."

Leon heard her take several short breaths in succession. "I…suppose that could be arranged, especially when I've never asked for it before."

"Bene." He checked his watch. "Now would be the perfect time to reach him at work." He handed her his phone. "Once you've talked to him, you'll be able to concentrate on our plan."

"I don't know what it is yet."

"Before I say anything else, we need to know if everything's all right for you to stay in Rimini. If not, I'll have to come up with another plan. While you do that, we'll head back to shore."

He raised anchor and started the engine. The sound prevented him from hearing much of her conversation. By the time they reached the dock, she'd finished the call. While he tied up the cruiser, he gave her a covert glance. "What's the verdict?"

"I couldn't believe he was so nice. He said for me to take all the time I needed. Not to worry."

"Eccelente."

One roadblock removed.

Belle handed him the phone and took off her life jacket, which he stowed away under the bench. She replaced it with her sweater. "When are you going to tell me the plan?"

"I don't know about you, but I could use some coffee. Let's go up to the villa and check on Concetta. Then we'll have the rest of the night to talk everything out."

"I admit coffee sounds good. It's getting cooler."

He helped Belle step onto the dock and they made their way back in silence. They might not be touching, but the sensual tension between them was palpable. Talia saw them in the hall and told him Concetta was sleeping like an angel.

Before heading for the kitchen, he and Belle went upstairs and tiptoed into the nursery to take a peek. Suddenly, both of them chuckled, because the baby was sitting up in the crib. She saw them in the doorway and started fussing.

"It looks like she was waiting for you to say good-night," Belle whispered. Leon crossed the room to pick her up and hug her. His heart dissolved when his child kissed him and patted his cheeks. "She adores you, Leon."

The sound of her voice brought his daughter's head around. To their surprise she reached for Belle, who caught her in her arms.

"Are you going to give me a kiss good-night, too? How lucky can I be? I love you, sweetheart." She walked her around the room. "I wish Concetta knew what I was saying, Leon."

"She doesn't need to understand English to know what you mean," he murmured in a satisfied voice.

"Is that true?" Belle kissed her again.

In the intimacy of the darkened room his daughter clung to her as if she were her mother. It added substance to an idea that had been building in his mind since the first time Belle had picked her up.

He'd planned to talk to her after they'd gone back downstairs for coffee, but his little girl had unexpectedly chosen the place and the moment for this conversation.

"Since she's not ready to go to sleep yet, I'll tell you my plan now. We need to get married right away to prevent my father from adopting you."

CHAPTER SEVEN

BELLE LET OUT a laugh that filled the nursery. She stood in front of Leon with the baby's head nestled against her neck. "Right away? As in…"

"Tomorrow."

"I didn't know it was possible," she mocked.

"I have a friend in high places."

"Naturally. So *that's* the solution to all our problems? From the man who's still grieving for his wife and never intends to marry again?"

Leon couldn't help smiling. "It's even stranger, considering that I've proposed to a woman who has declared marriage isn't an option for her."

Belle patted Concetta's back. "All right. Now that you've gotten my attention, let's hear what's really on your mind."

"You just heard it."

"Be serious, Leon."

He shifted his weight. "When you allow it to sink in, you'll discover it makes perfect sense. Our marriage will make it unnecessary for the adoption to take place, because you'll be my wife, mistress of our household, mother to my child."

His words caused Belle to clutch his little girl tighter.

"Concetta's tiny eyelids are fluttering, on the verge of sleep. That's how comfortable she is with you. She needs a mother, Belle. I've been blind to that reality for a long time. But seeing her with you is so right. Just now I heard you tell her you loved her. That came from your heart, so don't deny it."

Belle could hardly swallow. "I'm not denying it."

"If we marry, there'll be two desired outcomes, both of them critical. First, our marriage will enable you to have the full relationship you deserve with your mother for the rest of your lives, without moving into the palazzo. We both know that's Dante's territory and should remain so."

She hugged the baby closer.

"Secondly, it will prevent any more machinations on my father's part to see me married to the titled woman he's picked out for me. After all, who could be a more fitting bride than his wife's daughter? The beauty of it is that I'll be the one who takes care of you, not my father."

In a furtive movement, Belle walked over to the crib and tried to put the baby down. But Concetta wasn't having any of it and started crying again, so she picked her back up. "You need to go to sleep, little love."

A satisfied smile curled Leon's lips. "She doesn't want to leave your arms. It convinces me my daughter has bonded with you in a way she hasn't done with anyone else but me. You have to realize how important that is to me. She's been my world since Benedetta died."

"I'm very much aware of that."

"When I told Father I would never marry again, I meant it at the time. How could I ever find a woman who would be the kind of mother to Concetta that my mother was to me and Dante? But your arrival in Rimini has changed all that."

Belle buried her face in the baby's neck to shield herself from his words.

"Tonight I watched my daughter reach for you. With the evidence before my eyes, I know that with you as my wife, she'll have a mother who will always love her. I *know* how much you care for her already. I've seen the way you respond to her. It's the same way Luciana responds. Like mother, like daughter."

Belle kissed the little girl's head. "As long as we're having this absurd conversation, there's one thing you haven't mentioned."

"You're talking about love, of course. Since we both made a conscious decision not to marry, before we met, we won't have that expectation. But there's desire between us, as we found out yesterday. Which is vital for any marriage.

"Furthermore, we've become friends, who both love our families. Between us we can turn all the negatives into a positive, in order for you to be with your mother and calm Dante's fears." Leon moved closer. "Nothing has to change for you. Talia will continue to be Concetta's nanny. If the bank backs a new TCCPI outlet in Rimini, you'll be installed as the manager and can go on working."

"I guess it doesn't surprise me you could make that happen," she muttered.

"Let me make myself clear. I'd do *anything* to give my daughter a life that includes a mother and a father." Leon's voice grated. "Your journey to Italy to find your mother has convinced me you'd do anything to be close to her. If a career you've carved out for yourself will keep you here, then you can be a mother, have your career and stay near Luciana. Won't that be worth it to you?"

Belle shook her head. "I can't believe we're having this conversation. But for the sake of argument, what you're suggesting is that we enter into an arranged marriage."

He reached for Concetta and put her back in the crib. This time she didn't cry, but she held on to his finger. "Yes, but one in which we haven't been pressured by anyone. I realize I can't compete with your roommates for the companionship you enjoy with them, but I'm not so bad. We had fun watching the dolphins, didn't we?"

"That question doesn't require a response. What you're suggesting is ludicrous."

"Now you have some idea of how my parents must have felt when they had to enter into an arranged marriage. At least with you and me, we've both felt the fire. How long it lasts is anyone's guess. But if nothing I've said has made any difference in how you feel, then it appears the only alternative is for you to go back to your life in New York."

What life was that?

Leon lifted his head to appraise her. "While I stay with Concetta until she's asleep, why don't you go down to the kitchen and have that coffee you wanted? I'll join you shortly and you can give me your definitive answer."

"You think it's that simple?"

He grimaced. "No. I only know that we can't change what has happened, and a decision has to be made one way or the other."

"Like I said, I shouldn't have come to Italy."

"It's too late for regrets, and we've already had this conversation. The only thing to do is move forward. Just be aware that whether you stay here or go back to the States, my father plans to adopt you. He's been so eager to do it, only time will tell how that hurt has affected Dante. His relationship with our father and Luciana has been rocky at times."

"I don't want him hurt."

"Neither do I." Leon lifted his brows. "If you can think of a better way than marriage to prevent more pain from happening and still be close to your mother, I'll be the first one to listen."

"I'll go to your father and beg him not to do anything."

"It won't do you any good, Belle. On certain issues, my father is adamant. Where your mother is concerned, this is the gift he wants to give her, and no amount of tears or cajoling will change his mind."

"Not even for Dante's sake?"

"I'm afraid not. You heard my father. Dante's a grown man and should be able to handle it."

Belle was frantic. "You can't really mean what you've been saying…"

"Why do you think I married Benedetta in the dark of night?" he countered.

Belle's head jerked back. "But it's a feudal system!"

"I've been fighting it all my life."

At this point she was pacing the floor. Finally she stopped and turned to him. "What would we tell our parents? We've known each other only a few days."

"We'll tell them it was love at first sight. They won't be able to say anything. I happen to know Papà fell for Luciana the minute he met her. He'd never known a love like that with my mother."

Belle pressed her lips together. "It's so sad about your parents."

"They managed, but it's past history now. I can't speak for Luciana, but she must have had strong feelings for my father in order to get married again so soon after losing the man she'd first loved."

"You're really serious about this, aren't you."

"Serious enough that I've been on the phone with our old family priest, who married everyone in our family. He stands ready with a special license to officiate at the church tomorrow morning. All you'll need to provide is your passport. My staff will be our witnesses."

Belle stared blindly into space. "I was supposed to go out for the day with Mom...."

"Call her and tell her there's been a change in plans. Promise her I'll drive you to the palazzo later in the morning. When we arrive with Concetta, hopefully Dante and Pia will be there, so we can make the announcement of our nuptials in front of everyone."

"You don't just get married like this—"

"Most normal people don't. But we happened to be born to a mother and father with unique birthrights, who are married to each other, thus complicating your life and mine. With our marriage taking place, the idea of my father wanting to adopt you will fade, and take the sword out of Dante's hand. It might even improve our relationship. Much more than that, I can't promise. Only time will tell."

Belle edged away from him. "This is all moving too fast."

"The situation demands action. Father believes you're going back to New York on Sunday. When he announced he was planning to adopt you, I knew it meant he'd already been in touch with his attorney. He'll want your signature on the adoption papers before you leave. When he makes a decision, he acts on it before you can blink."

"You're a lot like him."

"Is that a good or a bad thing?"

"Please don't joke at a time like this, Leon."

Concetta had finally fallen asleep. He walked across the room to Belle. Reaching in his pocket, he pulled out a ring. She stared at the plain gold band. "What are you doing?"

He took her left hand in his. "Your engagement ring. Tomorrow it will be the wedding ring of Signora Arabella Donatello Sloan di Malatesta."

Belle pulled her hand away before he could put it on her. "I haven't agreed to anything."

He stared at her through shuttered eyes. "Then in the morning all you have to do is tell me you don't want it, and we won't talk of it again."

"Leon—you can't do this to me!"

"Do what? Offer to marry you so I can give you my name and protection? Help you to enjoy the mother you never knew? Give you the opportunity to be a mother to my daughter, who's already welcomed you into her life?"

"You know what I mean!" Belle cried.

"Don't you think I'd like to make up to you for the years of emotional deprivation? For the cruelty you received at your stepbrother's hands?" he demanded. "Don't you know your existence has changed destiny for all of us?"

His words scorched her. She wished to heaven she had someone to talk to. Ironically, now that she'd found her mother, she couldn't go to her. Not about this. It was worse than getting caught in the maze she'd seen earlier on the palazzo grounds.

"What do *you* get out of this?"

"I thought you understood. The most remarkable mother in the world for my daughter, and a possible chance to win back my brother's affection. When Benedetta became so ill, she begged me that one day I'd find happiness with someone else. At the time I didn't want to hear it, but she was right. Life has to go on. Our marriage will be a start along that path. Until you flew into my world, I didn't know where to begin."

Belle couldn't take any more. "I'm going to say goodnight." Without hesitation she bolted from the nursery and flew down the stairs to her bedroom.

For the rest of the night she tossed and turned, going over every argument in her mind. Could she really enter into a marriage when she knew Leon's heart had died after losing his wife? Belle couldn't hope to compete with her memory, but he wasn't asking for love. He wanted her to be Concetta's mother.

It was probably the only area in Belle's life where she felt confident. If she had that little baby for her very own, she could pour out all the love she had to give. Belle could be the kind of mother to Concetta she'd dreamed of having herself.

Leon *wanted* her to be his baby's mother.

That had to mean something, didn't it?

He was the most marvelous man. To think he trusted her with his prized possession!

Even if she was a virgin who'd had no experience with men, she could do the mothering part right. Maybe their marriage would help heal the wound between Leon and his family.

Marriage to him would ensure a close relationship with Belle's mother for the rest of their lives.

But what if Leon met another woman and fell in love?

Belle knew the answer to that: it would kill her. But would their union be so different from the many marriages where one of the partners strayed? It was a fact of life that millions of married men and women had affairs. There were no guarantees.

By the time morning came, she'd gone back and forth so many times she was physically and emotionally exhausted. But one thing stood out above all else. The thought of going back to her life in New York seemed like living death....

It was a beautiful, warm summer Saturday morning for a wedding in Rimini. In a veil and a white silk and lace wedding dress of her dreams, Belle stepped out of the bridal shop with Leon. They walked to his car where her bouquet lay on the backseat. He'd thought of everything. Belle heard the church bells of San Giovanni before they arrived. Though it was much more ornate than the church attached to the orphanage in Newburgh, Belle had the same sense of homecoming once Leon ushered her inside the doors.

Church had always been her one place of comfort, whether she'd been at the orphanage or the Petersons'. Except that this morning she was to be married to the dark prince of Rimini, as she'd first thought of him. Nothing seemed real.

He'd pinned a gardenia corsage to her linen suit before they'd left the villa. In the lapel of his midnight-blue silk suit, he wore a smaller gardenia. Belle could smell the fragrance she would always associate with being a bride, but she couldn't seem to feel anything. It was as if she were standing outside her body.

Leon's staff came in a separate car. They followed them down the aisle to the shrine in front, where the old priest was waiting in his colorful vestments. Talia carried the baby, who so far was being very good, and looked adorable in a white lace dress and white sandals with pink rosettes.

The priest clasped both of Belle's hands and welcomed her with a broad smile. "Princess Arabella?" She almost fainted at being addressed that way. "You look like your mother did when I married her and the count," he explained in heavily accented English. "Leonardo has advised that I perform this ceremony in English. Are you ready?"

"We are." Leon answered for them in his deep voice.

"If the witnesses will stand on either side."

Talia and Simona stood on Leon's right. He kissed his daughter, who kept making sounds. Carla stood on Belle's left.

"Arabella and Leonardo, you have come together in this church so that the Lord may seal and strengthen your love in the presence of the church's minister and this community. Christ abundantly blesses this love. In the presence of the church, I ask you to state your intentions. Have you come here freely and without reservation to give yourselves to each other in marriage?"

Without reservation? Belle panicked, but she said yes after Leon's affirmative response.

"Will you love and honor each other as man and wife for the rest of your lives?"

That wasn't as difficult to answer. Belle did honor

him. He was the one responsible for finding her mother. And there were many things about him she loved very much. The way he loved his daughter melted her heart.

"Will you accept children lovingly from God, and bring them up according to the law of Christ and His church?"

That was a question Belle hadn't been expecting. But how could she say no when she'd just admitted to coming here freely to give herself in marriage? She said a faint yes, but didn't know if the priest heard her.

"Take her hand, *figlio mio*."

Leon's grasp was warm against her cold fingers. He rubbed his thumb over her skin to get the circulation flowing. *That* she felt.

"Repeat after me. I, Leonardo Rovere di Malatesta, take you, Arabella Donatello Sloan, to be my wife. I promise to be true to you in good times and in bad, in sickness and in health. I will love you and honor you all the days of my life."

The next few moments were surreal for Belle, who could hear the words of the ceremony uttered by the priest, and their own responses. Concetta's baby talk provided a background.

Blood pounded in Belle's ears when he said, "You have declared your consent before the church. May the Lord in His goodness strengthen your consent and fill you both with His blessings. What God has joined, men must not divide. Leonardo? You have rings?"

Oh no. Belle didn't have one for him.

"We do."

"Lord, may these rings be a symbol of true faith in each other, and always remind them of their love, through Christ our Lord. Leonardo?"

Belle watched him pull the gold band out of his pocket. "Put it on her finger and repeat after me. Take this ring as a sign of my love and fidelity. In the name of the Father, and of the Son, and of the Holy Spirit."

It was really happening…

Leon reached in his pocket again and pulled out his signet ring to hand to her.

The priest said, "Arabella? Repeat after me. Take this ring as a sign of my love and fidelity. In the name of the Father, and of the Son, and of the Holy Spirit."

After saying the words, she was all thumbs as she put it on the ring finger of Leon's left hand. He'd removed his own wedding band. How hard that must have been, after the love he'd shared with Benedetta.

While she was still staring at his hand incredulously, Leon put a finger under her chin and tilted her head so he could kiss her.

"We've done it, Belle. You're my wife now," he whispered against her lips. "Thank you for this gift only you could have given, to help me raise Concetta. For that you will always have my undying devotion."

When his mouth covered hers, it was different from a husband's kiss. She didn't know what she'd expected, but it was more like a sweet, reverent benediction. Quickly recovering from her surprise, she whispered back, "Then we're even, because you've given me the gift of my mother and your precious daughter."

By now Concetta was making herself heard and getting wiggly. Belle saw Leon reach for her, and with a triumphant cry hug her in his strong arms.

The staff huddled around Belle with moist eyes to congratulate her. Their well-wishing was so genuine she was moved by their warm welcome as Leon's new wife.

Over their heads she looked at the baby. Leon caught her glance and brought Concetta over for Belle to hold. The child came to her with a sunny smile.

Belle's eyes closed tightly as she drew her close. This precious little girl was *her daughter* now! It was unbelievable.

The priest stood by with a smile, patting Concetta's head. "The *bambina* now has a beautiful new *mamma*." He made the sign of the cross over both of them.

"Thank you, Father."

They all moved out to the vestibule, where the priest asked them and the witnesses to sign the marriage document. With their signatures on it, everything was official. Leon took the baby from Belle, but as she leaned over the table to take her turn, two petals from her corsage fell on the paper. She looked around and discovered another petal still in Concetta's hand.

"She has the same sleight of hand as her *papà*. She'll need watching," Belle murmured.

His eyes gleamed molten silver. No man should be so handsome. Her hand shook as she wrote her signature. When it was done, she noticed the others were gone except for Leon. He rolled up the marriage certificate and put it in his pocket.

"Talia carried the baby out to our car. Shall we go, Signora Malatesta?"

Belle wondered if she would ever get used to her new name. He walked her outside to the church parking area.

"I looked up the meaning of your name in the library the other day, Leon. I knew *mal* meant *bad,* but found out *testa* meant *head.*" They'd reached the sedan where Talia had put the baby in the car seat. She was standing by the rear fender.

"If it meant bad people headed your family, then it had to have been a long time ago, because I've known nothing but good from your hands and your father's. I just wanted you to know that I'm proud to bear your name."

Some emotion turned his eyes a darker gray. "I'll cherish that compliment. Thank you." He helped her into the backseat next to Concetta, who was biting a plastic doughnut. Rufo lay at her feet, guarding her. Before Leon stood up, he planted a swift kiss on Belle's mouth, then shut the door. While he walked Talia to the car where the others were waiting, Belle ran a finger over her lips.

He was her husband. She needed to get used to this, but every time he touched her, she went up in flame.

In a minute he came back to the sedan. Once he was behind the wheel they drove away from the church. With the palazzo their next destination, Belle's thoughts darted to his family and their reaction when they heard the news.

Her heart ached for Leon. Though they both hoped the announcement of their marriage would help the situation with Dante, she knew her husband had been in pain over him for years. He had to be anxious right now.

"Leon?" she called to him in a burst of inspiration.

He'd been glancing at her and the baby through the rearview mirror. "Are you all right? You look worried."

"I am, because I have an idea, but I don't know how you'll feel about it."

"I won't know until you tell me."

Uh-oh. He *was* on edge. She could feel it. "The other day Mom told me Dante and his wife have their own entrance into the palazzo."

"That's right. They live in the other wing."

Her lungs constricted. "What would you think if we drove around to it first and dropped in on them, unannounced and unexpected? Under normal circumstances Dante would be the first person you'd run to with our news.

"Why don't you treat him that way instead of going through your parents? The element of surprise will catch him off guard, and might even please him if he realizes your parents don't know yet. It's worth trying—that is, if they're home."

For a long time Leon didn't say anything. "I don't know what they do with their Saturdays," he muttered.

Belle got excited when she heard that. "Then let's find out. What's the worst he can do? Slam the door in our faces while we're standing there with Concetta? I finally faced Cliff and look what happened!"

In the mirror, Leon's eyes flashed silver fire. "I believe you've got a warrior in you. If you're willing, I think your idea is rather brilliant."

"Grazie," she said in lousy Italian.

"First thing we're going to do is get you a tutor."

She laughed out loud. Miraculously, he joined her. It was the release they needed. When they entered the estate, he kept driving past the courtyard and on around to the other end. Belle saw a red sports car parked outside the entrance.

Pia's car was missing. That meant Dante was home alone. If Belle's suggestion was going to work, then it was better Pia had gone somewhere.

Leon pulled to a stop. By the time he'd gotten out, Belle had already alighted from the car with the baby in her arms. There was no hesitation on her part. Rufo rubbed against Leon's legs as they walked to the door.

When the boys were young, they had their own knock for each other. Rather than use the buzzer, Leon did what he used to do, then waited. Belle glanced at him. "Try it again."

He would have, but suddenly the door opened. To say that a disheveled Dante, clad in sweats, was shocked to see him and his entourage was probably the understatement of all time.

"Sorry to burst in on you like this, but I wanted you to be the first to know."

Dante squinted at him through eyes as dark a charcoal as their father's. "What in the hell are you talking about?"

"Belle and I just got married. We've come straight from the church."

"Be serious."

"I've never been more serious in my life."

A look of bewilderment crossed his face. "I thought you were still grieving over Benedetta."

Leon nodded. "I'll never forget her, but then something amazing happened when I met Belle. Papà is in for a shock when I tell him. You and I both know he has several women lined up, and expects me to marry one of them, but I could never do what he wants. I've never believed in titles."

A full minute passed before his brother said, "He'll tell you to annul your marriage."

"Not when he learns we fell in love the moment we met and haven't been separated since. I couldn't let her go back to New York tomorrow."

Dante took the scroll from him and unrolled it. After

studying it he said, "But to marry Luciana's daughter…" His eyes darted to Belle, who was entertaining the baby.

"We've never talked about it before, but I'm convinced the same thing happened to Papà when he met Luciana."

Dante swallowed hard. "I figured that much out when I got a little older. Papà never loved Mamma that way," he muttered.

"No," Leon whispered, glad his brother had come to the same conclusion. "That's why it hurt us so damn much when he got married that fast."

"It did that, all right."

Clearing his throat, Leon said, "There's something I've been needing to say for a long time. I hurt you when I went to school in Rome. I shouldn't have left you, but I was in so much pain, I thought only of myself. I'm hoping one day you'll be able to forgive me."

Dante eyed him with soulful eyes, an expression he hadn't seen since they were teenagers, but he had no words for him. Fresh pain consumed Leon. As Belle had said, it was worth a try.

He took the certificate from him. "We're going to go tell the parents now. It would be nice if you were there for a backup. You know how Papà feels when he sees either of us let our emotions overrule what he considers our duty. If he can't handle this, then Belle and I will be moving to New York with the baby."

An odd sound came out of Dante. "You'd go that far?"

"For my wife and daughter, yes." He reached out and grasped his brother's shoulder. "Thanks for answering the door. I purposely gave it our special knock to give you the chance to open it or not. Despite what you might think, you always were and always will be my best friend."

He turned to Belle and took the baby from her. "Come on, my little *bellissima*. We'll walk around to the other end of the palazzo and enjoy this wonderful day."

CHAPTER EIGHT

"JUST A MINUTE, Leon. I need to grab her diaper bag." When they were out of hearing range, Belle caught up to him. "No matter what happens, you spoke your piece and your brother knows you love him. It's up to him now."

Leon grasped her hand and squeezed her fingers. "That's what has me worried. Don't forget he's a Malatesta."

"Have you forgotten I'm proud to be married to one? Remember something else. He didn't slam the door in your face, either. That has to count for something."

Leon had married an angel. "Are you ready to face the parents?"

She nodded. "Be honest. You *are* a little worried about their reaction."

"You're wrong, Belle."

"Then what's the matter?"

His bride was highly perceptive, but he couldn't tell her the truth yet. He knew the reasons she'd entered into this marriage, but she didn't know all of them. When she found out, *that* was what he was worried about.

"Your life hasn't been like anyone else's. Not even your wedding day could be like anyone else's. I—"

"There you are!" Luciana called to them, cutting off the rest of what he was going to say. "I saw your car pull around the drive, but you were so long I came to see what was going on."

Belle ran to meet her mother and they hugged. "Leon wanted to talk to Dante for a minute."

"That was an awfully long minute, when I've been waiting for you. Sullisto went to the bank this morning, but he'll be home any second." They both gravitated to the baby. "Look at that outfit she's wearing! Where have you been?"

"To church," Belle answered with her innate honesty. "We were there quite a while. She needs a diaper change and a bottle."

Leon carried Concetta into the house, deciding it was the perfect segue for what was coming. He handed her over when Belle reached for her, and all three females disappeared into one of the guest rooms, while he wandered around the living room, looking at the many family pictures.

There was an eight-by-ten that he particularly loved—his mother on her knees in the garden. She wore a broad-rimmed hat and was planting a rosebush. Flowers were her passion. So were her two boys.

She'd poured out all her love on them. In the process she'd spoiled them, but Leon could never complain. His childhood had been idyllic. That's what he wanted for Concetta. He knew Belle would love her forever.

He picked up the framed photo. "Mamma? I wish you were here today. You'd love Belle the same way you loved Benedetta."

When he heard voices, he put it back and looked across the room at the stunning picture of the three

women in his life. They sat down on one of the couches
while Belle fed the baby.

"I know she's so good, but I'm surprised you took
her to Mass," Luciana said.

Belle flashed him a signal. He took the chair closest
to the couch and pulled it around. "Not Mass. We arranged a private meeting with Father Luc."

"Why?"

"This morning your daughter did me the honor of
becoming my wife." He drew the certificate out of
his pocket and handed it to Luciana. "Last night we
talked everything over. I asked her to marry me, so she
wouldn't go back to New York and meet some other
man. As you can see, Concetta is already crazy about
her."

With tear-filled eyes, Luciana looked at Belle. "I only
want to know one thing. Do you love him? Because if
you don't, darling…"

Leon knew what Luciana was asking. She was married to a man who'd done his duty with Leon's mother,
but the personal fulfillment hadn't been there. The
mother in Luciana didn't want that for Belle.

"It's all right, Mom," she said with a gentle laugh.
"When I first met Leon, I thought of him as the dark
prince of Rimini. He frightened me, but he also thrilled
me."

Her half lies thrilled *him*.

"I can understand that," Luciana murmured. "He has
a lot of his father in him."

"I tried not to be attracted, but that flew out the window, because we've spent hours and hours together.
Then I met Concetta. The three of us had such a wonderful time watching the dolphins we didn't want it to

end, did we?" She kissed his daughter's forehead. "We saw a lot of daddies there, but none of them had your daddy's way."

"Leon has been a remarkable father." Luciana's comment made him feel more ashamed of his prior behavior toward her.

"But I guess I didn't know how deeply I felt about him until he told me he wanted to marry me," Belle went on. "The thought of turning him down and flying back to New York was too devastating to contemplate. I felt the same pain at the thought of leaving you, after having just found you."

In the next breath Luciana jumped up from the couch. First she threw her arms around Belle and the baby, then Leon. "I'm so happy with this news, I can hardly contain it."

Leon's gaze fused with his wife's. If Belle had any doubts about their marriage being the right thing to do, they were wiped away by her mother's joy.

"Your father shouldn't have left. Why isn't he home yet?"

Leon had a hunch he'd been meeting with his attorney about the adoption. While he was thinking about that, they had a visitor. To his shock, his brother entered the living room, in jeans and a sport shirt, showered and shaved. "I just got off the phone with him." *Who called whom?* "He'll be here in a minute." Dante eyed Leon. "Don't worry. I didn't spoil your surprise."

He moved over to Belle and hunkered down in front of her. The baby had fallen asleep against her shoulder. "Belated congratulations. I would have invited you in earlier, but I wasn't decent."

"If you want to know the truth, when I'm at the apartment in New York, sweats are about all I wear."

Dante grinned. "Do you run?"

"As often as I can, before work."

That was news to Leon.

"We must be soul mates. Like you, I try to get in a run, but I usually do it after work."

"Does your wife run with you?"

"Sometimes."

"We'll all have to do it together."

"I'm afraid my brother swims."

Belle nodded. "So I noticed. Like a fish, I might add. Maybe I can train him by getting him to push Concetta in her stroller at the same time."

Dante roared with laughter.

"Where is Pia, by the way?"

"Visiting her mother, but I phoned her. She'll be back soon."

"Does her family live far from here?"

"No. Only a few kilometers."

"How lucky for both of them." Belle smiled at Luciana.

"They'll never know, will they, darling."

"No."

Dante studied them. "I bet it shocked both of you when you first saw each other."

Leon hadn't seen his brother smile or act this animated in years. Belle had that effect on everyone.

"When I was at the orphanage, I used to dream about what she'd look like."

Leon got up to take the baby from her. "Little did you know you saw her every time you looked in a mirror." He kissed his little girl. "I'll go put her down in the crib." Luciana had provided one for her after she was born. Leon hadn't brought her over often enough.

"I'll go with you. We'll be right back."

"Sure you will," Dante joked.

Belle followed Leon out of the living room and down the hall to the first bedroom. He put the baby on her back and covered her with a light blanket. Belle stood next to him at the side of the crib.

He reached for her hand, too full of emotion to speak.

"So far so good," she whispered.

"A miracle has happened today. It's all because of you."

"I'm afraid it's not over yet. We still have to tell your father." She eased her hand away. "If you'll excuse me for a minute, I need to freshen up, and will meet you back in the living room."

Much as he wanted to be alone with her, this wasn't the time. With another glance at his daughter, who was sleeping peacefully, he left the bedroom, and ran into his father in the hallway. The marriage certificate was in his hand. Leon had forgotten it had been left on the coffee table.

"It seems everyone in this house knows what you've done except me," Sullisto exclaimed without preamble. "Your powers of persuasion are phenomenal, to get Belle to marry you when you don't love her. You've even convinced Luciana."

Love for his stepmother seeped into Leon.

"She's only been here three days," his father added. "What did you do? Slip something into her wine?"

Leon bristled. That was below the belt, even for the count. "No. The trick of our ancestors wouldn't work on her. She doesn't drink, smoke or indulge in drugs."

"Belle's not an ordinary woman."

"Truer words were never spoken. She's made in the image of her mother, a woman who would have married the man of her heart if he hadn't been killed.... The woman you married after Mamma died because you wanted her at all cost."

His cheeks went a ruddy color. "How dare you speak to me that way—"

"I didn't say it to be offensive, Papà. I only meant to point out that true love makes us act with our hearts, not our heads."

His father's eyes glittered with emotion, but Leon had to finish what had been started years ago. "Mamma loved another man before she obeyed her parents and married you. I have no doubts my autocratic grandfather forced you into your first marriage."

"*Basta,* Leonardo!"

"I'm almost through. I was about to say it's possible *you* loved someone before you had to do your duty. I have no way of knowing, since you never shared that with me or Dante. But given a second chance, you married for the right reason. Every man and woman born should have that privilege. Concetta will grow up being able to choose."

For once in his life, Leon's father looked utterly flummoxed.

"Would you really condemn me to a loveless marriage with one of the titled women you've picked out for me, because it's what Malatestas do?"

"You're my firstborn son."

"You were *your* father's firstborn son, too. We'll both always be the firstborn, but in the end, what does it matter? In the Middle Ages it was a system devised for the aggrandizement of wealth. Surely we've come further than that in the twenty-first century."

"Leon is right."

Dante had suddenly materialized, seemingly out of nowhere. Sullisto swung around. "Were you in on this, too?"

"On what?"

"This outrageous marriage of your brother's." He thrust the marriage certificate at him. "When I phoned, you said nothing."

"Because I didn't know anything. But I can tell you this. When he showed up at my door, he looked happy like I haven't seen him since before Mamma died. Let's hope Luciana didn't hear you, or she might think you don't approve of her daughter. I happen to know you do or you wouldn't have invited her to come and live with you."

"So you're in his corner now?"

"This is his wedding day, Papà."

"A wedding set up to thwart me!"

"I doubt you were on his mind when he asked Belle to marry him," Dante interjected. "Just so you know, Luciana sent me to tell you lunch is ready on the terrace."

"I couldn't eat now."

"It would hurt Luciana if you don't come. In fact, it would be the height of bad manners."

Their father scowled. "I don't recall you having any the other day."

"The other day I wasn't myself." Dante shot Leon a pleading glance. "Since then I've repented."

"Why?"

"Since I've come to realize how much I love my brother."

Bless you, Belle, for your inspiration.

Leon smiled at him. "That goes both ways, Dante. Why don't you two go ahead? I'll find out what's keeping Belle. Maybe the baby woke up."

Their father still looked angry as he eyed both of them before walking back down the hall toward the foyer.

Dante clapped Leon on the shoulder. "That went well," he teased, sounding like the old Dante. "See you in a minute." He rolled up the marriage certificate and handed it to him.

"I owe you." Putting it in his pocket, Leon watched them go before he hurried into the bedroom. To his surprise, he found Belle standing at the side of the door. Rufo walked over to brush against his legs.

"I heard every word. I'm so happy you and your brother have reconciled. Between the two of you, I'm sure in time you'll be able to win your father around. Your master plan worked brilliantly, Signor Malatesta. Come on. Lunch is waiting." She slipped out the door, trailing the scent of gardenias, but she didn't look at him.

His marriage was in trouble.

He knew how deep Belle's insecurities ran. Leon had to hope his powers of persuasion were as phenomenal as his father claimed. Otherwise he was in for the kind of pain from which he sensed he'd never recover.

"Leon? How soon do you think you can arrange for TCCPI to set up a phone store here?"

Now that Concetta was awake, Belle had carried her out to the patio to play buckets with her.

He was standing by the railing, looking out at the sea. She feared he was brooding over his father. "I'll lay the groundwork next week," he told her.

"At first I couldn't believe you were serious, but since then I've found out you never joke about anything. I like a challenge. It would be interesting to see if I could make a success of it."

"What do you mean, *if?*"

Leon always complimented her. She decided it was in his nature, but she didn't deserve it. "When Mac learns I'm not coming back to the store, he'll be overjoyed, because he wants my job."

"That's probably the reason he won't get it."

She chuckled. "Spoken like a man who knows about business."

"I've been thinking about that and other things. I'll arrange to have your possessions sent from your apartment."

"Except for books and a few more clothes, I brought everything else important with me. One good thing about me. I travel light."

He didn't smile. She couldn't bring him out of his dark mood.

They'd just returned from the palazzo. Belle had forced herself to eat the fabulous meal Luciana had served them. For her mother's sake she'd acted like a new bride, and had kissed Leon several times for family pictures, while Sullisto looked on with only a comment here and there.

Pia had arrived in the midst of the festivities. Whatever Dante told her must have resonated, because she was very friendly to Belle. The party atmosphere continued after Concetta awoke from her nap and entertained everyone.

With the announcement that they were leaving to get ready for a short honeymoon, Leon brought the car around to the front. Rufo jumped inside before Belle's new husband helped her and the baby, after another hug for her mother. They left the estate and drove to the villa, where she changed into jeans and a knit top.

This was her home now, complete with the dearest, sweetest little girl on the planet and a husband to die for. There was only one thing wrong with this picture. Sullisto's words still rang in her ears.

Your powers of persuasion are phenomenal, to get Belle to marry you when you don't love her. You've even convinced Luciana.

She's only been here three days. What did you do? Slip something into her wine?

No. Leon didn't have to do any of those things. Belle had fallen instantly in love with him. He was the man she would have married no matter how long she had to wait. Of course he wasn't in love with her, but he'd been right about their desire for each other.

With every kiss over the past few days, she sensed a growing hunger from him. After having been happily married to Benedetta, it was only natural he craved the same kind of fulfillment. A man could compartmentalize his needs from his emotions.

Belle couldn't.

She loved him in all the ways possible. Today she'd made vows to be his wife. That was exactly what she would be to him. If not his love, he'd given her everything else, including a baby. There were trade-offs.

Belle could always be near her mother now. He and Dante were friends again. Sullisto was at war with himself, but it spoke volumes about how much he loved Leon, because he hadn't disowned him yet.

"Where are we going on our honeymoon?" That brought his dark head around. If she wasn't mistaken, her question had caught him off guard. "Mom offered to look after Concetta."

Leon's hand went to the back of his neck. She noticed he did that when he was weighing his thoughts carefully. "Where would you like to go?"

"Anywhere on the water. How about you? Or did you do that with Benedetta...?"

"No. We honeymooned in Switzerland, but I don't want to talk about her."

"I'm sorry. Would you rather we postponed a trip right now? Believe me, I'd understand."

"Understand what?" he blurted. "My father hurt you today. Do you think I'm going to forget that?"

"I didn't take it personally, not after his warm welcome the first night we met. He needs time. You're trying to change someone who was raised under a different set of rules."

Leon's eyes narrowed on her face. "How do you know so much about people?"

"Probably because I wasn't one of the participants of life. As I've told you before, most of the time I spent it observing other people. You learn a lot that way." She cocked her head. "Does your family own a yacht?"

"Yes. Shall we take it across the water to Croatia? There are some wonderful ruins in Dubrovnik and Split to explore."

"That sounds thrilling, but this is your honeymoon,

too. Since you've probably done everything, what would be your very favorite thing to do?"

His lips twitched for the first time. "That's a loaded question to ask a new husband."

"Humor me. I'm a new wife."

"Has anyone ever told you *you* live dangerously?"

Belle laughed. "I'm still waiting for your answer."

"Find a deserted island in the cruiser and do whatever appeals."

Her heart ran away with her. "An island? I'm glad you said that. I'll phone Mom and ask her to come over while we're gone. Concetta will be happier in her own surroundings, with the dog and familiar staff."

Belle picked up the baby, who'd become bored with the buckets. "Can we leave soon? It will give us more daylight to find the right island." That suggestion seemed to galvanize him into action. "I can see by your eyes you already have one in mind."

He actually grinned. When he did that, she was reduced to mush. "There's not much I can hide from you."

Yes, he could. He did! But being a Malatesta gave him special powers that rendered him inscrutable at times. Such as when he was pretending to be in love with her.

"I'll call Mom."

"While you do that, I'll pack the cruiser."

They pulled away from the dock at four, loaded with everything Leon could think of to make this trip one they'd never forget. Belle had been humoring him, to the point he could almost believe her gratitude to him for uniting her with Luciana wasn't all she was feeling.

He hoped like hell her physical response to him so

far wasn't a total act. If a woman as genuine as Belle could be playing a part for his benefit, then he no longer trusted his own judgment.

They headed farther down the coast. There were no islands of volcanic origin close to Rimini, but there was a sandbar. Those familiar with the area knew to avoid it. Others came upon it too quickly and in many cases ruined their hulls. Years ago Leon had come across it by accident and got in some of the best fishing of his life. If he'd had Belle with him back then…

Using his binoculars, Leon found the exact spot. He cut the motor and let momentum carry them all the way in. When sand stopped the cruiser, Belle gazed at him in surprise. "I thought we were going to an island."

"I lied. There isn't one around here. But with the sea this calm, there's enough sand exposed for us to sunbathe until tonight, and then moon bathe under the stars. No one else is around here for miles." He loved how she'd piled her hair up on her head. "If we'd taken the yacht, we'd have staff to contend with. These days it's almost impossible to get away from people."

Her mouth curved into a smile. "But you managed it." She stood up on the bench and looked around. "I love it! It's like being shipwrecked."

"Except that we have all the comforts of home on board and can leave when we feel like it."

"I don't want to talk about leaving. We just got here. I think this is the most romantic place for a honeymoon I ever heard of. Unique in all the world." The light in her eyes dazzled him. He wanted this to be real. "A little focaccia, a bottle of water and thou. It's evident Omar Khayyám hadn't been to the Adriatic."

Laughter rumbled deep in Leon's chest before he

picked her up and lifted her out of the boat to the sand. She started stripping as she ran. He did, too. They'd both worn their swimming suits beneath their clothes.

"If you'll stay close to me in the water, I won't make you wear a life preserver."

She sobered. "That rule applies to you, too, Leon. If you decide to go out alone, I don't want anything to happen to you."

Belle...

"Come on," he said in a husky voice when he could find it. They waded into the water, then started swimming. He loved her little shouts of excitement every time she saw a fish.

Several times they went in and out of the water, lying in the sun in between dips. Belle put on sunscreen and gathered some seashells. Leon got out his fishing pole and caught two mackerel. They cooked them in a pan on his camp stove, and ate them with salad and fruit brought from the villa. She declared she'd never eaten a tastier meal, and he agreed with her.

After the sun went down they covered up and lay back on lounge chairs on the cruiser. He turned his head so he could look at her. "When you told me earlier I'd probably done everything, you were wrong. I've never been here with anyone else."

"I'm glad you're making a new memory. I'm really glad it's with me. This has turned out to be the most fabulous wedding day a girl could ever want. To be surrounded by your family and my own mother. I can hardly express it." Belle's voice had caught in her throat.

"You're easy company, Belle. I've never enjoyed anyone more."

"I feel the same way about you." She sat up abruptly.

"Do you know I almost didn't go to your bank? Obviously the manager at Donatello Diamonds had advised me to go there for a reason, but I was so upset with him, I had to have a long talk with myself first."

Leon didn't even want to think about it, and turned on his side toward her. "What decided you in the end?"

"I knew that if I went home not being able to find my mother, it would haunt me that I hadn't turned over that one stone to see what was under it." Her way of expressing herself enchanted him.

"Tomorrow it will be a week since I flew out of JFK Airport, a single woman with no family, on a quest so overwhelming, I can't believe I followed through. Tonight I'm lying under the stars on the Adriatic with my Italian husband, knowing my mother is home watching your little girl."

"*Our* little girl now."

Belle nodded. "I know I'm not dreaming, but you have to admit the chances of all this happening are astronomical. You've been so good to me, Leon. If I spend my whole life thanking you, it won't be enough. I promise to be the best wife I can. Do you mind if I go downstairs now and take a shower? I'm a sandy mess."

"While you do that, I'll get everything battened down for the night."

Belle gathered up her things and went down the stairs to the lower deck. The twenty-one-foot cruiser had to be state-of-the-art. Leon had told her he liked a smaller boat like this. He could man it himself, and pull in and out of coves with ease. It made a lot of sense.

Beyond the galley was a cabin with a double bed.

One glance at it and her heartbeat tripled. She hurriedly took a shower and washed her hair.

Leon was giving her plenty of time, but now that she was ready, she felt feverish, waiting for him to come. Belle was the only one of her roommates or the girls at her work who hadn't been to bed with a man. Now it was her turn.

The mechanics of the act were no mystery to her, but it was a whole new world she was about to enter. Those few kisses they'd exchanged had already thrilled her, so much she couldn't wait to find out what it would be like to spend the night with him.

They hadn't talked about the consequences of sleeping together, but she'd made a vow to accept children lovingly. How would he feel about another child if she conceived? Or was Concetta enough for him?

This marriage had happened so fast, Belle was full of questions about the sexual side of their relationship. Only he could answer them. Why didn't he come? They needed to talk.

After another five minutes, she walked down through the hallway and called to him from the stairs.

"I'll be right there."

When he joined her in the bedroom five minutes later, he'd showered and was dressed in a T-shirt and lounging pajamas. The sight of his black hair disheveled after being washed had an appeal all its own. Her gaze dropped lower, to that well-defined physique she'd longed to touch all day. He was standing only a few feet away. She could reach out and touch him. Marriage had given her the right, but she needed a signal from him.

"Is there anything you need before I go back up on deck for the night?"

The question, asked in that deep voice, sent her down a dark chute with no bottom. The pain was so acute she couldn't hold it in. "I thought this was to be our wedding night."

His sudden grim expression chilled her, reminding her of the side of his nature that could be forbidding at times. "Under normal circumstances it would be."

She shook her head, causing her hair to swish across her shoulders. "These aren't normal? I don't understand."

For a moment she thought she saw a bleak look enter his eyes, but it might have been a trick of light. "You don't have to keep up the pretense any longer, Belle."

"Excuse me?"

"Your gratitude has been duly recognized. The truth is, I don't expect your sleeping with me to be a part of it."

She sucked in her breath. "Well, pardon me if I misunderstood. I thought this morning we took vows to become man and wife. You know—the kind who sleep together."

Now that she was all worked up, she couldn't stop. "You think you're so different from your father, but you're just another version of the same male. He was right. You don't love me. *That* I can handle. You've taught me that love at first sight is an absurdity, after all. I learn something new every day.

"Everyone knows real love takes years and years to develop. It's your lie about feeling desire for me that cuts to the quick, Leonardo di Malatesta. You faked it until I believed it, but now that it's crunch time, you've brushed me off the way I've been brushed off all my life."

"Belle—" A ring of white had encircled his hard mouth.

"I'm not finished. Do you have any idea how hurt I am by your rejection? How humiliated I feel after putting everything I am and feel out there on the line for you?

"Cliff was right about my being pathetic. Thank you for underscoring what I've always known about myself. But until just now I was looking forward to being with you tonight, to being in your arms.

"I thought my stepfather hurt me when he told me to get out of his garage and never step in it again. But you're the true master at turning the knife. Now that you've drawn blood, please leave *my* bedroom. We'll never talk about this again.

"In the morning I want to go back to the villa. Never fear, I'll go on being your wife and a mother to Concetta. I'll be there for your family day and night. You want to sleep in the same bed to keep up the pretense and avoid gossip? I'll do it. I'll stand by you at work, at home, until death. I owe you that. I made vows to do that."

She took a deep, painful breath. "But don't you *ever* touch me in bed, not even by accident."

Leon hadn't been sick to his stomach in years. But at two in the morning he slipped over the side of the boat and found a private spot. After being violently ill, he shook like a man with palsy. Until she heard him out, he wasn't going to make it through the night.

He decided it would be better to make noise on his way below deck so he wouldn't frighten her. Once he reached the bathroom, he brushed his teeth and drank some water. Then he tapped on the closed door. "Belle?"

"What is it?"

"We can't go on like this. I have to talk to you. May I come in, or do we do this through the door?"

"It's your boat."

It didn't sound as if she'd been asleep. He opened the door and a dim beam of light from the hallway fell across the bed, where her dark hair was splayed across the pillow. She was an enticing vision. How to begin repairing the damage?

Leon reached the end of the bed and sat on it. "When I came down here earlier, the last thing I wanted to do was go back upstairs for the night. But because of the speed of our marriage, I didn't want you to think that I'd 'purchased' you so I could claim my rights. I wanted to give you time to get used to me.

"Today was pure enchantment for me. I wanted it to go on and on. I was terrified that if you knew how much I'd been counting the minutes until we could go to bed together, it would frighten you. So I backed off. But to my despair, I unwittingly made the wrong decision, and I fear it has cost me my marriage.

"You have no idea how sick I was when I realized you'd overheard the conversation with my father. When we went into lunch, I knew the things he'd said had affected you. I felt helpless to do anything about it until I could get you alone. But when I came down the stairs to join you after your shower, I saw a woman who looked like the proverbial lamb going to slaughter.

"I thought of your bravery in leaving the orphanage to go to a strange home and adapt to someone else's lifestyle. You were so strong to do that and be able to handle it. Tonight I saw your strength in the way you faced me head-on, no matter what you might be feeling inside.

"Your trust in me was so humbling, I didn't want to do anything wrong. You have to understand I would never deliberately hurt you. How could I do that?" He tipped his head back. "There's something important you need to know, Belle."

"What is it?"

"This is about my mother. She had some last words for me before she died. I'll never forget them."

Belle stirred in the bed. "What did she tell you?"

"She said, 'You're so much like me, Leon. If you expect to ever truly be happy, then follow your heart.' Her advice sank deep inside me and helped free me from certain expectations, because I knew I had her blessing. When the time came to ask Benedetta to marry me, I didn't hesitate.

"Last night I asked you to marry me for the same reason. The *only* reason. I love you, Belle. I'm a man desperately in love. You're the most beautiful thing in my life. When we said our vows this morning, I kept thanking God for you in my heart. I can't explain why I fell so hard for you. The French have an expression for it—*coup de foudre*. A bolt of lightning. That's what it was like for me.

"Immediately I needed an excuse to keep you here for good. But the truth is, if there'd been no excuse—no baby, no Dante, no mother to find—I would have followed you back to New York until I could get you to fall in love with me."

Leon moved to the door, petrified he wasn't making

any headway. "As God is my witness, I love you. That's what I came to say."

He walked into the hallway and was about to shut the door when he heard the rustle of sheets. "Don't leave me."

Afraid he was hearing things, he turned around in time to see Belle move toward him. "Don't ever leave me." In seconds he felt her arms around his neck. "I'm madly in love with you, too, Leon. I love you so much it hurts. Don't you know that's why I said those cruel things to you?"

He came close to expiring with joy. "I do now." He picked her up in his arms and carried her back to bed, following her down with his body. The second their mouths fused, they began devouring each other.

Belle awakened the next morning before her husband. She lay halfway across his chest, with their legs entangled, and watched him in sleep. He was the most beautiful man she'd ever seen.

She loved his powerful legs, which kept her where he wanted her, even in sleep. The top cover lay on the floor, along with her robe and his clothes. She hadn't known pleasure like they'd given each other was even possible. It was too intoxicating to describe.

Unable to hold back, she kissed his eyelids and nose, the cleft in his chin. It was embarrassing how much she wanted him again. "Darling," she said against his compelling mouth, "are you awake?"

His hand roved over her back.

Delighted with that much response, she kissed his throat and worked her way to one earlobe. She slid her fingers into his black hair. Belle was on fire for him.

"I love you," she cried, out of need for the fulfillment only he could give. Her dark prince had to be the most satisfying lover alive.

His eyes opened at last. They were smoldering like wood smoke. *"Buon giorno, esposa mia."*

She smiled. "It will be a very good morning when you've made love to me again."

He rolled her on top of him so he could look up at her. "You're a shameless beauty. How lucky can a husband be?"

"Was last night as wonderful for you as it was for me?"

Belle heard him take a ragged breath. "Couldn't you tell? I ate you alive last night."

She smiled. "I'm still alive," she said breathlessly.

"I know. Come here to me, *bellissima.*"

It was several hours later when they surfaced. Leon kept a possessive arm around her hips while they stared into each other's eyes. "Where do you want to go today?"

"I want to stay right here. Is that all right with you?"

He laughed out loud. "You don't know much about men, but I have to admit I'm thankful I'm your first and only lover."

She traced the line of his mouth with her finger. It could go soft or hard depending on his mood. Right now there was a sensual curl. "I could look at you for hours. Do you think I'm terrible?"

He laughed again. "As long as I get to do the same thing."

Heat rose to her cheeks. "I think it's fun to be married. After being with you like this, I realize I grew up lonely. It worries me that I might be too needy. Promise you'll help me not to get that way."

He smoothed the hair away from her temple. "I think you're perfect just as you are."

"That's because we're on our honeymoon. But when you have to go to the bank, I don't think I'll be able to let you leave. Concetta and I will be miserable until you get home. Will you hate it if I bring lunch to your office sometimes?"

"What do you think?"

"I think you will."

After another burst of laughter he kissed her passionately.

"Leon?" she said, when he finally let her catch her breath. "I've given the idea of the cell phone store a lot of thought. The truth is I'd really like to be a full-time mother to Concetta. In order to do that, I couldn't manage a store, too."

He kissed a certain spot. "Especially if we decided we wanted to have another baby."

"You'd like that?"

"I want one with you. Concetta needs a sibling. My life was rich because I had Dante."

"You were lucky to have a brother. When do you think you'd like to try for a baby?"

Leon's shoulders shook with silent laughter. "Whenever you think you can handle it."

"If we tried pretty soon and were successful, that would make the babies maybe a year and a half apart. That would be perfect."

"Whatever you say, *squisita*."

"You're laughing at me."

Leon grew serious. "No. I'm laughing because I'm so

happy. The dark period I went through with Benedetta's illness and death took its toll. At the time I couldn't imagine feeling like I do right now. You've brought sunshine back into my life."

"You don't have time to hear all the things you've done for me—not before I feed you. While you lie here and miss me like crazy, I'm going to fix you breakfast in bed."

She tried to get up, but he pulled her back. "Don't leave me, Belle."

She pressed a hungry kiss to his mouth. "I'll only be as far away as the galley."

"That's too far."

"Now you know why I'm already dreading you going to work. I've decided I think it's scary to be married."

He took her face between his hands. "I've decided I adore you, Signora Malatesta."

CHAPTER NINE

.

Three months later

USING THE FRONT door key she'd been given, Belle let
herself and Concetta inside the palazzo. She'd put her
adorable baby in the stroller. "Mom? We're here!"

No answer. That was odd. After Sullisto had left
for the bank, her mother had called asking her to come
over. Luciana wanted help putting the finishing touches
on the birthday party she was planning for Leon's father that evening.

"Mom? Where are you?" She walked through the
house, pushing Concetta. "Hmm, maybe she's out in
the garden picking flowers. Let's go find your grandmother."

Belle was dying to talk to her mom and was thankful for the excuse to come over now. Leon had arranged
for an early business meeting so he could get home in
good time for the party, so she was free.

The housekeeper saw her in the hallway. "*Buon
giorno,* Belle. Your *mamma* is still in the bed."

Uh-oh. That didn't sound like her mother. "*Grazie,*
Violeta."

Belle pushed the stroller through the house to the master suite. She opened the door. "Mom?"

"Come in the bedroom, darling."

Curious, Belle hurried on through and found a slightly pale version of her beautiful mother lying against the pillows. "You're sick, aren't you."

"Not the kind I can give to Concetta. It's a good kind."

A *good* kind of sick?

What? All of a sudden Belle got it. She gazed down at her mother. "You're *pregnant!*"

"Yes..."

Belle sank down on the side of the bed. "Does Sullisto know?"

"No. He thinks I've got a bug of some kind."

"You *do!*" They both started laughing and then Belle hugged her mother in happiness. They stared hard at each other. "After all this time..." Belle looked at the baby. "Did you hear that, Concetta? In about seven months you're going to get a new aunt or uncle."

The two of them laughed for joy again before Luciana's eyes filled with tears. "It took finding you, darling. That's what the doctor said. You don't know how much I've wanted us to have a baby together, even if I am forty-two. You know, to cement things. This morning Sullisto almost didn't leave for work. I had to beg him to go."

Belle could relate, which was a change for her where Leon was concerned. But this wasn't the time to confide in Luciana. "How long have you had morning sickness?"

"For a few days. I've sworn Violeta to secrecy."

"Until tonight?"

"Yes. The doctor gave me some antinausea medicine. It's already starting to work."

"Sullisto's going to jump out of his skin with joy."

"I believe he will."

"I *know* he will. He loves you terribly, Mom, but being a Malatesta he wants everything to be perfect."

Her father-in-law had calmed down somewhat since Belle and Leon had come back from their honeymoon on the sandbar. But whether he'd forgiven his son for disobeying him a second time was something no one knew.

"Ah, you've already discovered that after being married to Leon. So tell me what's on your mind, darling, and don't say it's nothing."

Belle bit her lip. "When Concetta and I came over this morning, there was something I wanted to talk to you about, but now I can't."

"You mean that you're pregnant, too?"

Her breath caught. "Oh, Mom… I think I am, but I haven't done a home pregnancy test yet. That's what I wanted to discuss with you."

"I've suspected it since our family picnic the other day, when you couldn't eat."

"I didn't realize you'd noticed. If I thought I was carrying Leon's child…"

"Then he doesn't suspect yet?"

"No. I've had a few bouts of nausea, nothing terrible yet, but lately I'm so tired."

Her mother's delightful laugh filled the room. "You need to test yourself right now. There's a kit in my closet, hidden behind the shoes."

"You're kidding!"

"No. I bought two just in case. But the first one worked."

"I'll be right back."

"While you get the official word, I'm going to entertain my granddaughter. Come here, Concetta, and give your pregnant grandmother a big kiss."

Belle found the kit and went into the bathroom. A few minutes later she squealed for joy. Though she was barely learning the rudiments of Italian from her husband and the staff, she didn't need to read the words to understand what the color meant. She ran into the bedroom to show her mother.

"Congratulations, darling! Now that everything's official, we'll make our announcements tonight."

"We can't do that in front of Pia, Mom. It will hurt her too much."

"No, it won't. I know something you don't."

Belle blinked in shock and took the baby from her. "Are you teasing me?"

"No. She told me yesterday."

Yesterday... Belle was so excited, she could hardly stand it. "Does she know about you?"

"Yes, but our husbands don't know yet. Obviously, yours doesn't, either." Her mother flashed a secretive smile. "We decided to make this a real surprise party tonight. To know you're pregnant, too... Three in one family at the same time has to be some kind of world record."

"I agree. How do you want to handle it?"

"I think it should be something that shocks our husbands. You know how they love to be in control at all times. It's a Malatesta trait. Don't you think it would be fun just this once to throw them off base?"

She had an imp in her that Belle would never have guessed was there. "There's nothing I'd love more." She'd been standing by a window that overlooked the maze. Suddenly her brain started reeling with possibilities. "In fact, I've got an idea. First we're going to need poster board and hundreds of yards of ribbon in three colors."

"What on earth do you have in mind, darling?"

"A game. We love games, don't we, Concetta." She kissed her daughter's cheeks. "This one is going to be for all the men in the family to play. But this game will be different, because each man will end up getting the prize he's always wanted."

After a successful business meeting, Leon rushed home early to be with his family. The party wasn't scheduled to start for an hour and a half. That would give him enough time to enjoy his wife while his daughter had her nap. Up until this morning, when Belle had stayed asleep, she'd always been so loving and responsive, he knew he was the luckiest man on earth.

Disappointment washed over him in waves when he walked in and Simona informed him that everyone had left for the palazzo hours ago. The news hit him like a body blow. He'd been longing to lie in Belle's arms and forget the world for a little while. She made him feel immortal.

As he took the stairs two at a time to the master bedroom, he realized how empty the villa was without them. The thought of no Belle, his creative, adorable wife, was anathema to him.

All Leon had to do was shower and shave. He and Dante had gone in on a gift for their father. Sullisto had mislaid his old watch and hadn't found it yet, so they'd bought him a new one with their names engraved in it. Dante would be bringing it to the party.

For the occasion Leon had bought himself a new, light gray suit. Belle had told him several times how much she liked him in gray, the color of his eyes. Hating the silence of the house, he hurriedly dressed, and drove to the palazzo at a speed over the limit. He never drove this fast with Belle and Concetta, but he was in a hurry to see them.

When he pulled up in front, he saw his father and brother waiting for him in the courtyard, dressed in what looked like new suits. Leon levered himself from the driver's seat.

"*Buon compleanno,* Papà." He kissed him on both cheeks. "What's going on? Why are you out here?"

"We've been given our instructions, Leonardo." Sullisto didn't sound in the least happy.

Dante's dark brows lifted. "We were told to stay out here, and that when you got here, we were to go to the entrance of the maze to await further instructions."

Leon chuckled. He thought he could see his playful wife's hand in this somewhere. "Where's my family?"

"They're all inside," his father muttered, looking flustered. "Let's get this foolishness over with."

"It *is* your birthday, Papà."

"You're just going to have to be a good sport even if you are a year older," Dante teased.

They headed through the vine-covered gate to the maze. "I told Luciana I didn't want any fuss," Sullisto grumbled.

When they reached the entrance, there was a sign in Italian. Start Following Your Ribbon. Red for Sullisto,

Yellow for Dante and Blue for Leon. Don't Open Your Prizes When You Find Them. Bring Them to the Terrace, Where More Festivities Will Ensue.

Hmm. A prize. Just what did Leon's wife have in store for him? For the first time in years he got the kind of excited feeling he used to get as a child when his mother hid something they wanted, and they had to find it. He put a hand on his father's shoulder. "You go first, Papà."

"For the love of heaven," Sullisto mumbled.

With a grin, Dante followed him.

Leon brought up the rear. The ribbons led them on such a serpentine route, he started laughing. Dante joined in. Their father had gone on ahead and had disappeared. He just wanted to get the game over with.

"This is one game we never played in here," his brother quipped.

"Nope." And Leon knew why. Belle hadn't grown up with them. Her advent in his life had changed his entire world. "I guess this is where we part company. My ribbon has taken off in a new direction. See you in a minute."

"Call out if you get lost."

"That'll be the day, little brother."

Leon kept going until he came to a small package on the ground tied up with the end of the ribbon. Picking it up, he followed the ribbon back to the opening of the maze. Pretty soon his father emerged with an identical package.

"I think Dante must have gotten lost."

"I heard that, big brother." In the next breath Dante made his appearance with his own package.

Sullisto muttered, "I hope this is the end of the games. I don't know about you, but I'm hungry."

The three of them walked around to the terrace with the ribbons trailing behind.

"Careful you don't trip on those," Luciana called out from the table, looking particularly radiant in an ice-blue dress. "Happy birthday, my darling husband."

Pia sat next to her in a stunning pink outfit.

Leon's gaze sought his wife, who was wearing a gorgeous purple dress with spaghetti straps. She was so beautiful he almost dropped his package.

Luciana smiled at all of them. "As soon as you open your gifts, we'll eat."

Her smile was like the cat who'd swallowed the proverbial canary. Something was going on....

Leon opened his package. Inside was a small oblong box containing a home pregnancy device, of all things. His heart thundered in his chest before he even looked inside it. Belle's cobalt eyes had found his. They resembled blue fires, telling him everything that was in her heart.

It came to him then that everyone on the terrace had gone silent. When he looked around, he saw that both his brother and his father held similar boxes in their hands, and were totally dumbstruck.

Sullisto raised his head and looked at Luciana. "We're pregnant?" he whispered in awe.

"Yes, darling. It finally happened."

The look on his father's face was one Leon would never forget.

Pia's beaming countenance told its own story as she eyed Dante with loving eyes. "That trip to Florence," she reminded him.

Suddenly pandemonium struck.

Leon dropped the box and gravitated to his wife, pulling her from the seat into his arms.

"Concetta won't be an only child," she said against his lips. "I hope you're happy, Leon."

"Happy?" he cried. *"Ti amo, amore mio. Ti amo!"* He kissed her long and hard.

It was in this euphoric condition that he heard his father tap the crystal goblet in front of him with a fork to get their attention. Everyone broke apart and sat down while Sullisto remained standing. He lifted his wineglass toward Belle.

He had to clear his throat several times. "To my wife's firstborn, who came like an angel from across the ocean to bless the Houses of Malatesta and Donatello forever and make us all one."

"Hear, hear," an ecstatic Dante echoed, raising his glass.

Leon gripped Belle's thigh beneath the table with one hand, and picked up his wineglass with the other. "Amen and amen."

* * * * *

THE SLATER SISTERS
OF MONTANA

Nestled in the Rocky Mountains, the idyllic
Lazy S Ranch is about to welcome home
the beautiful Slater sisters.

Don your Stetson and your cowboy boots and join
us as these sisters experience first loves, second
chances and their very own happy-ever-afters with
the most delicious heroes in the West. No dream
is too big in Montana!

Out first in September 2013

THE COWBOY SHE COULDN'T FORGET

followed by the second in this fabulous
series in November 2013!

THE COWBOY SHE
COULDN'T FORGET

BY
PATRICIA THAYER

First published in Great Britain 2013
by Mills & Boon, an imprint of Harlequin (UK) Limited,
Eton House, 18-24 Paradise Road, Richmond, Surrey TW9 1SR

© Patricia Wright 2013

ISBN: 978 0 263 90139 9
ebook ISBN: 978 1 472 00524 3

23-0913

Harlequin (UK) policy is to use papers that are natural, renewable and recyclable products and made from wood grown in sustainable forests. The logging and manufacturing processes conform to the legal environmental regulations of the country of origin.

Printed and bound in Spain
by Blackprint CPI, Barcelona

Originally born and raised in Muncie, Indiana, **Patricia Thayer** is the second of eight children. She attended Ball State University, and soon afterwards headed West. Over the years she's made frequent visits back to the Midwest, trying to keep up with her growing family.

Patricia has called Orange County, California, home for many years. She not only enjoys the warm climate, but also the company and support of other published authors in the local writers' organisation. For the past eighteen years she has had the unwavering support and encouragement of her critique group. It's a sisterhood like no other.

When she's not working on a story, you might find her travelling the United States and Europe, taking in the scenery and doing story research while thoroughly enjoying herself, accompanied by Steve, her husband for over thirty-five years. Together, they have three grown sons and four grandsons. As she calls them: her own true-life heroes. On rare days off from writing you might catch her at Disneyland, spoiling those grandkids rotten! She also volunteers for the Grandparent Autism Network.

Patricia has written for over twenty years, and has authored more than forty-six books. She has been nominated for both a National Readers' Choice Award and the prestigious RITA® Award. Her book *Nothing Short of a Miracle* won an *RT Book Reviews* Reviewers' Choice award.

A longtime member of Romance Writers of America, she has served as President and held many other board positions for her local chapter in Orange County. She's a firm believer in giving back.

Check her website, www.patriciathayer.com, for upcoming books.

To my good friend and fellow writer Janet Cornelow.
The plotting group will never be the same without you.

CHAPTER ONE

Ana GRIPPED A handful of the horse's mane, lowered her head and gave the animal its lead as she flew over the dew-soaked meadow.

She felt the sting of the cool Montana air against her cheeks, but didn't stop. If she did she was afraid she'd fall apart. And Analeigh Maria Slater was always composed and calm. She had to be. She was the oldest daughter, and since her mother's desertion, the responsibility of her younger sisters had fallen on her shoulders.

Finally reaching her destination, she slowed her horse. The buckskin mare was reluctant to end the run, but obeyed by the time they reached the old, dilapidated cabin. The place Ana had come to as a kid when she needed to be alone, or needed to think. When she needed to cry.

She climbed off, and her legs nearly gave out as she hit the ground. It had been a while since she'd ridden, and she'd pushed it hard today. After tying the mare's reins to the post, she climbed the single step onto the sagging porch. Using her shoulder, she nudged open the weathered door and walked inside.

The cabin was just as dismal as she remembered. The one room was small, but serviceable. A sink and a water pump, a shelf overhead that still held canned goods. There was a set of bunks attached to the opposite wall, with filthy mattresses. The building would have been torn down, but her great-great-grandfather had built it when he'd settled in this area.

She walked to the one window and looked out at the view she loved. The lush meadow was green with new spring grass and wildflowers. She shifted her gaze to the side to see the Rockies, then in the other direction toward Pioneer Mountain and the national forest. In between were miles and miles of Slater land. Colton Slater's pride and joy, the Lazy S Ranch.

And at one time this ranch had been home to Ana and her three sisters. That had been a long time ago.

She brushed a tear from her cheek. But now with her father's emergency… Another tear followed. What was going to happen? What if Colt didn't survive?

She tensed at the sound of another horse approaching, then boots on the porch. She swung around, but didn't feel any relief on seeing the ranch foreman, Vance Rivers, stepping through the doorway.

The man was tall, with wide shoulders. Over the years, she'd caught sight of him without a shirt when he'd been digging fence posts. He'd earned the muscular chest and arms. Her gaze moved down to his flat stomach and narrow waist.

A black Stetson hid most of his sandy hair and shaded those deep-set, coffee-brown eyes that seemed to pierce right through her. She hated that he made her feel nervous and edgy whenever he got near.

"I figured I'd find you here."

"Now that you have, you don't need to hang around," she told him, and turned away. He had been the one who'd called her early this morning about her father's stroke. He also had been the one she found in the hospital room.

Of course that was who her father would want with him. "Shouldn't you be at Colt's bedside?"

Vance had always hated that Ana Slater could make his gut twist into knots. All that thick ebony hair and flawless olive skin showed off her Hispanic heritage, but her brilliant blue eyes let you know she was a Slater. All he knew was the combination made a perfect package.

He drew a calming breath.

Ana had never liked him much. Too bad he couldn't feel the same about her. "It's you who needs to be there when he wakes up."

Vance watched as she straightened, her shoulders rigid.

"Look, Ana, you're the only family here to make the decisions."

He thought about the other Slater sisters, Josie, Tori and Marissa, scattered after college. Not Ana. She might have left the ranch, but only to move into town and take a counseling job at the high school. Close enough so she could come out and check on the old man. On occasion, she saddled a favorite mount and went riding.

Ana finally turned around to face him. He expected to see anger, but instead he saw sadness mixed with fear in her eyes. Again his body reacted. After all these years this woman still had an effect on him.

He thought back to the day Colt Slater had taken him in, twenty years ago. He'd been barely thirteen. The man gave him a place to live. Vance's first home. Slater had only two rules: work hard and keep your hands off his daughters. No matter how difficult, Vance had kept those rules.

"Do you really think Colt Slater is going to listen to me?" Ana asked. "Besides, I'm not even sure if he can hear me."

"That's why you need to be there. Talk with the doctor and find out what you need to do. A stroke doesn't always mean he can't recover." Hell, Vance had no idea what he was talking about.

She shook her head. "You should be there, Vance. Dad will want to see you."

Although Colt was as close to a father as he'd ever had, he couldn't overstep any more than he already had. Whether Colt knew it or not, he needed his daughters.

"No, he needs his family. You have to get your sisters back here and fast. It's way past time."

It was an hour later when Ana and Vance got the horses back to the barn. Then he'd driven her into Dillon to the hospital, where her father had been airlifted just after dawn that morning.

Ana stood in the second-floor waiting area. She'd just left a voice message for her baby sister, Marissa. Tori and Josie at least took her call. The twins told her to keep them informed, but didn't offer to fly in from California. Both had made excuses about their jobs. So that left any decisions about their father's care up to her. She couldn't blame them. How many times had Colt Slater overlooked, rebuffed and just plain ignored these girls?

"Miss Slater?"

Ana turned around and saw the neurologist, Dr. Mason, walking toward her. "Has something changed with my father's condition?" she asked anxiously.

"No, he's remained stable since he was brought in this morning, and the test results are encouraging. I'm not saying that the stroke didn't cause damage to his right side and his speech, but it could have been much worse. He was lucky he got to the hospital so quickly."

Ana was relieved and thankful to Vance, since he'd been with Colt. "Thank you, Doctor. That's great news."

"He's not out of the woods yet. He'll need extensive

rehab to bring him back completely. We would like him to go to a rehab facility to help with improving his motor skills and his speech."

"Good luck with that," Ana said. "No one gets Colt Slater to do anything he doesn't want to do."

"Then you'd better start convincing him he needs this," the doctor suggested.

Before Ana could say any more the elevator doors opened and Vance stepped off.

As much as she hated that he was around, she knew if her father would listen to anyone it would be Vance. Sadness washed over her as she recalled the times Vance had gotten the one-on-one attention she and her sisters had begged for.

He strolled toward them with confidence; add in a little arrogance and you've got Vance Rivers, Ana thought.

"Ana. Doctor." He looked back at her. "Has something happened to Colt?"

"No, in fact it's better than I'd hoped." She went on to explain the doctor's rehab plan. "You need to get him to agree to go."

Vance just stared at her. "What makes you think I have any influence?"

"Well, he sure doesn't listen to me."

The doctor raised a hand. "When the time comes, whoever talks to Mr. Slater had better explain how important rehab is to his recovery." He said goodbye and walked away.

Vance wasn't sure why he was involved in this. He had enough to worry about taking care of the ranch. And he needed Colt's input on so many things. For one, he didn't know how to deal with the daughters.

"Look, Ana. You shouldn't have to handle this on your own. When are your sisters getting here?"

She shook her head. "They aren't coming back for a while."

"What do you mean?"

"Just what I said—they can't get home…right now. They want me to keep them informed."

Vance knew deep down that Colt had never been close with his girls. He more or less let Kathleen handle anything that had to do with the females. The housekeeper and one-time nanny had been with the family for over twenty-five years.

"Then let's go see Colt," Vance said. "For the first time ever, I'm hoping he's his usual cranky self."

Colton Slater blinked and opened his eyes, trying to adjust to the brightness. He glanced around the unfamiliar room. He saw the railing on the bed, heard the monitor. A hospital? What happened? He closed his eyes and thought back to his last memory.

It had been dawn. He'd walked out to the barn to feed the livestock. His arm had been hurt like a son of a bitch since he'd gotten out of bed; then he'd started to feel dizzy and had to sit down on a straw bale. Vance was suddenly beside him, asking him if he was okay.

No, he wasn't okay. Not when he woke up to find that he was in this bed with a needle in his arm, monitors taped to his chest. Worse, he couldn't move. What the hell was going on?

He tried to speak and the only thing that came out was a groan.

"Mr. Slater? Mr. Slater?" He heard a woman's voice. "You're in the hospital, Mr. Slater. I'm your nurse, Elena Garcia. Are you in pain?"

Again he could only groan.

"I'll give you something to help you."

Colt blinked and focused on the raven-haired beauty, and his breath caught. Seeing her heart-shaped face, those almond eyes, he sucked in a breath and opened his mouth to speak. "Luisa…" he whispered, then there was nothing.

Twenty minutes later, Ana walked into her father's hospital room. She held her panic in check on seeing the monitor and the IV connected to the large man in the bed.

She made her way closer. Colt Slater had always been bigger than life to her. The one-time rodeo star was nearly six feet tall, and muscular. The years of ranch work had kept him in shape. His brown hair was now streaked with gray, but even with the tiny lines around his eyes, he was still a handsome man. And she loved him. Maybe in his own way he loved her and her sisters, too. She felt a tear on her cheek and brushed it away.

"Oh, Daddy." She reached out and took his big hand, thrilled that it felt warm. She wanted another chance to get close to this man. Would he be around for that?

A nurse walked in and smiled. "Hello. It's good to see Mr. Slater has a visitor."

"How has he been?" Ana asked.

"He was awake not long ago."

Ana felt hopeful. "Really? Did he say anything? I mean, was he able to speak?"

Again the nurse smiled. "He said the name Luisa. Is that you?"

Ana gasped at hearing her mother's name. "No, it's not." She released her father's hand and hurried out of the room. Oh, God. He still wanted her mother. Ana couldn't stop the tears once she reached the visitors' room and found it empty. She finally broke down and began to sob.

Suddenly she felt a hand on her shoulder, then heard the familiar voice. She wiped her eyes and slowly turned around to see Vance. His dark gaze locked on hers and she saw the compassion. He didn't speak as he slowly drew her close. God help her, she went into his arms, letting his strength absorb the years of pain and hurt. She gripped his shirt and buried her face against his chest and sobbed.

Vance fought not to react to this woman. That was like saying not to take his next breath. Not to ache for something he'd wanted for so long and knew he couldn't have. Now, sweet Analeigh was in his arms.

The top of her head barely reached his chin, and it seemed every curve was pressed against him, tormenting him. He moved his hands over her back, feeling her delicate frame. She might feel fragile but she was far from it. He'd watched for years how she'd corralled her siblings, broke up fights, helped with school projects and even stood up to Colt for them.

He'd never seen her so broken as right now. "Hey, bright eyes, what's wrong? Is Colt worse?"

Vance reached in his back pocket, pulled out his handkerchief and handed it to her. She took it, but kept her head down. "C'mon, tell me," he coaxed. "Is it Colt?"

She shook her head.

"What's breaking your heart, Ana?"

She finally looked up at him. Her eyes welled with tears, her face was blotchy, but she looked beautiful. "He said her name."

Vance frowned. "Whose name?"

"My mother's. He said Luisa."

Vance wasn't shocked. "He's had a stroke, Ana. The man might be confused with the place and time."

She nodded, and as if she realized their closeness, she took a step back. "You're probably right. Sorry. It's just he hasn't said anything about our mother in years. I thought he'd gotten over her." She pointed to Vance's wet shirt. "I'll wash it for you."

Vance wondered if it was possible to wash her out of his head, his heart.

It had been a long day by the time Vance brought Ana back to the ranch. He drove up the circular drive and let her out of the truck. Then he took off toward the barn to check on the stock and the ranch hands.

Ana stood there and looked up at the large ranch house. It had been months since she'd been inside, but when the housekeeper, Kathleen, insisted she stay over tonight, she didn't have a choice.

She walked up the steps to the wraparound porch. Colt had built this house for his new bride, Luisa Delgado. It was well known about her parents' whirlwind romance, also about Luisa's disappearance twenty-four years ago.

Ana had been five years old at the time. She made herself remember the loving woman who'd hugged and kissed her little girls endless times. The woman who told those made-up bedtime stories, sat with her daughters when they were sick.

Not the woman who'd one day up and abandoned her family. All of them had been scared, including Colt. So much so, he couldn't even stand to be their father anymore. And today, Ana had realized he still wanted his ex-wife.

She walked through the front door. Everything was the same, including the large table in the entry, adorned with fresh cut flowers from Kathleen's garden. Ana glanced up at the open staircase with the decorative wooden banister, winding up to the second floor. She walked farther into the house, passing the living room. Two overstuffed leather sofas faced the river-rock fireplace. This was definitely a man's room. Her dad's office was next, then came the huge dining room with its high-back chairs and a table that could seat twenty. She moved on to her favorite room, the kitchen.

She smiled and glanced around to see the rows of white cabinets, which had been painted many times over the years to keep their high sheen. The countertops were also white, and the same with the appliances. The room was clean and generic. Long gone were any Spanish influences.

Kathleen walked in from the laundry room. The house-keeper was fifty-five and had a ready smile and kind hazel eyes. Her hair had been dark brown, but over the years had turned gray. She had never married, so Ana and her sisters were like the children she'd never had.

"Oh, Ana, I'm glad you're here. I'm hoping you'll be staying long enough for me to fatten you up. Child, you're too thin."

"I weigh the same as I always did, no more, no less."

Ana wasn't sure staying at the house was a good idea. There were so many memories she wanted to forget. But she'd be closer to the hospital. And since school was out for the summer, she was off work.

"Well, you still need to put on ten pounds."

Before Ana could protest, there was a knock on the back door. Kathleen went and answered it. "Oh, hello, Mr. Dickson."

Ana watched as the older man stepped into the kitchen. The distinguished-looking Wade Dickson was dressed in his usual business suit. He was not only Colt's lawyer, but his longtime friend. They'd gone to school together. And Uncle Wade had given the Slater girls more affection than their own father had.

He smiled when he saw her. "Hello, Ana."

She was still raw from today, and exhausted. "Hi, Uncle Wade."

He came closer and hugged her. "I'm sorry about your daddy. I was out of town when I got the news. But don't worry, old Colt is made of strong stuff."

She was touched. "I appreciate you saying that."

He released a long breath and guided her into the dining room, where they sat down at the table.

"I hate to do this, Ana girl, but we need to discuss what to do while your daddy is recovering."

She hated that term. "Vance is foreman. Can't he handle the ranch?"

There was another long pause. She could tell Wade was holding something back. "That's a temporary fix. I've been by the hospital, and right now your father isn't in any shape to make decisions. You girls will have to decide what to do for now."

"Dad will be okay," Ana insisted. "The doctor said… Well, he's going to need some rehab."

"I know, and I hope that will happen, too, but as his lawyer, I have to carry out his wishes. To protect his property and his family. And as of right now, Colton Slater is incompetent to run his business."

Ana felt her heart skip a beat. "So what do I need to do? Sign some payroll checks?"

"Well, first of all," Wade began, "Colt has a will, so he didn't put this all on your shoulders. You have a co-executor to help."

"Who?"

She heard someone talking with Kathleen, then a few heartbeats later, Vance walked into the room. He nodded to Wade. "Have you told her?"

The lawyer turned back to her. He didn't have to speak;

she already knew that her father had picked Vance over his own flesh and blood.

"So you've finally got what you wanted," she said. "Now all you have to do is change your name to Slater."

CHAPTER TWO

VANCE WORKED HARD not to react. He'd had plenty of practice over the years masking his feelings, especially around Ana.

"I'll let that pass, since I know you're upset. Colt named me because I've been foreman of the ranch for the past five years. This has nothing to do with me taking over."

Wade Dickson jumped in. "He's right, Ana. It wouldn't be any different if your father had appointed me to oversee things. And believe me, I'm grateful he didn't. Running a large operation like the Lazy S is a big undertaking, and I don't think you want to handle that. Do you?"

She didn't back down. "I've never gotten the chance to." Her angry gaze danced back and forth between the two men. "Dad didn't have any problem putting his daughters to work. Of course, he made sure we were limited to mucking out stalls or currying horses. And if we were really good at our jobs, we got to help with some of the roundups and branding. Yet once he thought we became a nuisance, he sent us off to the house."

Vance glanced away. He'd seen over the years how Colt ignored his daughters. The man had never been demonstrative, but he'd given Vance a chance at a life. Hell, the girls had been lucky. When their father noticed his daughters were getting tired, he'd made them stop.

Colt had never been that generous with him. The man was never abusive, but had sometimes worked Vance twelve- to fourteen-hour days when it came to roundup time.

"Colt didn't want you to get hurt," Dickson stated. "Ranching isn't an easy life."

Ana shook her head. "We both know the truth. Colton Slater just wanted sons. And he sure didn't want his daughters involved with his precious ranch." She shot a hard look at Vance. "What about you? Do you have a problem working with a woman?"

He frowned. "What exactly do you mean by *working?*"

She moved around the table. "I've waited twenty-plus years to be able to feel a part of this place. I have the chance and the time, since I'm not going back to work at the school until the fall, and I plan to use it. You can either help me or get out of my way."

Vance wasn't sure he liked Ana's idea. "What are you talking about?"

"You aren't going to have all the say-so around here. Dad gave me at least half control of this place."

Why was she acting as if this was war? "Up till now, the only person who had any control was Colt," Vance argued, trying to keep the anger out of his voice. "He's the boss. I still plan to carry out his wishes, because his situation is temporary. But if you want to work fourteen-hour days and smell like sweat and manure, feel free." He started for the door, but stopped. "Just don't plan for me to babysit you or your sisters, because the Lazy S is depending on this roundup." He turned and walked out.

Ana realized she might have overreacted a little. But Vance Rivers had always been the thorn in her side. There was no doubt that Colt had favored him over his own daughters. Well, not anymore.

She stood a little straighter. "It seems I'm going to be working this summer."

Wade Dickson shook his head. "I think you'd better get on that cowboy's good side, or it's going to make life difficult for the both of you."

That was the last thing she wanted. She hadn't forgotten the teenage Vance, with his bad attitude and swagger. He was good-looking and knew it. That day in the barn when he'd got her alone in the stall and kissed her until she couldn't remember her own name wasn't going to happen again. Nor was she going to run away like a scared rabbit.

Ana blinked, bringing her back to the present. "Dad's stroke is more than making things difficult. But I don't plan on ignoring my responsibilities to him or the ranch."

Wade shook his head. "I hope Colt appreciates your loyalty, but don't be too stubborn to think you can do this on your own. So you might want to find a way to get along with Vance. That's the only way this is going to work." The older man sighed. "Also, it might be a good idea to stop by my office tomorrow. There are some more details to go over."

"What details?" she asked.

"It can wait until tomorrow, but not much longer. Bring Vance with you."

Ana didn't like the sound of that.

"What about your sisters?" Wade asked. "When are they coming home?"

Ana had no idea. "Not right away. So this is on me for now." She tried to sound confident, but in reality she didn't know even where to start.

An hour later in the barn, Vance worked the brush along the flank of his chestnut stallion, Rusty. He was angry, more at himself than with anyone else. He'd let her get to him…again. How many times had he told himself to forget about Ana? The woman wanted nothing to do with him. He couldn't say he blamed her, not when their dad had ignored his girls all those years, while giving Vance the attention they should have gotten.

Many times he'd wanted to let Colt know how he felt about that, but the man had taken Vance in when he had nowhere else to go but into foster care.

Vance already had the stigma of having a father who'd been labeled no good for years. Calvin Rivers was well known as a man who couldn't hold down a job, and drank away his paycheck when he found someone willing to hire him. Vance's mother had gotten fed up and took off.

The strokes of his brush got more intense and Rusty expressed his irritation by dancing sideways in the stall. "Sorry, fella." Vance smoothed a hand over his withers and put the brush away. "I didn't mean to take out it out on you."

He walked out of the stall and headed down the center aisle of the large barn, passing the dozen horses stabled here. He stopped and talked to two of the ranch hands, Jake and Hank, giving them instructions for tomorrow's workday.

He said good-night and went through the wide door into the cool May evening. This had always been his favorite time of day. Work was done. The sun had gone down and the animals were all settled in for the night.

He knew his days on the Lazy S could be numbered. It was past time he left here, especially now that he had his own section of land. He'd already planned to leave in the fall after the alfalfa harvest. Now with Colt's stroke…

He headed along the path toward his place. A hundred yards away was the foreman's cottage. About four years ago, Colt had given him the three-bedroom house when he made Vance ranch foreman, after Chet Anders retired. Vance had been twenty-six and had just finished his college courses for his degree. That had been important to Colt. He was grateful, too.

Vance slowed his pace as he reached the house, seeing a shadow on the porch. He paused, then realized it was Ana sitting on the glider swing. Funny, for years he'd dreamed of her coming to visit him. He doubted this time was for the same reason he'd had in mind.

"You want another strip of my hide?" he asked, then kept walking into the house and flipped on the wall switch to light the compact living room.

He was surprised to see that Ana had jumped up and followed him, but stopped at the threshold. "No, I just want to talk to you about something. If you'll give me a few minutes."

Vance turned around to see the worried look on her face. He'd caught a glimpse of her vulnerability at the hospital today, but she also could have a cutting tongue. But he couldn't seem to take heed to the warning his brain sent as he glanced over her slender body, her rounded hips and long legs incased in worn jeans. He bit back a groan. She had just enough curves to twist a man's gut, making him want what he had no business wanting. Somehow Vance had to stop it if he planned to work with her.

Why couldn't he have these feelings for any other woman but her? Why hadn't he been able to move on? Forget the girl who hadn't cared about him years ago. By the looks of it, her feelings hadn't changed. Ana Slater didn't want him.

He was frustrated as he said, "Whatever I do or say, you attack my character. Even I have limits."

Ana knew her anger had gone too far. It wasn't Vance who caused the problem between her and her father. "I apologize. I let old feelings get in the way of what we need to do. And that's run this ranch."

When he stepped aside, she released a breath and made her way past the overstuffed sofa to look out the window that faced the barn and corral. It was easier than looking at Vance. He made her feel things whenever she got near him. It was strange because it had been years since the man had come close to her. Of course, she hadn't given him a chance.

"So you want to call a truce?" he asked.

She looked over her shoulder and nodded. "Wade pointed out we need to work together." She rushed on. "For the good of the ranch, and to help ease Colt's mind so he can concentrate on his recovery."

"We can't expect miracles."

Ana couldn't help but smile. "I'll settle for getting him to do what he needs to do to get back here." She released a long sigh. "I know you think that I don't care about my father, but I do."

"I never said that. In fact, I know how many times you've come out here and checked on him." Vance raised a hand when she started to deny it. "And no, Kathleen didn't rat you out. I've seen your car up at the house, and when you come by to go horseback riding. Why didn't you ever stay and talk with Colt?"

Tears formed behind her eyes. "That's a little difficult when Dad hasn't exactly welcomed me with open arms."

"Okay, his disposition has always been a little gruff, but maybe you can change that now."

Ana thought back to when life here on the Lazy S, with her mom and dad and younger sisters, had seemed about perfect. That had all changed overnight when Luisa Slater just walked out of their lives. It had been as if all the love was sucked away. The twins, Tori and Josie, were only three years old then. Marissa was barely a toddler.

If they hadn't found the note, they might have believed Luisa had been kidnapped. But no, there was no doubt that the woman wanted out of her marriage and to have no part of her children. That same day, Colt had changed, too. He'd closed up and shut his family out.

"He had four daughters who begged for his love. It's as if he blamed us for our mother's disappearance." Ana glared at Vance. "Were we responsible?"

He shook his head. "I can't answer that, Ana. I never met your mother. I've only dealt with mine. And April Rivers had no trouble packing up and leaving, too."

Ana gasped, realizing how closely their lives paralleled. "I'm sorry, Vance. I forgot."

"That's what I want people to do. Forget about my past." His dark gaze met hers. "It's the only way to move on."

Vance didn't want to rehash his past, because Ana and her sisters had the life of fairy princesses compared to his childhood. "Look, running the Lazy S isn't an easy job." He was aware of the toll it had been taking on Colt the past year. "We have the roundup soon. If you and your sisters want to help out, I'm not going to stop you."

"Like I said, I doubt my sisters will come home, but I plan to be around. In fact, I decided to move back to the house, at least over the summer or until Dad gets better."

Lord help him, Vance wanted Ana to stay around. The downside was she'd be here every day, reminding him of what he could never have.

"Okay, the day starts at 5:00 a.m."

She looked surprised. "I want to go see Dad by ten o'clock. And Wade Dickson wants us to meet him tomorrow afternoon in his office."

"Why?"

"I'm not sure. He said there are things we need to go over."

Vance nodded. "Then I guess you'd better get some sleep. Tomorrow is going to be a busy day."

She nodded. "I'll see you in the morning." She headed to the door.

Vance fisted his hands, wanting to call her back. And for what? To tell her he'd always care about her. That he'd wished those visits to the ranch had been to see him. No. To her, he was only the poor kid Colt had given a place to sleep. Even now, with his success, would she see him any differently?

Maybe over the summer she'd notice he was more than just another ranch hand.

The next morning, Colt felt the warmth of the sunlight on his face. Damn. Had he overslept? He blinked, opened his eyes and tried to focus. That wasn't the worst of his problems. He couldn't move. He groaned as he tried to lift his arm, and felt the touch of a hand, then a voice as someone said his name.

He turned his gaze and stared into her pretty face. He nearly gasped. Then he blinked and realized it was Analeigh. Oh, God, she looked so much like...her mother. No. He didn't want to think about Luisa now. But he knew that wishing wouldn't make it so. He'd given up on ever completely forgetting his wife. Correction, ex-wife.

Colt tried to pull away, but he didn't have the strength. What the hell was happening to him? He tried to speak, but all he managed was another groan.

"It's okay, Dad. We're here with you. You need to be still."

He groaned again.

"Please, Dad. You're in the hospital. You had a stroke, but you're going to be all right."

Colt could only look at her, then he relaxed when someone appeared next to her. Vance.

"Hey, Colt. Glad to see you're awake. The doctors have a handle on this. You'll be home before you know it. Trust me, everything will be all right at the ranch. I'll make sure of it. You just rest for now and get your strength back."

Strength. He was weak as a kitten. He closed his eyes as all the fight left him.

Just before noon, Ana sat in Vance's truck as they headed back to town to see the lawyer. She still couldn't get the picture of her father lying in the hospital bed out of her mind. Her chest was tight with emotion. This had to be hard for a man like Colt. He had always been physical, hardworking. Now, that had all changed. Would he be stuck in a wheelchair the rest of his life?

She thought about when she'd sat by the bed, praying he would open his eyes. Even his angry scowl was better than that blank look. No. She had to think positively. Her dad survived the stroke and he was going to recover.

He still hadn't spoken to anyone, except to say Luisa's name. At least he'd said something.

Ana felt Vance's presence, turned sideways and saw him sipping the coffee he'd gotten from the hospital.

He nodded to the one he'd brought for her. "Have some coffee. You look like you need it."

"Thanks." She reached for the cup in the console and took a sip. "This is good."

He smiled as he concentrated on the road. "Got it from the nurses' station. It's their own private brew."

She could just see Vance Rivers flirting with the nurses to get what he wanted. "Thank you."

"Let's talk," he stated, then went on to say, "It's only been forty-eight hours since Colt's stroke and he's still heavily medicated. You need to trust that he's going to get better."

She glanced out the windshield, watching the open ranch land, mountains for a backdrop. "He looks so helpless."

"Give it time, Ana. You need to be patient and not get your dad riled up."

"Riled up?" That hurt. "I don't plan to upset my father. How can you say that?"

Vance raised a hand from the steering wheel. "I only meant that you're too easy to read. Your emotions show on your face."

"I can't help that."

Vance nodded, knowing Ana had always had trouble hiding her feelings. She had a big heart and that was why it was breaking right now. She wanted so much to help. She'd tried so hard to keep the family together, but in the end her sisters all left anyway.

"You have to try, because Colt needs our help with his recovery."

Vance slowed the truck as they approached the small town of Royerton. Population was about five thousand in the ranching and farming community. He drove along Main Street, passing the small grocery, Quick Mart and the U.S. Post Office.

"And I plan to do exactly that."

"Good. Maybe we should keep the topic on the ranch. But not include that you'll be working with the other ranch hands."

"Like he'd care."

Vance pulled into a parking space outside the brick, two-story professional building. "Are you kidding?" He threw the gearshift into Park. "There were two rules that Colt enforced. One, work hard, and the other, stay away from his daughters."

Seeing Ana's surprised look, Vance retrieved his keys and got out of the vehicle. He wasn't about to tell her how difficult it had been to keep that promise, but he had because of the respect he felt for her dad. He'd been crazy about this woman for years. Could there be a second chance for him?

"I didn't know," she said when he opened the passenger-side door.

"There's a lot about Colt you don't know."

She took Vance's offered hand and stepped down onto the sidewalk. "That's not my fault."

"I didn't say it was." He opened the door to the lawyer's office and let her walk inside first. "I just wanted you to be aware of it."

"What about you? Did that rule apply to you?"

He nodded, wondering if she remembered that one time in the barn.

"Since you're still around, I guess you never told him that you accosted one of his daughters in the barn." She turned her back on him and walked into the reception area.

"Whoa. I wasn't alone that day, or the only one responsible for what happened. If I remember right, there was a certain young girl who'd been sniffing around a young teenage boy. Not a good idea. You know, raging hormones and all."

"I didn't have raging hormones," she retorted.

"Not yours. Mine." He studied the blush on her cheeks. He, too, was remembering the day she'd let him lead her into a stall and kiss her. If one of the other ranch hands hadn't come back early, he wondered how far he could have gone. He started to speak when Wade Dickson came out of his office and greeted them.

"Hello, Ana and Vance." He smiled. "Please come inside."

They went ahead of the lawyer into the adjoining room. Nothing too fancy, but there were nice comfortable chairs and a large desk. Wade had his law degree from the University of Montana hanging on the wall.

"Have a seat." He walked around the desk and sat across from them. He opened a folder and glanced over the contents, then looked at Ana. "Are you sure your sisters can't come home?"

"Not right away. Why?"

"I didn't tell you everything last night. There's a slight problem with the ranch."

Ana slid to the edge of her chair. "What is it?"

"As you know, the Lazy S is a sizable spread." He quoted the section amount. "Your father owns that land outright. But there's a lot of grazing acreage that is leased from the state. And the payment is past due."

"How is that possible?"

"Only Colt knows the answer to that." Wade paused. "I managed to get an extension from the state, but it's only bought us a few months to come up with the money. And if you don't pay it, someone else gets a chance to bid on the property."

Ana glanced at Vance. "Then we need to pay it."

Wade looked worried. "There aren't enough funds available."

CHAPTER THREE

ANA'S EYES WIDENED. "What do you mean, there aren't enough funds?"

Wade leaned back in his chair. "It means the Lazy S has had a rough few years. I just recently learned this because I've been notified by the State Land Leasing Board."

Ana turned to Vance. "Why didn't you say something?"

He was as shocked as she was. "First of all, I didn't know anything about the lease coming due. I knew beef prices were down and that we lost several head in that big storm last winter, but…" He'd never dreamed it had been this bad.

"What do you mean, you didn't know? You're Dad's foreman."

"I may physically run the operation, but Colt funds the business account. I use that money for payroll and for the feed and supplies. Colt kept the ranch finances."

He thought about the land that Colt had given to him a few years back. He'd planted an alfalfa crop on the acreage. It should be ready to harvest in about six weeks. That gave them the time, but would the profit be enough?

Wade broke into his thoughts. "Ana, I've been trying for years to get your father to diversify. He lost a lot of his savings when the market tanked a few years ago. In the past, that money had always been his cushion through the bad years."

Ana looked pale. "What do we do now?"

Vance wished he could offer a miracle, but he wasn't sure there was one. "Like Mr. Dickson said, we have nearly six months." His gaze met hers. "You can't do this on your own. I think you need to get your sisters together."

Thirty minutes later, Vance escorted Ana out of the Dickson law office.

"You look ready to drop," he told her.

"Gee, thanks. What every woman wants to hear."

He ignored her comment. "When was the last time you ate?"

"I had some toast this morning. I'm just not hungry."

"It's after one o'clock. You have a lot to deal with, so you need to eat." He placed his hand on the small of her back and immediately felt the warmth of her skin, but resisted the urge to draw her any closer.

She sighed. "You're right, but I should go home and figure out what to do about this mess."

Nixing her request, he guided her a short distance down the sidewalk to a small family-owned restaurant, the Big Sky Grill.

"First, you're going to eat." He held open the door. When she didn't move, he said, "I can keep this up all day."

She glared at him with those big blue eyes, then finally relented. "Okay. A *quick* lunch."

Once inside, they were greeted by the owners, Burt and Cindy Logan. Burt escorted them across the tile floor to a booth next to the picture window that looked out onto Main Street. Several patrons stopped Ana en route and wished her father well. When she finally got away, she slid into one of the bench seats while Vance sat down across from her and placed his hat on the space beside him. He pulled out a menu from between the salt-and-pepper shakers and went over the choices.

Cindy showed up with two glasses of water. "How's your daddy doin'?" she asked.

"A lot better. He's stable for now, but they're still running more tests."

The middle-aged woman placed her hand on Ana's. "Tell Colt that we're all praying for him."

"He'll appreciate that, Cindy. Thank you."

They gave her their order and she left them alone.

Ana shook her head. "I can't believe how many people care. Funny, isn't it? He seems to have gotten along with everyone except his own daughters."

Vance shrugged. "Why does that surprise you? The Slater family helped settle Royerton. Colt is well respected around here."

Vance knew how Colt had treated his girls. It wasn't that he was mean, he just pretty much ignored them. Over the years, Kathleen had always been the surrogate parent. "Okay, the man wasn't the perfect father." Vance leaned back in the seat. "So why did you stay, and not take off like your sisters?"

Ana stared at him with eyes that were the mirror image of Colt's. "I stayed for my sisters, then I got the job at the high school." She shrugged. "I'm not even sure it matters anymore."

Vance leaned forward. "Look, Ana, I don't know why Colt did a lot of things. There's no doubt he isn't a happy man. I've heard stories about how he was when he was younger, before your mother left."

He watched Ana stiffen.

He wasn't going to be put off. "Do you remember her?"

With a nod, she glanced away. "I was pretty young. But,

yes, I can remember how beautiful she was. Her voice, her touch." She turned back and he saw the tears in her eyes. "I wanted to hate her, but for years I just kept praying she'd come back and be our mom again."

He reached across the table and touched her hand. "That's understandable."

She looked down at his hand and slowly pulled hers away. "Is it? Do you wish your mother would come back?"

"Sure. Every kid does, especially when your dad isn't around to feed you and you're hungry." Vance blew out a breath. "And you can't go to school because you don't have shoes. Kids make fun of you for things like that. But sometimes you're just too hungry to care, when you know you'll get that free meal at lunch."

He caught the look on her face and realized how much he'd disclosed.

This time Ana took his hand. "Oh, Vance. I had…had no idea."

He shrugged it off. "No one did. At fourteen, I finally had enough and was trying to get away. I was big for my age and hoped I could go somewhere and get a job.

"I hid out in the back of a pickup truck in the parking lot so I could get out of town. I didn't know it belonged to Colt until I found myself at the Lazy S. I decided to sleep in the barn before starting my journey in the morning. Of course he found me."

Ana didn't want to feel sympathy for the kid who had a rotten life. "And you became the son Dad always wanted."

"As I told you before, I only wanted to survive," Vance stressed. "Colt was my only way out of a bad childhood. I'm sorry if you thought you had to compete against me for your father's attention."

She shrugged. It all seemed so juvenile now. "It doesn't

matter anymore. Colt made his choices a long time ago and that's why I can't get my sisters to come back here."

"Maybe if they know about the state of the ranch… I mean, it's part of their heritage, too. Their inheritance. Wouldn't they want to preserve it?"

Ana shrugged. "So far they haven't seemed too interested in anything to do with Colt or the ranch." She raised her gaze to meet his. "The trick is, how do I convince Josie, Tori and Marissa to come home?"

"Tell them the truth. Colt needs them and you can't do it all. At the least, you need help with his care." He paused, then asked, "Aren't they all living in California? You could go see them."

"Go there?"

He nodded. "If you show up on their doorstep they have to listen to you. They should help you with medical decisions about your father."

She frowned. "You don't know my sisters." This could backfire in her face. "So I think you should go with me."

The nurse raised Colt's bed so he could finally sit up. What he really wanted was to get the hell out of this place. Not an easy task, since he was still weak as a newborn calf and he couldn't move his right arm.

"Is that better, Mr. Slater?" the nurse, whose name was Erin, asked.

He grunted.

She smiled again as she put the call button next to his good hand. "Press this if you need me. Your daughter will be here, too. Plus, they should be coming to talk to you about your therapy soon."

He grunted again. What good was that going to do?

"It's going to take some work to get back in shape, Mr.

Slater, but you've got a good chance for a full recovery. But you'll need to work hard."

As if he hadn't worked hard all his life.

The nurse turned on the television to a game show, then walked out of the room, leaving him alone.

Most of the time he liked being alone. What choice did he have? Ranch work had filled in a lot of lonely hours. He released a breath and closed his eyes. What was he going to do when he didn't have the Lazy S anymore? Sit in a nursing home somewhere until he died?

Sadness overtook him as he closed his eyes and thought back over his life. His chest tightened when he thought of Luisa.

He could still picture her as vividly as if it were yesterday. Small and delicate, Luisa Delgado was beautiful with all that thick, black hair and large eyes. Her olive skin was flawless. When he first saw her, at a rodeo, he'd thought she was an angel. When she walked up and talked to him, he figured he'd died and gone to heaven.

After they'd married, weeks later, he'd thanked God every day, and especially when they were blessed with the babies, every one of them a beauty like their mother.

The tightness in Colt's chest worsened as he recalled the evening he'd come in from the range, so anxious to see his girls. Luisa had been moody and distant of late, with caring for the children. He'd offered to get her someone to help, but she said she wanted to be their mother full-time. Later that night he'd found her crying, and had asked her what was wrong.

She'd only said, "Just make love to me so all the bad things will go away."

Colt released another sigh, recalling how intense their loving had been that night. When he'd walked into the house the next afternoon, there was a babysitter and his wife was gone. All that he had was a short note, telling him she no longer wanted a life with him and their daughters.

He'd searched for her, wanting to beg her to come home, but he never found her. Then he got the divorce papers. That day his life as he knew it had ended.

Two days later, Vance sat next to Ana as the plane landed at LAX. He had no idea how he'd gotten roped into going to California.

For one thing, he hated large cities and the crowds. Secondly, if there had been any animosity between him and Ana, it had been worse with the younger sisters. He had to just keep remembering he was doing this for Colt, and for Ana.

The plane taxied to the terminal. "I'm not sure this visit will change anything," Ana said, feeling a little nervous. Maybe it had something to do with the close quarters. Vance was a big man, and that didn't leave her much room. "What if Tori and Josie refuse to help?"

"Then we go back to Montana and figure it out on our own." His hand rested against his jean-covered thigh. She was suddenly intrigued by his long, tapered fingers.

He went on to say, "And we will figure out something. I promise."

She glanced at his face and saw his sexy smile. Her heart went *zing* and she had to look away. No! She wasn't going to even think about this man like that. Okay, so maybe it was normal, since she hadn't been in a romantic relationship in a while. That was still no excuse to think about Vance Rivers that way. She was no longer that dreamy-eyed teenage girl who wanted his attention. No way was she getting involved with him.

When the plane stopped at the gate, she unfastened her seat belt as Vance stood and reached up into the overhead compartment. He took down her carry-on and his duffel, along with his cowboy hat. He stepped back to let her out into the aisle. The small space made it impossible not to brush up against him. She inhaled his scent and could feel his hard body. Again the zings. Okay, so that hadn't changed over the years; he still appealed to her, a lot.

Since they had their only luggage with them, they went straight to the car rental booth. Vance got a midsize sedan and started to climb into the driver's seat.

Ana looked at him. "Can you drive the L.A. freeways?"

He took off his hat and tossed it in back. "We'll soon find out."

"Here's the address for Josie's business."

Vance took the paper and entered the address in the GPS, then headed for the 5 Freeway. They ended up in the older section of Los Angeles not far from Griffith Park. It was a two-story stucco building with a Spanish design.

They got out of the car and walked up to the directory on the wall. It didn't take long to find the right office. The sign on the glass door read Slater Style.

"Catchy name," Vance said.

"That's what Josie's all about." Ana released a breath. "Okay, let's get this over with."

Vance nodded, opened the door and allowed her to step in ahead of him. The small reception area consisted of a desk and chairs that lined the opposite walls. But there wasn't a soul in sight.

Vance checked his watch. "I guess everyone's at lunch. Did you tell Josie you were coming?"

"No. I didn't want her to find an excuse to keep me away."

Suddenly the door opened and a familiar woman, carrying a take-out food sack, walked in. However, it wasn't the twin they expected to see here.

Vittoria Slater had dark hair, the same pretty smile as her older sister. "Ana? What are you doing here?"

"Tori?" Ana rushed to her and they hugged tightly. "I think you know my reason for coming to L.A. But what are you doing at Josie's office?"

"Well, as of a few months ago, it's my office, too. I quit my job and decided it was time I went out on my own." She nodded. "Josie offered me office space here. I decided to give my own web-design company a chance."

Tori had their mother's coloring, the olive skin, midnight-dark eyes and ebony hair. Her hair was shorter now, cut just below her chin.

Ana was excited for her sister, knowing how unhappy she'd been with her previous company. But Ana was a little sad that she hadn't shared this with her.

"That's great. So how is business?"

"Good. Several of my old clients came with me, and I like being my own boss." Tori finally noticed Vance across the room and she blinked in surprise. "Vance, good to see you." Her smile faded. "Wait a minute, has something more happened to Colt?"

"No, your dad is still the same," Vance told her. "I'll let your sister explain the rest."

"We need to talk about what to do," Ana stated. "Dad isn't going to get better right away, so we've got to discuss…some things. The ranch, mainly."

The anger was evident in Tori's eyes. "It can dry up and blow away for all I care. I hate that place."

Ana wasn't surprised by her sister's reaction. "Tori, you can't mean that. It's our home."

The younger twin shook her head. "It was just a big, old house to me. Dad was happier when we finally all left."

Ana wasn't surprised by the animosity toward their father. "I understand your feelings, but right now, Colt can't speak, or make decisions for the Lazy S. I'm going to remind you that the ranch has been in our family for three generations."

Tori began to speak when the office door opened and another sister walked in.

"Hey, Tori, it's about time—" Josefina Slater stopped and stared. "Ana! What are you doing here?"

"Is there an echo in here?" Ana hugged the other twin. Josie had fair skin with long, golden-brown hair and the Slater blue eyes. Except for the shape of their faces and their smiles, the two twins couldn't look less alike.

"To answer your question, since you didn't come home, I thought I'd come here."

Josie's gaze went to Vance as he nodded in greeting. "And you felt the need to bring reinforcements? Hi, Vance. It's been a long time."

He smiled. "Good to see you again, Josie."

Ana turned back to her sisters. "Vance is here to help convince you both of the seriousness of the situation." She wasn't foolish enough to think this would be easy.

Josie's frown told her that she wasn't going to be easily swayed. "Like I told you when you called last week, I have a big event coming up. I can't leave right now."

Ana was sad that they wouldn't come back home for their father. "I understand that, being an event planner, you need to be here, but I'm talking about our father. We're a family."

Josie shared a glance with her twin, then said, "It seems you and Vance have it under control. You two seem to make a pretty good team. We'll give you permission to make any decisions. So there's no reason you had to come here and try and rope us into going back home."

And it wasn't getting any easier, Ana thought. "We came here because we need to make some decisions about Dad."

"Has something else happened?" Josie asked.

Ana saw the flash of concern and was encouraged. "No, he's the same, and he'll start physical therapy soon."

"That's good, isn't it?" Tori asked.

Good, there was more concern. "The reason we're here isn't so much about Dad as it is about the ranch."

"What do you mean?" Josie asked. "Can't Vance handle things while Colt recovers?"

He gave a nod, but didn't say anything.

"It's more than running the ranch." Ana started to explain, then said, "I wish Marissa was here, too. She should be in on this."

"Maybe I can make it happen," Tori said, and motioned them into her office. Vance, Ana noticed, sat down in the reception area.

Her sister went behind the desk and opened the laptop. "If she's not out on a location, Marissa should be home." After several keystrokes on the computer, a picture came up, then the real thing.

"Hey, Tori."

"Hi, Marissa."

"What's going on?"

"Quite a bit, actually. Got someone here who wants to talk you."

Ana stepped in front of the monitor. She felt tears burning her eyes as her baby sister appeared on the screen, sitting at a desk. "Hi, Marissa."

"Oh, Ana," she sighed. "You're in California?"

She nodded. "I only wish I could see you in person, too. How about I come down to San Diego? If you'll be around."

She saw the panic in her youngest sister's eyes. "Well... maybe, but it's not a good idea right now. I'm going to be out on a shoot all this week. How long are you planning to be here?"

"I need to get back soon to take care of Dad."

Marissa hesitated, then asked, "How is he?"

Ana glanced across the office at Vance, happy for his support. "He's holding his own. That's why I'm here. Uncle Wade came to see me a few days ago. Since Dad is temporarily incapacitated, there needs to be an executor to take over."

"So Uncle Wade is the boss now?"

"No, he isn't. Dad named Vance and me."

The twins shot a look across the office at him. "Why doesn't that surprise me?" Josie said. "He's always treated Vance like family."

Vance didn't say a word for a moment. It was true, Colt had always treated him fairly. Although he wasn't happy about the man's treatment of his daughters.

"Seems I'm the only one who knows about running a ranch," he said eventually.

"That's not our fault," Tori retorted, then all the girls began to argue. That was when Vance put his fingers in his mouth and let go with a loud whistle. It got their attention.

"I didn't ask for the job," he told them. "But since I have it, I'm going to do everything possible to keep the ranch."

Josie looked at Ana. "What does he mean?"

"It means the ranch is in financial trouble. Big trouble." Ana told them about the amount of money owed for the lease, and their six-month extension. "So we need to come up with some ideas."

"Dad doesn't have the money?" Marissa asked.

Ana shook her head, knowing this wasn't going as well as she'd hoped.

"Well, we don't, either," Tori stated. "Everything we have is tied up in the business here."

"It's not only money we want," Vance said. "We need some ideas to add income to the ranch so this doesn't happen again. So tell me, is the Lazy S important enough to you sisters to help save it? Can we count on your support?" After giving them his two cents' worth, Vance turned and walked out of the office.

Tori sighed. "I have to say that cowboy of yours sure knows how to get a woman's attention."

"He's not my cowboy or anything else."

Josie looked at her twin and they both grinned. Then their baby sister's voice said via the computer, "If you say so, sis."

Ana was frustrated, having to defend herself. "I do say so. Vance and I have to work together."

Tori shook her head. "Too bad. You've had that guy tied into knots since you grew breasts."

What? Ana opened her mouth to deny it, but refused to add fuel to the fire. They had other problems. "We need to direct our attention to the ranch."

There was silence and Ana saw the confused looks on her sisters's faces. Of course they were torn. Colt never appreciated anything his daughters had ever done. Tori and Josie had been top students all during school. They'd even won academic scholarships. Marissa had been a star athlete, but over the years their dad had said little in the form of praise or encouragement to any of them. So why should they go back to Montana now?

Ana couldn't make them, but didn't want them to have any regrets, either.

"Okay, sisters," she began. "If you won't do it for our dad, I have another idea." She glanced at the twins, then at Marissa on the computer screen. "Let's do it for ourselves. Let's show Colt Slater how his girls can run the ranch."

CHAPTER FOUR

THREE HOURS LATER, Ana kissed her sisters goodbye and she and Vance left the Slater Style office. She regretted that she hadn't been able to convince them to come home.

She sat in the passenger seat as Vance drove them to the airport hotel. "Go ahead and tell me how badly I handled things."

"No, I'm not saying a thing. Your sisters will have to decide on their own if they want to come home." He stopped at a traffic light, and his dark gaze locked with hers. "I understand how they feel. I've watched for years how Colt treated you girls."

Ana froze. "But you never did anything."

"I can't say I liked it, but I was a kid, too. I liked having a roof over my head, food in my stomach."

Ana remembered the night when Vance had showed up at the supper table, a skinny teenager with a lot of attitude. At first, she felt sorry for him, knowing he had been beaten by his drunken father. Their dad had never laid a hand on them, but it was almost worse when he directed all his positive attention to Vance. It should have come to his daughters.

"We both can agree that Colt never had a sweet disposition," Vance went on. "Truth be known, he doesn't deserve your and your sisters' loyalty. But if I know you girls, you inherited a fair amount of stubbornness and determination from that man. You four aren't about to let the Lazy S fail."

Before Ana could disagree, he pulled up in the circular drive of the large chain hotel. The valet came up to the car and opened her door. "Good evening, ma'am."

She got out and thanked him, while Vance popped the trunk and another attendant helped with the bags.

They arrived at the front desk. A pretty blonde with Jessica printed on her name tag smiled at Vance. Why wouldn't she? He was a handsome man. Dressed in a pair of cowboy boots and creased jeans, he would turn any woman's head. Ana glanced away, hating that she wasn't immune, either.

He placed his hat on the counter. "Hello, ma'am. We need a couple of rooms for tonight."

"Do you have a reservation?"

"I'm sorry, we don't. This was an unexpected trip."

The woman frowned and began to search the computer screen. "We're pretty full tonight."

His dark gaze never wavered as he moved closer. "I'm sure you can find something."

Jessica sighed and went back to her search. "Oh, good. I do have a one-bedroom suite available."

Before Ana could refuse to spend the extra money and the night with this man, Vance said, "We'll take it." He pulled out his credit card, and before Ana recovered, they were riding up in the elevator.

Vance held his breath as they stepped out onto their floor. He was surprised that Ana hadn't fussed about sharing a room. Of course, he hadn't given her much choice. He found their suite and slid the key card into the slot, then pushed open the door and allowed Ana to step in. His body immediately responded to her closeness. He caught her scent as she brushed by him. He sucked in a breath and gave himself a quick talking to, then followed her inside.

The room was fairly spacious. There was a sofa, which was no doubt going to be his bed. He went into the next room to find an inviting king-size bed. *Don't even go there.* He turned and walked away from the temptation.

"You take the bed. I'll sleep out here."

Ana shook her head. "You're too tall for the sofa. You take the bed."

He didn't want to fight about this. "Do you really think you're going to win this argument?"

He could tell she was thinking about it. "Fine. Sleep wherever you want."

What he wanted was not an option. He went to the phone and pressed the button for room service. "What do you want to eat?"

"I don't care." She rolled her suitcase into the bedroom and closed the door.

"It's going to be a long night," he breathed, then said into the phone, "I'd like to order two steaks, medium rare, with baked potatoes and green salad."

They told him thirty minutes. Restless, he went to the mini bar and opened it to find beverages. He bypassed the bottles of beer for a soda. Opening it, he went to the window and drew back the curtains to reveal the millions of lights of Los Angeles. He suddenly missed the isolation of the ranch. Not many lights out there, just millions of stars in the sky.

He turned and found Ana standing across the room. She was still wearing her dark slacks and print blouse, but she was barefoot. "I called the hospital. Dad is resting comfortably. That's a good thing, since he starts therapy tomorrow. I'd like to be there."

"Not sure Colt will be happy about that. I doubt he wants anyone to see him weak."

"Well, he's going to have to get used to it, because he doesn't have a choice."

Vance couldn't help but smile. Ana was definitely her father's daughter.

"I also want to apologize to you."

He liked her being feisty; it helped him keep a safe distance from her. "For what?"

"For arguing about the room. We're both too tired to go looking for another hotel. We're adults and can handle sharing a space for one night."

He nodded, but wasn't so sure. He hadn't been able to spend much time with Ana in the last few years. He'd hoped that would dim his feelings for her. No such luck. He ran his fingers through his hair. "Seems we've been thrown together in an awkward situation. It's been years since we've spent any time together. I can see where you'd feel we're strangers."

She fought a grin. "Yeah, you're the brother I never wanted."

He'd never felt brotherly about her. "Was that why you pretty much hated my guts?"

She frowned. "*Hate* is a strong word. Angry, maybe, because of the attention you got from Dad."

"I wish I could have helped that situation."

Ana shook her head. "No one crossed Colt Slater."

Not true. Vance had one time, when he'd broken that promise to stay away from Colt's daughters. Ana had been the only one who tempted him, that day in the barn when he'd kissed her.

He shook away the memory. "I wish I could have helped, anyway."

A knock sounded on the door. "That's fast." He answered it, expecting supper, but found a bellman with an ice bucket holding a bottle of wine and two glasses.

"Mr. Rivers. Compliments of the management," he said, and waited as Vance stepped aside for him to enter the room. The man set the wine next to the table and began to uncork the bottle. He poured a small amount in a glass and held it out to Vance, who took a taste and nodded. "Very good."

"Thank you, sir. It's from a local winery just north of Los Angeles."

As he filled both glasses, Vance took out some bills and handed them to the waiter, who then left.

"Seems you made an impression on a certain desk clerk," Ana said.

Vance picked up one glass and handed it to her. "Jessica is the assistant manager."

Ana hesitated, but accepted it. "I'm not much of a drinker."

"Nor am I, but I think tonight one glass wouldn't hurt." He raised his glass to her in a toast, then took another drink. "Come see the L.A. stars."

Ana wasn't sure if drinking alcohol was a good idea, but she didn't have to go anywhere. She walked to the big window. "Where?"

He pointed downward. "They're down there. See all the lights."

She smiled, aware of the big man standing very near to her. "Oh, my. That's a lot of houses."

"It looks crowded, too. How do they stand being so close together?"

Ana took another sip, enjoying the taste as the liquid slid down easily. She sipped again and her body began to relax. "And the noise? How do they stand all the noise and traffic?"

He shrugged. "I have no idea. I feel I was pretty lucky to end up at the Lazy S."

"I know." She faced him, feeling overwhelmed by everything that had happened the past week. "I don't want to lose the ranch, Vance. I can't."

He looked down at her. "I promise, Ana. I won't let that happen."

"So you'll help me?"

She realized that his gaze dropped to her mouth. And she suddenly remembered another time when he looked at her that same way. Right before he kissed her. "You don't even have to ask, bright eyes."

His deep, husky voice caused a warm shiver to rush down her spine. She took another sip and suddenly felt light-headed, not knowing if it was the wine or the man. She reached out and touched his forearm to steady herself. Big mistake, looking into his dark eyes. "I like when you call me that." Did she really say that out loud?

Vance frowned. "I think you need to eat something." He took their wineglasses and set them on the table. "Come to think about it, you didn't finish much of your lunch."

Reality came back full force. "Arguing with my sisters always causes me to lose my appetite." She felt the tears welling up. "They are so angry with Dad, but I can't blame them."

He gripped her upper arms. "Look, Ana, you need to give them some time. I have a feeling they'll find their way back home."

She hesitated, so aware of his touch. "Will you leave the ranch if Colt doesn't get better?"

"Do you want me to leave?"

Ana couldn't imagine the Lazy S without him. She shook her head. "No. You have to stay. I mean, you know the operation, the cattle and the crops."

Vance knew that Ana was exhausted. The last few days were beginning to take a toll. Mix in wine and that could mean trouble. What he did like was how agreeable she was with him, and so close. It would be easy to lean down and kiss that tempting mouth of hers.

Whoa. He quickly shook away the thought and stepped back. "Then let's come up with a way to make money."

She picked up her wineglass and took another sip. "What about the roundup?"

"With low cattle prices and our smaller herd, it's not enough. Besides, there's something you girls need to know...." He paused as Ana looked at him with her deep blue eyes. The last thing he wanted to do was give her any more bad news.

"What?"

"It's just that we need more than a temporary fix. Since I've been foreman, the ranch profits have been dwindling. I know there aren't funds to help out with the lean years. We might have to downsize, sell off stock. Norman Stanton would pay dearly for Red Baron."

"Our prize breeding bull?"

Vance nodded. "And there are the horses. Our stallions, Night Ranger and Whiskey King, would bring top dollar."

"Oh, not the horses. Do you really have to sell them off?"

"We might not have a choice. They're a luxury, unless we're going to breed them."

"And sell the foals?"

"That'll take time that we don't have now. We could advertise our studs. It would be more money coming in."

Ana shook her head. "I can't believe that Dad hasn't covered any of our broodmares. Who's the stable manager?"

"You're looking at him. Colt let Charlie Reynolds go last year," Vance told her. "That was a shame, because Charlie had great instincts and was a good trainer. Now our stable is about half of what we once had."

"Did you ask Dad why?"

"Question your father's decision? Not me."

"Something must have happened," she said absently. "It's not like him to be careless about the ranch."

Vance had noticed it, too. "Maybe he wasn't feeling well even then."

Ana didn't like to think her father might have been sick all this time. "Well, he can't tell us now. We just have to find a solution on how to fix it."

A knock sounded on the door. Vance went to let the bellman in with the cart carrying their supper. After being handed the signed receipt, the waiter left.

Vance went back to the table and pulled out Ana's chair. "Let's eat."

She walked over and sat down. "Thank you." She took another sip of her wine and watched as Vance sat down across from her. Yes, the man was handsome. Those deep-set brown eyes, his square jaw covered in a dark shadow from his day's growth of beard. He'd been handsome as a teenager, but as a man he was even more so, being self-assured and confident.

Her focus zoomed in on his mouth. His lower lip was full and had her wondering how it would feel....

She glanced away. What was she doing? She couldn't think this way about Vance Rivers. Not to mention the fact that over the years, he'd had several women on his arm and probably in his bed.

Besides, they had nothing in common but saving the Lazy S. That alone put Vance Rivers way off-limits.

By the time the plane landed the next day, Ana was exhausted from the trip. She hadn't gotten much rest, thanks to the man sleeping just outside her bedroom door.

Vance had parked his pickup at the airport lot before their trip, so they drove straight to the hospital. The ride there was a quiet one, for which Ana was grateful. She had a slight headache, which she contributed to that second glass of wine, one Vance hadn't shared with her.

They got off on the second floor and went directly to Colt's room. There she found the bed empty and her father sitting in a wheelchair.

"Oh, Dad. Look at you." She went to him, and felt the urge to hug him. Instead, she placed her hand on his arm. "How are you feeling?"

Colt only looked at her, then glanced away. Pain shot through Ana's chest. Rejection was something she should be used to, but it still hurt.

A young man wearing dark scrubs walked into the room. He smiled at her. "Well, Colt, seems like you're attracting the ladies today." The man's smile widened as he held out his hand. "Hello, I'm Colt's occupational therapist, Jay McNeal."

Ana shook it. "Ana Slater. Colt's daughter."

Jay glanced down at Colt. "You didn't tell me you had a beautiful daughter."

Ana pulled her hand away. "Has my father had a therapy session yet?"

"Yes, he did," Jay said. "And he did very well."

Vance stood across the room, watching this guy. He never liked his type, always smiling when a woman was around. Vance walked over to Colt and pulled up a chair so he'd be eye level with his mentor-father figure.

"I'm glad to see you up." He glanced at Ana and the therapist as they walked to the other side of the room. "I know this has been rough on you, Colt, but I want you to know that I'm taking care of things at the ranch. I'll hold down the fort until you're well enough to come home."

No response.

Vance decided to try something else to see if he got a response. "Ana and I just got back from Los Angeles. We went to see Tori and Josie, to let them know about your condition."

That did it. Colt shot a look at him and made a groaning sound. Good, a reaction.

"That's right, Colt. Ana is trying to bring them home."

Another groan.

"There's no choice, we need help to run the ranch. Come on, they're your family, and you're lucky to have them." Vance stood and turned toward the door. Stubborn man. Well, Colt needed to get over that real fast.

Frustrated, Colt tried to call Vance back, but he was helpless to speak. Dammit. He couldn't let this happen. His daughters were better off without him. Without a bitter old man who couldn't get over the woman who'd deserted him and their daughters.

From the day their mother left, it had been like that. He knew nothing about raising girls. To make it worse, every time he looked at his beautiful Ana, Tori, Josie and Marissa, all he could see was their mother in their faces. God forgive him, he hadn't been able to get over Luisa's betrayal.

He closed his eyes, wishing for the millionth time that he'd done something that would have changed the past. That he could have gotten his wife to stay, for their daughters at least.

He regretted so many things. The worst had been making his girls suffer because he couldn't deal with his own failure. He glanced down at his useless hand. Now it was too late. He didn't care about the ranch anymore, but he couldn't stand to see the hurt in his daughters' eyes. He'd caused them enough pain. It would be best if they could forget all about him.

The next morning, Ana woke up early and, after Kathleen's insistence on breakfast, drove into town. The first thing she needed was some clothes for her long stay at the ranch.

She stopped at her apartment and packed up her jeans and boots. Suddenly she felt excited that she was going to be living back at the Lazy S for the next few months. She could ride everyday, not just when she could find the time, or figure out when her dad wouldn't be around. She thought about another man who'd be there constantly. Vance. They needed to work together. Not that she had a choice, but this wouldn't be an easy chore. And they still needed to come up with something to help bring in income.

After locking the front door to her one-bedroom apartment, she carried her suitcases to her small SUV. She had two months until her job started back at the high school. If need be she could take off more time, but that was a wait-and-see. They might need her income if the ranch couldn't be saved. Not to mention her father's medical bills.

She shook away that dismal thought and climbed into the car. She drove back through town, down Main Street, passing the many storefronts that made up Royerton. The 1920s buildings housed businesses like the Big Sky Grill, a clothing store, Missy's Boutique, and an antique shop, Treasured Gems. On the corner she saw the familiar brick facade of Clarkson's Trading Post and Outfitters. And smiled, thinking about her close friend Sarah Clarkson. They'd known each other since kindergarten. She was the third generation Clarkson to help run the store.

Ana pulled into a parking space out front and got out. She wanted to thank her friend's family for the flowers and sweet note they'd sent for Colt.

She walked into the shop and was greeted with racks of clothes and walls lined with fishing and hunting equipment. The large store was crowded with customers, this being the height of fly-fishing season. It was a big part of the revenue for the store and the town.

She glanced around and spotted Hank and Beth Clarkson behind the counter, waiting on customers. Sarah had just come out of the back room along with one of the store's licensed outfitters, Buck Patton.

Sarah spotted her and smiled. She held up a finger, asking her to wait, then turned back to the group with Buck and gave instructions. A few minutes later, they all shook hands, before the guide walked the group out the side door to the waiting van.

Sarah rushed over and greeted her with a hug. "Oh, I'm so glad to see you. Is your dad okay? We tried to stop by the hospital but we couldn't see Colt."

Ana nodded. "He's better. He started therapy. I wanted to tell you that I'm moving out to the ranch for the summer."

The pretty redhead blinked at that. "Why? Is your dad coming home so soon?"

Ana shook her head. "No, but I need to help out. It's going to be a long road for Dad's recovery, and since he's incapable of running the ranch right now, I've been named as one of the executors."

"That surprises me. Colt Slater giving anything to his daughters, even responsibility, surprises me."

Sarah knew the history of her family. "Well, I'm not exactly doing this on my own. The other executor is Vance Rivers."

Sarah gasped. "Now, that's no surprise. So are you going to play nice?"

Ana sighed. "We'll be too busy to think about anything

other than running the Lazy S. We have a roundup coming in a few weeks."

Sarah eyed her closely, but before she could make comment, her parents came up to them. They exchanged more hugs. As a kid, Ana used to wish they were her parents, too.

Beth asked, "How's your Dad, Ana?"

"Better, thank you. He has a long rehab, though."

It was Hank who spoke up. "If anyone can do it, Colt can. He's too stubborn not to come back from this."

Ana smiled. "He is that."

"You don't need to tell me," Hank said. "For years I've been trying to get him to allow my outfitters on his land." The man shook his head. "You have one sweet fishing spot on the northern section just going to waste."

"You wanted to fish on the ranch?"

Hank nodded. "I wanted to make your dad some money, too. Colt always said no. He liked his privacy."

Suddenly an idea popped into Ana's head. *Oh, my, could this work?* "Do you still want to fish on our property?"

Hank paused. "Are you serious? That section of the Big Hole River is incredible. I could send out day groups. Of course, the real money is doing overnight trips and weekends."

He showed her the chart with the going rates that fishermen paid for these kinds of trips. She nearly fell over.

Ana asked Hank if he could stop by the ranch and they could go over the section of property in question. When he agreed, she knew all she needed to do was convince Vance. Would he go against Colt and side with her? She shrugged. This was for the sake of the ranch, so they would deal with the repercussions later.

CHAPTER FIVE

LATER THAT EVENING Vance drove to his house and parked his truck. He'd been at the hospital to see Colt. Not that it had done much good, since the man barely acknowledged his presence. He'd tried to discuss what was going on at the ranch, but Colt seemed disinterested, so Vance had called it a night and left.

On the way back home, he'd stopped by the Big Sky Grill and picked up some dinner. All he wanted tonight was some food and a bed. When he got out of the truck, he heard someone call his name. He turned and saw Ana hurrying along the path from the barn.

His gut tightened as the long-legged brunette headed his way. In his many fantasies, she would be running into his arms, happy that he was home.

She shot him a smile and his pulse began to race. There went his sleep for the night. "What's your hurry?"

"I'm excited," she told him, her breathing a little rough as she held up a manila folder. "You have a few minutes?"

"Sure." He raised his sack. "Mind if we go inside so I can eat my dinner?"

"Oh, sorry. You should eat." She waved at him. "I'll come back."

He reached for her arm to stop her departure. "Don't

go. I mean, it's silly for you to go all the way back to the house. Come inside."

"Only if you eat while I talk."

Together they walked up to the porch. "Sounds like a plan."

Inside, Vance turned on the overhead light and walked to the dining area, put his food sack on the table and his hat on the hook by the back door. "Can I get you something to drink?" He opened the refrigerator. "I have soda and milk."

"Nothing, thank you."

Ana glanced around the room, surprised to see so much detail in the decor. Okay, it was a man's house, but it was clean and organized. The walls were painted a golden hue and the woodwork and trim stained dark. She walked to the large Western painting hanging over the brick fireplace and quickly recognized the signature of a local artist. Then she studied a bronze statue of a horse on the mantel.

"Does it meet with your approval?"

She swung around to Vance. "Sorry, I never thought of you in a house."

He set two soda cans on the table. "Just in a room upstairs in the barn."

She quickly realized how harsh she sounded. "No, I don't see you in the barn. It's just that you have good taste…in decorating." She came back to the table and sat down. "And for the record, Dad should have never let you live in the barn, anyway."

"I think he was trying to protect his four daughters. And it was the apartment over the barn."

Suddenly she was glad for the extra soda, and took a drink. "Please, eat."

Vance sat down across from her in the ladder-back chair. He popped the tab on the can, took a long drink, then unwrapped his meat-loaf dinner from under the foil. "Okay, what's so important you needed to talk about it tonight?"

"Did you know that Dad refused Hank Clarkson's offer of pay to bring fly fishermen on the property?"

With a shrug, Vance scooped up a piece of meat. "A long time ago I heard rumors. I thought it was a friendly disagreement between the two."

She opened the folder. "It's a friendly disagreement that would have brought in a lot of money for the ranch."

Vance continued to eat. "I'm listening."

"Earlier, I drove into town to pick up some clothes from my apartment. Afterward I stopped by Clarkson's Trading Post to see my friend Sarah. Hank Clarkson asked about Dad's condition, then said something about the section of the Big Hole River on our property."

Vance watched as Ana tilted her head, mesmerized by her thick ebony hair brushing against her bare shoulders.

"Seems Hank has several clients who want to fish in a private section of the river." She opened the folder and took out a paper with the going rate anglers pay. "We could be making a portion of that amount."

"Is that before or after the guide and Hank's commission?"

"Well, before, but he's supplying the boats and the guide. It still leaves a lot of money. Hank also said we could make a lot more if he had lodging for overnight trips."

Seeing her excitement, Vance began to realize there could be possibilities, too. "I've fished along the river and the trout are big. It might not be the answer to all of our problems unless…"

Her rich blue eyes lit up and he couldn't look away. "Unless what?"

"A lot of things," he managed to answer. "Do you want

to do this temporarily, or is this going to be a permanent addition to the ranch?"

"Seems that with the ranch having so many bad years, I think we should see where this could take us."

He liked the idea better and better. "Do you want to hire our own guide? Build structures to house the customers?"

She shrugged. "I don't know. What do you think?"

"Shouldn't you talk to your sisters?"

She shook her head. "First, I probably can't get them to make a decision. This is something we can do right now. Hank assured me that he can get some paying customers pronto and I don't want to lose this opportunity." She looked at Vance. "Is it crazy to invest in something like this?"

"Since there isn't a lot of money to spend on investing, maybe we should tread cautiously. See how it works for day fishing first."

"So you like the idea?"

"Yes. It's something that doesn't cost us anything to start with. But we have to do a trial run to see if the investment is worth expanding before we think about building some cabins."

She looked thoughtful. "What about some of our existing buildings? The bunkhouses?"

"They could work, but they'll soon be filled up with the extra hands for the roundup."

She nodded. "Okay, we'll start with day trips. I told Hank that he could stop by tomorrow and check out the best sites. Do you want to come along?"

It would probably be better if he stayed clear of her, but he was pleased that she even asked him. "We're moving the herd down at dawn," he told her. "I guess I could meet you there along the river."

Since the day Vance Rivers had shown up at the Lazy

S, Ana had never wanted to think anything good about him. He'd been the kid who took so much of her father's attention. In all honesty, Vance never had much to do with her dad's decision making. Colt Slater made sure that his word was law. Until now.

She smiled. "Good. I want you there to help in case I have to make any decisions. I don't know the ranch like you do."

"I'm sorry for that."

"It's not your fault, Vance. That was Dad's choice."

"Well, looks like you're involved now. And you have every right to any make decisions about the ranch."

"I'm doing this for all of us." She sighed. "Right now, I'm not sure if my sisters care if the ranch survives or not. But I'm hoping that will change. This is our heritage."

Vance grinned. "Then I guess we better keep the Lazy S going."

Suddenly she felt warm. Undoubtedly, she was attracted to the man, even after all these years. Not a good idea, not when everything depended on them working together.

The next day, Ana had made an early trip to the hospital to see her father. Colt was just as cold and distant as he'd always been. So she left wondering why she even bothered with a man who didn't care.

Glad to be out of the hospital, she checked her watch as she pulled off the highway and onto the river road. It took about ten minutes to get to her destination, where she saw Hank Clarkson walking along the riverbank under the grove of trees. He wasn't alone. The younger, blond man with Hank was Mike Sawhill. She hesitated to get out of her SUV when she recognized him, a man she'd been foolish enough to go out with a few times. When Mike had wanted to push things faster than she wanted to go, things didn't end well.

She climbed out and walked through the high grass to the riverbank, glad she wore her jeans and her cowboy boots. "Hi, Hank." She nodded at the other man. "Mike."

"Hello, Ana. It's been a long time."

She ignored his comment. "Sorry I'm late."

"Not a problem," Hank assured her. "Mike and I were just trying to find the best spot to launch a boat." The older man took off his hat and wiped his brow. "We might need to clear out some brush."

They walked toward the wide river that ran through the Lazy S. She felt the cool breeze off the water, remembering how as kids, she and her sisters would go horseback riding here. They'd strip down to their underwear and get in the cold water.

She brushed aside the fond memory. "Will that be a lot of work?" she asked, trying not to notice that Mike was staring at her.

Suddenly she spotted a horse and rider coming across the pasture. She smiled when she recognized Vance. "Good, he made it."

They all turned as the rider came closer. The man sat in the saddle as if he were born to it. There was an easy familiarity in the way Vance handled the large animal.

He slowed Rusty as he approached them, then walked his mount to the area behind the vehicles and climbed down. After tying the reins to a tree, he strolled over to the group, decked out in working cowboy gear: leather chaps, dusty jeans and boots. Oh my, Vance Rivers looked good.

He pushed his hat back off his forehead. "Sorry I'm late. I had to move a herd." He shook hands with Hank.

"It is roundup time," Hank said, then introduced Mike. "We just got here ourselves."

Ana watched something flash between the two men, and stepped in. "Did everything go okay?"

"Yeah, just had to chase down a lot of strays." He smiled at her. "What did I miss?"

"Hank's a little worried about the steep bank and brush, for launching a boat from here."

Vance caught Mike Sawhill's close attention on Ana. He didn't like it. "There might be a better spot about a quarter mile downstream. I've caught my share of browns and rainbows there."

They took off and walked the distance. After being in the saddle all morning, Vance didn't mind stretching his legs. In between answering questions from Hank, he also watched Ana's uneasiness around Mike.

Vance didn't know the angler guide personally, but he'd seen him around town, especially in Montana Mick's Bar, usually with a lady.

He suddenly felt protective, and called to Ana. She turned around, and he asked about her visit with Colt. It distracted her from whatever Sawhill was saying to her.

They finally reached their destination. "Here it is," Vance announced as they turned toward the bank. The area was shaded by leafy trees, and the bank wasn't as steep and had a small clearing.

"I've fished here a few times, but never launched a boat. So you'll have to tell me if it will work."

The two men went to examine the bank closer, giving Vance a chance to talk to Ana. "Is Sawhill someone to you?"

She glared at him. "No!" she muttered, keeping her voice down.

Vance could see there had been some history between them. He didn't like that, not at all.

When the two men walked back, Hank was smiling.

"It's a great spot. There's plenty of shade and the water is deep." He looked at Ana. "How soon do you want your first customers?"

Ana glanced at Vance, then back at Hank. "Is there anything we need to do to get ready?"

"Not to begin with. I have several locals who've been itchin' to cast a fly in this section of the river. No angler wants to compete in a crowd." Hank looked at Mike. "Day after tomorrow?"

Mike nodded. "I have a group of four. We'll be testing the water to see what we catch. Thing is, the Big Hole River is all good."

Hank smiled again. "Is that okay with you?" he asked Ana. Her eyes widened. "Sure."

The older man shook his head. "Relax, Ana. We're doing all the work. Now, if you had lodging, there's a group coming in this weekend. I'll have to put them up in the local motel."

Vance was suddenly curious. "How many anglers, and what do they expect in accommodations?"

"It's a group of four who are pretty easy to please. A roof over their heads and a bed. A bonus would be to not have to cook."

Vance glanced at Ana, then said, "I've got a house at the ranch, and if Kathleen will cook a little extra, we can throw in a few meals, too."

Ana shook her head. "No, Vance. You can't give up your place."

He shrugged. "Not a problem." He shot a look at Mike. "I'll just move up to the main house with you."

"I can't believe you said that," Ana said as she marched up to Rusty's stall an hour later. She was not happy with Vance.

She leaned against the wooden slats as he began to brush the animal.

"I don't see the problem," he told her. "It's my house to give up."

"You know that's not what I'm talking about. You made them think that there's something going on between us."

"Can I help what they think?"

"You can when you direct them there," she countered.

"Okay, you're right, but I didn't like the way Sawhill was looking at you. And admit it, you're uncomfortable around him."

"I can handle any problem with Mike."

Vance paused in grooming Rusty. "So you admit there's a problem."

"Look, we only went out a few times. I didn't feel anything for the guy so I didn't continue seeing him. He didn't like that."

"Did he bother you today?"

"No. So I don't need you to intervene. But now you made it so people think I'm…"

"Involved with that wild Rivers kid," he finished for her.

"I didn't mean it like that." She released a sigh. "Don't we have enough to do without adding to it?"

"I don't see I'm adding to anything. I solved a couple of problems. One, I got Sawhill off your back, stopped him thinking about trying to start up something again."

"I'm not interested, anyway." This man was infuriating. "It was only a few dates, a few kisses," she said, lowering her voice, wanting to walk away. She wasn't going to discuss another man with him.

Vance put away the brush. "Secondly, we have paying customers, and add in lodging, there's a lot more money coming in. Say, 'thank you, Vance.'"

Ana knew she was being stubborn about this. Why did

she have a problem with him staying in the house? Maybe because there were just the two of them, and with the attraction she was feeling, it wasn't safe. "Okay, thank you."

Vance stroked Rusty across his back, then walked out of the stall. "It's only for a week, Ana. Could you put up with me that long?"

They started down the barn aisle. At this time of day the men were out doing chores. So besides the horses in their stalls, they were pretty much alone.

"Or should I move back into my old room in the barn, or the bunkhouse?"

She stopped. "I can't let you do that. Of course you can move into the house."

Vance's eyes softened, then he gripped her hand and pulled her into the empty corner stall.

"Vance, what are you doing?"

With a tug of her hand, he had her suddenly against his body. "I thought since you don't want to be seen with me, we shouldn't let anyone see when I do this." His mouth closed over hers, and Ana wanted to cry out for him to stop, but that would be a lie. She'd wanted this since Los Angeles. His mouth slanted over hers and her arms wrapped around his neck as the kiss deepened.

A soft moan escaped her lips as she moved closer, so close she could feel the hard planes of his chest. Oh, God. Her body was betraying her as she eagerly returned his kiss.

He finally broke away and looked down at her. His dark gaze was heated. "It seems your kissing has improved over the years."

The room was dark, as much as a hospital room could be. Colt couldn't wait to get out of this place. To be able to sleep in his own bed, in his own house. He closed his eyes and realized that might never happen.

If he didn't get better, he couldn't go back to the ranch— that was a fact. So he needed to get his strength back, to relearn to walk and talk again. It had been barely a week since his stroke, since his entire life fell apart.

God, he was only fifty-four years old. What had happened? Lousy habits for one, along with stress and endless hours of work. That wasn't any kind of life. He thought back over years of not caring about anything. He'd lost so much, he hadn't wanted to go on, especially after the girls left home. Hell, he'd driven them away, and ended up all by himself. Vance was the only one who'd hung in with him and the ranch. Now Colt was pretty sure he would lose the Lazy S and rot away in some nursing home.

He thought back to the early years and the joy he once had in his life. Luisa and their beautiful daughters. They were all gone, except for Ana. For some crazy reason she wanted him to survive. He felt a surge of hope. Maybe he could salvage something and at least have part of a family.

He needed to get better. He glanced down at his lifeless hand and recalled what his therapist, Jay, had said: "You have to put in the time and hard work."

Colt stared down at his hand again, willing it to move. It seemed to take forever, but he finally lifted two of his fingers. Then he dropped his head back on the pillow and smiled, feeling for the first time in a long time that he wanted to do this. He thought back to his rodeo days and the determination it took to climb on a bull, to ride the eight seconds.

Colt opened his mouth, working to form something more than a grunt. "Sss…second ch…chance," he said in the silent room.

The small accomplishment brought more joy than he'd

felt in years. Suddenly, he didn't want to just lie down and die. There were things he needed to change and correct before he checked out of this world.

He closed his eyes, and this time sleep finally came, but so did a dream of his beautiful Luisa.

She stood in the doorway, then it seemed she floated across the room to his bedside. She leaned in closer and he could see her face, her beautiful face.

"Colton," she whispered.

Her voice touched off so many feelings, feelings he'd suppressed for years since she had abandoned him. Yet the pull was too strong to deny. "Luisa." He tried to open his eyes, but couldn't. "Luisa."

"I'm here, Colton." She touched his face. "I've always been here."

CHAPTER SIX

"I'M SO SORRY, ANA," Sarah said as they sat at a corner table in the Big Sky Grill the next day. "I had no idea Mike was the guide going with Dad yesterday."

"It's not a problem," Ana told her friend. "It's not like I'm going fishing with the group. So we won't cross paths again."

Sarah munched on a French fry, then said, "Mike can be a pain in the butt sometimes with his flirting, but he knows if he steps over the line he'll have to deal with Dad." She leaned back in her seat. "And he likes his job too much for that."

Ana had always envied her friend's relationship with her father, their closeness. "It wasn't a problem. I can handle Mike."

Sarah leaned forward and lowered her voice. "And it didn't hurt to have Vance Rivers come to your rescue."

Not hungry any longer, Ana pushed her club sandwich away. "I didn't need to be rescued at all." She shook her head. "What is it about men that makes them think they need to compete against each other, and I'm the prize?"

Sarah smiled. "I'd say you're a pretty lucky girl. I wouldn't mind having someone like Vance around...just in case."

Ana tried not to think about him that way. "Sarah, you know we have to work together. That's all that's going on."

"So you don't have any feelings for the man? No sparks between you two?"

Ana shook her head, knowing she was lying. Yesterday's kiss in the barn proved that there were sparks. Okay, more like fireworks. But what about Vance? Was he trying to prove a point by kissing the boss's daughter, as he had all those years ago?

Sarah's voice quickly brought Ana back to reality. "I would think a man as handsome as Vance would get your juices flowing."

"I can't afford to get anything flowing. We have to focus on the ranch. And there's Dad to think about. I have too much on my plate right now to think about him or any man."

"I'm sorry, Ana. Is there anything I can do to help?"

"You're a good friend, Sarah. Thank you, but unless you want to drag my sisters back here, there isn't much you can do." She smiled. "Taking me to lunch was the best. Thanks for calling and insisting I come into town."

"A lot of good it did." She nodded to the nearly untouched sandwich. "You aren't eating enough."

Ana sighed. "I'm not very hungry."

"Well, make yourself eat. Colt needs you to stay strong."

Did her father even care? She knew that he needed her at the ranch. Whether he wanted her there or not, she wasn't sure. But she wanted him well and back home to run the Lazy S. Then she could go back to her life. Her job. Except for the kids at the school, there was no one special waiting for her.

The following morning came far too soon for Ana. She got up with the sun, ate toast for breakfast and drank down some coffee, then headed out to the barn. She was going to do whatever needed to be done.

She was ready to face Vance, whom she hadn't seen in two days. Once inside the barn, she found a list of chores hanging on the door of the tack room, but no Vance around. The note stated that he'd gone out with most of the ranch hands, who were moving the herd.

She shook off her disappointment that she hadn't been asked to go along, then went to start her tasks. At the feed bin, she began to scoop out the morning's rations of oats for the horses. With Jake's help she got the job done within the hour. Then the cleaning began, the mucking out stalls and hosing down the center aisle.

She even had the buckskin, Blondie, in the washing area. By the time she was finished with the bathing, she was as wet as the horse.

It felt good to do physical labor. It took her mind off everything except the job at hand. She walked Blondie back to her clean stall. The horse nudged her for more attention.

"If I have time later, it's you and me headed across the meadow." She gave the affectionate horse one more rub and left the stall.

Jake walked by, whistling. "Thanks for the help, Ana."

"Not a problem. What's next?"

The twenty-one-year-old smiled. "We're finished for the morning."

"Good, then I think I'll go up to shower." Ana wrinkled her nose. "I can't stand myself any longer."

She took off toward the house, then paused to admire the huge stone and brown-clapboard structure. The original two-story house had been built for her mother, but over the years, they'd added on as each baby came along. Now it looked big and empty and in need of some tender loving care.

Ana walked up the stone path to the back door, to find Kathleen folding clothes in the utility room.

"Hold it right there, young lady. You're not going into the house wearing those filthy clothes." The housekeeper handed her a towel from a stack of clean ones. "Strip and put everything in the hamper." She shook her head. "This sure brings back memories. You always could get the dirtiest of all your sisters. I miss those times," she said, lifting a basket of clean clothes and walking out.

Ana smiled as she kicked off her boots and unzipped her jeans, shimmied the wet fabric down her legs and tossed them into a hamper. That was the benefit of staying for the summer: she got to be around the horses and live here at the ranch. She pulled off her sweatshirt and threw it on top of the jeans. She was shivering by the time she got out of her soggy panties and bra. She reached for the towel and wrapped it around her just as the back door opened.

Ana gasped in shock when she turned around and saw Vance step into the small room.

"What are you doing here?" she demanded, gripping her towel tightly.

He didn't answer right away, but his gaze took a slow journey up her body. "Right now, I'm enjoying the view."

She felt warmth surge through her. "Well, stop it."

He tipped his hat back and leaned against the doorjamb. "That's a little hard to do." He shook his head. "Damn, if you don't look good in a towel."

"Oh, grow up." She hated that he made her feel so anxious. "I'm going to take a shower. So if you need anything… I mean, is there something I can do—"

"Believe me, a lot is coming to mind, but right now I just need to move in." He grinned. "Looks like I'm going to be enjoying my stay here."

Ana didn't have a comeback, so she swung around and

marched off with as much dignity as she could manage in a towel. All the way reminding herself that there would be a man in the house. A man she definitely needed to stay clear of.

Vance enjoyed the view from the back almost as much as the front. But if he wasn't careful, and if he came on too strong, Ana would run far and fast. He frowned. The wise thing to do might be to back off completely, as he'd been doing for years. Yet all he could think about was the kiss they'd shared in the barn. No other woman could tie him in knots like Analeigh Slater.

Hell, he'd thought the years apart would lessen his appetite for the pretty brunette. But all she had to do was flash those big blue eyes at him, and once again he couldn't remember his name.

He grabbed the duffel bag outside the door and walked into the kitchen just as Kathleen was coming down the hall.

She gave him a bright smile. "So now I know what's got my girl so riled up." The housekeeper paused. "A word of advice, Vance. Don't push too hard."

He played innocent. "I only came by to drop off some things in my room."

The older woman shook her head. "Yeah, I know. Just be warned, Ana is vulnerable right now. She's been fighting for her daddy's approval all her life." Kathleen pushed her finger into his chest. "I don't think you'd ever break her heart intentionally, but…just tread softly."

Vance felt his chest tighten. That would be the last thing he would ever do. He was more worried that she would destroy him.

An hour later, Ana came out of the same bedroom she'd slept in since she was a little girl. She was freshly showered and shampooed, realizing she'd be sharing a bath with Vance at least for a few days.

In the past four years, she'd seen Vance Rivers only in town. They would nod in greeting, but rarely exchanged words. Now she had to work with the man, and she'd be sleeping a few doors down the hall.

Okay, it was a big house. There were four bedrooms upstairs and a master suite at the opposite end. They could go their separate ways, except when they needed to come up with ideas to help the ranch.

She headed for the stairs and saw her sister Marissa's bedroom door was open. There was Vance, taking clothes out of his bags and putting them in the dresser drawers.

In the walk-in closet there was a row of shirts hanging neatly. Well, he was making himself at home. Ana closed her eyes. He had every right to be here. He'd been a part of this family for years. He should be like a brother to her. So why didn't she feel sisterly toward him?

Just then Vance turned around, and she zoned in on the tall, broad-shouldered man with that lanky cowboy build a woman couldn't take her eyes off. Her gaze moved to his handsome face with those deep-set, coffee-colored eyes. His sandy-brown hair was thick and wavy, and maybe a little on the long side.

"See anything you like?" he asked.

"Well, you were checking me out downstairs. I thought I'd turn the tables and see how you like it."

He dropped his stack of T-shirts and came toward her. "I like it a lot, especially from you," he told her.

She fought to move away, but he was so close, and so tempting. "This playing around isn't a good idea, Vance."

"Who said I was playing?" he challenged.

Her heart started to pound as she met his intense gaze.

She managed to step back. "Whatever it is, stop it. We need to concentrate on other things. Are you settled in?"

"I'm getting there. Back at my house, I put away all my personal things. Jake and Gary moved beds from the bunkhouse into the other two bedrooms. So the place now sleeps four to five adults. Kathleen is going to put on the bedding and add some special touches."

"Thank you, Vance. Thank you for doing this."

"It's not a big deal. The house is part of the ranch. It's not even mine."

"But it comes with your job as foreman."

Vance had plans to have his own place soon. The dream might be pushed further into the future than he wanted, but he wasn't giving up. He had the land, and the crop nearly ready to harvest, and soon he'd be able to build his house. He looked at Ana. Question was, would he ever have the girl?

"I can handle living here," he said, wanting to change the subject. "I bet your sister would have a fit knowing I'm sleeping in her room."

Yeah, and so close to me. Ana suddenly remembered the kid who used to sleep in the barn.

"Like I said before, Colt should have never made you stay out in the barn," she said.

Vance raised an eyebrow. "He didn't make me stay anywhere."

"A boy shouldn't have to live with animals."

"It wasn't that bad. Really. My room was upstairs. It was a big area, and finished just like a regular house."

"But you were a kid," she insisted. "You needed adult supervision."

"I was fourteen," he told her. "Chet was close by. I had pretty much been living on my own for years. Though my mother left, my dad was around most of the time. I liked being at the ranch, because he wasn't there taking a swing at me." Vance glanced away. "It was heaven to have a warm bed, three square meals and clothes."

Ana felt the tears building.

He gave a frustrated sigh. "Don't you do that! Don't go feeling sorry for me. I've had a good life here. Your father took me in, helped me learn about horses and cattle. He gave me a chance at a good life, Ana. So just drop this."

Seeing her frown, he quickly changed to another topic. "I heard you worked pretty hard today."

"Isn't that what you wanted? There was a list."

He folded his arms over his chest. "I post a list every day, but I didn't expect you to do it all."

"I want to help out."

"You don't need to go overboard, Ana. There are men who get paid to do the job."

"You can't expect me to sit around and do nothing."

He hesitated. "Then how about taking a ride with me this afternoon? I need to help with the herd."

She was excited. "You're not just making the trip up for me?"

He shook his head. "I don't have time for that. I wouldn't have come in, except I needed to get my clothes out of the house. I'd planned to go back out after lunch. You can come along or not." He went back to putting clothes away in the dresser.

"I'll come," she agreed.

"Then let's have some lunch and go."

She smiled, and he found there was nothing sweeter.

There was nothing like the view of the mountains and feeling the cool breeze against her cheeks as she raced across the pasture. Blondie loved to run, so Ana gripped the horse's mane and let her have her lead through the high grass.

She glanced over her shoulder and saw Vance on Rusty only a slight distance behind her. He could easily catch her, but she was glad he allowed her the freedom to do her thing.

Finally, he rode up beside her and pointed toward the pasture, where cattle dotted the landscape.

"Fun is over, it's time to go to work," he called to her.

Ana pulled back on the reins and her mount slowed. They approached the herd of Hereford cows with their babies, and she immediately heard the calves bawling. She smiled at the familiar sound, and inhaled the scents of cattle and fresh grass.

Vance closed the space between them. "You ride in with the herd. I need to check for strays."

With her nod, Vance kicked Rusty's sides and they took off after an errant yearling. Ana couldn't help but smile, seeing the gelding react like a pro cutting horse. She knew Vance had entered Rusty in many competitions.

The horse and rider were putting on a show now. They headed off the calf, and a dance of wills began between the equine and cow, until Vance managed to direct the little guy back to the herd and his mama.

Ana walked Blondie along with the herd, careful not to startle any of the cows. Vance soon fell in beside her.

"Pretty impressive work."

"Thank you, ma'am." He tapped the brim of his hat with a gloved finger. "You want to play cowgirl?"

She nodded. "Show me what to do."

"Watch Gary and Todd," he told her.

She leaned over her saddle horn and spotted two young cowboys with lariats in their hands, using the ropes to keep the cows in a tight group. Before she could ask, Vance handed her a bandanna from his pocket.

"Tie this around your mouth. It keeps out the dust."

She did as he told her, then he handed her a rope and rode with her to the back of the herd. "We're going to ride drag, but the dust shouldn't be too bad, since it rained last night."

"It's okay," she said. "Where are we taking them?"

"A good mile to the branding pens." He looked concerned. "Will you be okay?"

She nodded, though she wasn't sure. "I can do this."

He winked at her. "I don't doubt you can." He stayed with her, sending Gary and Todd to flank the herd, and they continued the slow process of moving the cows.

Nearly two hours later, they finally reached the large pens. They got the herd through the gate, where Gary had feed waiting for the hungry cows. Once the last one was inside and the gate shut, Ana climbed down from her horse.

"Oh," she cried, as her legs started to give way, but she felt someone grip her by the waist and hold her upright.

"Whoa, there," Vance said against her ear.

"I'm okay." She held on to the saddle horn, hoping he'd release her.

"You sure?"

"Let go and find out."

He did. And by a miracle, she managed to stay on her tired legs. "I guess I'll need to toughen up."

"Not too much." He tossed her a wide grin. "I kind of like your soft places."

Before she could say anything, he walked off to help the men. She decided that she would stay and rest a minute or two, or a hundred. Oh, boy. She moved very gingerly to the shade of a tree and leaned against the trunk. How would she pull this off tomorrow?

She smiled. She didn't care. All the aches and pains were so worth it. For once she felt she was a part of this ranch, and decided she was going to find a way to stay and be a part of this operation. She looked at Vance walking to his horse. He wore leather chaps over his jeans and a cowboy hat low on his head.

The man took charge as if he were born to the job. Well, so was she. She just needed a little practice at being a cowgirl, and couldn't let one good-looking cowboy distract her.

By the time they got back from the cattle pens, they were both exhausted and dirty. After taking care of the horses, Vance went into the bunkhouse for a shower, leaving Ana a chance for some privacy. Not that he wanted to be apart from her. He'd enjoyed spending the day with her, and wouldn't mind more.

He stripped down and walked into the large shower stall. He closed his eyes as the warm spray hit his tired body, but he wasn't too tired to think about Ana. The picture of her standing naked in the big tub at the house flashed into his head. Water would be slicing over her slender frame from the overhead spray, her soapy hands moving over those sweet curves. His mouth went dry as he remembered the taste of her mouth, and he ached to sample the rest of her.

With a frustrated groan, he reached out and turned the faucet to cold, and quickly finished washing. He got out, dried off and wrapped himself in a towel. He cursed, knowing Colt would have a fit if he knew Vance had been thinking this way about his oldest daughter.

He walked out of the shower area, stood at the mirror over the row of sinks and ran his hand over his two-day growth of beard. He'd no sooner reached inside his shaving kit for his razor when he heard a gasp.

He glanced in the mirror and saw Ana standing in the doorway.

What the hell… "Ana. Is something wrong?"

Looking embarrassed, she shook her head. "Jake told me… He said that there was some liniment…in here." She shuddered. "He said it would help with my soreness."

Vance glanced over her long legs encased in a clean pair of jeans. By the looks of her still-damp hair she'd already showered.

"Your legs hurt?"

"Along with other body parts," she murmured.

He tried not to think about the parts she didn't mention. It didn't work.

"I want to be able to help with the branding tomorrow, so I need to do something to help my aches and pain."

She was staring at him as if she'd never seen a man in a towel before. He liked the interest he saw in her eyes. As much as he wanted to see where this would go between them, this wasn't the time.

"Maybe you should just take a day or two off," he suggested.

She frowned. "But I want to help."

"You don't need to prove anything, Ana." He opened the counter drawer, searched around and found a tube of ointment. He held it up. "You're already sore from today's ride."

She straightened, then crossed the room and took the tube from him. "Then let me prove it to myself. I can handle tomorrow."

He gripped her by the wrist. "I just don't want you to get hurt in the process."

She looked both sad and angry. "So you expect me to just stand around?"

"I want you safe. Those calves can be downright ornery

when they're riled." He stepped closer, reached out and touched her cheek. "I don't want this pretty skin bruised."

He saw the pulse pounding in her neck, and her breathing changed, too. "Vance…"

He looked into her deep blue eyes and a sudden jolt rocked his gut. He wanted this woman. "Damn, Ana, what you do to me."

She started to glance away, but his touch drew her back as he lowered his head and brushed his mouth across hers. She drew in a sharp breath, but he didn't stop, just went back again. He teased her lower lip, then moved to kiss the corners of her mouth. But before he could get seriously into her, the sound of voices drew them apart.

He cursed and she jumped back. "I've got to go."

She hurried out of the bathroom, leaving him aching for what he wanted but might never have. Yet he couldn't give up on this chance. He only needed to convince Ana.

CHAPTER SEVEN

THAT NIGHT, DINNER was quiet. Ana attributed it to being tired from the long day. And the kiss. What did she say to the man when he acted as if it had never happened?

She thought of her invasion of his privacy in the bunkhouse shower. He'd been practically naked. Okay, he had on a towel, but his muscular chest and wide shoulders were exposed for the world to see. So she'd stood there ogling him like a silly teenager. Not that it had bothered him at all. The big mistake was when she let him kiss her. Again. What was it about this man that drew her? That made her so aware that she was a woman?

She glanced at Vance. He was sitting in the same seat he'd been assigned when he first came here to live. Right next to Colt. She also remembered how right after the meal was finished Vance would carry his plate to the kitchen, then go back to his room…in the barn. He had never been allowed to join in anything with her and her sisters.

And from the minute the young, moody Vance set foot on the ranch, Ana had been aware of him. As a preteen girl she'd thought it was just an annoyance and would go away when he left. But Vance never left the ranch, and for a long time she'd blamed him for taking Colt from his family.

Once in college, she'd met and gotten engaged to Seth. Things should have been perfect, but then he'd wanted to move to a larger city. Despite Colt's rejection, she wanted to live close to home, to her sisters, even her dad…and Vance?

He glanced up. "I can hear you thinking."

"What?" she said too loudly, then lowered her voice even though they were alone. Kathleen had gone to play her weekly bingo game. "I'm just tired." Ana pushed her plate away.

He tossed her a grin. "Or maybe you're thinking about earlier. It's nice to know that you were affected by the kiss."

She worked at slowing her breathing and heart rate. "It was barely a kiss."

"Give me more time and you won't have any doubts."

She raised her hand. "No. Not a good idea."

He hesitated, not looking happy. "You're right. We've been denying this between us for years, so why not continue?"

Was she ready to face this? No. "Just because there's an attraction between us doesn't mean we should act on it."

"Right again." He slid his chair back and stood. "I'm needed in the barn."

"Vance," she called.

He stopped and turned around. "If I don't leave now, Ana, I'm going to do my damnedest to prove you wrong." His dark eyes bored into hers. "You ready for that?"

She hesitated, feeling the heat from his gaze. Was she ready for this? She did the safe thing and shook her head.

He turned and walked out.

The next day, Colt listened as Dr. Mason went over his progress with Ana. He liked what he heard, except for the part that said he needed to go to a rehab facility to finish his therapy.

Great. He was headed for the nursing home to be left

to rot. He glanced at Ana and saw the concern etched on her face.

"Why can't Dad come home?" she asked.

Dad. She'd always called him Colt. He felt his chest tighten and his eyes water.

Ana looked at him and smiled. "Why couldn't we just have an occupational therapist come to the ranch?"

The neurologist shook his head. "He'll need a full-time nurse along with a therapist. And unless you're independently wealthy, that's expensive. The insurance companies don't pay for full-time in-home care."

"I didn't know." Ana was silent a moment, then said, "So going into the rehab center is the best option?"

Madison nodded. "And Jay McNeal will still be working with him."

Ana turned back to Colt and touched his arm. "Would you like that, Dad? For Jay to keep working with you?"

Hell, the guy was tough as nails, but Colt didn't want him to back down. With a groan, he nodded, and was rewarded with another smile. Her pretty face lit up. Suddenly, Luisa came to mind. No. He wouldn't let that woman get to him ever again. She'd already helped destroy his relationship with his daughters. No, that was the one thing he couldn't blame on his ex-wife. He had done that all by himself.

The doctor and Ana walked across the room to where Vance stood. Colt noticed that Vance couldn't take his eyes off her. There was no doubt about the desire burning in the kid's eyes. This time it looked as if Colt was going to lose Analeigh to another man.

Two mornings later Vance was up before dawn. He had a date with about a hundred calves that needed to be branded and castrated before they were hauled off to the feedlot. He climbed out of bed and slipped on his jeans and shirt.

He'd had a lousy night's sleep. *Thank you, Ana.* But he knew he'd created his own problem and had to deal with it. He needed to stay away from the temptation. Not a problem. They had the roundup the next two days, and with the anglers arriving this morning to stay at his house, that should be plenty to keep him distracted.

Sitting on the edge of the bed, he grabbed a pair of socks and worked them on, then stuck his foot into the boot shaft and tugged his jeans down over the decorative stitching. He stood and ran his fingers through his hair, then made a quick stop in the bathroom.

He'd just stepped into the hall when Ana's bedroom door opened and she appeared in a skimpy pair of boxer shorts and a tank top. *Whoa, dogie.* His body immediately reacted, making it difficult to speak.

"Vance." She said his name in a low, sleep-laced voice. That didn't help the situation.

"Why didn't you wake me?" she asked.

He swallowed, knowing that would have made matters worse. "I was going to, but thought you could use a little more sleep and head out later."

She nodded. "Just give me two minutes and I'll be ready."

He was hoping for a different answer. "The anglers are coming today," he called. "Wouldn't you like to stay around and greet them?" Truth was, he didn't want her getting hurt, or worse, distracting him.

"Hank's taking them fishing first thing this morning. I'll welcome them tonight." She disappeared back into the bedroom, leaving the door partly open, so he saw her shirt go flying, along with her boxers. Great. He was supposed to sit in a saddle all day with the picture of a naked Ana in his head?

A minute later the door swung open and she came out dressed in jeans and socks, buttoning her blouse over a tank top. She ran across the hall into the bathroom and shut the door. Vance leaned against the wall, wondering if he should go on ahead, but seconds later she walked out, grabbed her jean jacket and began to tie her hair back. "I'm ready."

He liked her fresh look—no makeup, not fussing with her hair. "We'll grab some breakfast at the bunkhouse."

She smiled and reached for her boots at the back door. Sitting down, she worked the scuffed buckskins on, then grabbed an old cowboy hat off the hook and headed with him toward the barn. Suddenly, he was looking forward to spending the day with her.

When they arrived, they found Jake loading up the truck. "Is there any food left?" Vance asked.

"Sure." The kid nodded. "Morning, Ana."

"Good morning, Jake."

They kept on walking to the bunkhouse. They heard the men talking, and some were joking around, but when Ana stepped through the door, silence blanketed the room.

"Hey, don't stop on my account," she said.

Todd got up and motioned to her to take the spot. "We were just sayin' how this roundup won't be the same without Colt."

Vance caught Ana's sadness. "You know he wishes he could be here," she told them. "With the way the rehab is going, I'm sure he'll make the next one. So you guys will just have to put up with me today."

Pete Cochran stood. "I'll say you're a lot better looking than old Colt. Your daddy would be proud of you, Ana."

She blushed as he handed her a plate. "You'd better eat. You've got to show these guys you're a Slater."

By noon, Ana was tired and smelled of sweat, dirt and cows, but had never felt better. She couldn't work as hard as the men, but she'd done her share.

She stood at the pen gate and watched as the roper, Todd, lassoed another calf and dragged him over to the branding area, where Vance wrestled him to the ground. Next the heeler held down the hind legs as Pete did the quick job of castrating the calf.

"Okay, let's brand this guy," Vance called.

Ana went into motion, hurrying out with the iron and pressing it against the calf's hind quarter. The smell of burning cowhide filled the air as the Slater brand was engraved onto the animal. She pulled the iron away and saw the sign for the lazy S.

"Next," she called, as they released the animal and he ran off to his mama.

"Good job."

She looked at Vance, feeling a sense of pride for what she was accomplishing and for the generations of Slaters who'd come before her. "Thanks."

She stood back and watched the men work together. She knew she got the honor of branding only because of Vance, but she'd take it.

Suddenly, the sound of the dinner bell rang out. "Lunch break," Kathleen called.

They turned around and found that the housekeeper and some of the men had set up tables under a group of huge oak trees.

The ranch hands started walking over, eager for some of Kathleen's famous fried chicken and rice and beans.

There were several salads to choose from, so something had to be to their liking.

Ana smiled when she arrived to wash up. Once her hands were clean she got in the food line.

"Land's sake, child," Kathleen called to her. "Have you been playing in the dirt?"

Grinning, Ana looked down at her mud-spattered jeans and boots. "You could say that," she agreed as she moved on with her heaping plate. She walked toward the shady area and spotted two high school students, Billy Kramer and Justin Patchett. She stopped and talked with them, then moved on past another table. She recognized a few of their neighbors and thanked them for helping out. One in particular, who was seated at the end, she hadn't seen in years—Garrett Temple. The tall, dark-haired man had been their closest neighbor, and according to Colt, their biggest enemy.

"Garrett."

He raised his head and his smile died as he slowly rose to his feet. "Hello, Ana. It's been a long time."

"Yes, it has. Are you helping with the roundup?"

He nodded. "If this isn't a good idea, I'll leave."

She recalled that Colt and Garrett's father, Nolan, had had a feud going for years. So had Garrett and Josie, but theirs was a more personal one. Ana hadn't been happy about the way Garrett treated her sister, but that had been years ago, back in their first years of college.

"Why would I want that?"

With that, Garrett smiled. "Considering our families' history, I don't want to cause any trouble."

She didn't want to rehash anything from the past. "Colt isn't here."

"I know. I'm sorry to hear about his stroke. Vance said he's doing well."

It was nice that Garrett asked. "He's going through rehab now. We're hoping to have him home soon."

"That's good to hear."

Ana smiled, then said, "Maybe for you, but Colt isn't the easiest man to deal with, and trying to keep him down during his recovery will be nearly impossible."

Garrett laughed at that. "I know. My dad is just as stubborn."

Vance heard Ana's laugh and turned around to see her with Garrett. A funny feeling came over him when he saw how she was looking up at his friend. Her eyes sparkled, as if she was hanging on his every word.

"Hey, boss." Todd walked over and asked him a question about the afternoon crew.

By the time Vance looked back at the couple, he found that Ana had sat down at the table with Garrett. No, he didn't like this one bit.

He grabbed a plate, filled it and made his way over to the table just as the pair looked up.

"Hey, Vance, sit down," Garrett said. "Ana and I were just catching up about the kids we knew."

Well, that was one conversation he couldn't join in. "That's good."

Garrett grinned. "Can you believe that she's working at the high school?" He turned back to Ana. "Do the students give you as hard a time as we gave the teachers?"

"Some of them do, but for the most part, they're pretty good kids."

Vance concentrated on eating, but his food was suddenly tasteless. He had nothing in common with Ana or Garrett. He'd been ahead of them in school, and they hadn't run in the same social circles.

The reminiscing continued between the two until Vance

couldn't take any more. He stood, and Garrett looked at him. "You're leaving?"

"Some of us have to work." He walked off, knowing he was acting like a jerk. But that didn't seem to stop him.

Okay, so this place might not be so bad.

Colt looked around the rehab facility's community room with its large, flat-screen television and several card tables set up for socializing. His bedroom wasn't so bad, either. He'd been here only a few days, so he'd reserve judgment on how he felt about the place.

He did like having familiar faces around. And Jay made sure he was working hard on his exercises, even had him up and walking with the help of the parallel bar today. Colt also had a speech therapist now. It was a little crazy to start making sounds as if he were a baby, but it seemed to help him.

He just wished someone could help ease his frustration. No one would tell him how much this was costing, or how long he'd be staying here. All he knew was he couldn't afford it if he had to pay. He might as well sign over the Lazy S, because there wasn't much money left in the bank.

He sighed. Even if he got better what good would it do him? Would he ever be able to climb on a horse again? Ride across the land he loved so much? How could he check his herd?

He closed his eyes and thought back to the financial mess he'd left before he had the stroke. He'd planned to try and fix it, but hadn't gotten the chance. Now it was too late.

With the Lazy S gone, he would have nothing....

"Dad?"

Hearing Ana's voice, he opened his eyes. She was smiling at him as if she really wanted to be here.

She was so pretty. He raised his hand to touch her, and

she gasped. "Oh, Dad. You can use your hand. That's wonderful." She hugged him. He closed his eyes against the emotions, suddenly realizing how starved he'd been for the contact.

After the way he'd treated her and her sisters, how could she be so loving toward him? He didn't deserve it, but he never wanted to give it up. Yet, he knew he would have to. Ana would be around only until he got better.

CHAPTER EIGHT

THREE DAYS LATER, Ana sat at her father's desk going over the ranch's finances. Things still weren't in great shape, with the extra payroll going to the men on the roundup, but thanks to the neighbors volunteering to help out, it could have been worse. Of course, the Lazy S would be returning the favor when those ranches needed help.

Vance had also worked out a deal with Garrett to transport the yearlings to the feedlot. In exchange, Vance was going to plant the Temple Ranch alfalfa crop next year.

She frowned, thinking about the first day of the roundup, and how patient the man had been with her. All these years her father had never wanted to make the effort, but Vance had taken the time to teach her about the operation.

She leaned back, thinking about the handsome cowboy with those deep-set eyes, the cocky smile and a mouth that tempted her. She never knew if he was serious about her or if she was just a challenge, the boss's daughter he'd always been forbidden to go near.

She liked to think that those shared kisses meant something to him, too. Yet since the roundup he'd been distant, staying far away from her, including the house. Okay, he'd been busy. Did that mean he had to spend all his time at the bunkhouse? Then today he'd moved back into the foreman's house.

She'd known it would happen sooner or later. What she didn't expect was to miss him so much. It was more than missing him; she'd come to care about Vance. More than she wanted to admit. If she let herself, she could fall in love with him. She suspected it was already too late.

The phone rang, bringing Ana out of her daydream. "Lazy S Ranch," she answered.

"You sound so official," a familiar voice said.

"Josie?"

"Yes, it's me," her sister said. "You're the only one who ever knew my voice from Tori's. How are things in Montana?"

"Looking better every day, " Ana fibbed a little.

There was a long pause, then Josie asked, "How is Colt doing?"

Ana had kept in touch with her sisters about everything going on. "I went to the rehab center yesterday. He's doing well. The therapist says he's improving every day. It won't be long before he comes home."

"That's good," Josie said, then asked, "How did the roundup go?"

Ana smiled. So her sister had been reading all the emails she'd sent. "The yearlings were shipped off to the feed-lot." She didn't mention Garrett Temple's help, knowing the twosome's history. Not if she ever wanted Josie to return home.

Ana rushed on to say, "And we're booked solid for fishing through the fall. Even the foreman's house is rented the next two months."

Josie finally rejoined the conversation, "That's good, Ana, but as you say, we still need more income. Have you thought about expanding?"

"Expand how?" Ana asked, happy that one of her sisters, at least, cared.

"I've done several corporate events in the past few years. The most requested is to set up something in a different locale, where it's quiet and restful, a sort of retreat. If you are serious about having another income for the ranch, there needs to be more housing for larger gatherings. Then the ranch could be rented out for corporate functions, for special fishing events, or even for small weddings.

"That sounds like an expensive undertaking," Ana said, knowing they didn't have the money for such a big venture. "How are we going to finance a project of that scale?"

"Tori and I are working on that," Josie admitted.

Ana loved that the twins wanted to help, but how long it would take, and how much money, was a big worry. "Do you know someone with deep pockets?" she asked, half teasing.

"You might be surprised. Adding a silent partner could be an option."

"Not sure about that," Ana told her, then looked up and saw Vance standing in the doorway.

He leaned against the doorjamb, just watching her. She tried to focus on what her sister had to say, but the man's presence was distracting her. When his dark gaze locked on hers, her heart began to race so fast she had trouble concentrating. "Why don't you email me the information?"

Vance stood across the room. He knew he had acted like a jealous jerk, but he couldn't stay away from Ana any longer. And since he'd talked with Garrett, he knew there had been nothing between the two. His friend admitted he'd cared about Josie.

So Vance needed to apologize. He also knew it was time to find out how Ana felt about him. From the second she'd returned to the ranch, all those long-ago feelings had been stirred up again. He had to know if he was wasting time. If Ana didn't care about him at all, he needed to move on.

When she looked at him with her sapphire eyes, he couldn't seem to think about much of anything, except how much he wanted her. Before he lost his nerve, he walked into the office and closed the door behind him, his gaze never leaving Ana's.

She continued to talk to Josie, but if he had anything to do with it, the conversation was about to be cut off. He went around the desk and Ana's eyes grew large, but he didn't stop. He placed his hat in the overstuffed chair beside her, then took the phone from her hand.

He sat on the edge of the desk directly in front of her as he spoke into the receiver. "Hello, Josie. This is Vance. I have something important to talk to Ana about, so you'll have to call her back. Later." He hung up the phone.

Ana looked shocked. "Why did you do that?"

He pulled her to her feet, settled her between his legs as his arms went around her waist, bringing her even closer. "So I can do this."

He dipped his head and captured her lips. She remained stiff for a second or two, then slowly sighed as she melted into him. Soon she raised her hands around his neck and threaded her fingers through his hair.

Good Lord. No woman had ever felt as good as Ana. His tongue slipped inside and tasted her essence, only making him want her more. He finally tore his mouth away and looked at her.

Her eyes were wide with desire. "I take it you don't hate me anymore."

"I never did." He leaned his forehead against hers. "Just jealousy rearing its ugly head. I'm sorry."

"Why would you be jeal—"

He cut off the words when he kissed her again, and again. "Because I want you, Ana. I care about you."

Her eyes rounded. "Oh, Vance…" She drew a shaky

breath. "I'm not sure. If things don't work out between us…"

"How will we know if we don't give it a try?"

Her gaze searched his face. "What about Colt?"

"He's not here."

"He will be," she stated.

"Suddenly you need your daddy's approval?"

"It's not that, it's everything else. Along with Dad, we have a ranch to run together."

Vance was hurt that she had so many excuses, but he hid it with anger. He held her back so he could stand. "I guess that tells me what I needed to know." He reached for his hat, and was heading for the door when she called to him.

"Vance, it's not that…. I mean, if it doesn't work out…"

He gripped the brim of his hat. "Ana, why don't you think about it, and give me a call when you decide what you want?" He turned and walked out. A man had to have some pride, even when it came to love.

Sometime in the early morning, Ana got tired of rolling around in bed, and finally got up and went downstairs. She glanced at the clock; it wasn't even 4:00 a.m. Great. She poured herself a glass of juice and went to the large picture window behind the kitchen table.

She kept playing over and over in her head what Vance had said to her. *I want you.* She wanted him, too, but she was scared, scared to give her heart to a man. No, it was just this man. Vance had the power to hurt her, because she already cared about him.

She heard a noise behind her, then Kathleen appeared. "Sorry, did I wake you?"

"I was getting up anyway." Still in her pajamas and robe, the older woman came up to her, looking concerned. "Are you okay, Ana?"

"Yeah, I'm just a little restless."

The housekeeper had been a mother and a friend. "I suspect it's more than that."

Ana started to deny it, but Kathleen interrupted. "Could you be missing a certain man since he moved out of the house?"

"Crazy, isn't it? Most of the time we can't even be civil to each other." Ana couldn't stop thinking about what had happened in the office earlier.

Kathleen sighed. "Sweetheart, you two have been dancing around each other since you came back here to live." In the predawn quiet, Ana could hear Kathleen's humor. "So have you decided to do anything about it?"

Was that it? Did she feel safer dancing around the issue without risking her heart? "Me? Why should I do something?"

She was met with silence.

"Maybe I'm scared," Ana admitted.

"Love is scary. Don't let what happened to your parents stop you." Kathleen turned to her. "All I can tell you is what I know. Vance Rivers is a good man. But when it comes to love there are always chances things won't work. You have to decide if you're willing to take it."

Ana never was one to take risks. She was the oldest, the sensible daughter. She always tried to do the right thing. So why was she walking across the compound to Vance's house just before dawn?

She was afraid to answer that question. She was shaking as she walked up the steps, but before she could chicken out, she knocked on the door. She stood there a few minutes and almost felt relieved when there wasn't an answer. Just as she started to leave, the door opened and Vance stood there, wearing only a pair of jeans and a towel draped around his neck.

Oh, God. She loved looking at this man. She met his eyes and tried desperately to speak, but nothing came out of her mouth.

"What the hell." He reached for her, pulled her into the house and closed the door, pushing her back against it. A soft light came from over the stove in the kitchen, letting her see the look of desire in his eyes.

"What are you doing here?"

"I didn't like how we left things last night."

"So you thought coming here before dawn was a wise thing to do?"

"I couldn't sleep."

"Join the club, lady. You've kept invading my dreams since you've come home."

His honesty shocked her. "Really?"

In answer, he lowered his head and covered her mouth with his. With a soft moan, she gripped his bare arms, feeling his strength. Yet he held her with tenderness as he placed teasing kisses against her lips.

"We could bring my dreams to life if you like," he told her before he gave her another sample. He captured her mouth in a deep kiss, causing her knees to give out.

He wrapped his arms around her, pulling her close. "I got you," he whispered.

She laid her head against his chest, feeling his rapid heartbeat. "I want you, Vance," she breathed.

He pulled back and looked down at her. A slow smile crossed his face. "That's nice to know, but your timing is rotten. I promised Garrett I'd help him out this morning."

"Oh…" What should she do now? She pulled away. "Okay. Sure. I should leave and let you get going."

"Wait." Vance tugged her back into his arms. His gaze

moved over her face as his hand cupped her cheek. "I'm just as disappointed as you are. When I make love to you, Ana, I don't want to rush it. I want to take hours," he breathed as his lips brushed over her ear. "I want to spend all night making slow sweet love to you." He raised his head and covered her mouth again. He was breathing hard when he drew back. "I don't want to leave you right now."

She shivered, her own breathing rapid and her imagination running wild. "I don't want to go, either," she admitted. Suddenly she didn't have any pride when it came to this man.

"Tonight. Come to dinner with me, tonight?"

"A date?"

His smile faded. "Is there a problem with going out with me?"

"No. It's just…that I promised Colt I'd drop by tonight."

"I should be back from Garrett's by three. I can go with you, then we could have dinner."

She suddenly brightened. "I'd like that."

"Okay, it's a *date*," he said, leaving no doubt that he wanted to spend time with her.

"A date." She started for the door, but he quickly pulled her back and covered her mouth again. By the time the kiss ended she was light-headed. "I'll see you later."

She managed to walk out the door, but she wasn't sure if her feet ever touched the ground as she made her way back to the house.

Ana hadn't been out on a date in so long she was having trouble deciding what to wear. She settled for white linen trousers and a sleeveless, peach-colored blouse and heeled sandals.

When she came down the steps, Vance was waiting for her. He was dressed in black Wrangler jeans, a slate-gray

Western shirt and shiny boots, and had his black Stetson in his hand.

His smile sent a warm shiver up her spine. "You look beautiful." He stepped forward and took her into his arms. His head dipped, and he placed a tender kiss against her lips.

"Thank you," she said. "You don't look so bad yourself." She was reaching for her purse when Kathleen walked out.

"You two have a good time," she called.

"We will," Vance said as he escorted her to his clean truck. The inside was spotless, too. "Someone's been busy today," she said as he climbed into the driver's side.

He leaned across the console. "I have this special girl I was hoping to impress." His mouth brushed over hers again, and she sucked in a breath. He pulled away before it got too intense. "Have I succeeded?"

"I'll let you know later."

Thirty minutes later, Vance escorted Ana into the rehab center. He found he was nervous. What would Colt think about him going out with his daughter? Even though Ana was an adult, Vance still couldn't help but wonder if Colt would think he was good enough.

He shook off the feeling. Neither he nor Ana were planning to make an announcement to the man. There wasn't anything to say, anyway. Not yet.

At Colt's room they found the door partly opened and the speech therapist inside. Vance froze when he heard the sounds coming from Colt.

"Dad," Ana cried as she went into the room. "You're talking."

Colt's therapist, Carrie Woodridge, stood up. "Ms. Slater, I wasn't expecting you."

Vance noted the panicked look on Colt's face. He wasn't

ready to share his accomplishments. "Ana, why don't we leave until Carrie is finished?" He took her by the hand. "We'll come back."

He looked at the therapist and she signaled about thirty minutes. With a tug on Ana's hand, he managed to get her out the door.

"But, Vance… I want to help."

"But your father doesn't want you to hear him stumble over his words. You know how proud Colt is."

Smiling, Ana nodded. "He's talking, Vance. I can't believe how much progress he's made since coming here." She glanced around the state-of-the-art facility. "I'm just worried about the cost."

"Isn't the insurance company covering it all?"

She sighed. "Finding that out wasn't on the top of my list when Dad needed a place for rehab."

Vance had some concerns, too, but he didn't want Ana worrying. He glanced at his watch. "Let's go and check with the billing department. It's early yet. And if we discover there's money owed, we'll figure out something. Colt needs to be here."

They walked back to the reception area and asked to speak to someone in the accounting department. Moments later, a young, dark-haired woman came through the double doors. She saw them and smiled. "Ms. Slater. I'm Allison Garcia. I understand you need to discuss your father's coverage."

"Yes. We're not sure what the insurance covers on his bill."

The woman nodded, then escorted them back to her office and had them sit down in front of her desk.

"First of all, are you happy with your father's care here at Morningside Rehab Facility?"

"Very much so," Ana said. "He's been improving at a remarkable pace."

Allison smiled again. "Good."

Ana exchanged a look with Vance. "We're just wondering about the cost."

The accountant turned to her computer and brought up the file. "Your father's insurance is handling eighty percent."

"So twenty percent is our responsibility?"

Allison looked over the paper. "It appears there's been an adjustment in the bill." She glanced at Ana. "A lot of times, they adjust the cost for patients."

"So there isn't a balance owing?"

"As of right now, there isn't." Allison smiled. "We're a new facility, and we're trying to build a reputation in this area. I'd say your father is a recipient of this good fortune, so the cost has been adjusted."

"That's wonderful," Ana said as she stood, then thanked the woman for her time and left.

"Do you feel better now?" Vance asked as they walked out into the reception area.

"I don't know. It's nice that Dad has the cushion of a discount, but I'm afraid of all the other bills that are coming in. We're trying to keep the ranch afloat and we're barely making it."

Vance took her by the hand and directed her into a deserted passageway. "You've got to stop this, Ana. You can't do it all alone." He leaned down and brushed his mouth over hers. "I'm here, too. We'll figure this out together. Somehow we'll come up with other ideas about making money."

She nodded. "Thank you."

"Stop thanking me. We're in this together. I don't want to lose the Lazy S, either. It's been my home for nearly eighteen years." He touched her cheek. "That's how long I've cared about you."

* * *

Colt was exhausted from his speech session, and from having Ana walk in. He hadn't been ready for anyone to know that he could speak, especially Ana. Not yet.

He could still see the look on Vance's face. He would be harder to fool about his progress. Colt never could put much past that boy. Of course, Vance River was a good man, and Colt also saw the way he looked at Ana. There was no hiding his desire for her. And there was no doubt there was something going on between them.

Colt grabbed his walker and worked to stand up, then managed to get himself over to the window to look out at the mountains he loved.

He thought back over his life, to the happiness of those first few years with Luisa and their daughters, until everything had fallen apart.

Vance had come into his life by accident. Having him show up at the ranch had distracted Colt from a lot of his pain. He'd had to concentrate on the kid, who'd been so wild he barely had table manners. Vance had also been suspicious toward anyone in authority. Colt couldn't blame him. Everyone who'd said they loved him had just abused him.

The one thing Colt had had to do was keep Vance away from his daughters.

He glanced down into the parking lot now and caught a glimpse of the couple walking toward the truck. Vance tugged on Ana's hand and pulled her into his arms and kissed her.

Colt couldn't stop them. He smiled. Of course, why would he want to?

CHAPTER NINE

AT SEVEN O'CLOCK, Vance escorted Ana into a small restaurant just outside Dillon that was nestled up to the river's bank. The Riverside Inn was well known for its seafood and prime rib.

The hostess led them across the small, intimate dining room to a booth with a view of the river. Ana slid into her seat and Vance sat down across from her. She looked out at the picturesque scene, the late-day sun reflecting off the flowing water, creating a golden glow.

She smiled at her date. "It's lovely here."

"You've never been here?"

She shook her head. "I really don't go out much."

"So Sawhill never brought you here?"

She was taken aback by the question, but quickly shook her head. "As I said before, we only went out a few times. We usually just went to Montana Mick's for drinks, and dancing."

Vance reached across the table and took her hand. "I apologize. I had no business asking you about your personal life, but you deserve better than a guy who thinks that a few drinks is a way to treat a lady."

She knew that, but Mike had been the only man asking to spend time with her. "It was just a casual thing."

"Well, I want to make some special memories with you,

Ana. And if you want to go dancing, I'll take you to Montana's, or anywhere else."

Suddenly, she found it difficult to breathe. "I like being right here…with you."

He gave her a big smile. "I can do that, bright eyes."

Another catch in her breath. "Why do you call me that?"

He shrugged. "Because your eyes are the prettiest blue…and so expressive. They were the first thing I ever noticed about you."

She blinked at his admission. "You mean when you came to live at the ranch?"

He nodded.

"You were barely fourteen. I was twelve."

He winked. "That's old enough to be attracted to a pretty girl." He squeezed her hand again. "And now she's turned into a beautiful woman."

Ana found her heart pounding, not over the compliment, but that she was feeling the same attraction. And less than twenty-four hours ago she'd gone to Vance's house in hopes of ending up in his bed.

Oh, God. What had gotten into her? She'd never approached men. Maybe that was why she'd spent so many years alone. Wasn't it about time she went after what she wanted?

"You're going to wear yourself out, thinking so hard."

She felt the heat rising to her neck. "It's Colt," she said, wanting to change the subject. Facing her feelings for Vance wasn't something she was ready to deal with. "Did he seem okay to you when we went back to his room?"

Vance wasn't sure if he should say anything, because he didn't want to change her good mood. "Your father is fine, outside of the fact that he knows I have a thing for his daughter. I'm not sure he likes the idea." Vance raised her hand to his mouth and placed a kiss against her knuckles. "He saw how I looked at you today."

Ana's mouth dropped open. "Why would he care?"

"I think that Colt has always cared about you girls. He was just afraid to show it."

"Afraid? We loved our dad. We showered him with affection until he pushed us away so many times we couldn't handle any more rejection."

Vance felt Ana's sadness. He leaned closer and lowered his voice. "I only knew about Luisa from Kathleen."

Ana tensed at her mother's name, and he gripped her hand tighter. "It's hard to figure why she left her husband and four daughters, but there was no doubt that Colt loved her." Vance stared into Ana's eyes. "Someone you care about deeply isn't so easy to get over." His gaze locked on hers. "I know."

He watched her throat work. "There's been a special woman in your life?" she murmured.

He wanted to lay his heart out then and there and tell her of his feelings, but all he could manage was a nod before the waitress appeared at their table. Vance ordered prime rib rare and Ana asked for the same.

"Will there be anything else? A drink from the bar?"

He turned to Ana. "Would you like a glass of wine?"

"Only if you are, too," she said.

He shook his head. "I'm having iced tea."

"I'll have the same."

After the waitress left, Ana asked, "Is the reason you don't like to drink because of your dad?"

Vance released a breath, trying to stay relaxed. His past was something he never liked talking about. "I haven't considered Calvin Rivers my father for a long time. But yes, he's the reason I don't drink in public. I don't want to give people the chance to think I'm anything like him."

Ana nodded. "Do you keep in touch?"

He shook his head. "Are you kidding? He lit out of town right after Colt took me in." The last thing Vance wanted was to bring up the past to darken the mood. "Why don't we make a pact tonight and not talk about any family?"

She smiled and agreed.

"What about you, Ana? You like your job?" He already knew a lot about her life. He'd made it his business to know about the woman he'd never managed to forget. The woman he couldn't get over.

She smiled again. "There isn't much to tell. You already know I'm a counselor at the high school. I love my job. At first I thought I wanted to teach, but I enjoy helping the students with their long-term goals. So many people want kids to pick a career, but never take the time to guide them and show them all their options."

He loved hearing her enthusiasm. He'd seen firsthand the respect and admiration Ana generated when he'd talked with two of her students, Billy and Justin, at the roundup.

"And I would say you're good at your job."

She shrugged. "I hope I am, because the kids mean a lot to me."

Vance leaned forward, wishing he could get closer to her. "You coming tonight means a lot to me, too, Ana. I hope I can convince you just how much."

He watched her eyes grow wide, but before she could say anything, their food arrived. He'd put his feelings out there; now it was her move.

Over the next two days, Ana couldn't stop thinking about her evening with Vance. It had been incredible. When they'd driven back to the ranch, however, he'd walked her up the steps to the house, gave her a toe-curling kiss, then said good-night and left. She hadn't seen him since.

With a sigh, she sat down at the desk in the office. On paper the Lazy S was showing some profit. The bills were getting paid, and a lot of the back payments for the lease were being made up. As for the day-to-day operations, they still needed a steadier income. There was nothing in reserve.

Ana printed out the email her sister Josie had sent her yesterday. It was a list of different websites Ana could go to and see advisements from other ranches that had gone into side businesses. Some had added the dude ranch element; another showed a large, all-purpose structure they rented out for corporate retreats, small weddings, even quilting workshops. All these places were also working cattle operations.

Ana had to admit there were some good ideas. Problem was, they would need capital to build the extra structures. She doubted that any bank would loan them money with the ranch barely making it.

There was a knock on the door and Vance stuck his head in. He'd been out working, because he still had those sexy leather chaps on over his dusty jeans.

She felt the heat move through her body as he smiled, removed his hat and asked, "You busy?"

"Nothing that can't wait," she managed to answer.

He walked in and came around the desk and tugged on her hand so she would stand. "First, I need to do this." He lowered his head and his mouth captured hers. The kiss started out sweet, gentle. It quickly changed when he took charge and pulled her closer as their need intensified. By the time he released her they were both breathless.

"I've missed you," he said.

"I've been here, but I didn't know where you were." Okay, so she was a little hurt that he couldn't make time for her. Or maybe he'd decided that he didn't want to carry things between them any further.

"I've been at Bill Perkins's place. He broke his arm last week so I've been helping with the roundup. I was going to tell you yesterday, but you'd already left to go see Colt. I told Kathleen."

"Oh, I haven't seen her today." Ana knew she was being foolish, because Vance hadn't made any promises to her.

He smiled and she got all warm and achy inside.

"So you missed me?" he drawled.

She smacked his arm and pulled back. "Don't get a big head about it. Besides, we have a ranch to run, so it's nice to know where you are."

Vance wasn't happy to have to report in to her, as if he couldn't do his job. "The men were taking care of things, but you're right, I should have called you directly to let you know." He kissed the end of her nose. "I tried to finish up at a good time yesterday, but it didn't work out that way. As badly as I wanted to talk to you, it was too late to phone." He pulled her close and nuzzled her neck, sending shivers up her spine. "Do I get points for not being able to think about anything but you?"

Oh, yes. "Maybe."

"Were you thinking about me?"

"I've been too busy." His lips were touching all the right spots. "Oh, Vance," she gasped.

He raised his head and gave her a cocky smile. "Seems I hit a sensitive spot. How many more do you have?"

She was in big trouble. She managed to step away. "I need to get back to work."

Vance let her go, but he wasn't about to leave yet. He pulled up a chair and sat down beside her at the desk. He liked inhaling her scent, and would like to keep tasting her, but she'd probably throw him out if he pushed too hard.

"So I hear we have more guests arriving this weekend. That has to be good."

She nodded. "The business we've gotten from the anglers is good. But we still need to expand to make enough to keep the ranch going." She showed him some of the websites of ranches branching out with things other than just raising cattle.

He liked the ideas, but what would Colt think about it? "Have you talked with Hank Clarkson about this, to see if it would be worth the expense of expanding?" Vance asked. "Would we be able to fill more rooms than just the foreman's house?"

Ana looked at him. They were so close he could lean in and kiss that sweet mouth of hers. He watched her eyes darken. It was nice to know that she was feeling the same heat.

She turned back to the computer. "There are other groups we can cater to than just anglers. Josie suggests we think on a larger scale. If we build a main structure, we should think about doing corporate retreats. We could handle small weddings, quilting retreats. Surprisingly, there are all sorts of groups that enjoy time in the country."

Vance looked back at the screen. "It sounds like there are a lot of options."

She nodded. "Problem is we don't have a lot of money for construction." She sighed as she pointed to the log cabin–style building in the picture. "This would be perfect by the group of trees beside the river. I've even come up with a name, the River's Edge."

Vance liked these suggestions. "We could talk to a contractor and get an estimate on costs, then present it to the bank."

Ana's eyes lit up. "So you think it's worth it?"

"Yeah, I do. We can't get crazy, but maybe we could

start off with a central structure." Vance pointed to the log house on the screen. He, too, was caught up in the idea. "The downstairs could have a main meeting room, plus a kitchen, and the upstairs, three or four bedrooms. That would bring in some money. Then later we could add some cabins along the river, for the anglers, or for corporate functions. Between the foreman's house and a few cabins, we could double our income."

She rewarded him with a smile that made his gut tighten in need. He wanted to take her into his arms and make her forget about everything else but them. Soon. They had a lot to deal with right now. But one day, it was going to be all about them. He wasn't going to let her leave the ranch again. Not without a fight.

The next evening, Ana watched Vance walk toward the house carrying his duffel bag. Once again he'd moved out of the foreman's house for a group of anglers coming in for the weekend. This time, instead of going to the bunkhouse, he was back at the main house. A welcome sight for her, but also frightening, since closeness could mean their relationship could move to the next level.

Was she ready for that? She recalled her early morning walk to his house a week ago, when she'd been more than willing to move ahead with a relationship. It had been Vance who'd slowed things down. He'd gone with her to visit to her father, taken her on the roundup. And there was their date the other night. She shivered, recalling when he'd showed up in the office and kissed the daylights out of her. He seemed to care about her.

She was definitely falling hard for this man. What frightened her was she didn't want to be just one of Vance River's women. A few years back, the man had been seen with several different women, but none of them ever seemed to last long.

What did he want with her?

All Ana knew was that she had come to care about him, a lot. She could admit it now. She'd cared about him years ago, but also resented him for taking her father's attention. She couldn't blame him any longer. That was all Colt's doing.

So what should she do now?

She heard a sound and turned around as Vance walked into the kitchen.

He smiled and winked, then walked up to Kathleen. "Smells good. Is supper about ready?"

She nudged him out of her way. "Sit down and I'll bring you a plate."

Ana had the table set and ready, but was she ready for this man? She couldn't ignore the feelings she had whenever Vance was close to her.

"How was your afternoon?" he asked.

"I stayed busy."

He placed the napkin on his lap. "Did you get in to see Colt?"

She nodded as Kathleen brought over the pot roast and potatoes. "It was a short visit, but he was sitting in the recreation room."

Vance paused. "No kidding. Was Colt making friends?"

She shook her head. "He was watching television."

They continued to share their day, and Ana enjoyed the relaxed time with him and Kathleen. But every so often, she'd catch Vance watching her. She couldn't stop the blush and he'd smile.

"Kathleen, the meal was great. Thanks." He looked at Ana. "I'm going to the barn to check on the horses before turning in."

She nodded and helped Kathleen finish loading the dishwasher.

"My, my, seems a little warm in here tonight. Are you two any closer to admitting your feelings?" the housekeeper asked when they were alone.

Ana looked at her. "Vance has been keeping his distance since our date. So I'm not sure what he wants."

"You might try pushing the issue."

Ana wasn't sure if she could pull off a seduction, but she wanted Vance.

After taking her shower, she put on a gown and the bathrobe Kathleen had given her for her birthday. The lightweight, rose-colored silk felt cool against her skin. She was brushing her hair when she heard someone coming up the stairs. Vance.

Her heart raced at the sound of him entering the bedroom down the hall. She sighed in relief, until once again there were footsteps, coming in her direction, and ending at the bathroom across from her room. Soon the water came on in the shower.

Ten minutes later, Ana took a breath and released it as she opened her bedroom door and waited. Somehow, she had to let Vance Rivers know she was ready to have a real relationship.

Vance quickly dried off and realized he hadn't brought any clean clothes with him. He'd been so distracted by Ana he wasn't sure what he was doing, or what he wanted to do. Although it was killing him, he couldn't rush her and mess this up. Maybe moving back to this house wasn't a good idea.

He wrapped the towel around his waist and gathered his dirty jeans, then opened the door, to be met by Ana standing in her doorway.

"Hey. Sorry, I didn't mean to hold you up from using the bathroom."

"You didn't." She came toward him. "I was waiting for you."

Oh, boy. His gaze moved over her short, silky robe and bare legs, and his body stirred to life. So much for the cold shower.

Giving up any idea of backing off, he walked up to her. "I've been waiting for you forever, Ana. So be sure this is what you want, because I'm not going to give you up."

Ana worked to swallow the dryness in her throat. This step could be disastrous, but she also knew it could be wonderful, and she was willing to take a chance on this man she'd fallen in love with. Maybe she'd even loved him for years.

She nodded. "I want to be with you, too, Vance."

He took her hand and walked her to his bedroom, then pulled her inside and closed the door. He tossed his dirty clothes aside and leaned down and captured her mouth. She went willingly and kissed him back with the same fervor. She was quickly consumed by desire for this man as his tongue slipped past her parted lips, making her body crave even closer contact.

He finally released her, but his mouth moved to her ear and he whispered, "I want you, too, bright eyes. And I plan to prove just how much when I kiss every delicate inch of you." His lips moved over her jaw, placing tiny kisses as he went. Next he trailed a path down her neck, causing her to shiver. When her knees started to give out, he caught her. "I got you, Ana."

Her lips parted as she worked to breathe against the rush of feelings he created inside her. Her hands went to his chest, moving and stroking over the hard planes of his bare skin.

He was busy, too, working on the knot of the belt on her robe. When it parted, he pushed the garment off her shoulders, then stood back to gaze at her. Finally, he reached up and tugged on the straps of her nightgown, pulling it down her arms to drop at her waist.

"God, Ana, you're beautiful."

He tugged her into his arms and kissed her deeply. Then he swung her up, carried her across the room, set her down beside the bed and took off her remaining clothes. Once she was naked, he stood back and eyed her closely.

She reached for his towel and let it drop, then touched his bare chest. "You are beautiful, too." She felt shaky as she placed kisses along his skin. He sucked in a strained breath as he cupped her face, then his mouth covered hers again.

He finally pulled back. "Are you sure about this, Ana?" His gaze was dark and riveting. "This isn't a game to me. Once we're together, I don't plan to let you go."

She took that leap of faith, trusted her feelings for this man. "Yes, I'm sure. I want you, Vance, only you."

Sometime around dawn the next morning, Ana rolled over in bed and blinked as she saw Vance pulling on his jeans. She smiled, then realized he was leaving.

"Vance?" she whispered in the darkness.

He turned and she took in his broad shoulders and chest. Once again her heart set off racing.

"Hey, I didn't mean to wake you. I need to go get the men started for the day." He sat down on the bed. "I'm already running late as it is."

She sat up and slipped her arms around his neck, causing the sheet to drop to her waist. "Then it shouldn't hurt if you stay with me a little longer."

"What about Kathleen?"

"Let her find her own man."

Ana placed her mouth against his and did her best to distract him. With a groan, he surrendered, wrapping his arms around her and deepening the kiss. By the time he broke it off, they were both breathless.

"Lady, you don't play fair." He stood. "I really need to go. Not just for me, but for you, too. I know the men aren't going to think anything about me walking out of this house, but I would like to keep this between us for the time being. I want this special for us."

Suddenly, Vance had some doubts. "Unless you don't want any more than last night."

She looked at him for what seemed like an eternity, then rose up and punched him in the arm. "You didn't say that, did you?"

"Hey." He rubbed his biceps, but was happy she was offended by his remark. "I'm just giving you options."

"If you don't know me better than that, then we're done here."

He reached for her and pulled her back into his arms. Closing his eyes, he reveled in the feeling of her pressed again him. "Hey, cut me some slack. Last night was special to me. More than you'll ever know. I don't want you to have any regrets."

She raised her head. "For me, too, Vance." She touched his face. "I want to be with you, and not just here." Then those beautiful baby blues looked at him. "I care about you."

"I care about you, too." He leaned down and kissed her. He was a goner when it came to this woman. As the kiss deepened, he pressed her back against the mattress, needing to feel closer to her. He couldn't leave Ana now, maybe never. Just this once, he'd let the men handle the work, and he'd take the morning off.

CHAPTER TEN

"YOU KNOW YOU can't keep fooling everyone much longer."

Colt sat in his wheelchair and stared at his therapist, trying to act clueless about the accusations. But Jay knew him too well. The young man hadn't been intimidated, and matched Colt's stubbornness throughout the past month.

"Your daughter is going to discover your secret before long."

Colt wanted to tell him to stay out of his life, but knew what he said was true. He shook his head. "N...no."

Ana had been coming to see him nearly every day. Would she keep visiting him if she knew that he was improving so quickly?

"N-not r-ready yet."

The young man placed his hands on his hips. "Do you realize, Colt Slater, how lucky you are to be recovering at this rate? Whatever your reason for playing helpless, it's going to backfire. Ana's been so worried about you."

"Sh...she said that?" Colt raised his arm. It was still weak, but he could move it now.

The last thing he wanted was to lose Ana again. She'd moved back home to help out. Every visit, she talked in detail about what was going on. It had been a highlight of his day—not hearing about the ranch, but hearing it from her. He knew it was a long shot, but he hoped he could start to rebuild their relationship. He just didn't know where to begin.

All those years he'd wasted on bitterness toward the girls' mother, he'd lost any connection to his daughters. He didn't want to go back to that big, empty house. "Sh-she won't c-come to see me any...anymore."

Before Jay answered, a knock at the door distracted them. Vance peered inside. "I don't mean to disturb you. I can come back later."

"No, we're finished for the day," Jay said, then looked back at his patient. "Think about what I said, Colt."

Vance walked into the room. Alone. "Ana couldn't make it today. She had to go to a meeting at the school."

Vance didn't miss the disappointment on Colt's face. So he *did* want Ana to visit. Maybe the stroke would change some things between father and daughter. Maybe he would finally realize what he had.

"Sorry, you get me instead."

Colt made a groaning sound and turned away. Vance wondered if the man's attitude had something to with him having a relationship with his daughter.

Jay checked his watch. "I need to go to my next session. I'll be by tomorrow, Colt. So behave until then."

Vance said goodbye, then grabbed a chair and placed it in front of Colt's wheelchair. He straddled it and rested his forearms on the back.

"So what's new?"

Colt frowned. "Y...you t-tell me."

Vance was thrilled that Colt was talking. "You know most of it from Ana. The yearlings were branded, shipped and sold last week. The foreman's house has been rented out to three anglers for the weekend, and Hank Clarkson is taking them fly-fishing to that sweet spot at the river where your daughters used to swim."

"Wh…where?"

"Don't play dumb, Colt. We both know you used to go check on the girls."

Again he frowned.

Vance ignored it. "We're showing a decent profit from the fishing, so we can probably pay off the leases. It's not enough, though. Your daughter Josie is talking about branching out."

Vance went on to explain about some of the changes they'd been talking about, the ideas about building a new structure.

He saw the angry look on Colt's face before the older man glanced away.

"Don't be upset. We're doing this to help save the Lazy S."

Colt looked back and nodded. "T-take c-care of Ana."

Vance was surprised by his words. "I will, always. I care about her. She will be pleased to know you're able to talk."

Colt raised his hand. "No! D-don't tell her. Keep my s…secret."

Vance stared at him a moment, then said, "I will, but I think you're making a mistake."

Colt wanted a chance to repair some damage, praying it wasn't too late. He needed Ana there at the ranch when he returned home. "N…not the first one."

Later that day in the barn, Ana could sense Vance even before he touched her. His hands slipped around her waist, and she stopped brushing Blondie's coat, then leaned back as he pulled her against his hard body. "I missed you," he whispered against her ear as he placed kisses along her neck.

"You saw me this morning," she told him, recalling how he had climbed out of bed after making love.

"Five o'clock was a long time ago. Do you have any idea how hard it was to leave you?"

"Oh, Vance." She shivered as his mouth caused goose bumps along her skin. Unable to stand much more, she turned in his arms and quickly brushed her lips across his.

Vance released a groan as he captured her mouth in a deep, searing kiss. He finally released her. "If you're going to greet me like that, I should go away more often."

Ana didn't want him to leave her ever, but she knew that in a few more weeks she had to go back to her job and her life in town. She had no clue as to what would happen with their relationship. Was it even a relationship? There hadn't been any declaration or promises.

"No, this ranch couldn't run without you."

He cupped her face. "You're doing a good job, too. The men seem eager to do whatever you want."

Good, maybe he was a little jealous. "Does that bother you?"

He placed a quick kiss on her lips. "Not if they're doing their jobs. And if they aren't trying to steal my girl."

His girl. Ana froze, trying to draw air into her lungs. Suddenly the horse shifted and nudged them against the stall railing.

He chuckled. "I think we're crowding Blondie. I know of a better place," he suggested. "It's about a twenty-minute horseback ride. You game?"

Blondie whinnied and Ana smiled.

"I take it that's a yes."

Thirty minutes later Ana was on Blondie and racing toward the meadow. She glanced over her shoulder, seeing Vance atop Rusty, closing on her.

"Come on, girl. We can't let them beat us." Ana leaned forward and nudged the mare with her heels. Feeling the wind on her face and being in rhythm with her horse gave her a feeling of peace. She caught sight of Vance coming up beside her, but she stayed the course and didn't let the gorgeous man distract her.

She smiled. He'd already distracted her. She'd fallen so hard, she couldn't think about anything else. When the small cabin came into view, she pulled back on the reins. Blondie slowed and finally stopped next to the sagging porch.

Vance rode in, climbed down, and after tying his horse to the rail, walked toward her. "You are one sexy lady, but when you're on horseback, you are incredible." He bent down and kissed her.

She loved that she could make him feel this way. "Don't try and distract me with your compliments."

Vance refused to let her go. "So I can distract you. That's good to know." His mouth came down on hers once more. This time he took her lips in a hungry kiss, knowing how quickly this woman could go to his head, not to mention his heart. He'd lost that to her at about age fourteen. He drew her to him, and she sank her sweet body against him. He ached for her. It also reminded him of the intimacy they'd shared last night and this morning. How much he wanted to have her that close always.

He broke off the kiss. His breathing was labored as he took a step back. "We'd better slow down or…" He stopped talking and walked toward the shack.

She followed him. "Vance?"

He turned around and could see the question in those beautiful blue eyes. "You keep looking at me like that, Ana, and I'm going to forget all my good intentions."

She smiled. "What are your intentions?"

"Look, last night was incredible."

She didn't seem happy. "But…?"

He went back to her. "There is no but, Ana." He gripped her by the shoulders. "I just don't want to mess up what's going on between us. I care about you."

"And I care about you, too."

He liked that, but was still worried. They had a lot of baggage between them. There were things she needed to know, about him and about this land. "There are a lot of things we have to deal with before it's just about us."

She nodded, then grabbed his hand and pulled him toward the shack, pushing open the stuck door. "Come with me to my special place."

They went inside the dusty, one-room cabin.

"I don't think we can use this place for the anglers," Vance joked.

She smacked his arm. "Nor would I want you to. This is mine. I know it's not much, not perfect, but it has this."

She went to the window over the rusted sink and pulled back the curtains, exposing an incredible view. Before them was the green, grassy meadow, encircled by glorious, tree-covered mountains that seemed to reach all the way to the big, blue Montana sky.

"It's perfect, Vance."

He heard the reverence in her voice as he came up behind her and wrapped his arms around her. "Yes, it is." He never doubted that Ana loved the Lazy S Ranch as much as he did. How would she feel if she knew that he was intruding on her heritage? He had his own plans for this meadow, and soon, he wanted to share them the woman in his arms.

Ana glanced over her shoulder and smiled at him. "I can imagine a hundred years ago, when my ancestors stood right here in this spot and gazed out at this same view. This cabin was built by my great-great-grandfather, Owen Colton. He and his bride, Millie, settled right here. Dad is named after that side of the family."

Vance envied Ana's connection to her roots. "So it wasn't Slaters who settled here."

"No, but not long after, my great-grandfather, George Slater, arrived on the scene."

"Did Colt tell you all this?"

She frowned. "Not hardly, but I looked it up in the town history. The Coltons and the Slaters practically build Royerton."

"What about your mother's side?"

He caught Ana's reaction. "I don't know anything about her."

"I think you do, just that you don't want to talk about her."

She glared. "Not any more than you want to talk about your parents."

He found he could trust her. "You can ask me anything you want."

She turned around and leaned against the sink. "Do you know where they are?"

"My father, no. My mother lived in southern Oklahoma with husband number three until she died about five years ago. Her drug-induced lifestyle finally caught up with her." He shrugged, purposely leaving out a lot of details. "Too many bad choices."

"I'm sorry, Vance."

"Like I said, she made bad choices." He released a breath. "Now, you. Where is your mother's family from?"

Ana wasn't sure she could talk about Luisa Delgado. Then she looked up into Vance's eyes and saw the compassion there. "Colt never spoke much about our mother's family. All I know is that she came from Ciudad Juarez, Mexico. At least that was the name of the town that was on the divorce papers."

"You saw the divorce papers?"

She shrugged. "It was a few months later. One night, I woke up, hearing some yelling downstairs. I came out of my room and saw the lady who used to take care of us, Mrs. Copeland, and Dad. She had her suitcase packed, and walked out the door. I hoped she was going away for good, since I didn't like her much.

"After a little while I went downstairs looking for Colt and found him lying on the sofa. He'd been drinking and was mumbling Luisa's name over and over again, saying she was never coming back. I stayed with him until he fell asleep." Ana brushed away a tear. "On the coffee table were some papers. There wasn't much I could recognize, except for the words *divorce decree* and the names Colton Slater and Luisa Delgado Slater."

His chest tightened, feeling her pain. "Have you ever thought about going to find her and ask her why she left you all?"

"Only every day during my childhood. I desperately wanted to find the woman who used to hug and kiss us every morning and every night. Who told us repeatedly that she loved us. Then one day she was gone." Ana felt tears welling in her eyes, but refused to let them fall. "But I couldn't will her to come back to her little girls. The worst thing was she took our father away, too. Colt never got over his sadness."

Vance pulled Ana into his arms. "I'm sorry, Ana. I wish I could do something." He leaned down and kissed her, wishing he could take away the pain for both of them. He wanted to erase all the hurt from the past and look toward the future. Would he have that future with Ana? Would there be more nights like last night when he got a glimmer of that dream? Yet there was so much that could keep that from happening for them.

"We should get back. It's getting late."

She looked disappointed. "But I don't want to leave. I like it here." She wrapped her arms around his waist. "It's magical."

"Magical?"

"As a girl, when I got the chance to go horseback riding, I came here. This meadow always made me feel better, so I named it the magic meadow." She smiled and shifted in his arms. "And now you're here."

Vance glanced around at the filthy room. "Not that you aren't tempting, Ana, but when the sun goes down, it won't seem so magical. Come on, I'll take you out to dinner, then we'll turn in early."

"Really?" Ana was excited that Vance was asking her out. "But I'm sure Kathleen has fixed us supper."

He shook his head. "It's her bingo night, so we're on our own for the evening. I thought we could go into town to the Big Sky Grill. I have some news about a contractor."

She gasped. "Tell me."

He shook his head. "We'll talk about it over supper. Right now, I want to take my girl out."

His girl? She tried not to turn all giddy on him. "Okay, it's a date. I'll race you back." She took off for her mount, suddenly loving her life at the ranch, and her man. The bad memories were turning into good ones.

An hour later, Vance walked Ana into the Big Sky Grill. Several heads turned in their direction. Okay, so they would be labeled a couple now. Good, he wanted everyone to know that Ana Slater was his.

They got the circular booth in the corner. He slid in on the other side from her and they met in the middle. She glanced over the menu, then closed it.

He stared. "So you know what you want?"

She nodded slowly and a sexy glint appeared in her eyes. "I have for a while."

Suddenly his heart began to race. "So have I. Ana..." He started to reach for her hand, but the waitress appeared and set down their water. After taking their order, she left.

Ana turned to him. "What were you about to say?"

Now wasn't the time to talk about their personal life. He glanced around at the crowd. "I'll tell you later. Let's talk business first."

She sighed and sat up straighter. "Yes, tell me about the contractor."

"Nothing is settled, but we talked a little about the building we want, and how our timeline is before winter, when the snow comes. His company is in Butte, but he's working from here now."

"Who?"

"Garrett Temple, from G. T. Construction."

Ana was shocked. She had no idea that Garrett was a contractor. "Garrett's in the construction business?"

Vance nodded. "There wouldn't be any reason for you to know. He's only been back the past few years, just part-time until his father got ill and Garrett had to make the move permanent."

Ana shook her head. "I guess I haven't been keeping up on the town news."

"Is it a problem? I mean, with Josie and their past together?"

Ana shrugged. "My sister lives in L.A. Why would she care if Garrett did the work or not? Especially if we get a good deal. Will we get a good deal?"

"We can cut costs if we do a lot of the work ourselves, and contract out only what we need to have done."

"It's still going to cost a lot of money, isn't it?"

"That's why we need to go to the bank," he said. "We have an appointment at one o'clock on Friday with the loan officer, Alan Hoffman."

"So we're really going to do this?"

"I thought you wanted to, Ana."

"I do. It's just a big step, and what if we fail? We'll jeopardize the ranch even more."

"The ranch is already in trouble, and if we don't bring in more revenue it will be taken away. Tomorrow, Garrett is stopping by to go over the plans and the cost. If you feel it's too much, then we can come up with something else."

Vance took her hand and squeezed it. "I would never ask you to do something that made you uncomfortable. And we'll run it all past your sisters, too."

Ana nodded. How could she not love this man, when he worked so hard to make sure she was included in everything? "What about Colt?"

"I mentioned some of this today during my visit, but of course he didn't say anything. I would like to take the plans to show him, if you and your sisters agree to the idea."

It was hard to keep her focus on business when all she wanted to do was kiss the man. "So is the business portion of this date over?"

He frowned, then a smile stretched across his handsome face as he placed her hand on his thigh. "Yes. We can finish any business tomorrow. I have other plans for the rest of the night."

"You do? Care to share?"

He lowered his head and his voice. "Oh, darlin', if I told you what I'm thinking about doing to you, you might run for the hills."

She looked into his dark eyes. "I doubt that. In fact, I have a few ideas of my own."

* * *

Two hours later, Vance helped Ana out of the truck at the house. He was a little nervous as they walked up the steps and went inside. The house was quiet, and he knew Kathleen had already retired to her residence off the kitchen. She had left a light on in the hallway.

"I guess Kathleen has already gone to bed," Ana said. "I could make some coffee, or something else if you want."

He could tell she was as nervous as he was. He turned her toward him. "Ana, I don't want to put any pressure on you. Last night was incredible, but that doesn't mean I take for granted that there will be a repeat."

Her large eyes locked on his. "What if I want a…repeat?"

He reached for her and pulled her against him. "I'd say I'm a pretty lucky guy."

She smiled. "Then that also makes me a lucky girl."

He couldn't kiss her, because he would never get her upstairs. "Maybe we should finish this discussion in the bedroom."

Vance took Ana's hand, loving the feeling of her beside him, making him think of the possibility of a future together. Once inside his bedroom, he stopped and kissed her, long and deep.

"I want you, Ana." His breathing was labored. "I also want you to know that I care about you, too. A lot. I've never felt this way about anyone before. When we get through this with Colt and the ranch…"

He shivered as she placed tiny kisses along his jaw. "You're talking too much, Vance." She started to unbutton his shirt. "Just show me," she challenged him.

He walked her toward the bed and paused to look down on the beautiful woman before him. "I don't think there's enough time, or the words to say how you make me feel."

"No words, Vance. Make love to me."

His mouth closed over hers and all worries were put aside for another time. This was all about them.

CHAPTER ELEVEN

THE NEXT AFTERNOON in the ranch office with Vance and
Garrett, Ana studied the building plans laid out on the
large desk.

She turned to Garrett. "I'm surprised by how quickly
you came up with a design, and a very impressive one."

He smiled. "I have a good team."

Garrett Temple was a handsome man, with his nearly
black hair and gray eyes. Just a little shorter then Vance,
he was still over six feet. He and Ana had been in the
same class in school, but back then he'd only had eyes for
Josie. The pair broke up when they both went to different colleges.

"So you like the design?" Garrett asked.

She suddenly realized she hadn't said anything. "Oh,
yes. I love it. It's more than I could ask for, but it's the cost
that worries me."

Garret directed her attention to the construction bid.
"This cost includes the large main structure and also six
one-bedroom cabins. As I explained to Vance, we'll be
able to complete the exterior of the main building, also do
the rough electrical and plumbing before the bad weather
sets in. I broke down the costs for that. And I'll leave the
option open for the cabins until the spring."

Ana studied the amount they needed to begin. She knew

they were getting a great deal, but it was still a lot. "I appreciate this, Garrett, but I'm not sure we can come up with the money."

Vance finally made his presence known. "Ana, we're going to see Hoffman at the bank on Friday. We could get a construction loan."

"Or you could get a partner," Garrett added. "This is a sound investment. Something I'd seriously consider investing in."

Oh, boy, Josie would love that. Her ex-boyfriend helping them save the ranch. "Not that we don't appreciate the offer, Garrett, but I'm not sure a partnership is something we're looking for right now." She wanted to be honest. "And there's Colt. We haven't discussed this new idea with him."

Garrett slowly nodded, as if he realized she was thinking about Josie. "Okay, I'll leave the plans with you, and when you decide, let me know. Just don't wait too long." He picked up his hat and headed for the door, then paused and turned around. "I hope you'll consider letting me help, Ana. Don't let the past cloud your decision. I'd hate to see you lose everything."

"I don't want that, either, Garrett. I'm doing everything to keep that from happening."

Would Josie feel that way, too?

That afternoon, Vance left Ana in the office, talking on the phone with her sisters, while he went back to work. Hours later, when he came in from the barn, she was still in there. "Hey, this isn't good," he said as he walked into the office. "You can't keep working like this."

"I just got off the phone with Josie. I had to send her a copy of the plans."

He crossed the room, pulled Ana to her feet and brushed

a kiss across her mouth. He didn't miss how tired she looked. "Well, now it's time to stop for the night and eat some supper."

"I'm not really hungry. I think I'll just go upstairs to my room."

He didn't like that idea. "First you eat." He escorted her to the kitchen, where Kathleen had beef stew simmering in the Crock-Pot, and fresh biscuits.

Ana went to her place at the table and sat down. "Okay, maybe I'll have a little."

The housekeeper smiled. "That's my girl." She set a bowl in front of her and Ana dug into her food.

Vance concentrated on his meal, too, since she didn't seem to be interested in anything but the stew. Had something happened since the meeting?

They finished supper and Ana carried her bowl to the sink. "If you don't mind, I'm going up to bed. I'm exhausted. Good night." She walked out of the kitchen.

Vance watched her depart, a little hurt that she didn't even acknowledge him outside of being polite.

Kathleen brought two mugs of coffee to the table. "She's carrying a lot on her shoulders right now, so don't take it personally."

"Can't she let me help her?" he said, unable to keep the frustration out of his voice.

The housekeeper frowned. "Our Ana is independent. All the girls are for that matter. Blame Colt for her being so leery about trusting. She needs a man to treat her like she matters. Be honest with her, Vance, and the trust will come." Kathleen smiled. "She'll know your true feelings."

Be honest. That was the problem; he hadn't been completely honest with Ana. He needed to fix that and fast.

After helping Kathleen with the dishes, he went upstairs. He walked by Ana's room and paused, but decided to shower first and come up with a way to tell her about the land Colt had given him.

Fifteen minutes later, he slipped on a pair of pajama bottoms and made his way to the room across the hall from the bathroom. Did she want to step back from what was growing between them? He refused to let her shut him out, not until he said what he had to say. He needed to have everything out in the open.

He knocked on the door, then didn't wait for an invitation, but walked in. She was already in bed, looking over more papers.

"Vance." She said his name in the breathy way that caused his body to tighten with need.

He walked to the bed and took the papers from her, then set them on the night table.

"Vance, I'm still making notes."

"Not tonight, Ana." He sat down on the edge of the mattress, facing her, then leaned closer and covered her mouth in a tender kiss. "You said you needed to rest, but you're not resting." He kept teasing those sweet lips until she finally moaned and wrapped her arms around his neck.

"What do you have in mind?" she whispered, taking her own nibbles.

"I thought I could help you…relax." He pulled her to him, craving her closeness as much as his next breath. His body tightened with need for her. "I give a great back rub, or whatever else you have in mind." He began to demonstrate, and she soon was making purring sounds as his hands stroked slowly over her back.

"Oh, Vance, that feels wonderful," she moaned. "You can stop in about a hundred years."

He smiled. He wanted a lifetime with her, too. "Ana, we need to talk." He stopped the movement of his hands and pulled her against him.

"Okay." She dropped her head on his shoulder.

"About five years ago, I graduated college."

She yawned. "I know. Kathleen told me."

"First of all, I want you to know it wasn't my idea. Colt bribed me, because he knew how badly I wanted my own place someday. So he said he would give me some land if I got my degree. When I did, he deeded me three sections of the ranch. I've planted alfalfa on two of those sections. The third is the north meadow." He paused. "It's your magic meadow."

Tense, he waited for Ana's reaction, but there was none. Then he heard the soft sound of her breathing, which told him she had fallen asleep.

He closed his eyes as his head fell against the bedframe. What should he do now? Wake her up, make her listen to his confession again?

He'd tell her tomorrow. He reached over the shut off the light, then slid down in the bed and pulled Ana against him. He had to make this right, because he didn't want to think about how hurt she would be when she found out.

Ana shifted in his arms. "Vance," she breathed. "I'm glad you're here."

He pressed a kiss on her lips and knew that he'd never have to give her up. "So am I, bright eyes, so am I."

Friday afternoon, at five minutes to one, Vance pulled the truck into the bank parking lot. He turned off the engine and looked at Ana. He saw the worry on her face as she continued to glance over the loan application. Nothing he'd said or done over the past few days could ease her fears.

He reached across the bench seat, unfastened her safety belt and pulled her to him. "Ana, stop worrying. It's going to be fine."

"I can't help it, Vance. This income is crucial."

"Then let me help. You don't need to do everything yourself."

She laid her head against his shoulder. "Sorry, I haven't been the best company."

He took her hand, raised it to his mouth and kissed her fingers. "You can be as grumpy as you like. Just don't turn away from me. I want to share the good and the bad with you."

She nodded.

"No matter what happens today, we'll figure out another way to go," he said, trying to reassure her. "Do you believe me?"

She raised her sapphire gaze to meet his and smiled.

"That's my girl." He pulled her into a tight embrace, loving the feeling of her closeness. He kissed the side of her face along her jaw, moving slowly toward her tempting mouth, but resisted. "I think we better get out of the truck before we draw a crowd."

Vance opened the cab door and blew out a breath to calm his thundering heart. He walked around to the passenger side, trying to tamp down his fears about getting this loan. It wasn't only for the ranch, but for a future with Ana. Something they could build on together.

He wanted more than just to be the kid who'd always been looking in from the outside. He wanted to be her partner, and not only at running the Lazy S.

Ana got out of the truck and began to walk toward the bank, feeling Vance's reassuring hand at the small of her back. She was glad he was with her. Funny, how much her life had changed. A few months ago she'd been content in her career at the high school. Her life had been predicable and a little boring.

Now she couldn't imagine living away from the ranch, away from Vance. Life without him, not seeing him every day. That could happen if they didn't pull this off. She felt his strength next to her, and it helped boost her courage.

She released a long breath as they walked into Royerton First National Bank. The building was over a hundred years old, and not much had changed on the inside. She hoped their view on loaning money to women had.

Vance directed her to the reception desk, where a young woman, a onetime student of hers, Cari Petersen, was waiting for them. "Hello, Ms. Slater."

"Hi, Cari." They exchanged some pleasantries, but her nervousness didn't subside. "Is Mr. Hoffman in?"

The girl nodded. "He's expecting you." She raised the phone to her ear and announced them. Then she stood and escorted them down the hall, where they were surprised to find Alan Hoffman Jr. waiting for them. He'd gone to school with Ana, too. Wasn't he too young to hold this position, make these decisions? She'd thought they would see his father.

"Hello, Ana, Mr. Rivers."

They shook hands, and then he escorted them into the large paneled office and directed them to the chairs in front of the desk. Alan took his seat behind it.

"First of all," he began, "how is your father doing?"

"He's recovering nicely, thank you," Ana said. "He should be home soon, in fact."

Alan grinned. "My dad will be happy to hear that. Colt is one of our favorite customers."

"One of the reasons we're here," Ana began, "is because we want to keep the Lazy S solvent." She rushed on to say, "There have been some rough years with the economy, so we'd like to expand the family business. I believe you have our proposal in front of you."

They sat and waited as the banker skimmed over everything and asked several questions about the project.

Vance gave a pitch about their profits with just the limited business so far.

Alan took off his glasses and leaned back in his chair. "This all looks good on paper, but money has been tight the last few years. New businesses have come and gone with this economy." He glanced at Ana. "Are you planning on using the ranch as collateral?"

Ana froze. She'd been afraid of this; she couldn't risk the ranch, especially since they could possibly lose their leased grazing land. "That's a consideration. Of course, I will have to discuss that with my father before I do anything."

Alan nodded. "I understand. Let me present this to the loan board and get back to you."

All three stood. Alan turned to Vance. "Mr. Rivers, have you ever thought about selling any part of your land?"

Ana turned to him. Vance owned property?

Vance shook his head. "Sorry. I have plans for those sections."

"Well, if you ever change your mind, I might know of a development group who would pay top dollar for that sweet piece of meadow acreage."

Vance's face paled. "Like I said, it's not for sale."

What meadow? *Her* meadow? Ana's heart sank and she suddenly felt sick. Somehow she managed to hold it together until they were out of the building. Then she took off down the street. She could hear Vance calling her name, but Ana didn't stop. She couldn't breathe.

All these years she'd done everything to be the perfect daughter but her father had never wanted her. Why would he, when he had Vance?

Her long stride ate up the distance along the sidewalk as she headed for her apartment. She needed to be alone. Someplace where she could deal with the pain, the hurt. She felt Vance's hand on her arm and she turned around.

His gaze was intense. "Ana, talk to me."

"It's a little late for that, don't you think?"

He didn't budge. "I'm not going away until we talk."

"Well, you're going to have a long wait."

"This isn't going to solve anything, Ana. I'm either going to speak to you right here or we go someplace private."

Ana saw the curious looks of people passing by. She smiled at them in greeting. "Okay. My apartment is three blocks away."

With a nod, Vance fell into step beside her, but he remained silent as they made their way to Elk Drive. She went up the steps to her one-bedroom apartment and took out her key.

Vance knew he had to explain, but he seriously doubted he could find the right words to convince Ana he wasn't trying to take over the ranch.

He followed her into a small room that included both a living and kitchen area. Hardwoods covered the floors and the furniture was in earth tones. He glanced around the generic apartment and realized just how isolated Ana's life must be.

He stopped in the middle of the living room. "I'm sorry, Ana. I never meant for you to find out this way. Colt deeded me a few sections after I graduated from college three years ago. I tried to tell you the other night, but you fell asleep."

She didn't look convinced. "That was convenient for you."

"It's the truth. I never meant to deceive you. A month ago, I didn't think you'd care. It wasn't until we went riding to the meadow that I realized that wasn't true."

She wouldn't look at him in the eye. "Who else knows

about the land transfer? Am I the only one in town who was kept in the dark?"

"No one knew, except Wade and whoever else Colt told."

She was silent for a long time.

"Colt probably wouldn't have done it if any of his girls ever came back to the ranch."

"You have to feel welcome to want to come back." Vance could see Ana was fighting tears. "It's still our heritage," she told him. "Not yours."

Her jab hit him hard, but this time it came from someone who truly mattered to him. Right when he was beginning to think he could be a part of her life.

"Dammit, Ana, I can't change what happened over twenty years ago. I'm sorry as hell that your mother took off and left you. And I'm also sorry that Colt wasn't there for you. But I won't take the blame for it. I worked hard to make my place on the Lazy S, but I never tried to take anything away from you or your sisters."

This time her eyes were ablaze. "You didn't have to— it was given to you. You truly became the son Colt always wanted."

Vance tried to block out the hurt from her words. It didn't work this time, despite years of practice. He'd already lost, when all he'd wanted was to love her.

Two hours later, at the ranch, Vance saddled up Rusty and led his horse out of the barn. He climbed onto the chestnut cutting horse and rode across the corral. He needed to clear his head, to clear his heart of the one woman he could never have in his life.

Once through the gate, he kicked the animal's sides and the race was on. Rusty loved to run, and Vance wanted to get to a place where the hurt didn't reach him any longer. Problem was, he wasn't sure he could run that far.

Run from the mother who'd never wanted him, or a father who had no use for him except as a punching bag. Twenty years later, he still hadn't been able to outrun his past.

The river came into view and Vance suddenly realized how far he'd gone. He slowed his horse, then stopped when he saw another rider standing by a black gelding at the riverbank. Garrett.

He climbed down. "Hey, Garrett, what are you doing here?"

"I'm doing some surveying for the building. You here to chase me off Slater land?" he said jokingly.

Vance shook his head. "I have no authority to do that. But you might be wasting your time. The bank wasn't very receptive about the project."

Garrett tipped his hat back as their horses drank from the river. "Then find another source for the money."

Vance wasn't in the mood to talk about this. "I doubt Ana is interested anymore."

Garrett tied his horse's reins to a branch of a tree and leaned against the truck. "What happened? You two have a lovers' quarrel?"

Vance head shot up. "How...?"

His friend laughed. "You're not good at hiding much, Rivers. Whenever Ana comes around you get all tense and can't take your eyes off her." He sobered. "I take it she's the one you want to share that new house of yours with."

Vance froze. Now that the words were spoken, it made him realize how crazy he'd been to even think they could have a future together. "You have those designs finished already?"

Garrett gave a nod. "Take some advice and show them to her before you break ground. A woman wants to add her own touches."

"The way things look now, I need to hold off on thinking about anything permanent."

His friend studied him a second. "That serious, huh?"

He nodded in turn. "Thanks to Colt, Ana isn't going to ever trust me again."

Garrett shook his head. "I know that feeling all too well."

Vance saw the strange look on his friend's face. The man had his own past troubles with a Slater woman.

"I'm not a good one to ask for help with your love life, but I might have some ideas about the business side," Garrett stated.

Vance knew that was pretty much all he had left. He needed to concentrate on the ranch, and leave anything personal out of it. Could he do that? Could he give up on the woman he'd loved all these years? It seemed Ana had already answered that question for him.

The next afternoon Vance stormed into Colt's room, to find him sitting by the window.

"Colt, you need to do something," he said. "To start with, you can't keep letting Ana or any of your daughters think that you don't care about them."

"What h-happened?"

Vance paced the room. He hated that he had to do this when the man was still recovering, but everything was falling apart.

"What didn't happen? Ana has been trying to come up with a way to pay off the lease." He went on to explain about the idea for bringing in more revenue. He told Colt about the plans for building cabins to bring in more anglers. Not knowing if there was still animosity between the Slaters and the Temples, he conveniently left out that Garrett was heading up the project.

"Whether you like the idea or not, the Lazy S needs to make money, and Ana and her sisters have been working hard to make that happen. She needs some encouragement from you."

Colt frowned. He hadn't seen Ana in the past two days, but thought that was because she'd been busy. She had told him some things about the project and he had enjoyed hearing her enthusiasm. Something wasn't right between her and Vance. "What d-did you d-do?"

The younger man stopped and glared at him. "What did I do? I did nothing. You're the one who teamed me up with Ana to run the place, when it should have been your daughters in charge. I'm an outsider. Not family."

Colt hesitated. Was that how Vance felt? "You know the r-ranch."

Vance sent him another glare. "And whose fault is that? Your daughters would like to know how the ranch runs, but you refused to show them."

Colt fought not to look away.

"I watched for years how you treated them," Vance said. "How you barely acknowledged them. Why, Colt? What did they do that was so wrong?"

Colt was ashamed of his lousy parenting. After Luisa left, he'd wallowed in self-pity, ignoring the girls until they stopped depending on him for anything. It had been easier that way. He wouldn't be hurt again when they left.

"Do you know that Ana can't trust another man because you've never been there for her?" Vance crouched down in front of his chair. "Ana feels lost, Colt. She's hurt because of the land you deeded to me. Now she hates me because she thinks I matter more to you than she does. And I don't blame her. But unlike you, I care about her."

Colt's chest ached. He hadn't wanted this to happen.

"So you can't hide any longer. You need to tell her the

truth. Let her know how you feel before it's too late." Vance turned and walked out of the room, leaving Colt alone.

He sat there in the deafening silence. Was this what his life had become? He'd pushed just about everyone who ever care about him away. Maybe he deserved to lose everything and to end up a lonely old man.

Memories flooded into his head. The good ones early on, then years and years of bad memories. Years when he could have made a better life for his girls, but had chosen not to. He'd stood back and let someone else care for them; someone else got Ana's, Tori's, Josie's and Marissa's kisses and hugs. Someone else got their love.

He brushed a tear from his face. "It's your own damn fault, old man," he chided himself, not wanting to go back to that life. He wanted Ana to stay at the ranch, and try and bring the other girls home, too.

He turned his wheelchair and reached for the phone on his bedside table. He got the operator. "I need the R-Royerton First National Bank." He waited until a woman's voice answered. "Alan H-Hoffman Sr."

"Who's calling, sir?"

"C-Colton Slater," he said. Although the effort was exhausting, his speech was clear.

Hoffman's booming voice came over the line. "Well, you old son of a gun, how are you?"

Colt smiled, hearing the familiar voice. "B-better. N...need a favor, friend."

"Okay. What's going on?" Sarah stepped into Ana's apartment two days later.

It was after ten o'clock in the morning, but Ana hadn't showered or gotten dressed yet. "What are you talking about?" She shut the door behind her friend.

"Why are you staying here instead of the ranch? Don't

you usually have a hundred things to do out there? Dad said the fishing has been incredible. Word has gotten around and the anglers are asking to go out to your place."

Ana hadn't been back to the ranch since Friday. Besides not being able to face Vance, she didn't have her car.

"They're taken care of," she said. "I'm sure Vance can handle anything that comes along."

Sarah studied her. "Speaking of that good-looking man, you two seemed to be getting pretty chummy."

She wasn't that surprised by her friend's observation. "How did you know?"

Sarah smiled. "So you are dating?"

Ana shook her head and headed for the small apartment kitchen. "No. I'm not sure if we really ever were." She began to fill the coffeemaker. "I mean, we were so busy with the ranch and Dad. We just kind of fell together."

"But it was getting serious, right?"

Ana couldn't talk about it. "Not anymore. I mean, it never was. I should have stayed focused on the ranch and taking care of Colt." She leaned against the counter. "Then it wouldn't hurt so much."

"Oh, honey, I can't believe Vance doesn't care about you."

Ana shook her head. "No, but it doesn't change the fact that he's always had Colt's attention."

"And you blame Vance for that?"

Ana looked at her friend and brushed her hair away from her face. "No. Yes. I don't know."

"I do," Sarah said. "Vance was only a kid when he showed up. Okay, Colt took him in, but I bet whatever Vance got from your father he earned with hard work."

"What about me, Tori, Josie and Marissa?" Ana knew she sounded like a spoiled child. "Don't we deserve anything?"

"Of course you do. And isn't it about time to finally confront Colt about this issue?"

Ana's bravado began to fade. "But what if he finally tells me the truth? What if he tells me that he doesn't love me?"

CHAPTER TWELVE

OVER THE NEXT week Vance tried to stay busy with the day-to-day running of the ranch, but all he could think about was Ana. Then to top it off he'd gotten a call from Hoffman at the bank, who asked to see him. Vance called Ana, but she didn't answer, so all he could do was leave a message telling her about their appointment.

He wasn't surprised when he walked into the bank lobby and she wasn't there. Not that he expected her to be able to forgive him, but he had hoped that they could at least work together for the ranch. He'd thought wrong.

He walked into Alan's office and was greeted by a smile. "Hello, Vance. Good to see you again."

Vance hoped the man was feeling this good for a reason. They exchanged handshakes.

"Glad you could come in. Will Ana be joining us?"

"She couldn't make it today," Vance said. "I'll relay any news to her."

"That's right, the school year is starting soon." The loan officer looked over the papers on his desk. "Well then, I guess you'll get the pleasure of telling her the good news. We've approved the loan."

"You're giving us the business loan?"

Alan nodded. "Yes, and for the amount requested. I have

the paperwork right here. Since you're partners, I'll need Ana's signature, too."

"Of course." Vance was caught off guard by the news.

"We could get your signature today, and if you take the papers to Ana to look over, she can return them at her leisure." Alan smiled. "Just have her call to arrange a time to come in and sign. We need to make sure it's notarized."

The banker sobered. "Vance, about the other day, I overstepped when I mentioned your property. From Ana's expression, I take it she didn't know that Colt had deeded it over to you."

Vance nodded. He remembered Alan Hoffman from high school, but they hadn't been friends. Not with his father being the bank manager. Many parents didn't let their boys associate with that good-for-nothing Rivers kid. "I was surprised when he gave it to me."

Alan held up his hands. "You worked hard for Colton over the years. If he's anything like my father, you earned every acre."

Vance shrugged. "I only did my job."

"I'd say you did a lot more than that."

"You mean despite being Calvin Rivers's son?"

"Okay, we all knew of your dad's reputation, but I hope you know we're not looking back. The people in this town respect you, Vance. You made a place for yourself in this community."

Vance should be happy with this man's praise, but without Ana none of it mattered to him. "Thank you."

Hoffman nodded. "So that being said, I do know of a buyer for your land if you're interested."

Vance thought back to the day he'd ridden to the meadow with Ana. He could still hear the wonder in her voice as she'd looked over the land of her ancestors. "Sorry, it's not for sale." He took the loan papers, said his good-byes and walked out.

Once outside of the bank, Vance stood on the sidewalk. What was his next move? So far, he'd lost the most important thing to him—Ana. No matter what he planned to do with the land, she wouldn't give him a chance to tell her.

He walked two blocks to the office of Wade Dickson, Attorney at Law. Vance removed his hat and walked inside to the receptionist's desk. "Hello, Mrs. Smart. Is Wade in?"

The middle-aged woman smiled. "I'll see, Vance." She went to the door, knocked, then peered inside. After an exchange of words, she motioned for Vance to go in.

He walked into the office. Before the lawyer could even stand, Vance stated his case. "I need some advice."

Wade made an effort not to smile. "Ana?"

He nodded.

"Have you tried to tell her how you feel about her?"

Vance wished he had the chance. "I don't think any amount of sweet words are going to fix this."

After trying for the past two days, Vance didn't know where else to go to look for Ana. The only place left was the high school, since classes were starting the following Monday. It might be his best shot to catch her.

Memories flooded back as he walked through the double doors and down the hall to the main office. As a fourteen-year-old, he'd spent a lot of time with the principal before Colt had given him a home and adjusted his bad attitude.

A woman coming out of an inner office told him where Ana's office was, and he set out on a search. He walked the short distance to the counseling center, where he spotted her right away.

Through the glass partition he could see she was busy

talking with another teacher. She wore her dark hair pulled
back in a ponytail, with short bangs across her forehead.

He zeroed in on those big eyes that had mesmerized
him for years. No wonder blue was his favorite color. Ana
blue. He shifted his gaze to her full mouth, and quickly
his hunger grew.

The sight of her delicate jaw and long slender neck
had him recalling how he'd trailed kisses down her body,
raising goose bumps on her heated skin. He treasured the
memories of their nights together, with her pressed so close
to him. How she'd given herself so freely, never asking for
anything back. Yet he wanted all of her.

Ana raised her gaze to his, her cobalt eyes as cold and
unwelcoming as a mountain stream. She didn't look happy
to see him. Somehow he had to change that, get her to forgive him.

She said something to the other person, then walked out
into the hall. "Vance. What are you doing here?"

"You wouldn't take my calls, so I came here to see you."

"That's because we have nothing to talk about."

It hurt that she could so easily ignore what they had.
"Yes, we do, Ana." He took a step toward her. "So either
we discuss it here or go inside to your office. But we're
going to talk."

Ana worked to stay calm, hating that Vance could cause
such a reaction in her. She didn't need to spend any time
with him. She still hurt. She might never get over his deception.

She moved away from the doorway and let him inside.
She closed the door, though there wasn't much privacy,
which was a good thing. So why did it feel so intimate?

He sat down in the only chair besides hers, and she
caught his familiar scent, a mixture of soap and pure
Vance.

He placed an envelope on her desk. "It's the loan papers."

"Loan papers?"

"The bank came through with our building loan."

She tried not to appear surprised. "They're giving us the money?"

Vance nodded. "And since we're still joint executors of Colt's estate, we need to make a decision. Do we move ahead with the lodge?"

Ana didn't know what to do. She hadn't told her sisters any more because she'd doubted they were going to get the loan. "I need to talk to Tori, Josie and Marissa."

He nodded. "What about Colt? He's still head of the family."

She stared, openmouthed. Had they really been a real family? She was more doubtful now than ever before.

It took two days before Ana got the nerve to go to the rehab center and see her father. She thought it would be better to wait until some of her anger subsided. There had been so much hurt over the years, but nothing compared to this. Every glimmer of hope she'd had these past weeks about reconciling with her dad began to fade away. She had to let it go.

She blinked back the tears as she made her way down the hall to his room, knowing this discussion should have happened years ago. It was time to figure out where she stood with the man. She wasn't going to beg Colt Slater for his love.

She knocked on the door and looked inside. Colt was seated in his wheelchair, staring out the window. She felt her pulse pounding and her stomach tighten, but she refused to leave. They had to deal with this problem.

Colt was a handsome man for his age. Of course, fifty-four wasn't old by most standards. His rough-cut jaw was cleanshaven and his thick graying hair trimmed neatly. His eyes were deep set and a brilliant blue. His shoulders and chest were broad and his stomach flat. She had no doubt that the ex-rodeo star could still attract women.

Ana crossed the room, sat down in the chair beside him and glanced at the view of the Rocky Mountains. The two of them sat in silence for a few seconds, then Ana said, "We got the loan to start building the lodge and cabins."

She threw it out there to see how her father would react, good or bad.

"Good."

She was a little surprised. Colt had always been a private man. He'd never wanted anyone on his land.

"So you're okay with this business venture? There will be anglers and other guests on the ranch."

He nodded.

"You want me to go ahead with this?"

Colt turned and looked at her. "Y-yes, Ana, I w-want you there v-very much."

She blinked, surprised at the clarity of his speech. "You're talking."

He nodded again.

"How long?"

"It's b-been getting b-better every day."

She smiled. "Oh, Tori and Josie and Marissa are going to be so happy."

He shook his head. "No, p-please don't tell them. Y...yet."

"Why?"

"They won't c-come back."

Ana was confused. "You want them to come home?"

There was a flash of sadness in his eyes before he glanced away. "'Cause, I m-miss you all."

Ana felt angry, though tears gathered in her eyes. She

shook her head in disbelief. "No, don't say that if you don't mean it."

Her father reached for her hand. She could feel the strength, the calluses on the pads of his fingers. "I m-made m-mistakes. I need to fix them."

Part of her wanted to run, but the other wanted to embrace this man. "Why now? You never seemed to want us around when we were growing up. We did everything to try and please you, but it wasn't enough. It was never enough." She jumped up and moved to the other side of the room. "And now you suddenly want us to act like we're one big, happy family."

"No!" he said, his voice strong. "I w-want to make it up to you." He held her gaze. But there was so much emotion showing on his face she had to look away. Why was he doing this to her?

"Ana, I'm s-sorry. I wasn't the f-father I sh-should have been to you girls. Please give me a second ch-chance to make it up to you."

Her chest hurt so badly she couldn't breathe, but Ana wasn't about to cry. The last thing she needed was to let him see how much she cared that he'd finally said the words she'd ached to hear all those years. Could she forgive him? Would her sisters? She pushed that aside as more hurt surfaced.

"If you loved us so much, why did you give away our land to Vance?"

Colt looked startled by her words. "Ana...I—"

"No, don't say anything." She waved her hand. "I've got to go," she said, and hurried from the room. She didn't want to deal with any of the men in her life.

The next day, Ana realized she couldn't handle everything on her own. She picked up the phone in the ranch office and called her sisters.

"Slater Style," Josie answered.

"Hi, Josie, it's Ana."

"Hey, I was about to call you. Wait, let me get Tori and put you on speakerphone."

After about thirty seconds, Ana's other sister came on board. "Okay, Ana, tell us what's going on," she said. "You have any news from the bank?"

Ana was sad that they hadn't asked about their father. That was when she realized that telling them of his speedy improvement wouldn't bring them home anytime soon. And that was top priority.

"Yes, they approved our loan."

There was a pause, then Josie said, "That's great. So when do you and Vance break ground on the project?"

"I'm working with Vance as little as possible."

"Wait a minute," Josie began. "I thought you and he were the ones Colt put in charge."

Ana wasn't sure she wanted to tell them about the land. "Let's just say we disagree on a lot of things. That doesn't mean we can't go ahead with this project."

"Are you sure?" Josie asked, concern in her voice.

"Yes, G. T. Construction is ready to break ground next week." Ana prayed her sisters wouldn't ask any questions about the contractor. "We can't delay it much longer or we'll run into bad weather. I want you all involved with this."

There was silence again and Ana knew the twins were trying to decide what to say next. "How involved do you need us to be?" Tori asked.

"I'll appreciate any and all of your input and support, because there will be a lot more decisions to make. Next week, I go back full-time to my job at the high school. I won't be here 24/7 to oversee things."

"Wait a minute," Tori interrupted. "What about Vance? He'll be around, won't he?"

Ana closed her eyes and released a breath. "Yes, he's here, but he's also busy with the ranch business. Right now, he's cutting the alfalfa crop." She released another breath, relieved he wasn't around. She'd seen him on the mower in the field when she drove out to the ranch this morning.

"Isn't he going to help you supervise this project?" Josie asked.

Ana wasn't sure of much anymore. "Vance will be acting as the ranch foreman. That's his job. I'll oversee things with the contractor."

"So you can handle this by yourself?"

"I don't have a choice. We need the revenue or we lose the ranch, and we all agreed that this was a good way to bring in more money. Even Colt agrees."

"Colt?" Josie said. "How did you get him to agree with the idea?"

That had been more of a courtesy than their father had given her when he deeded away Slater land. "I just told him something needed to be done." Ana couldn't help but think about how much of an improvement he'd made. "Speaking of our dad, he'll be released from the rehab center and be coming home soon. That means we have to think about hiring some help, or one of you needs to come home."

That got the twins stammering about how their businesses needed their full attention at the moment. They promised they would take it up with their youngest sister.

Ana finally let them off the hook and told them she would handle things. After she hung up the phone, she realized what a job she'd taken on. And unlike before, she would be handling it alone.

She got to her feet, deciding she was hungry. It was already after one o'clock and she needed some nourishment to face her meeting with Garrett. She walked into the kitchen, expecting to find Kathleen, but instead saw Vance looking in the refrigerator.

With him in that position she got a good look at the jeans pulled tightly over his rear end. His shirt was sweat streaked and clinging to his muscular back. Her pulse started racing and her mouth went dry. Great. All she needed was an out-of-control libido.

She'd started to back out of the room when he turned around with his arms full of sandwich makings. He raised his dark eyes to hers. Then, surprisingly, he smiled at her.

"Hi."

"Hi. I was looking for Kathleen," she fibbed. "Is she around?"

"She's off today. If it's important, she's at her sister's in town." He put everything down on the counter. "Can I help you with something?" He came around the island and crossed to her.

Ana refused to back up. "No, thank you. I'm handling it." She decided to change the subject. "I saw you cutting the alfalfa."

He nodded. "I think the crop should bring in enough money to cover the rest of the lease money."

She shook her head. "It's not all Slater land. Part of that crop is yours, since it's on one of your sections."

He shook his head. "No matter what's on paper, Ana, it goes into the same pot."

She didn't want to discuss this. "Were you planning to be here as foreman all your life?"

Vance couldn't get enough of looking at Ana. He'd missed her over the past few days. "No. I was going to have my own place."

"And I expect you to continue with those plans. You

have your land and your crop. I'd say that's a pretty good start on a new life."

Her rejection hurt. Ana had that power over him, especially now that she'd given him a glimpse of a life he'd only dreamed about.

Well, she wasn't going to walk away from something they both wanted, without feeling what he was feeling. He took a step closer to her and inhaled her sweetness. "Sometimes things that seem perfect are far from it, especially when no matter what you do, you still can't have the most important thing."

He reached for her and drew her against him, causing her to gasp. He took advantage of that and covered her mouth with his. In an instant the heat was turned up. He had this one chance to let her know what a good thing they had. He cupped her face and tilted her head so he could deepen the kiss. When she breathed a sigh, his tongue slipped into her mouth, tasting her addicting sweetness.

Ana's arms slipped around his waist in surrender to the kiss, and he took advantage again, pressing his body against hers. He was fighting dirty, but he was about to lose everything. This was all he had.

She finally broke off the kiss with another gasp. He looked down at her eyes, laced with desire. He could continue the seduction, but she'd only end up hating him more. He had to walk away or lose his mind.

"Goodbye, Ana." Vance turned and headed out the door. He didn't need to be hit over the head to realize how crazy it was to think he could fit into her life. He'd always be the kid who was outside looking in, looking for a place to belong.

CHAPTER THIRTEEN

THE NEXT DAY started out with problems. Ana not only thought about Vance most of the night, she overslept, and had to begin her morning rushing to her appointment at the bank to sign papers. When she finally arrived, she found Wade waiting for her. Her father's lawyer explained that he was taking over as executor. Vance would no longer be her partner for the project.

Ana couldn't hide her surprise. Something was going on, and no one was telling her anything.

"Isn't this what you wanted?" Wade asked her.

She thought about Vance's deception, but for him to walk away... "Maybe, since I can't trust him."

When Alan walked out of the room to make copies, she asked Wade, "Why didn't you tell me Dad had given land to Vance?"

The lawyer frowned. "That choice was your father's. I'm sorry he never discussed it with you."

"But those sections were an important part of the ranch."

Wade gave her a confused look. "That may be, Ana, but they were Colt's to give away. And although your father recently had a stroke and is *temporarily* incapable of running the operation, he had every right back then to deed that land to Vance."

In her head Ana knew Wade was correct, but her heart

was broken over it. "You're right, Wade. Colt can do whatever he wants. He'll be home soon, so he can take over again."

Wade sighed. "You know, Ana, you can be as stubborn and bullheaded as your father. And I'm going to tell you the same thing I told Colt. To take this time and try to build a relationship."

Tears blurred Ana's vision. "I've tried."

Wade hugged her. "Oh, darlin', I know you have, and that old cuss is more to blame than anyone." The lawyer stepped back and she wiped her tears away. "Colt might not deserve this chance, but life is too short not to try and work this out. Not just with your dad, but with Vance."

She nodded. She didn't want to think about Vance, but her heart had other ideas.

Thirty minutes later, the loan money had been put into an escrow account so they could start the construction. So why didn't Ana feel excited about the project?

She walked outside with Wade, who hugged her again, then said, "Don't be too hard on Vance. He's a good man." He smiled. "And I think you'll learn that sooner or later. Hopefully, not too late."

Before Ana could say anything, Wade started back to his office, leaving her confused about so many things. But she had to put all that aside for now.

She walked across the street toward the Big Sky Grill for her meeting with Garrett. Then she had to return to the ranch and help set up the downstairs guest room for her father's return home. The living room needed to be stripped of furniture, which would be replaced by physical therapy equipment. Jay would come by three days a week to help with Colt's workouts.

Ana was excited and nervous about her father's homecoming. Was Wade right? Was Colt ready to build a relationship?

She walked through the door of the restaurant and a flash of memory hit her. Vance had brought her here and they'd shared a hamburger and fries like a lot of other couples. Had they been a couple? Whether they had been or not, her problem now would be to turn off her feelings for the man. Seeing him every day was going to be hard, so she hoped he'd concentrate on the cattle operation and stay out of her way.

She didn't need be reminded of what they'd had together, or what she thought they'd had. Their kisses, their nights together. She wanted to hate him, but yesterday in the kitchen he'd looked lost. She shook away any sympathy. He still had lied to her. He had to know how much she loved that section of land.

She heard her name called and looked toward the booth in the corner. She put on a smile and crossed the restaurant.

"Sorry I'm late." Ana slid into her seat. "It took longer at the bank then I thought."

Garrett smiled back. "Not a problem."

He got the waitress's attention and ordered coffee. "Is everything okay with the loan?"

She nodded. "I signed all the papers, so do you want to talk about a starting date?"

"I sure do." He leaned toward her. "I can have a crew there by next week. If the weather cooperates, we can get those slabs poured before the end of the week."

Good. Colt would be arriving home then. "That fast?"

"As they say, time is money. And my guys want and need the work."

She released a breath. The way it looked, she was handling this project alone. "Okay, let's do it."

Garrett stood. "I'll have a crew there in the morning." He checked his watch, then made a quick phone call on his cell and finalized the arrangements. He hung up. "It's all set. How about some lunch to celebrate?"

"I don't want to hold you up," she said.

"You're not. In fact, if I was home right now, I'd be pacing around."

The waitress appeared and they put in an order for burgers and fries.

"You got a hot date later?" she teased.

He shook his head. "My son is coming to visit me."

Ana was caught off guard by the announcement. "I didn't know you had a son. You're married?"

Garrett shook his head slowly. "I'm no longer married. And yes, Brody is eight years old. He's coming to live with me. I'm hoping it's going to be permanent."

Ana was still caught up with Garrett having an eight-year-old son. How could that be? Garrett had been dating Josie back in high school and part of their college years before they'd suddenly broken up.

Garrett saw her questioning look. "I take it Josie never told you why we split up?"

Oh, boy. "Only that you met someone else."

"It hadn't been the wisest behavior, but my son is a result of that action. Although my marriage didn't survive, Brody is and will always be the joy of my life." Garrett studied Ana. "I hope this won't affect our business relationship."

She quickly shook her head. "No. This has nothing to do with the past. You're helping us build our future. And besides, Josie isn't going to be any more involved in this project than via phone calls. She's already made that clear to me several times."

That seemed to make Garrett relax. "Then I guess we start work on Friday."

"That sounds perfect." Ana hoped her words turned out to be true, or she could be in a lot of trouble, and not only with the ranch.

* * *

By late that afternoon, Vance had packed up most of his personal things, nearly twenty years' worth. He'd send for the rest later, because he had only so much room in his truck. He just wanted to get the hell out of there, the sooner the better.

He carried the last box outside and loaded it in the truck bed, then slammed the tailgate. He glanced around the compound and toward the big red barn where he'd first lived, in the apartment upstairs. His gaze moved to the bunkhouse, then to the corral where Rusty was prancing around, hoping someone wanted to go for a ride. Vance wished he could take his chestnut gelding with him, but for now he wasn't sure where he would be living. Would he buy some land, or find another job as foreman?

"Goodbye, fella," he called, and waited to hear the answering whinny. Then he climbed into the truck and started the engine.

He'd already said his goodbyes to the guys, and put Todd in charge of the ranch hands, knowing he'd get them to follow orders until Ana found another foreman.

Putting the truck in gear, he drove the short distance up the gravel road to the house, but followed the circular driveway until he made his way around back. He parked by the kitchen door and sat there a minute, recalling so many years ago when he'd first walked inside the Slater house. All the meals he'd shared with the family, but nothing else.

Over the years, Vance had done the work Colt gave him, and had stayed away from his daughters. He'd broken that rule recently, when Ana moved back home to help out. He must have lost his mind, because he finally admitted to himself that he had loved her all these years. He released a sigh. Well, it was past time for him to wise up. He didn't fit in here, never had.

He would leave, but not before he broke off the last tie to this place. He picked up an envelope from the seat, got out and walked up the back steps. Through the screen door he saw Kathleen at the stove, probably cooking supper.

She turned when he walked in. "Hi, Vance. You're early for supper."

"I didn't come to eat, Kathleen." He paused, then said, "I'm leaving."

She frowned. "For how long?"

He shook his head. "For good. I've already cleared my things out of the foreman's house, except for the furniture. You can keep that for the renters. Todd knows what to do for the rest of the week. The alfalfa is cut, and most of it's baled. Todd will have the men finish the job."

He kept talking, because he knew it would be too easy to change his mind. Kathleen would try to convince him to stay.

The Slaters' housekeeper had been the closest thing to a mother he'd ever known, and he never doubted that she loved him. He felt the same way about her.

"Vance Rivers, you stop this foolishness and tell me what's going on."

"It's for the best, Kathleen. I should have left here a long time ago. Ana is more than capable of handling things. She doesn't want my help." He had trouble getting the words out. "Wade can step in if she needs him. Besides, the other sisters need to pitch in, too. If I'm not here maybe they'll come back to their home."

Kathleen didn't look as if she believed any of his speech. "What about Colt? He's being released in a few days."

Vance forced a smile. He still needed to talk with Colt. "That's good. He needs to be home with his daughter. Not me."

"But you're like a son to that man. You have to know that."

Colt had been good to him, but as he did with his daughters, the man kept everyone at a distance. At the very least Vance hoped something good would come out of this and Colt would repair the relationship with his daughters. Vance needed to leave for that to happen.

"They'll never be a family with me around. I'm part of the problem. It's time, Kathleen."

Tears filled her eyes. "Where will you go?"

He sighed. "I have a place for now, but I promise I won't leave the area without saying goodbye."

He pushed away from the counter. "I'll be right back." He walked down the hall to the office, and placed the envelope on the desk. He returned to the kitchen. "I put something on the desk for Ana. Tell her…" He didn't know what to say. "Tell her I'm sorry."

"Vance, you need to tell Ana yourself. At least tell her how you feel, and fight for her."

"She doesn't want to hear anything I have to say."

"Then make her listen. If you care about her you'll stay and help her through this."

"I wish that was possible, but it's not. It's too late."

But before he could leave, he heard the front door open and close. He froze, knowing it was Ana. He started to make his exit, but Kathleen grasped his arm.

"You talk to her." Her grip tightened. "Let her know how you feel."

He shook his head. "It would never work between us." Not when Ana thought he was trying to take the ranch from her.

The sound of the footsteps caught their attention. "Is that your pot roast I smell?"

At the sound of Ana's voice, Vance tensed and started to leave, but Kathleen stopped him.

Ana walked into the kitchen, but her smile disappeared when she saw him. "Vance…"

"Ana." His gaze took her in like a starved man. Her dark hair curled around her face, but her pretty blue eyes looked tired. He started to speak and explain things, but he saw the hurt in her expression. He didn't see that anything he could say would change anything. "Look, I was just leaving. Goodbye, Ana."

He'd blown his chance with her, and now it was too late. It was time to let the dream end. He turned and walked out.

Ana could only watch as Vance left. The sound of the screen door hitting the frame made her panic, and for a split second she considered going after him. But what good would it do? If he truly cared about her wouldn't he try to work things out?

"It seems you could have talked to the man," Kathleen said. "Hear him out."

"We've tried. Vance got what he wants."

"Oh, sweetheart, if you think that then you don't know Vance as well as I thought. All he's ever wanted was to belong somewhere."

"So do I, Kathleen."

Ana fought tears as she walked out of the kitchen and down the hall to the office, where she closed the door. She could escape for now, but knew she would be seeing Vance often, even with her going back to work at the school. He would be at the house with Colt. How could she act as if everything was normal?

She walked to the desk to email her sisters about the starting date for construction. Sitting down, she saw an envelope next to the desk from Wade Dickson, Attorney at Law. What was Uncle Wade sending her? She opened the envelope and took out the papers. On top was a note.

Ana,
It was never my intention to take anything from you.
You were right, the land should stay in the Slater family.
    I only hope you can convince your sisters that Lazy S is more than just land.
Good luck,
Vance

Her hand trembled as she set the note aside to glance over the papers, feeling her stomach tighten. Oh, God. It was the deed to all three sections of land, including the meadow, and they were all signed over to Analeigh Maria Slater.

Later that night, Colt was restless, so he took the offered medication to help him sleep. Lying in the dark, he still wasn't sure if going home was a good idea. He'd liked having everyone come here to visit him, but what would happen when he got back to the house? Would Ana go live in town again? He wouldn't get to see her every day like he did now.

And what about Vance? There were problems between him and Ana, Colt knew. Problems that he had created when he gave the boy part of the ranch. Colt knew why he'd done it: Vance had cared about the Lazy S, and he'd earned it.

In Colt's eyes that made it right to give him part of the place. Colt hadn't been able to take credit for much after his marriage failed, but putting Vance Rivers on a straight path had been his one shining accomplishment. He wasn't going to apologize for giving the boy the land for his dedication and hard work. Only now, it had caused more trouble.

Colt felt his eyes drifting shut and thought back to the decades of loneliness. If he had just held on to his little girls instead of pushing them away, how different things might have been for Ana, Tori, Josie and Marissa.

He brushed a tear off his face.

"Oh, Luisa," he breathed. He could still see her beautiful face when he closed his eyes. He still dreamed of her, of them together. Thought about all their hopes of a future together. But their seemingly perfect life had quickly changed when Luisa walked away.

"No puedo vivir sin ti. Te amo," he whispered in the darkness. *I can't live without you. I love you.* He'd said those words so often to his bride during their short six years together. It had been well over twenty years since they'd parted.

He fisted his hands tightly. Why hadn't he ever been able to put her completely out of his head, his heart? Why did he keep hoping she'd show up and beg him to take her back? Then he could tell her to get the hell out of his life.

"Te quiero con toda mi alma. Siempre." The female voice was a breathy whisper in the silent room. *I love you with all my soul. Always.*

Colt froze, but didn't open his eyes. He couldn't even breathe when he heard the familiar words, *"Tu eres mi vida." You are my life.*

"Luisa," he gasped, and jerked up as he glanced around the room, his eyes working to adjust to the darkness. He heard his heart pounding in his chest as he caught a faint female scent. His gaze searched every corner of the room, but found no one.

He was alone, just like always.

CHAPTER FOURTEEN

ANA SPENT THE night at the ranch, but she didn't sleep at all, not after Kathleen told her Vance had resigned and moved out of the foreman's house. Ana was haunted by the fact that she was the one who'd driven him away from his home. He'd given it all up.

Because of her.

She was ashamed that she had refused to listen to anything he had to say, and had believed the worst about him. In the end, Vance gave everything to her so she could be happy. Well, she was miserable, because he was the only thing she wanted.

Oh, God. She had to find him, to get him to stay. To make him understand that he was the one who belonged at the Lazy S. She couldn't imagine never seeing him again.

At daybreak, she began calling his cell phone. Every time, it went straight to voice mail, but she couldn't get herself to leave a message. Anything she had to say would sound so insincere. She needed to talk to Vance in person. At least to tell him she was sorry for those awful things she'd said.

She came downstairs to the kitchen to find a flurry of activity. Three ranch hands were busy moving sofas against the walls in the living room, making space for the therapy equipment being delivered in a few hours. There was a delay, and Colt wouldn't be coming home for a few more days. At least that would give Ana more time to get things together.

Todd came over to her. "It's good to see you, Ana."

"Hi, Todd," she said pleasantly.

The new foreman smiled. "I know you'll be busy, with Colt coming home and all, so if there is anything else you need, let me know."

Bring Vance back, she cried silently. "I appreciate that, Todd. I hope everything is going smoothly with the operation."

He nodded. "Of course we miss Vance, but we're handling things."

Did the men know what had happened? "Have you spoken to him?"

He nodded. "I call him when I have questions." The new foreman shrugged. "He's been here so long, no one knows the Lazy S like he does."

Ana fought her tears. "I know. I'm hoping that, with Colt coming home, things will get back to normal."

A big grin appeared on Todd's face. "The men are looking forward to the boss being home."

The young man went back to his task and Ana escaped to the kitchen, where Kathleen was busy mixing up a batch of her oatmeal raisin cookies to give the men for their help.

The housekeeper wiped her hands on her apron and came around the table. "What's wrong?"

Ana shook her head. "Oh, Kathleen, I've made a mess of everything."

"Come on, we talked about this, Ana. Your father needs to take blame for this one. In fact, he and I are going to have a long discussion when he gets home. One that I wish

I'd pushed for twenty years ago. Maybe things would have been different today."

"I don't want to rehash the past. I want to start fresh with Colt, but I'm not sure I can until I get things straightened out with Vance."

"You will, honey. Give him some time."

"No, I can't. I drove him away from his home." Ana didn't want to think of all the awful things she'd said to him. The man she cared about. The man she loved. Oh, God, she loved Vance so much. How could she have done this to him?

Kathleen led Ana to a chair at the table and sat her down. "You've had a lot to deal with since your dad's stroke. Your sisters haven't been here to help you, either. Can't blame them, though. There was a lot of resentment because of Colt's neglect. You needed someone to blame."

"You would think as an adult I would understand that what Colt did was never Vance's fault."

Kathleen sighed. "Do you think you stayed angry with Vance for another reason?"

Ana wanted to deny it, but she couldn't. She was afraid.

Kathleen smiled. "I watched for years how Vance stood back from the family, but he always had eyes for you. A crush at first, but every time you came home from college, he seemed to make excuses to show up at the house. He went through a real dark mood when you got engaged."

Ana thought back to their first kiss, when she was fourteen, and how angry he'd been with her. "I didn't think he liked me back then."

"You have to understand him. He was afraid of your father finding out. He fought to find a place to belong." Kathleen leaned forward. "To not be that kid from the wrong side of town. He's worked so hard to lose the stigma."

"Oh, God, and I put him right back there."

"No, Colt didn't handle it right. He was wrong not to tell you girls, but he wasn't wrong to give Vance part of this ranch. Don't you think the man worked hard enough to have a place where he belonged?"

Ana's heart ached. She'd messed up everything and she had to make it right. "I need to fix this, Kathleen. Please tell me where Vance is. Please tell me he didn't leave the state."

"No, he's close by." Kathleen sighed and hesitated, then said, "He's staying at Garrett's place."

"Working at the ranch?"

"No, he took a job on the construction crew."

Vance had been up since five that morning. He'd been at the lodge site, helping the men unload lumber off the flatbed truck and carry it to where the concrete slabs had been poured yesterday morning. Today they were going to frame the first floor of the structure, so there wouldn't be any break in the workload anytime soon.

He never minded hard work. It had gotten him through some rough times. Times when he hurt so badly nothing distracted him from the pain. Times when people thought he wasn't worth saving, but he'd worked to prove them wrong. Times when he loved someone so deeply that he had to bury his feelings in work.

Work wasn't doing the trick to hide what he felt for Ana. That was why he couldn't stay here.

"Hey, don't kill yourself. I have plans for you."

He looked up to see Garrett smiling at him.

Vance removed his hard hat and wiped the sweat off his forehead. "I'm only doing the job you hired me for."

Garrett motioned for him to follow him off the site.

Once under the shade of a tree, but before Garrett began to speak, Vance said, "Hey, I know I'm not as qualified as your regular guys, but I appreciate the work."

"You are qualified. In fact, my men are complaining that you're making them look bad. Slow down, Vance. Stop letting what happened between you and Ana drive you so hard you get hurt."

Vance straightened. "I'm not."

Garrett glanced over Vance's shoulder. "Well, that's good to know, because you're going to be tested on that theory." He nodded and Vance turned to see Ana walking toward them. Garrett made his exit.

Vance's chest tightened as she moved through the high grass toward him. She was in her usual attire of jeans and a blouse tucked in at her narrow waist.

"Hi, Vance," she said.

He nodded. "Ana. Is there a problem at the ranch? With Colt?"

"No, Todd is handling everything and Colt is fine." She raised her gaze to his. "I came to see you. Can we talk?"

He didn't want to rehash anything. "I really need to get back to work."

He'd started to leave when she called to him. "Please, Vance."

Her plea worked and he waited for her to speak.

"I'm sorry for all the things I said," she told him. "I took my anger out on you when I should have directed it at Dad. You have every right to the land."

He didn't want to say anything, but muttered, "You think I give a damn about that land? Well, I don't. It was never what I wanted."

Ana's eyes filled. "I know that now. And I'm sorry,

so sorry for the way I treated you." She glanced away. "I didn't trust what I was feeling for you. I got scared, Vance."

He walked a few feet away, then came back. "You don't think I wasn't scared? The problem, Ana, was you couldn't trust me. You wouldn't believe anything I said."

With her silence, all he could hear was his pulse pounding in his ears.

"I would now," she confessed.

Her words were encouraging, but still he hesitated. "I can't go back to the past, Ana. Things are different now."

She looked disappointed, but before they could say any more, one of the men called to him. "Hey, we need another pair of hands here."

"I've got to get back."

She reached out and touched his arm. "I'm not giving up, Vance. Can you give us one more chance? It's your choice what happens next."

He glanced away, not wanting her to see how she affected him. "I'll come by later. Meet me in the barn, say, four o'clock."

Ana smiled. "I'll be there." She walked off, leaving Vance aching to run after her.

Garrett came over. "So you worked things out?"

"We're just going to talk, later."

His friend sighed. "Take some advice. The less talking the better."

At four o'clock Ana walked out toward the barn and found Vance in the corral, with Rusty and Blondie saddled.

She nearly ran into his arms. "Hi."

He nodded. "Hi."

"Are we going somewhere?"

"I thought we'd go for a ride, somewhere we wouldn't draw so much attention."

Ana looked around and saw several of the men watching them. Good, she'd have him to herself. She took Blondie's reins from Vance and climbed on her mare.

Vance mounted Rusty, then together they walked the horses out the corral gate, thanking Todd for closing it.

It didn't take long before Ana picked up the pace and they were both racing across the pasture. She soon began to relax and enjoy her ride, not wanting to think that it could be their last one.

They rode past the alfalfa fields and Ana knew where Vance was directing her. It wasn't long before they ended up in the meadow, approaching the small cabin.

Once there, she pulled on Blondie's reins and the horse came to a stop. Vance did the same with Rusty. After tying the animals to the railing near the rebuilt lean-to, he went to the pump and began to fill the old trough with water.

Ana glanced around and noticed some subtle changes. The boards had been replaced on the porch floor, and there were new shingles on the roof, too.

Vance pulled a plastic cup from his saddlebag, filled it with water and offered it to her. "Here, this is so much better than bottled."

Ana drank about half, then gave it back, and he finished it. She wasn't feeling as sure about this talk as she'd been when they left twenty minutes ago. She looked out over the meadow, wishing it would give her some magic right now. Then suddenly the wind kicked up and clouds moved overhead, and soon came the raindrops.

"Come on. We better take cover." Vance grabbed her hand and pulled her onto the porch, then opened the door and got her inside the cabin.

"I guess we should have checked the weather," she said.

"It's not bad." Vance went to the small table and lit the kerosene lamp. "The rain should pass over in a few minutes."

Removing her hat, Ana wiped the moisture from her face and jeans jacket, then looked around. There were changes inside, too. The room had been cleaned for once. The bunks and old mattresses were gone, replaced by a large wrought-iron bed with a colorful quilt covering it. Her gaze quickly searched the rest of the room. The kitchen area had been cleaned, too. There were more canned goods on the shelves, and fresh curtains in the window.

"Who did this?"

He folded his arms across his chest and leaned against the sink counter. "It all depends, if you like it or not."

"What's not to like? Are you living here?"

He shook his head. "This is yours, Ana."

She felt her throat close up. "You did this for me? When?"

The rain continued to come down. "A few weeks ago," he told her. "I knew you liked to come here when you went riding, so I thought why not make it livable."

She walked to the bed. "Where did you find this?"

Vance wasn't sure he could pull this off. Being here with her was killing him. "It was in the barn, up in the attic." He paused. "It used to be mine, but the mattress is new. And I bought the quilt from Mrs. Hildebrand at the Country Days Festival."

"Oh, Vance." Ana's fingers traced the double wedding ring embroidered on the quilt. "How did you get everything out here?"

"In that old wagon behind the barn, and with a lot of help from Todd."

"But why?"

"I know what this place means to you, Ana." This was his chance. "And you mean a lot to me."

Her gaze rose to meet his, and Vance could see the glistening of tears.

"I don't deserve this," she choked out. "I said so many awful things to you."

He fought the urge to go over to her. They needed to talk first. "We both made mistakes. I should have told you about the land. Believe me, I tried. That night I came to your room, when you were going over the loan papers? I confessed it all to you, then realized you had fallen asleep before I finished my explanation. The next day was when Hoffman spilled the news to you at the bank."

Ana watched him. "I should have listened to you that day. I should have believed in you. I'm sorry for doubting you." She looked away. "I know I messed up everything. I drove you away from your home. Please believe that I never wanted to do that."

All at once the rain stopped and the sun came out. Ana released a long breath. "We should get back." She went toward the door.

Vance had to act quickly, and caught her before she got too far. He pushed the door closed easily. "You notice that I fixed the hinges? I even put a lock on the door." He slid the bolt to prove a point. "I'm not finished yet, Ana. I have a lot more to say to you."

She looked up at him, her eyes wide with hope, and with love. That gave him the courage to go on. "Eighteen years ago, I showed up at your house, that kid you and your sisters wanted nothing to do with."

When she started to speak, he raised his hand. "I need to say this, Ana." At her nod, he continued. "I didn't blame any of you for resenting me. So much of that was because of Colt, but we have to let that go, too. All I cared about for all those years was you. How much I wanted to see you every day."

"But after you kissed me that first time in the barn, you pushed me away."

"Colt would have thrown me so far off the ranch, I could never find my way back. I kept my distance, hoping that my feelings would fade away, like an adolescent infatuation." Vance shook his head. "They only got stronger, Ana. I couldn't stop caring about you even if I wanted to. And when you moved home this time, I knew I couldn't deny it any longer."

"Oh, Vance."

He shifted closer. "I care about you, Ana." He brushed his mouth cross hers. Once. Twice. "Do you want me to show you how much?"

She sucked in a breath. "Showing is good."

His mouth closed over hers, and he wrapped his arms around her waist and drew her against him. She whimpered and slid her hands up his chest, combing her fingers through his hair as she deepened the kiss. Finally he broke away.

His gaze met hers. "I love you, Analeigh Slater. I think I fell for you at fourteen, and never recovered."

"Oh, Vance, I love you so much." She rose up on her toes and kissed him again. "And I don't want you to ever recover from loving me. Because I never have. I know now that I loved you back then, too."

He cupped her face. "I don't plan to. And because of that love, I needed to give you back this land."

Ana hesitated, but knew they were both being honest, so she needed to say what she wanted. "No, we have to share it." She hesitated. "What were you planning to do with this meadow?"

He took her back to the window. "In a few years, I want to build a home here. Maybe start a small herd of Herefords, but my main love is horses, both breeding and training them."

"Funny, that's pretty much what I want to do, too."

He grinned at her, and a warm shiver raced through her. "I thought you had a career in town."

"I can multitask. I'm a Slater. There's ranching in my blood."

"I think there's a lot of stubbornness, too."

She loved the feel of Vance's arms around her. "And I don't plan on making anything easy for you, either. I wouldn't want you to get bored with me."

He grew serious. "That would never happen. I can't imagine my life without you in it, Ana." He smiled, but couldn't hide the nervousness. "I want to wake up every day with you. Live right here on this land where your ancestors settled a hundred years ago. I want children with your blue eyes and incredible beauty." He sank down on one knee on the old wooden floor. "Analeigh Maria Slater, will you marry me?"

Okay, that did it. She couldn't stop the tears as she nodded. "Oh, yes." She knelt down and wrapped her arms around Vance's neck. "Yes! Oh, yes, Vance, I'll marry you."

He kissed her, and by the time they broke apart, they were breathless. "Later, we'll go into Dillon and pick out a ring."

She could hardly wait to do that, then she remembered. "Oh, Colt comes home tomorrow. Maybe we should tell him first."

Vance smiled as they got to their feet. "Your father already knows how I feel about you." He grinned. "I think a better idea is staying here and enjoying the daylight we have left." He backed her up against the new double bed. "Don't you think we should celebrate our upcoming wedding?"

"As long as it's a private celebration."

His head lowered to hers. "Whatever the lady wants."

She took a teasing bite of his lip. "This lady wants you."

"I aim to please."

Ana wanted this time with her man in her special place. Now they'd both found somewhere they belonged.

Somewhere they could begin a life together, looking forward to another generation, in this magical place.

EPILOGUE

THE NEXT MORNING in the meadow, Vance and Ana walked out of the cabin. He drew his future bride into his arms and kissed her in the bright sunlight.

"I like how you say good-morning," she purred.

"And I liked how you said good-night." Vance recalled how he'd held Ana until dawn, and soon, they would be able to start their life together. "I'd keep you here longer, but I'm afraid they'll send out a search party."

He reluctantly released her, and they mounted the animals he'd saddled earlier, and headed toward the ranch. Once they arrived at the corral, several men looked in their direction.

Vance didn't care that everyone knew they'd spent the night together. Ana was going to be his wife, and if he had anything to say about it, they'd have a lot more stolen moments at the cabin. He had to agree with her, the meadow was magical.

"I think our secret's out," she said.

"You're not my secret, Ana. You're going to be my wife." He grinned. "And I want to shout it to the world."

Smiling, she climbed off her horse. "Well, my husband-to-be, I'd like to *shout* it to my family first. Do you mind?"

He came around Rusty. "Of course we should tell Colt and your sisters first." He stared into her blue eyes, and nearly lost it. He pulled her close. "You want me to tell them what a lucky guy I am? How much I love you?"

She reached up and touched his cheek. "No, just keep telling *me*." She brushed a kiss against his mouth. "Come on, let's go up to the house."

Once in the barn, they handed their horses over to Jake. The young man gave them a big smile and walked off with the mounts. In fact, they got several greetings along with smiles as they made their way to the house.

"I guess we never discussed what my job is," Vance said as they approached.

Ana stopped. "We want you to have your job back, of course. The Lazy S can't survive without you."

He loved the ranch, but he didn't just want to work for Slaters. "I think maybe I should invest in the operation."

She paused. "What do you mean?"

"If I'm going to be part of this family, I should contribute more. Make an investment in the future."

"You mean like money?"

He nodded. "I'm not some broken-down cowboy. I could invest in a few broodmares. I've managed to save some over the years."

She smiled, liking the idea. "That's nice to know. But you already own part of this ranch." When he started to dispute it, she raised a hand. "Why don't we discuss this with Colt?"

With that decided, they made their way up the drive to the back door and found Kathleen in the kitchen.

The older woman folded her arms over her chest. "I take it you couldn't get to a phone to tell me that you weren't coming home?"

Vance pulled Ana into a tight embrace. "I guess we were thinking about other things."

"It better be to tell me that you two have come to your senses."

Vance kissed Ana. "I think you can say that. How do you feel about helping with a wedding?"

Tears sprang to the housekeeper's eyes. "I've been waiting a long time for that to happen." She hugged Ana and then Vance. "Maybe that will get your sisters home."

Ana gasped. "Oh, no! Dad! We need to go get him." She checked her watch. "I have to shower first."

Kathleen held up her hands. "No need. Wade is escorting him home, along with Joel. You two just get cleaned up and give Colt the good news when he gets here. I think if anything will make him happy, this will." She rubbed her hands together. "Oh, it's going to be a good day. Now, you two run upstairs and get showered. I'll keep your breakfast warm."

"Yes, ma'am." Vance took Ana by the hand and they hurried through the house to the stairs, hearing Kathleen's words about no dallying. He stopped on the landing and kissed Ana. "I'm happy Colt is arriving home today, but I wanted to keep you all to myself for a while longer. You don't know how badly I want to steal you away and head back to the meadow."

Ana's gaze searched Vance's handsome face. She couldn't believe how much she loved this man. She also knew how close she'd come to losing him. "We'll go back to the cabin soon. Remember, we're going to build our home there."

"That has a lot to do with getting our business off the ground. How soon are you going to marry me?"

"Tomorrow?" she teased, but she was dead serious.

"Sounds great to me, but I think you'd be happier to have your sisters here for our wedding."

She arched an eyebrow. "Would you mind?"

He shook his head. "I'm just not sure your sisters are going to accept me into the family."

"That's their problem. You're the man I chose, the man I love. And if I know Tori, Josie and Marissa, they'll come around to love you, too."

Vance pulled Ana against him. "As far as I'm concerned, you're the only Slater sister that's important to me right now."

She smiled. "I'm the lucky sister." She brushed her mouth over his, stirring the flames. "Give it time. My sisters will grow on you."

He swung her up into his arms. "Like I said, you are the only one I want to marry, to be the mother of our children, to spend the rest of my life with."

"Oh, Vance. There's nothing I want more than to build a life with you."

He carried her down the hall to their room. There wasn't going to be "hers" or "his"; it was going to be "theirs" from now on.

Colt was pushed into the kitchen by Wade. He'd been home for a little over a day, and found he hated being in the wheelchair, but knew that he sometimes had to use it. But not for long, he decided. Now that he was finally home, he was going to recover. To get back as head of the ranch, head of his family. With some changes, of course.

Wade walked around him to the coffeemaker. "You need any help getting settled in?" his friend asked as he filled two mugs. He handed one to Colt.

"You d-don't have to hang around."

His friend arched an eyebrow. "Are you trying to get rid of me?"

Colt shook his head. "Get a life. You sp…ent too m-much time with me."

"I would like to think if this happened to me that you'd stick by me. We're friends, Colt. No matter how stubborn you are, or disagreeable, that will never change." The lawyer leaned back against the counter. "I only hope you take advantage of this second chance."

Colt smiled. He couldn't be happier. "Ana's marrying Vance."

Wade nodded. "I'd say that's a perfect match. But you still have to repair the problems with your three other daughters. You got any ideas?"

He held up a finger. "One at a time. I learned my lesson."

"It's about time."

Two days later, Vance walked out of the barn and saw Ana's car pulling up at the house. He picked up his pace and got to her as she was climbing out of the driver's side. He leaned down and kissed her.

"Oh, I like this kind of welcome home," she told him as she let him have her briefcase.

"Always. How was your first day back at school?"

She kissed him again. "Well, outside of talking about you, and showing off my new engagement ring—" she flashed the square-cut diamond on her left hand "—there wasn't time for much else." She grinned. "Have I told you how much I love the ring and what a special guy you are?"

He nodded. There was a time when Vance hadn't felt special. Hadn't felt he belonged. It was Ana who made him feel as if he could do anything. "I always want to be that guy for you, Ana."

She pressed her lips to his. "Just love me, Vance. No one else does that as well as you do. And I couldn't love another man as much as I love you."

He placed his head against hers. "I love you, Ana. We're going to make such a great life together."

The look in her eyes told him she believed in him. That was all he needed, that and her love.

He kissed her again—a kiss so sweet he didn't even hear another car pull up. When they finally broke apart, he noticed a familiar-looking woman climb out.

She was small, with sandy-brown hair, and they were close enough that he could see those Slater-blue eyes.

Ana gasped. "Oh, my God, Josie."

Her younger sister came around the car, staring at them both. "I guess I surprised you."

"What are you doing home?" Ana asked.

"I thought you said you needed help with Colt." She continued to watch Vance. "And there seem to be some things you left out." A tiny smile tugged at the corners of her younger sister's mouth. "How many other surprises are there that I don't know about?"

Ana shot a glance at Vance and caught his wink as he drew her close to his side. "Let's just start out with saying welcome home, Josie. And secondly, it seems Ana and I are going to need your services as an event planner." He gave her a big smile. "Do you do weddings?"

* * * * *

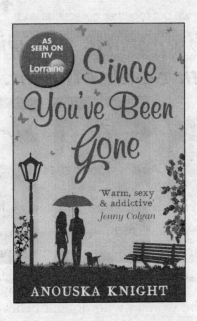

Special Offers

Every month we put together collections and longer reads written by your favourite authors.

Here are some of next month's highlights— and don't miss our fabulous discount online!

On sale 20th September

On sale 4th October

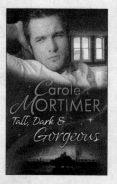

On sale 4th October

Save 20% on all Special Releases

The World of Mills & Boon®

There's a Mills & Boon® series that's perfect for you. We publish ten series and, with new titles every month, you never have to wait long for your favourite to come along.

Blaze
Scorching hot, sexy reads
4 new stories every month

By Request
Relive the romance with the best of the best
9 new stories every month

Cherish
Romance to melt the heart every time
12 new stories every month

Desire
Passionate and dramatic love stories
8 new stories every month